ALSO BY J. E. HIGGINS

OTHER GUN FOR HIRE BOOKS

The Devil's Shadow

THE SAUWA CATCHER SERIES

The Dublin Hit

The Bosnian Experience

Cyprus Rage

You can find J.E. Higgins at www.thehigginsreport.com, where he writes monthly reports on international political trends.

THE MONTEVIDEO GAME

A GUN FOR HIRE THRILLER

J. E. HIGGINS

MERCENARY PUBLISHING

Copyright © 2018 by J E Higgins

All rights reserved.

No part of this book may be reproduced in any form or by any electronic or mechanical means, including information storage and retrieval systems, without written permission from the author, except for the use of brief quotations in a book review.

CHAPTER 1

The power of the orchestra mesmerized the audience. They were overwhelmed by the sheer force of the *Black Swan* overture at the Teatro Colón Auditorium. Even without the aid of strategically placed amplifiers, the orchestra paid respect to the music's creator. The performing ballet troop danced with precision and beauty.

Elloy Mendoza expressed this opinion while enjoying the evening's festivities from his box overlooking the whole auditorium. Mendoza relished the classics. He had never held much regard for the modern genres of music — rock, folk, or the ghastly collection of sounds originating in the Americas like rap, country, or Latino. Unlike many of the wealthy elites who attended the evening's performance to see and be seen, for him just listening to the classics was invigorating.

He hated the 'keeping up appearances' attitude of so many of his kind. His interest in the classical lifestyle was genuine, and something that had been difficult to justify to his covert masters, the Cuban Directorate Generale Intelligensia (DGI). As CEO of the prestigious Bolivar Investments

& Acquisitions, what would be even more difficult to justify was his growing side business — selling intelligence services to other interests for a sizable profit.

Echoing from mid-air, a voice interrupted his hypnotic delight in the music. "I could never enjoy the noise of the old European composers," the voice, saturated with a Middle-Eastern accent, spoke in perfect Spanish. "Maybe I have too much of a sense of personal, national sentiment to enjoy the cultural delights of others. Still, I regard this type of music as obnoxious."

Undeterred by the mockeries from the man sitting behind him, Mendoza said, "This is a rather unorthodox meeting. I was under the impression my agent was going to meet you to discuss the details."

"Your agent is a fool," the voice stated with vehemence. "His choice of a meeting place was something out of a cheap spy novel. He wanted to meet in some low-end dive in a section of town where my colleagues and I were sure to stand out. I decided to forego dealing with him and come straight to you. An unexpected meeting at one of the most prestigious locations in Argentina would be most difficult for the authorities to maintain surveillance, especially at the spur of the moment. Low paid civil servants would be out of place among the social elite of Buenos Aries."

Mendoza was begrudgingly impressed with the gentleman behind him. It was a good move. The cover of a wealthy Persian in a place like the Teatro Colón Auditorium was far less conspicuous than a low-end brothel being watched by the authorities. It was a reminder that the DGI operative was not dealing with an amateur. He needed to rethink the type of people he sent to act as liaisons.

"So now, Sẽnor, I wish to know if all is in order."

Mendoza leaned back in his chair and, with his hand placed over his mouth to avoid attracting attention, he answered. "I have the information you require. Everything you requested: names, contacts, more in-depth reports, and intelligence. I was able to meet all your requirements, but I have one question. Are you going to require a system for money transfers?"

"Did we request money transfers as part of our requirements?" It was a rhetorical question. "Please do not take me for a fool. I am well aware of your intelligence connections to Cuba and that the information you are receiving and the networks you are making available are through them. The fact that you are purely a mercenary selling access to your own government's intelligence services is not unnoticed. When can this information be made available to me?"

"Tomorrow at a place of your choosing."

"It will be at your office. We have real estate issues to engage your services and payment will be made through our usual channels."

"Very well. I will receive you in our conference room."

"That will suffice," the voice retorted. "Tell me, does it bother you collecting and selling your government's resources in such a capitalistic fashion?"

"Does it bother you?" Mendoza responded smugly.

The meeting ended, and Mendoza returned his attention to the orchestra. He was slightly irritated he had lost so much of the program from an interruption of trivialities. Behind him, he heard the creaking of the chair as the shadowy figure rose to make his exit.

Ali Anwar al Qalmini left the auditorium through the door leading to the box seats. He brushed past two of Mendoza's bodyguards manning the entryway. The bodyguards had learned to use their judgment for when to let acquaintances through and when to bar access. An expensively dressed and well-groomed Persian flanked by a small entourage of his own protective detail who could slip into such exclusive places was certainly one not to be challenged.

As the door shut, Qalmini found himself alone in a rather narrow hallway. His guard detail had taken up strategic positions at either end of the hall. Far from burly, muscled thugs who knew little more than bar fighting, these men were solid professionals. Qalmini had known them from when he commanded the Quds teams supporting the resistance movements in Iraq against the American aggressors years earlier. He had shed blood and survived several combat engagements with these men and, more than anyone, he trusted them with his life. As he rose through the echelons of the officer corps of the Pasdaran—the Iranian Revolutionary Guard Corps—he had brought them along.

Saying nothing, Qalmini made his way down the hallway toward an exit point. The two guards controlling the exit point moved ahead and repositioned themselves outside. A quick nod to Qalmini as he approached alerted him that the outside area was clear of any threats. Behind him, as he was about to enter the outer room, the two other guards withdrew from their positions on the other side of the hall and followed their charge.

Qalmini's dislike for the music of the old composers was partly because he had no personal taste and partly because it was a continuation of his all-encompassing hatred toward the western world. Still, appearances had to be maintained and leaving the concert early after much difficulty getting in would create suspicion. Besides, he had another pressing engagement he had yet to attend.

Qalmini was no Islamic puritan like so many in his government or his organization. He relished his pleasures: good food, occasional tobacco products, and the enjoyment of high-class living. But like many of his breed and generation, he saw Iran as the only viable challenge to the US and European imperialism in the Islamic world.

Qalmini and his escorts navigated the marble stairs leading to the main hall. They crossed the velvet carpet and ascended up an adjacent flight of stairs. Within minutes, he was at the door to the private box seats he had reserved for the evening. There, he was met by three more men who completed his security detail.

One of the men stepped forward. "The lady has been waiting for you, sir," the guard said in a rough Persian dialect used by many of his men from desert and village lineage.

"Is she upset?" Qalmini inquired.

"No, but she asked when you would arrive."

Qalmini stepped through the door into the box with two of his guards in tow. Inside he found a stunning woman sitting in one of the plush velvet seats. She was elegantly dressed in a satin gown of shimmering silver that draped all the way from her milky white shoulders, across her large, firm bosom, and ended just below her feet. A slit along the side of her gown allowed a perfect view of her long toned legs encased in black silk stockings and gleaming black leather heels. Her golden hair was tied up in a well-sculpted knot atop her head with strands strategically freed alongside the circumference of her face. This was all held together by a few jeweled ornaments and strategically placed combs. She was a beautiful woman with sensual looks and an athletic figure.

Taking his seat next to her, Qalmini said, "Did the Contessa feel neglected?"

With a crooked smile from her full cherry lips, she said, "I was concerned I would look jilted. I was also concerned your meeting might have turned out badly given my understanding of your contact."

Qalmini focused on the orchestra, aware of her gaze on him. "I maintain my reservations about him. Reservations I may be forced to act upon."

The Contessa shifted her gaze toward the orchestra. "I do hope if such action becomes necessary, it will be discrete. I wouldn't want you to think you are still in southern Lebanon or Syria."

Qalmini snickered. "You think me so primitive as to not understand the difference?"

"Buenos Aires, you will find, is not nearly so accommodating or understanding of the methods you might employ."

"I would assume not. Now, my dear, to our business."

"I have covered my end," she said with the same self-assured smile on her face. "You will find I have those you need for this operation."

Content with her answer and with the business of the evening, Qalmini prepared himself to endure the evening's attraction. Begrudgingly, he found himself somewhat impressed with the presentation, but his deep loyalties to his own culture would never allow him to admit it.

The muggy, tropical climate was different than what Micha Cohen was accustomed to. He had lived his adult life in the dry desert world of the Middle-East and, before that, spent his childhood in the harsh coldness of the Soviet Union. Looking over the balcony of his penthouse suite, he took time to enjoy the serene view. The glistening waters of the Pacific Ocean provided an excellent backdrop for the luscious, vegetated land. Perhaps the Zionists should have made the Jewish nation in South America, he thought as he took in the picturesque scene.

Twisting the Ashton mild cigar burning between his teeth, he swirled the brandy in the glass snifter. The brownish red liquid twirled like a whirlpool in the ocean. His life and current career had been spent in the rough living of refugee camps, third world locations, and a childhood in the squalor of Soviet working-class accommodations. His past had given him a deep appreciation for the finer things in life, and he never missed an opportunity to enjoy them.

His moment of contentment was interrupted by the simulated sound of a throat clearing behind him. The sound had become all too familiar. He didn't have to turn to know it was Kafka Dayan. Without breaking his pose, Micha said, "All is well, I assume?"

"The meeting is still a go," the young man said with a slight twinge of concern. "The respective invitees have all confirmed their attendance for nine o'clock here in your hotel room."

"You still have reservations about this, Kafka?" It was a rhetorical question. Cohen already knew the answer. He turned to find himself looking at a tall, slender man fitted into a tailored gray business suit worn with casual disdain. With his rough Middle-Eastern features and a scraggly crop of black hair, Kafka looked more like some Arab rascal than an Israeli special operations soldier. Still, such things were what made Kafka Dayan so good at his work.

Kafka spoke bluntly. "I think you are playing a dangerous game, one you may not win."

Cohen knew his young protégé was right. He was about to embark on something that could very possibly get the community of the world's powerful intelligence agencies in an uproar. Yet, what he was about to do needed to be done. If his own people would not support him, he had made his peace with God and would do it on his own.

He looked at Kafka — the young man he had known since he was a boy from a North Israeli Kibbutz. Micha had watched him grow up to become a strong and determined man. Kafka had joined the Israeli Defense Force, graduated, and served with distinction in the elite anti-terrorism unit, Shayetet-13 — the navy's seaborne comparison to the IDF's better known Sayeret Matkal. It was Micha Cohen who recruited the young soldier for this special operation and introduced him to the shadowy world of espionage and clandestine warfare.

Kafka was no fool. He understood the risk when his old mentor recruited him for this particular mission. However, he had a deep loyalty to the old man that would not let him walk away. "I just feel we need to tread lightly," Kafka confessed.

"Normally, I would agree. But, in this case, time is something we don't have and that means taking risks that otherwise would not be considered."

Kafka folded his arms and tapped his finger against his bicep, a nervous action.

Cohen wanted to offer words of assurance, but he had

none. Kafka was too astute to believe them if he did. Finishing the last small gulp of his drink, Micha Cohen placed the glass on a nearby table and gave his complete attention to the remainder of his cigar.

The clock off to the side read 8:15 AM.

CHAPTER 2

The offices of the Buenos Aires branch of Bolivar Investments & Acquisitions were an interesting attempt to mix modern architecture and a professional infrastructure while trying to stay consistent with a turn of the century colonial design. The building was constructed with a traditional gray brick exterior and polished mahogany: doors, window frames, paneling, and designer flooring. Over the years, great care had been taken not to destroy too much of the existing infrastructure when modernizing such problems as old wiring and plumbing. The hallways and general offices had kept their historical integrity by maintaining the gas-powered lights lining them and keeping the original railing and floors.

The artwork was well chosen with several copied pieces from well-known Spanish and French artists who had been in Argentina during the late nineteenth and early twentieth centuries. Interspersed with the artwork was a well-sequenced pattern of framed photographs from 1905 through 1940 depicting the city. The city was proud of their advancements into a modern society.

After his previous dealings with Sẽnor Mendoza, Ali Anwar al Qalmini had lowered his expectations for future encounters, but the professional cover of the building intrigued him. The offices were tasteful, low key and conservative, redeeming the Cuban somewhat.

Arriving on the top floor, Qalmini and his entourage walked down a dark corridor illuminated only by antique gas lamps. He reached a set of ominous looking, heavy double doors, stopped, and took a moment to study the ghastly looking carvings on the door, which seemed to be inspired by medieval Christian art. In this case, the theme was the fiery bowels of Hell with a sculpting of skeletal demons devouring the souls of unrepentant sinners.

One of his men snickered. "Maybe they're keeping holy crusaders with swords and armor behind the door."

"If so," Qalmini said smoothly, "I promise the 'infidels' will not find the Holy Land so easily conquered this time around." His remark earned him a collection of chuckles as they waited.

The doors opened with a loud and rather eerie creaking. They were met by a tall, slender man with a crop of slicked back, heavily oiled hair and thickly lined face. In his dark black suit, the man looked like some horror movie villain. With a slight bow, the man motioned them inside. The Iranians filed in and found themselves in a large room with a long polished table in the center. Like the rest of the building, the lighting from gas lamps had been converted to use electricity. Early twentieth century paintings lined the walls. A large portrait of the former Argentine President, Juan Peron, was placed high and looked down, Godlike, on everyone in the room.

Elloy Mendoza strolled in with a flamboyant swagger

through a pair of doors from the other side of the room and joined them. Unlike his bland looking associate, the Cuban took pride in his appearance and was wearing a gray silk suit and matching vest. The shirt sported pinkish-red buttons and a red velvet tie. The silver cufflinks, that were nearly impossible to ignore, looked expensive. For an operative of the *People's Utopia,* Mendoza was certainly unopposed to enjoying the higher class of living his cover provided him.

"I know Muslims are opposed to indulging in libations. Something, I am sad to say, causes you to miss out on one of life's greater pleasures. I hope the teachings of Mohammad do not prohibit the indulgence of fine tobacco," Mendoza strutted over to a large, oak humidor sitting on a table at the far end of the room.

"The Prophet was not as stringent or puritanical as some of his less enlightened followers would suggest," Qalmini said, and joined Mendoza, leaving his guards to stand fast.

The humidor held a vast assortment of fine cigars. The aroma of fresh, manicured tobacco filled Qalmini's nostrils. Producing a CAO mild bullet head from the pile, Mendoza obliged his guest by clipping the end and lighting it with a polished silver lighter. It was a majestic show of wealth designed to impress his clients.

"If we could please get down to business, Sẽnor," Qalmini exhaled a thick cloud of grayish-blue smoke.

"Yes, of course," Mendoza motioned to his assistant, the dullish figure that Qalmini mentally dubbed the 'Mortician'. The assistant promptly stepped out of the room and returned carrying a black leather valise. Placing it on the table, he produced several packets which had been inserted in manila folders. He placed them in a neat line directly in front of the lead chair. When he had finished, the Mortician grabbed the valise and quietly backed into the corner.

With another wave of his hand, Mendoza motioned the Persian to the table. Qalmini thought this presentation amateurish. He expected important information to be delivered on a disk or USB stick.

Sensing the client's disdain, Mendoza said, "We have all this information on a stick for your convenience. I just felt these packets allowed you a chance to view your merchandise immediately. After all, you paid good money for it."

Qalmini found the Cuban's smug demeanor irritating but, since he already disliked the Cuban, he simply ignored him. Seizing a random folder from the table, he perused the first couple of pages before sitting down and flipping to the next page. Mendoza had taken steps to produce the information in Spanish and in Persian. "Your research and preparation are quite thorough. I am impressed." Qalmini said with a tinge of respect.

"I have a feeling your organization will be requiring a great deal more services in the near future. I like to keep the better-paying clients inclined to employ my resources." Mendoza smirked.

"A very capitalistic notion. A servant of the people's state should be wary." Qalmini raised an eyebrow.

"Communism was a dead dream when it started. It is only truly supported by the elites of any society." Mendoza rolled his Ashton Black between his fingers. "I enjoy the life of the elite, and I have no taste for the *nobility*,"—Mendoza's upper lip twitched as he said the word—"of a working-class life. I enjoy the functions of capitalism as most realists in my position do."

Qalmini turned another page. "These people seem to

have all the right backgrounds and connections for what I need. Are they approachable?"

"Yes," the Cuban said. "You will note their profiles explain what motivations you could use to appeal to each person. Will you need our assistance with negotiations? I'm sure you would want to reduce your organization's exposure."

"Arrangements for that have already been made. My final question is regarding the land purchases."

"As you requested," Mendoza took a puff from his cigar, "three sizable properties in the south of Brazil and two others in Argentina were purchased. All of them are in thick jungle environments far from any civilization but close enough to dirt road networks to maintain consistent supply lines and maneuverability. You'll find all the details in the final two packets. I have purchased and reviewed the properties through an unaffiliated firm we work with from time to time. There should be no trace back to me or you."

Qalmini retrieved one of the last folders. Inside, deeds, recent photos, and detailed maps supported Mendoza's claims. "How far from Uruguay is the border?"

"The Argentine properties place you twenty kilometers from the border, and the Brazilian properties are no more than forty-five. As you can see by the maps my surveyors drew up, you will enjoy a honeycomb of trails and roads that exist through the most remote areas of the countryside and give you ample means to cross undetected."

"Good, I can see these people have the means to operate, but are you sure they're approachable? Can they be recruited?"

"Yes, they were all very carefully vetted. What you are looking at is information and histories compiled from both

DGI and their various South American service records. In addition, there are personal reports from my own people who have been tracking these people just to be absolutely thorough." Mendoza puffed out his chest, proud, a confident man.

Content with the answers, Qalmini smiled. "I am satisfied. This is fine work, Sẽnor." Waving his hand at his entourage, he stood. His entourage strode forward and collected the documents.

Mendoza produced a small thumb drive from his jacket pocket and handed it to the Iranian. "This should conclude our business, I believe."

Taking the thumb drive, Qalmini said, "It does, for now. The rest of your money will be sent via the arranged transfer. Saleed United Real Estate & Acquisitions will be retaining the services of Bolivar Investments & Acquisitions for our purchase of the Paraguay property in Cuida de la Sol. I believe the agreed price was six million to be paid in Euros?"

"Yes."

The property to which he referred was in a low-end neighborhood in one of Paraguay's larger cities. Altogether, it was conservatively estimated at maybe a half million Euros. Still, it was a great way to make payment for Mendoza's services without raising any serious suspicions. The Iranians had figured this tactic out years ago as the IRGC was building up a war-ravaged Iran with large, profitable business portfolios that expanded into the international markets.

Qalmini smiled, dusted an imaginary piece of lint from the sleeve of his bespoke suit, and promptly made his exit.

CHAPTER 3

The first knock came at 9 o'clock.

Kafka Dayan strode to the door and peered through the eye hole. He saw a short, pudgy man in a bland, brown suit, wearing glasses. The man was in his mid-fifties and appeared, from his physical shape, to avoid exercise and healthy living like a vampire avoids a garlic farm.

Opening the door a crack, Kafka scanned the surroundings.

"I am alone, sir. I did not bring anyone. I have no intention of attracting any unwanted attention. Now, open the blasted door and let me in!" the pudgy man snapped. "I feel like a fool standing out here like a bellhop."

Kafka was taken aback at the unexpected demand. He had expected to be calming a room full of edgy businessmen and attorneys, but this plump-figured person was not the slightest bit intimidated or nervous. Kafka opened the door, and the exasperated man brushed past him without hesitation, making straight for the liquor. The new arrival poured himself a drink before landing in one of the armchairs.

"Time is of the essence, my dear boy. I hope I'm not the

only one you invited here," the man said with the same disgruntled attitude.

Kafka was too bewildered to know how to respond.

"No sir, there are others I expect to be here." Micha Cohen emerged from the bedroom in a dark, professionally tailored pinstriped suit. His hair was slicked back, and he looked like a CEO of some big corporation. Cohen's strength was his ability to play to the environment he was in. "I thank you for coming," Micha extended a hand. "May I ask how we should refer to you, and who you represent?"

The man's expression changed from disgruntled to satisfied, as he took a moment to scowl at the young man who had received him. The look said, 'that's how this is done you impertinent little bastard'. Kafka brushed it off.

The pudgy man's attention focused on the meeting's presenter. Sizing Micha Cohen up, the man said, "For the purposes of this meeting and future contact, I will be 'Mr. Greentree', and I represent the interests of our Friends on the Island."

"Thank you for coming, Mr. Greentree. I promise your client's time will not be wasted by indulging me." Cohen's voice was soft but professional. Mr. Greentree was anything but a novice at such meetings. By the way, the two older men spoke to each other, it appeared that they both had considerable experience in this arena.

Moments later there was another knock at the door. Taking his previous security precautions, Kafka slowly opened the door and stood like a warrior preparing for a fight.

"Dear Lord!" Mr. Greentree exclaimed. "This one is a damned commando! We're not in a blasted war zone. Anyone who would want to do people of our caliber harm would have the resources to know who we are. Which means, they would be better served attacking us on the street or sneaking a bomb up here. They certainly wouldn't stack up against the door of a penthouse in a well-secured hotel with state of the art security systems and cameras everywhere."

Kafka bit his tongue and thanked himself for holding his temper. He decided he did not like the little man referred to as Mr. Greentree. As he opened the door, he found himself facing another sullen figure. With ghoulish features and pale white skin, this man might never have seen sunlight a day in his life. A thickly lined face, sagging jowl, puffy eyes, and a thinning crop of salt-n-pepper hair gave him an air of the recently deceased. His black pinstriped suit added to this unnerving appearance. Kafka labeled this man 'Boris Karlov'.

Without a word to Kafka, the ghoulish figure crossed the room to where Micha Cohen was standing. The sullen Mr. Karlov cracked a smile as he and Cohen hugged each other exuberantly.

"Good to see you!" Cohen said as he relaxed his embrace.

"It has been a long time, sir," Karlov replied somberly.

"Too long," Cohen agreed warmly. "Am I referring to you as Cincade again?"

"I see no need to change." Karlov shrugged his pin-stripped shoulders. "And in the spirit of expediting things, I am representing the 'Morning Coffee Club."

"That will suffice, my old friend," Cohen replied.

Karlov — who was now Mr. Cincade — slipped into a seat across from Mr. Greentree and acknowledged Kafka pleasantly.

There were two more knocks within the next twenty

minutes. The first yielded a middle-aged man of Nubian linage hosting a distinct but well-polished French accent. He was introduced as 'Mr. Lupon', a representative from the 'Investor's Party'. The final guest was a sharp contrast to the others. He was tall, athletically built with a well-proportioned body, well-groomed, and sporting a conservative gray suit. Unlike his colleagues, who looked to have a history going back to the first Israeli War, this young man was in his mid-thirties.

Shooting past Kafka, the latest guest cracked a grin. "No weapons here mate, and I certainly didn't bring friends with me."

Kafka stood his ground, but the young man waltzed his way into the room to Cohen. He grabbed his host's hand. "For this operation, I'll be 'Mr. Comfort.'" Mr. Comfort took a moment to scan the other occupants, who eyed him and his flamboyant behavior disdainfully.

Kafka presumed that Mr. Comfort was a new addition to this informal social club of intrigue. Mr. Comfort released Cohen's hand and said, "I speak for the 'Chess Players'."

Mr. Comfort helped himself to a glass of bourbon before taking his seat next to Mr. Greentree. Greentree offered a scowl of disapproval. For this reason alone, Kafka couldn't help liking Mr. Comfort.

With all the guests accounted for, Micha Cohen moved to the center of the room to begin the meeting. Taking his cue, Kafka locked the front door, closed all the windows and glass doors and pulled the curtains closed, leaving the room darkened. He finished his security precautions by turning on a small machine located in the corner of the room. Kafka signaled the premise was secure. Then he went to the study and picked up a black leather satchel and brought it into the main room, placing the satchel on the coffee table.

Micha Cohen began his presentation.

"I wish to thank all of you and whom you represent for coming." Micha stopped for a moment to observe his audience. "I realize my request is entirely unorthodox and outside the typical procedure. However, I promise this is of the utmost importance and, after my briefing, you will understand the need for concern."

Cohen turned back to Kafka. His assistant responded by moving to the table, removing a gray laptop from the satchel, and logging into the system. As he worked, Micha went on. "Last year, as part of another mission we were conducting in the Beka Valley in Lebanon, our intelligence picked up a collection of sensitive documents. Many of these documents were communiques with the Pasdaran, more commonly known as the Iranian Revolutionary Guard Corps, and the Hezbollah military strategist, Amir Walli Akman. In one of the dispatches, a high-ranking officer in the Pasdaran was requesting a meeting to discuss Hezbollah's ability to augment 'high level' operations Iran might wish to undertake in the Western Hemisphere, particularly in the region of South America."

"This isn't new or revealing," Mr. Greentree snorted. "We are all well aware of Hezbollah's extensive network throughout the world. In South America, they have been carrying out terrorist operations targeting the Jewish community."

"I agree," Mr. Lupon concurred softly. "This is not something unusual."

Around the room, the other members agreed.

"Normally, I would reach the same conclusion, however,

we chose to investigate this matter a little more closely. If you please?" Cohen said facing his young assistant.

The laptop came to life and displayed an image on the far wall. The audience was now looking at the photograph of a man dressed in a combination of olive green military fatigues and traditional Islamic robes. His crop of bushy salt-n-pepper hair and snarled, unkempt, graying beard suggested the photo was taken in a hostile environment.

Cohen put a name to the picture. "Amir Walli Akman is currently wanted in Argentina for the bombing of a Jewish community center in Buenos Aires. He is also wanted for questioning in Brazil for his role in the assassination of a well-known detractor to the late Venezuelan dictator, Hugo Chavez, and by extension the outright killing of two Mossad Katza in the same timeframe. This picture was taken six months ago in Syria where he is commanding a Shia Lebanese unit in support of the Assad regime in the Syrian civil war."

He paused. "I wish to add, as part of this secret briefing, he is a target of opportunity for Israeli intelligence."

Micha Cohen now had the complete attention of the audience. "The significant thing about this man is he was for many years assistant to the late Imad Mughnivah who is helping to establish Hezbollah's tentacles into South America. After Magniya's assassination in 2008, this man stayed on managing the organization of the South American branch before repatriating back to Lebanon. Several agencies of the Israeli intelligence community have determined he currently maintains the strongest contacts of any Hezbollah leader to South America, their South American base, and the Lebanese communities scattered throughout the countries of Argentina, Brazil, and Paraguay."

The audience was waiting for more. Cohen took special note of the young Mr. Comfort, who seemed proud of his importance at being at such a sensitive meeting. In his mind, the veteran Israeli operative guessed Comfort would be difficult to manage, intoxicated as his ego was on the power he currently wielded. Still, it was all part of the game. Cohen signaled to Kafka, who promptly changed to the next picture. "The other person of interest is this man."

This was a more polished figure, mid-fifties with neatly cut, shiny black hair and a thick mustache that complimented his well-manicured features. Unlike the previous figure, this man looked like a corporate CEO wearing a sleek, black business suit minus the traditional Iranian necktie. "He is Ali Anwar al Qalmini, a Colonel in the Pasdaran Quds element. He was the senior Iranian officer reaching out to Walli Akmann. Considered one of the major operatives of covert operations, he is credited with such activities as masterminding the training and logistical support for several of the Shia militias in Iraq during the American occupation and, more recently, was one of the senior figures directing a special behind the line's campaign in Syria against the anti-Assad forces. I say more recent because four months ago he completely dropped out of all operations both in Syria and Iraq."

Again, Cohen paused, observed. He knew his audience was waiting for more. "I realize this action, on its own, is not conclusive. However, eight months ago we did receive another interesting communique from the Iranian embassy in Buenos Aires, Argentina. It was in response to a requested study regarding various countries in South America, the stability of their governments, and the potential for a possible coup d'état from any dissident elements within the government or from outside. From what could be gathered, this was not isolated to their embassy in Venezuela but was part of a larger study encompassing all their South American diplomatic missions.

"I have been looking more closely at Colonel Qalmini, who has been a most elusive and, until recently, mysterious figure. He seems to operate in the shadows of Iranian international affairs. When his name was mentioned in our intelligence reports, it was usually in concert with the more complex and large-scale operations being carried out by their intelligence community.

"What is particularly interesting, and what I wish to bring to light is something else I discovered. Colonel Qalmini has always been involved in Iranian covert operations. In the 1980s, he was part of the Pasdaran liaison team working with the Iranian Ministry of Intelligence and Security, better known as the VEVAK, the intelligence arm of the Iranian State. This was during the days of Ali Falloni when he was initiating the infamous 'Chain Murders' across the world. As part of this liaison team, Qalmini was part of a military intelligence joint research team where he studied and wrote a paper discussing the idea of toppling a government by fomenting coups and rebellions consisting of leaders who would prove to be more favorable to Iran's agenda. This study was largely directed toward neighboring Islamic states in the region, particularly the Sultanates of Qatar, United Arab Emirates and Oman — countries that have sizable Shiite populations.

"Qalmini authored an addendum exploring the possibility of extending this strategy to overseas areas. The objective was to gain a greater strategic position against the United States by establishing Iranian friendly 'puppet' governments in the Western Hemisphere. He states using such methods would create a greater equilibrium between the two powers. Inevitably, the US will be more influential in the Middle East, but Iran would have governments beholden to them in the Western Hemisphere."

Cohen could already identify those whom he had convinced and those he would have to joust with for their support. Mr. Lupon, ever cerebral and no novice to such intrigues, was nodding his head as was Mr. Cincade, as the pieces were all coming together.

As expected, Mr. Comfort seemed a little unsure and, given his apparant inexperience, was determined to prove he was worthy of the task he had been given by powerful people. He asked a plethora of questions suggesting he had a keen strategic prowess for this sort of affair.

It was Mr. Greentree who would prove to be the significant complication. He was neither a novice nor was he impressed by Cohen or his sort of people. He was not the type to be drawn in by intrigue and secrecy and was experienced enough to intelligently challenge any analytical conclusions that might affirm a need to react. While this was expected, Cohen's concern was that Greentree would have the ability to sway the others as well.

Cohen moved around the room. "This brings us to what is happening now. After Qalmini withdrew from operations in the Middle East, he became the CEO of Saleed United Real Estate and Acquisitions. It is an established Pasdaran company mainly geared toward acquiring and developing real property assets primarily in South America. As of last month, our intelligence assets have traced Qalmini to Argentina accompanied by several persons we have identified as longtime operatives of the Quds Special Forces."

"So you think Iran is looking to orchestrate a coup somewhere in South America?" Mr. Lupon, concerned, held his fingers to his lips. "Where, do you believe?"

"We don't know," Cohen knew that was not the answer they wanted to hear. "That is the issue that bears further examination."

"Let's stop," Greentree interjected. "Are you speaking for Israel? Is this analysis the official conclusion held by the Israeli Government?"

With a sigh, Cohen replied, "No."

There was a rumble of confusion as the audience exchanged bewildered glances.

"This is not what Israel believes, and you are not speaking for them?" Mr. Cincade asked in astonishment. He was quickly joined by Mr. Comfort. "How can we possibly entertain this project, if it's not backed by your government? This is purely your theory — a conjecture." Mr. Comfort was a mixture of a man expressing concern and enjoying a moment to participate and posture in front of his more seasoned counterparts.

As predicted, Cohen could see the growing indignation of both Cincade and Lupon. "Gentlemen, if I may be allowed to explain myself." The room fell silent, all eyes on him. "No, Israel does not draw the same conclusion I did from the analysis. I am speaking not as an agent of my government but more precisely...." Cohen trailed off as he prepared his next words carefully. "I guess you can say I am acting as a rogue operative who sees this situation as a threat. Because my government does not see any reason to act, I come to you and those whom you represent to aid me."

The room remained silent. Kafka felt apprehensive. By all the stone-faced looks, he believed they were all going to simply stand up and walk out the door. Watching the old covert operative, he found Micha Cohen somber and resolved. Cohen had his hands in his pockets and was rubbing his lips together as he waited for the next question.

Mr. Greentree did not disappoint. "If your government doesn't believe what you are saying, why should we?"

Calmly, Cohen said, "Governments, like the most powerful corporate entities on earth, can make mistakes. In the world of politics — with a government that is constantly vacillating between pursuing aggressive covert warfare as a means of combating the enemies of Israel and worried about the repercussions of being caught carrying out these operations — it is inclined to consciously want to ignore uncomfortable findings or to explain them away. To concur with such findings would require some type of response, and because this is in the Western Hemisphere and not the Middle East, political and strategic leaders in Tel Aviv are apprehensive to support any conclusion that presumes what I just explained to you gentlemen."

"This is a serious risk you are asking us to buy into." Mr. Cincade spoke up.

"It is," Cohen said. "I would not have called this meeting if I had any other avenues available."

"Presuming we agreed to support your cause," Lupon interjected, "What then? Exactly what do you intend to do about this problem?"

Cohen took another moment to formulate his words. This question was crucial and had to be answered without equivocation. "The response is to initiate operations against whatever they are trying to do. This would mean establishing an independent network of intelligence and covert operations. No state assets can be used. This must be a black operation from the financing to acquiring resources and recruiting personnel. The operation will be carried out in three stages: first, acquiring knowledge of their exact intentions and who, specifically, they are targeting; next, identify their network here — who they are working with, where they are being resourced, and where they are operating from; and, finally, we engage them through whatever means are most feasible to effectively neutralize the threat."

"That all seems extreme to me," Mr. Comfort exclaimed, feeling his bravado. "I understand the intelligence aspect of this. What I cannot understand is why we should have to engage anyone as opposed to exposing them and letting the respective governments and authorities deal with it?"

Cohen fixed his eyes on the young man. "That would seem like an obvious answer. Yet what you fail to understand is that since we ourselves don't have a full picture of their operation, the first question is how can we convince the various governments here? More to the point, many of these countries have enough of their own civil unrest. They may lack the resources and would require better evidence than what we could produce. Furthermore, we may be informing the very people the Iranians are recruiting to carry out the operation. In which case, we have to assume there will be blood we must draw against the enemy. This may also be an operation that will be carried out over several countries across the continent."

The audience again displayed a mixture of facial expressions. What was being discussed was a vast divergence from the usual orthodoxies and protocols that commanded these secret meetings.

"How do you propose setting up this network? I assume

it will have to be expedited in a swift fashion," Mr. Lupon asked with a reserved tone.

Cohen was relieved the men were conversing as opposed to walking out. "I have already developed a list of various persons and entities that can be approached for either in-depth or temporary service for this operation. My assistant has a great deal of experience in this sort of operation and will be my resource on the ground. He will carry out mission executions and use of persons while I oversee and manage the overall mission."

"Him!" snorted Greentree, his finger pointing at the young commando managing the laptop. "He may have experience in the desserts and villages of the Middle East. This, however, is South America and an entirely different animal than dealing with a bunch of ragheads, sheiks, and whatever kind of sand nigger he is generally accustomed to dealing with. I'm not comfortable with some Israeli commando playing cowboy down here in this part of the world. There are considerations."

"Mr. Greentree," Cincade interrupted. "I do not see the relevance of geography at this juncture. An operative is an operative capable of fighting a hostile foe. And hostility is certainly as uncontrolled here as in the Holy Land."

With an angry look, Greentree folded his arms and sat back in his chair. Cincade ignored him as he contemplated the information he had been fed. Cohen spoke to the men as a whole. "This will not be a simple affair. What I need is money, money that will not be missed or traced and can be moved easily into the shadows."

"You mean millions of dollars that you will never have to be accountable for," Lupon interjected.

"Yes, that is exactly what I'm talking about," Cohen

replied. "What I need in order to embark on this project has to be easily dismissible. If any part of this plan gets compromised, we must be able to dispense with it easily. Those you represent mustn't have anything linking them to us and that means no connection to the money or the resources we will use." Lupon slumped down in his chair, clearly uncomfortable with the suggested arrangement.

"So, you are asking us to back your own personal operation with millions of dollars that you intend to just have disappear?" Comfort was practically out of his chair. "You're asking us to give you money that you could run off with."

"If I were to do that," Cohen said evenly, "I would be putting a huge target on my back. One phone call from those you serve alerting the Institute about any criminality on my part would be signing my death warrant. Not only would your masters pursue legal means to recoup their stolen losses but, if Israeli intelligence lost valuable slush accounts for their clandestine operations, they would be motivated to track me down and make an example of me. I would not consider it out of the realm to have some of their own people shadowing our operation to ensure the money is being effectively used."

The group shifted, glanced at one another, calmed. Their collective body language suggested they accepted Cohen's answer as sufficient. Kafka sat back silently. As a soldier, he understood the importance of knowing when to keep quiet. He took his time evaluating each man in the room. He had learned long ago that careful evaluation of a subject could be crucial in dire moments.

Over the course of the meeting, Kafka had decided he didn't like Mr. Greentree. Though an old hand in these matters, he was too pompous and discriminatory. Kafka had fought and killed those 'sand niggers' the little man referred to so arrogantly. At that moment, he felt a greater kinship to those he had battled against in the Palestinian Hamas or the Lebanese Hezbollah than he did to those 'fine-suited gentry' Cohen was busy trying to win over. He felt the same animosity toward the young, ego-driven 'Mr. Comfort', so pleased with himself for being asked to the meeting and determined to play up his importance.

Maybe Kafka's reaction to these men was due to a youth spent on a kabutz farming collective in the rugged lands of North Israel along the Lebanese border where hot summer days were spent tilling the dirt and tending the livestock. Nights were spent listening to the teachings of the Torah mixed with a healthy dose of Marxist communism while huddled in a shelter from the storms of Kassam and Katyusha rockets fired from across the border in Lebanon. Or maybe, it was due to the years of adulthood fighting an endless war behind the lines in the various neighboring countries of his homeland, assassinating terrorists in their safe havens and debilitating the militaries of those who posed a threat.

No matter how he rationalized it, he found both men obnoxious. They considered attending a secret meeting in a plush penthouse of an upscale hotel an adventure. He would like to see them smugly holding such a meeting in Beirut or in a militia controlled location in Iraq. Mr. Cincade, though more professional in his manner and inclined toward asking intelligent questions, had the air of a man who had seen the true world of violence and conflict; however, he had only viewed them from the vantage point of safety. Kafka could not hold any disdain for Mr. Lupon. Unlike his colleagues, Lupon seemed more familiar with the world in which both

Cohen and Kafka Dayan lived. A small collection of scars Kafka had noticed on Lupon's neck were recognizable. He had only seen those on survivors of grenade or mortar attacks.

Cohen proceeded with the presentation. Kafka dutifully changed the images to complement the briefing. "I will need a minimum of twenty-million in dollars," Cohen said. "I will also need assistance establishing a shell company — an already established venture capital and real estate firm or one that can be set up and given credentials."

"So in addition to money, you want us to help you set up and legitimize a front operation?" Mr. Comfort asked, shocked.

"That is reasonable," Cincade interrupted, keeping his young colleague from wasting time posturing.

Embarrassed, Comfort sank back in his chair realizing he had just revealed his level of his inexperience.

Cohen ignored the interruption. "In order to effectively move around, I will require a cover that explains constant movement from country to country as well as the movement of vast sums of money. I will also need names and introductions to arms and equipment providers. We will not be relying on any government support, and I am not familiar enough with the Western Hemisphere to establish contacts on my own. I believe the 'Morning Coffee Club can best assist in this department, Mr. Cincade."

Cincade said nothing, only indicated his agreement with a light grunt.

Mr. Lupon asked, "Upon completion of this mission or in the event of being compromised, how do you plan to liquidate your network and, more to the point, what protection will our clients have from exposure?"

"Those recruited off the market will be done through me and my associate." Cohen waved to acknowledge Kafka. "They will have no further contact or knowledge beyond that. For all they know, they will be working for the US or Israeli intelligence community. Furthermore, they will assume there is some special interest in South America with an agenda to keep foreign meddlers out of the country. Should our operation be compromised at all, the only serious issue will be the loss of the money put into this action, everything else can be dropped. Without me or my associate around to answer questions, they will have a network of rogue mercenaries and nothing more."

"You forget the part about our clients helping to legitimize your front companies," Mr. Greentree interjected, scowling. "Will that not open them up to some considerable exposure?"

"Not really. A few open contacts to give the impression that we are legitimately operating or perhaps scouting discretely for some larger interest should be enough to cause any already busy government to ignore us. That can all be done by accepting a few phone calls. In the end, any investigator would assume this would merely be old friends talking or our company fishing for business. Either way, they can easily be explained to anyone prying." Cohen examined the audience again. It was obvious nothing would be decided today.

A few more questions — for which Micha Cohen offered up educated yet vague answers — and the meeting ended. The men filed out of the room. Greentree and Comfort made a hasty exit, while Lupon and Cincade offered respectful goodbyes to their host before taking their own departures.

Now alone in the penthouse, Kafka expressed his confusion to Cohen. "All right, what was all that we just went through? Who were those guys, and who the fuck were the people they were representing? The 'Chess Players', the 'Investor's Party', the 'Morning Coffee Club'; this all sounds like a bunch of old grandmas sitting in a kitchen."

Cohen headed for the collection of booze. "Not really. It's more like a gathering of some of the most powerful Jewish capital interests in the world."

Kafka took a seat and waited for the old spymaster to elaborate further. Cohen obliged. "In the early days of World War II, several German-Jewish expatriates escaped the Nazis and infiltrated the financial powerhouses of New York and London. They recognized the threat posed by Fascist saboteurs and sympathizers long before the British and American governments did. On their own, they began to organize their own counter-intelligence operations which the Jewish financiers personally bankrolled. These expats became a private operation to combat Nazi threats. When the war ended, and the horror of the Holocaust was made known, several of these bankers and financiers continued maintaining their private operations.

"When the first Arab-Israeli War broke out in 1949, and the world left us to fend for ourselves, these financiers realized that Jews needed to help Jews because the world has and will always turn its back on us. Those groups mentioned were some of the consortiums of those financiers. We approach them from time to time to help finance our covert operations, move money around, and provide cover for our operatives when necessary. Those men are a special type of attorney. They are professional covert representatives. Because the most powerful bankers and moneymen in the world cannot logically be seen attending meetings in a place like this or with people like us, these 'special envoys', attend for them. They listen to our pitch, evaluate our plan, and then coordinate the necessary arrangements."

Kafka found himself confused. This was an alien world Micha Cohen was introducing him to. "I don't understand. What do you mean 'pitch' or evaluate our plan? What's for them to evaluate?"

Cohen sighed gently, "You will notice that we had four different consortiums represented at this meeting."

"I was able to gather that much, yes."

"Well, this mission can easily be financed and supported by just one of them with no real difficulty. However, like any good businessmen, they don't like to simply throw good money toward bad situations. In the past, Israel has pitched some rather ludicrous, if not heavily compromising ideas that might not be practical or feasible for one group but could be handled by another group. Moreover, not all our covert plans are that good. We may all be Jews fighting for our homeland, but that does not mean they are a cash cow that unquestionably bankrolls everything.

"The men you have just seen have spent years as lawyers dealing in various international affairs that give them extensive knowledge and experience in these types of missions. The consortiums they represent entrust them to act as proxies. It's as if we were entrepreneurs looking for investments in our company — asking for investments for our operation. We asked several of these consortiums to this meeting understanding that some may decide against helping us. If we get even one to 'invest', we will be fine. However, this is more a business negotiation than anything. One may offer to finance but abstain from our other request which would be to help establish and legitimize our cover. For this, another consortium may offer to cover that portion of our operation. So we must wait and see who responds and find out what they are willing to offer."

Kafka leaned back in his chair. "Well, this all seems to be a perfect model for chaos. What happens if two groups offer to bankroll us unbeknownst to each other?"

Cohen poured himself a small glass of gin. "These consortiums have been around much longer than Israel. They know each other and stay in regular contact. Before they speak to us, they will discuss amongst themselves our proposal and reach a conclusion."

This was truly a remarkable situation for the young soldier. It was all so complicated and yet so simplistically organized. "When will you expect to hear an answer?"

Swirling the liquid contents in his glass, Cohen raised his eyes toward the ceiling as if expecting the answer to be there. "If we don't hear from them in a week, I would consider this operation dead."

"And if they contact Israel about this?" Kafka asked with a hint of concern.

"We already told them this is outside of Israel, and the consortiums are not beholden to our government. Hopefully, they won't feel the need to spread this knowledge. However, if they do, then we will most likely see the end of our careers."

Kafka grimaced as the old spymaster's words sank in. Cohen began sipping his drink leaving his young comrade deep in thought.

CHAPTER 4

What was it about the weathered, water stained ceiling that captured Nouri al'Marak Surriman's attention? Laying on the rickety collection of rusty springs and bent framing under a thoroughly worn mattress, he lazily stared up at the twirling blades of the creaking ceiling fan. At the moment, it was the most intriguing thing in his life.

In this cheap hotel room in Asuncion, Paraguay, his mind wandered, yet he was careful to avoid thoughts of the last few years where he had seen nothing but blood and carnage, first in Lebanon and then Syria. He also shut out images of the mysterious Iranian he had met in the battle-ridden hollows that had once been the Syrian city of Aleppo. The Iranian had sent him to a special training camp just outside of Tehran where he received extensive operational training. Now the Iranian was suddenly back in South America. Perhaps Surriman should wonder why. But, at this moment, the fan creaking, it was all inconsequential to him.

His restful bliss was interrupted by the light rapping at his door. It was a controlled knock, not fast like a friend or delivery boy but precise and well-timed, the way a businessman or a cop would knock.

The clock on the nightstand read 3:42 am. The rapping stopped and was not followed up with any voice announcing a reason for such an intrusion so early in the morning. Slowly Nouri al'Marak Surriman slid off his bed causing the rusting metal to screech, most assuredly alerting the person outside to his existence and location. Reaching for the gun he kept hidden under a newspaper next to his bed, he stepped softly over to the door.

The intruder rapped again in the same precise way. By now, Surriman was sure whoever was on the other side had no intention of barging in or deceiving him. Lowering the Para-Ordinance 45 automatic to his side, he looped his way around the small barricade of chairs he had staged in front of the door as a stopper for anyone who was not so patient or courteous. Through the small eyehole, he saw an all too familiar man. He opened the door to a bulging, middle-aged man with thinning hair, and a scruffy white beard.

"Come in," Surriman said as he stepped out of the way to allow the man through. Surriman couldn't help gawking at the man's choice of apparel — a flowing purple flowered shirt and tan cargo pants. It was a bad attempt by a man who had never been to this city, let alone this region of the world, to try and blend in. The sight was comical to Surriman who held back the temptation to laugh.

The older man gave him a disapproving sigh as he took in the features of the room. "Your choice of lodging is highly questionable," he opened in a gruff tone and thick Middle-Eastern accent.

Surriman shut the door and walked over to the nightstand to collect the pile of clothes he had randomly tossed there. "It was cheap. I know the neighborhood very well and, as you no doubt noticed, it is mostly inhabited by Lebanese — my people." Taking another look at the pudgy, older man, Surriman added, "our people." The older man tried to hide his disgruntlement at the statement. Surriman gathered his clothes and said, "So the likelihood of attracting attention is greatly reduced."

The older man grimaced. He was accustomed to a far higher standard of living and looked upon this room as a most disagreeable arrangement.

Ignoring the older man's displeasure, Surriman asked, "So what is the situation, Maruk?"

Maruk inspected the young man before him. Surriman was bare except for a pair of gray boxers and a black string necklace. Maruk took note of the collection of battle scars on the young man's body. Shrapnel wounds and patched over bullet holes were a memoir of the Surriman's past couple of years serving Hezbollah in the various conflicts in the Persian Gulf. His lean, toned body was a testament to his athletic prowess. It was easy to see why the IRGC al Quds unit chose him for this mission.

Sweeping back the thick mane of long, curly black hair framing his oval-shaped face, Surriman looked back at the older man who was still staring at his markings. "They're just battle scars, my old friend. Nothing many of our countrymen don't have as well."

That he was so nonchalant only embarrassed Maruk who came quickly to the point. "I have your instructions and necessary information." Producing a thick, white envelope from under his shirt, he tossed it on the bed. "The colonel will be personally assuming command of this operation if that is any indication of the significance placed on it."

Picking up the envelope, Surriman's eyes widened, his only response to the news he had just been given. "Well then, this should be history-making," he said in his usual casual manner as he calmly got dressed.

Maruk, a lifelong administrator and political hack, found such behavior from the younger man almost insulting. "Your role in this will be made clear by him when he and his team arrive in Paraguay."

Slipping into a pair of jeans, Surriman fastened his brown leather belt. "What cover will we be operating under?"

"You'll be taking your instructions from Saleed United Real-Estate and Acquisitions. You will be contacted by that company when they are ready to use you."

"How involved will you be in this operation?"

Maruk took a breath as he raised his eyes. "Oh, I leave tonight for Oman. My only involvement was to make the necessary arrangements."

Surriman threw on a wrinkled cowboy shirt and buttoned up the front. "Off to work with the Syrian expats in preparation for the Assad regime reassuming control of the country?"

"Something like that," Maruk muttered, looking around the room. "Either way, I'll be back in the real fight." He stopped when he caught Surriman's gaze. "I mean I'll be back on the battlefield I know best." He tried to recoup himself. He tended to forget that his young cohort was not necessarily a son of the Holy Land but had been raised in the deep jungles of this very continent.

Surriman maintained his sullen look. "Then you've delivered your information. Anything else I should know before you leave?"

Maruk paced within the tight confines of the room. "Your

code name for this job will be '*Rascal*'. You will initiate contact with one who will go by the name *Porthos.* Are there any issues with this?"

"No." The younger man pulled on his socks. "Who will initiate contact, me or them?"

"You will go to the park the day after tomorrow but not before noon." Maruk said waving his finger to emphasize the point. "At the park, you will find a park bench that has Farsi writing carved on the side of it. From there you will go to the nearest tree. At its base, you will find a box containing a disposable cellular phone. You will be called at 1800hrs that night. You will answer the cell phone using your code name. They will answer with theirs. From there, you will be given further instructions. Are you clear on this?"

"Yes." Surriman slipped on his hiking boots.

Such indifferent behavior only worked to annoy the older man. "I can only assume you think of me as some money pusher who rubs shoulders with wealthy donors. I must emphasize the importance of this mission. It's not a game. We have intelligence that the enemy has already gained knowledge of this operation and have deployed operatives to disrupt it."

Leaning his head to one side, Nouri Surriman looked off into the distance for a moment as he reached for a bottle of water. "To the contrary. I remember hearing a sermon from some Christian missionary years back when he said ever so loudly, '*Death comes unexpectedly!*' A few years later I was in a club in Europe having a drink with a Palestinian contact, a lawyer. The old boy had never been active in this whole affair other than the protests he took part in while at the university. He had lived the straight-and-narrow life and had only occasionally done favors for the 'cause'. As he left and crossed the street to get into his car, he got hit by a drunk driver and died after three hours of excruciating pain. This was no different from what you would see on any battlefield. It also taught me that death really does come unexpectedly.

"So, my good friend, this plan will either work or fail. I will either live or die, and that is all that can come of it."

Satisfied he'd communicated all instructions, Maruk said his last goodbye before leaving the young operative to finish getting dressed.

Surriman remained seated gazing up at the ceiling. At that moment, all was quiet, and his mind was free to ponder. He thought back to where his life had changed paths, and where he would have been had he been a fruit grower instead.

CHAPTER 5

Qalmini took a moment to enjoy the view out the window of the Andes Mountain range set against the clouded sky. If nothing else, this beautiful scene was worth the trip for this meeting.

Feeling a presence behind him, he stepped back from the window. One of his men quietly informed him that all the meeting's attendees had arrived. Helping himself to one last glimpse of the mountain range, Qalmini sighed and faced his man. With a nod, the two strolled out of his room.

It seemed a mockery, the Iranian thought as he walked through the halls and various rooms of the sizable ranch house. The variety of expensive European art, the priceless artifacts on the walls, and the polished mahogany tables contrasted greatly with a like number of icons to the communist years — pictures of the known leaders like Lenin, Mao, Fidel Castro, and the ever-popular Che Guevara, plus a few lesser-known people such as Fusako Shigenobu of the Japanese Red Army days and Abnel Guzman of the homegrown Shining Path.

As a rule, Qalmini despised Marxists, not just because of

their bad history in the Holy Land, but because he found their supporters to be a combination of professional sycophants who believed in their sense of undeserved entitlement. These disingenuous elites, such as the owner of this very home, espoused the virtuous working-class revolution so long as they didn't ever have to get their own hands dirty or actually associate with the 'unwashed' field hands.

Perhaps it was the experience of his youth in the early years of the Islamic regime when Khomeini established the Association of Radical Mullahs as a socialist/Marxist front. It was a fictional counter-challenge against the more right-wing Society of Radical Mullahs that existed as the spectrum to appease the pro-business Iranian faction of society. It gave the illusion of existing political competition. Instead, they were both organized and secretly led by the same powers under Khomeini. In the end, those that espoused the evils of wealth and the virtue of humble living for others never denied themselves such ostentatious sinfulness.

Arriving at a large dining hall decorated with gorgeous chandeliers and stained-glass windows depicting the medieval themes seen at Mendoza's office, Qalmini joined a large group of men gathered loosely around the long dining table in the center of the room. While a few of the party were undeniably of Latin American lineage, the majority were his own countrymen representing the various departments of the IRGC, the military and VEVAK operations functioning in South America. He was aware they had all been contacted by their respective superiors in Tehran and mysteriously ordered to attend or send high ranking subordinates to this ranch deep in the mountains of Peru. They had been told little except that they would be briefed in detail at the meeting and given further instructions.

The Iranian Revolutionary Guard shared a complicated history with VEVAK. Known also as the Ministry of Intelligence and Security (MOIS), VEVAK enjoyed the position of being the primary internal and external intelligence agency in service to the Iranian State. However, the IRGC, better known as Pasdaran, was the organization with the mission of safeguarding the revolution and as such, reported directly to the Supreme Leader himself. Though both organizations often operated in cooperation to fulfill co-assigned operations and responsibilities, the IRGC was typically given an operational ranking. This had led to some unfavorable rivalries between the two organizations.

Walking into the room, Qalmini noticed sealed packets lined up across the table in front of each seat. He was happy to see that his men were attentively watching the table to ensure the packets were not disturbed by unauthorized parties. Before taking his seat, Qalmini took another moment to observe his guests. As expected, they were dispersed informally into groups of their respective agencies with the military 'advisors' congregating in one corner and the VEVAK operatives adjacent to them. His own IRGC colleagues stood the furthest away — on the opposite side of the table. This was a reminder that despite the same country and similar mission, the relationship between the revolution's protectors and the country's regular intelligence and military forces remained cool at best. The few Latins in the room represented intelligence agencies of friendly regional powers: Cuba and Venezuela. It would not do to carry out such an operation without their knowledge or their unofficial blessing even though Qalmini would tactfully omit any mention of Mendoza's involvement from his briefing.

"Gentlemen, if you would please take your seats,"

announced his aid. All the guests responded by slowly migrating to the table. As with their social associations, the attendees took their seats maintaining their agency allegiances.

Sitting at the head of the table, Qalmini was flanked on either side by two of his aides: Majors Rashid al' Akim and Semir Ali Essouri. Both men had served with him for years in the al' Quds unit in various campaigns and had contributed significantly to the planning and development of this operation. Always the consummate bureaucrat, Major Essouri, a small mousy man with wire-rim spectacles and receding hairline, sat hunched over a stack of papers taking care to review all the details — like an actor reviewing a script.

With everyone seated, all eyes were now on Qalmini. Taking his time, he thought out his words carefully. Silence had now descended upon the room with the final sounds of the security detail shutting the doors to the outside world.

Placing his hands on the table in preparation, Qalmini looked to his aide, Essouri, who looked up and nodded slightly indicating he was ready. With a deep breath, Qalmini began. "I thank you all for attending this meeting. I know you have all been given vague explanations as to why you are at this meeting and the high importance Tehran has placed on it."

The room was silent, all eyes were fixed on Qalmini in anticipation. He continued. "We are about to embark on perhaps the most audacious and radical endeavor in the Western Hemisphere. This plan is part of a new strategy by which we, the Islamic Republic, intend to significantly change the geographic strata of the world's balance of power."

The buildup was proving successful, and the audience was still attentive. "The intention is to bring the conflict to our enemy, the United States, by creating hostility directly in their own backyard — here in their own part of the world, if you will."

As expected, the last statement was met with a diminished sense of interest, and grumblings across the table. Qalmini gave the audience some time.

"What is so new about this idea?" growled one of the VEVAK operatives at the far end of the table. "We already are fighting the battle over here."

Qalmini had prepared himself for dissension. "I realize at some marginal level we have found a means to indirectly engage the US with rough alliances — the criminal organizations in Mexico and building extensive Hezbollah networks amongst the Lebanese communities that exist in South America. However, in the long run, this accomplishes only minor threats and, at best, agitation that is far disproportional to what they inflict on our regional security in the Gulf. Now several high-ranking figures back home concede that in order to undermine American hegemony abroad, it is necessary to threaten their stability within their own immediate shores."

By now even Qalmini's own IRGC colleagues were unsure of where this discussion was leading. They needed more information, which Qalmini patiently provided. "Though insurgency in sizable scales can be effective against smaller countries such as Israel, it does not pose a threat to a power like the United States. The Americans are a military culture best celebrated in terms of conventional wars and nation-state geographic politics defining their enemies.

Therefore, it is necessary to promote a strategy that addresses the situation in that context."

Confusion all around. One of the military advisors rose to his feet shaking his head. "What context? We have no army over here unless you are talking about taking over a country so we can gain a foothold to threaten the Americans. That is the only way I can see this conversation going."

"And you would be correct," Qalmini said calmly. Shock reverberated around the table. Qalmini took a breath, "The only way to create a genuine threat to the Americans is by giving them a threat in the context of a nation-state that resides within their own backyard."

"I hope you are not suggesting this strategy with the goal of enlisting us," spoke the man representing Venezuela. "While we are glad to help you economically and diplomatically, what you are asking is something our government can ill afford to engage in. Such provocation would be detrimental."

"I agree," the representative from Cuba added. "The strain of the cold war days is still strong in the echelons of our leadership. They would want nothing to do with any military provocation toward the US. With a decaying infrastructure and growing hopes of economic development, such a concept would be unrealistic to even consider."

"Or attain. Yes, I would agree," Qalmini said again in his cool reserved manner. "That is why we would only ask your quiet cooperation in this matter — your blessing, unofficially of course, and your cooperation in certain diplomatic ways to help secure a successful outcome."

The buildup was going as expected. Confusion gripped the room as the intrigue mounted. Qalmini let it foment a little longer before adding, "Again, as I say, the plan is most audaciously conceived, but one that has been considered the most practical means to accomplish our agenda."

The room was silent. All eyes were on Qalmini who was now confident he had made his pitch well. "I'm speaking of creating our own proxy nation-state, built from the ground up, beholden to us and can be an indirect threat from us."

Like a chorus, the men simultaneously gasped then followed with mutterings and shocked commotion. "Please everyone," Qalmini interrupted, "indulge me if you would."

The room went quiet as Qalmini raised his hands. "We have already made the case that it is essential we have proxies in the Western Hemisphere. This is vital in order to create the needed atmosphere against the United States and protect our actual allies here as well."

"What country are you looking at to turn into a proxy nation-state?" asked one of the VEVAK representatives.

"For our purposes, we have chosen the country of Uruguay," Essouri suddenly interjected leaning over his pages of figures. While Qalmini was the mastermind, it was Essouri who had been his researcher. He was the one who had the sharp, encyclopedic mind and could find all research pertaining to an operation and quote it at will for the right occasions. With a slight nod, Qalmini turned the briefing over to the mouse-like major who checked his notes.

"Uruguay presents a perfect opportunity for this operation. It is situated on the Atlantic Coast with a large seaport. Its largest city, Montevideo, is the capital and chief economic center for the country. With a national population of three plus million people, one-third of the country resides within this city as well." Essouri straightened up and removed his glasses as he went to address the room. "In other words, gentlemen, if we are looking at this strategically for all the complexities of orchestrating a coup, this location is definitely the most feasible both logistically and militarily. We only need to construct our plan around this city for it to be successful."

"What also needs to be appreciated is that the current reigning president, Jose Mojica, is readily accessible. He doesn't take pay for his presidency. He resides on a small farm with virtually no security. I would further add that militarily the country has only a combined service of 15,000 or so, and it is extensively involved in UN peacekeeping missions. This can be both useful and problematic — useful in that the military is stretched thin and could be minimized as a threat to our mission, problematic in that they have an officer and NCO corps that has fresh combat experience."

"This is a good update," interjected one of the military advisors waving his hand. "But I still see several problems, both politically and militarily. Can we assume anyone in their military could be recruited to undertake this mission? If so, can we assume the military has the ability to even assert control over the country?"

Essouri leaned back in his chair. "Sir, we have deduced from our research that the military is not a feasible option for exactly the concerns you raise. We have no one available who could or would carry out this mission. To answer your other question, we believe that ultimately getting the necessary military support to effectively assert control is not at all probable."

Another military advisor cut in. "So, your remedy to mitigate this problem is?"

Essouri turned back to his commander who waved his hand reasserting his control of the briefing. "In order to carry out this plan, we would need to build an external force outside the country that will give their loyalty to whomever we establish as the new master of the country. We have already obtained the land under the cover of sub-contractors and are building small city-like training areas that resemble the types of structures encountered in Montevideo. This force will be a compilation of mercenaries and unemployed locals who can be easily recruited with steady paychecks and political bullshit. A chapter out of Mao's strategy, if you will — take a populace disconnected from the outside world, and they have no alternative but to do what you tell them."

"So, barring the military," one of the IRGC representatives spoke up, "who do you have in mind to be our future president?"

Qalmini rose from his seat. "Gentlemen, if you please. I will explain my full plan." He began to move from the table shifting his eyes between the audience and his two aides still seated at the table. "This whole operation will have to be built from the ground up. The person we intend to recruit is a sitting member of one of the larger opposition parties in the country's Parliament. We have identified him as a rather ambitious politician who has a greater taste for power than ideology and no patience for the traditional practice of rising through the political ranks. The thought of being handed the country without the grueling irritation of getting elected or having to answer to any other political bodies will be quite appealing."

Qalmini paced around the room. "The reality, gentlemen, is that to be successful in this endeavor, we must write this operation as if it were a play in a theater. We must write the entirety of this story from beginning to end. To ensure the Americans are deprived of any excuse to intervene militarily, we must be deceptive so our hands remain only indirectly involved. To do this, we will work through well-chosen intermediaries to control this operation. We will use no direct assets. We will not call upon our Hezbollah allies in this region, nor will Quds or any other Iranian military advisors be on the ground. We have pools of professional soldiers not affiliated with us that can handle the training and organization of the force. The coup must look entirely domestic and not at all influenced by us.

"This brings up another complication we need to address. Uruguay is a relatively stable society that has not had any significant political upheavals since the 1970s. Elections are held frequently. As stated before, military coups are highly irregular. What would be a viable reason for a coup to occur that would be perceived as logical?" Qalmini paused. "We would have to create one."

With that comment, Essouri took over the brief again. "We would have to build a radical element entirely from the ground up. Like the coup plotters, this would have to be made up of the indigenous populace to avoid suspicion of outside interference. Like the camps we discussed, that are being built to train our 'established' army, we will establish a group of left-wing radicals. We will indirectly train and resource this group with the purpose of carrying out a terror campaign in the country that infuses hysteria in the country's right-wing political elements. This group will create the environment for our coup to occur under the guise of establishing law and order and protecting private business owners who will be concerned about the threat of a communist insurgency toward their economy."

"What makes you think this will not empower the people further to get behind their president and government?" the IRGC representative asked.

Qalmini cleared his throat and retrieved command of the brief. "President Jose Mojica has an interesting history politically. First, he is an outspoken atheist. This is something that does not sit well with the religious elements of the country. What is even more interesting is throughout the turbulent years of the seventies, he was an active member of the famed Tupamaros urban guerrilla movement. He spent several years as a political prisoner for those terrorist activities. When we kick off this insurgency, we intend to raise the suspicion that these terrorists are working at the behest of or, at the very least, with the blessing of the current president. This suspicion should create the alienation and instability we need. This can be done by recruiting the leadership among the disaffected relics who are still seething in dark corners and would jump at the chance to relive their glorious heydays."

"I assume you already have someone in mind?" asked another military advisor.

"We do," interjected Rashid al' Akim, who didn't wait for his commander to wave him on. Unlike his colleague Essouri, Major Akim was a bear of a man with a large muscular frame and remarkable height. He towered over everyone as he rose to his feet to address the audience. His salt-n-pepper facial hair was bordering between stubble and a full beard. Unlike Essouri, Akim was a field man, an officer in the al' Quds force who had spent his life, since his teenage years, on the battlefield — first as a young recruit in Khomeini's jihad against Saddam Hussein's Iraq and later in Lebanon. Lately, he had trained Shiite guerrillas in their war against the American occupation and fought in Syria against the heretic Sunnis trying to depose Assad. Although he saw Qalmini as a brother, it killed him to see his commander outfitted in the 'soft clothes' of a bureaucrat, when he knew the Colonel should be in combat fatigues like the soldier he was. Though overjoyed when he was chosen to be part of this operation, being in a room with 'comfortable' men did not bode well for the veteran fighter. He was more at home in the rough lands and war zones engaging with insurgents and guerrillas.

Qalmini was well aware of his cohort's decorum and political skills and stood aside to let the big man speak. "We have found a couple of these 'left-overs' that seem right for recruitment into this operation and have a close pulse on true believers who can be brought into this affair. And just so you don't ask, we will neutralize this threat when the coup kicks off by sending in our own attack teams to eliminate their bases over the border. Since we will have helped set up the safe houses and logistic networks, our coup conspirators will be able to clean up the domestic network."

Audience expressions had changed from shock and bewilderment to signs of approval. They were beginning to see the viability of the plan.

When he was sure Akim was done, Qalmini said, "Following the takeover of the country, our new president will quickly extend a leaf of friendship to Iran. We will then begin a military partnership starting with advisors and technicians and graduating to military equipment and, hopefully, progressing eventually to missile launching bases. All of these actions will cause panic in Washington because this coup was not officially orchestrated by us and because of the political sentiment in the world. The Americans will be poised to act militarily, but they will have to recognize the threat now posed directly to their homeland."

Qalmini looked over at the Latin American representatives. "This stage brings me to you. For this to succeed, we will need political legitimacy as well. If your countries are quick to recognize this new government as the legitimate government of Uruguay, this will make it harder for any serious political action to be taken by the Western Powers."

The Latin Americans nodded approvingly. The Cuban leaned back in his chair. "As long as we don't play up the left-wing or right-wing politics outside of what is necessary, I cannot see anything wrong with Cuba making a public statement recognizing your man."

"Neither do we," the Venezuelan chimed in.

"Good, then it is all settled," Qalmini said taking his seat.

CHAPTER 6

It was the same tired lecture she had heard countless times. Contessa Selena de Alvarez sat quietly in the darkened far corner of the sizable lecture hall at Uruguay University. The lecture room was cast in the traditional European design reminiscent of a Roman Colosseum. The lectern was placed in the center at the base of the gradually rising rows of wooden chairs.

At the lecture platform, Professor Raphael Patrica cut a distinguished figure. Seventy-five years of age, the trim, athletic man looked more like he was in his late forties. His neatly groomed crop of silky black hair was combed straight back, lining his rounded face and square jaw. Professor Patrica presented a nearly theatrical performance in discussing the Marxist concept of economics.

The Contessa listened quietly, trying to hide her boredom. She had heard such dissertations before, first from her brother Marko during his rebellious teenage years and later when she attended university. At the elite world of her private Spanish college, she would hear the rants from various academics and fellow students espousing the nobility of the laboring class and the evils of the aristocratic elites. As a rule, she considered politics boring and largely pointless. For her, governments and societies succeeded or fell based on the pragmatism or stupidity of their leaders and systems — not on philosophies and theories based on fanciful idealism.

It was a stark contradiction watching Professor Patrica deliver his impassioned lecture on the virtues of communism while wearing expensive brown slacks, matching vest and a dark brown sports coat. The classroom, she noticed, was nearly full. The Professor was known to have quite a following among the student body. Many of the class attendees were the expected crowd of spoiled rich kids who, by the look of their greasy hair and punk clothes, were more interested in getting stoned or laid. She did identify a collection of a dozen or more kids who seemed honest believers of the Professor's words. More than nodding, they diligently took notes, scribbling away in their notebooks and listening intently. The Contessa had noticed true believers at previous lectures delivered by Patrica. This pattern was the proof she required. Raphael Patrica was the man she needed to carry out the first stage of the operation.

After his lecture ended, the Professor entertained several questions from eager students before releasing everyone for the day. Waiting patiently as the students hurried out of the classroom, the Contessa slowly rose to her feet and glided down the narrow wooden steps.

She watched. No one was paying any particular attention to her. A radical like Patrica could always be under some form of surveillance from the security forces tasked with keeping order within the state. To her relief, she got nothing but lustful glances from hormonal youths who could never be lurking security agents.

Quietly slipping into a chair in the front row, she waited patiently as the professor navigated the attention of eager students gathered around him like rock star groupies. Several minutes later the crowd dispersed until there was only one young girl left talking to him. The Contessa took note of the young woman who possessed unique attributes that intrigued her. Unlike most of the other students who indulged in the latest designer apparel, this girl was dressed in a simple gray T-shirt, a men's light blue dress shirt, Wrangler blue jeans, and cowboy boots. Her hair was long and tied loosely in a knot behind her head. Her features were not necessarily mestizo — the distinctively prevalent ethnic features in most South American countries. Instead, she had a lighter coffee skin tone denoting her Basque ancestry.

The girl had first caught the Contessa's attention at the beginning of the class. She was part of the small group that seemed intensely interested in his lecture. She took copious notes and her attention never wavered. Yet she possessed a quiet resolve to analyze the information and draw her own conclusions. She was obviously not one to give into blind obedience. She seemed to assume a strange mixture of a contrasting persona. She carried herself as someone who had obviously been raised in the world of elites. However, her dress and seemingly free-spirited nature gave rise to the assumption she was no stranger to rough living and menial work nor was she at all afraid of it.

Even now, as the Contessa waited for the conversation to end, she heard the girl calmly discuss the lecture. Her questions were direct and intelligent, her contentions were not the outburst of an arrogant youth but the results of additional study and thought. The conversation finally ended with the girl taking up her brown canvass school bag and ascending the steps toward the exit. The Contessa's eyes followed her all the way out of the room.

The Contessa rose from her chair and made her way to where the professor was busily gathering his books and papers. "Professor Raphael Patrica?" She asked as she approached with a feigned hesitancy.

The Professor cocked his head to one side perhaps attempting to place the attractive blond approaching him. "Madame? I'm afraid you have me at a loss. I don't ..." He stopped, waving his finger and widening his eyes. "I have seen you a few times. You attended some of my open speaking engagements and, yes, I believe a couple of classroom lectures too."

His mind worked to complete the cerebral dossier he was forming in his head while taking in the stunning beauty dressed in slacks, T-shirt, and light brown sweater vest. Even with attempts to hide behind a set of wide framed glasses, no make-up and hair tied neatly in a bun, she still was a stunning beauty. "You always sit in the far back rows... almost always in the shadows. You don't seem to be an aspiring student."

"I'm not, Sẽnor," the Contessa replied, smiling. "We have a mutual acquaintance, you and I." The Professor gave her a puzzled look. The Contessa's gaze never wavered. "More precisely, in the Basque country. He should have contacted you about my wish to meet you."

The Professor's eyes widened. "Yes, he did mention someone. A woman he knew and trusted wished to discuss some things with me."

"Well, here I am," the Contessa raised her hand. "Please call me Reina for this occasion."

"An alias, how intriguing." The Professor took the young woman's hand and gave it a gentlemanly kiss. "So how may I be of service?"

The Contessa retrieved her hand. "Our friend told me you were one who could best be consulted on some rather technical matters I'm interested in researching. They are of a particularly dangerous nature."

The Professor said nothing, suddenly cautious. "I would not recommend we continue this conversation here. My office would be much more appropriate."

The Contessa agreed, and the Professor retrieved his documents, stuffing them into his leather case. "Shall we go?"

"Before we go," the Contessa stopped him. "Who was that young lady you were just speaking to?"

Throwing the case strap over his shoulder, the Professor struggled to remember back through the faces of the last few minutes. "The girl who was just here?"

"Yes, the girl in the jeans and T-shirt."

Raking through his mind, the Professor was slow to answer. "That was, that was Illana Muricia. She comes from comfortable means. Her father is a lawyer for the big shipping companies operating in Montevideo." The Professor shook his head, "I used to have great hopes for her. Unfortunately, she reads so much garbage about establishment economics — Fredrick Bastiat, Milton Friedman, and the other worshippers for the Bourgeois."

"In other words, she reads beyond what you tell her," the Contessa replied. "At least she is not a drone who espouses beliefs devoid of any independent thought."

He grimaced as he started out the side door. The Contessa followed quietly making a mental note to look further into the young Ms. Muricia at a later time.

The Professor's office was well kept but, as expected, it was a museum dedicated to a heyday long since passed. The walls were awash with photos of the Professor in his much younger years adorned in olive green combat fatigues and, in most of the pictures, holding some kind of weapon in a triumphant pose. A few others showed a defiant young Patrica serving his time in prison for his revolutionary activities. The rest of the pictures were the decorations common to most committed Marxists; Che Guevara, Mao addressing the humbled masses, or Lenin delivering a speech. The bookshelves were filled with the Spanish version of various works of Socialist literature. Strangely, his academic honors were few and posted directly on the wall behind his desk. Raphael Patrica, despite his success as a respected university academic, still yearned for his glory days as a valiant revolutionary.

He continued to decry corruption despite two decades of free elections and open government with his old comrades holding the presidency and a controlling majority in the Parliament. His kind was stuck in a world they never wanted to end. Contessa Selena de Alvarez had picked the right person for her needs.

"You really seem to miss it." She indicated the display of pictures on the wall.

"I feel the intended goal never came to fruition," the Professor replied with a hint of nostalgic remorse. "Those I called brothers in the Revolution now live comfortable lives as government power brokers. They betrayed what we set out to do."

The Contessa mentally rolled her eyes. Given the Uruguay President, Jose Mojica, himself a former Tupamaro guerrilla, personally chose to reside in a small farm raising chickens as his sole means of income made the wealthy professor seem even more disingenuous. "Yet you seem to hold onto the idea of the revolution."

"Of course. It will come back. It is just a matter of time, of energy."

"And of resources and support from a powerful benefactor," the Contessa interjected.

The Professor grew wary, disbelieving, his eyes blinking.

The Contessa smoothed her voice to a hypnotic purr. "You are right. I have been in many of your lectures, heard much of your brilliance and observed the crowds of listeners. I don't wish to be excessively flattering, but you are one of the few who legitimately keeps the flicker of life left in the ideas you still fight for. I see many in your lectures who are genuinely awakened by your teachings." She watched as the Professor tried to hide his growing bravado at all her compliments.

"Well, I don't know. I thank you for your perception," he beamed slightly trying to maintain his composure.

The Contessa slid into one of the smaller chairs on the other side of his desk. "The issue is when discussing a movement of any real consequence, the essential elements are access to steady resources, protection, and a flow of solid recruits committed to the cause."

Leaning over with his elbows firmly on the table, the Professor collapsed his hands under his chin. "What are you getting at?"

She crossed her legs in a feminine yet authoritative pose. "I am getting at the rebirth of your revolution, only I have the means for it to be more than a simple annoyance. To actually have the force to deliver the changes this country needs."

The Professor listened intently as she drew him in. "You of all people have your thumb in all the right places. Places to revive the movement and build the army you need. What I am offering is access to the resources to make it all a reality."

"This is a lot to take in," he sat back in his chair wiping at the light perspiration gathering on his face. "How do I know that you are genuine and can deliver what is needed? How do I know you are not security police?"

The Contessa lifted her hand to interject. "I can show you the land already exists that can be used for your base camp and training facilities. It will be developed for both rural and urban warfare. I am able to obtain seasoned military advisors who can give your recruits practical first-hand military training. In addition, I can offer a near limitless supply of armaments to wage the fight."

Shaking his head nervously, the Professor raised his finger. "No, no, this is too much; it is too easy. I need to know who this benefactor is: Cuba, Venezuela, perhaps even Argentina or maybe even Nicaragua. I need to know who you are representing and why they feel the need to be so benevolent."

"My dear Professor Patrica," the Contessa said gently. "Do not make such foolish requests. You have been in the game long enough to know that such requests are not possible to honor. You must not know those details for your protection and the protection of those I represent. All you need to know is that I can offer you the revolution you have always dreamed of, and this offer is being made by those who still feel a kinship to the Tupamaros and the cause you support. I can show you the land, the money, and the armaments already on site for your use. All you need is to recruit and organize a movement."

The Professor balled his hand into a tight fist as he pondered everything the woman said. Though he didn't want to admit it, what she was offering had been his life's ambition. He missed the heroic days of his youth — fighting the junta establishment for the peasants and the lower class. This was what she was offering. "I want to see this land and equipment you are offering first. I also want to know who you are offering as these *advisors*."

With a bow of her head and humble lowering of her eyes, the Contessa softly replied, "I wouldn't have it any other way."

CHAPTER 7

Kafka Dayan had never been one to participate in the greater pleasures of life. His rugged existence on the Kabutz followed by the tough conditioning by the Defense Force had made such luxuries an unrealistic and alien concept. Customarily, his mind was focused on the mission at hand. Sitting at the coffee table, that only a few days before had hosted the meeting of four shadowy figures, he pored over the collection of reports and dossiers he had scattered in front of him.

As part of his responsibility, Cohen had sought his counsel regarding the establishment of a team of mercenaries to operate clandestinely for this mission. Obligingly, Dayan had discussed the talents, training, and experience that would be required given the circumstances. Strangely, the old man had discussed this basic question hypothetically months before in Haifa over drinks in a bar. But it was a complete surprise when Dayan arrived at the hotel suite, after receiving a cryptic message from his old friend, and found a memory stick containing the professional histories of people that generally fit the requirements he had outlined.

In preparation, mostly to keep himself busy, the veteran commando carefully reviewed the documents. He saw several impressive resumes accompanied by classified intelligence reports from various intelligence services discussing their assessments. In the week he spent reviewing the information, he found six potential recruits for this operation.

He kept a small notepad beside him in which he wrote down questions and notes on any thoughts pertaining to the operation. He wrote all the information in Hebrew so any curious eyes would find it difficult to decipher. Taking further steps, he intermixed his notes with a cooking recipe and made his notes cryptic enough that an initial translation would conclude the writing was purely innocent. Using this system, he could keep the notebook handy without worrying about a security breach if it was stolen.

Cohen entered the room. He was ecstatic and acted as if he had just won a fortune at the gambling tables. Sinking down on the couch directly across from his young comrade, he placed his black leather satchel on the coffee table. With an excited look, he regarded Dayan. "We have an investor."

"Who? How much?"

Producing a laptop from his satchel, Cohen turned it on, connected to WIFI and began typing. Moments later he looked up. "Apparently, Mr. Lupon was in favor of our plan. I received this message from Leohem & Cohel finance house."

Twisting the laptop in Dayan's direction, Cohen pointed to the screen that showed an official-looking email from this Leohem & Cohen:

To the board of Las Creveous:

We have reviewed your plan and proposal for establishing

your operation. After our evaluation, we have concluded that you are a sound investment and would like to offer up to $20,000,000 financing of your operation to be paid to you in US dollars and converted to whatever alternative currency your firm finds necessary to properly establish your business.

Sincerely,

L. U. Pon

Treasury Investment Officer

Kafka read the note. It fascinated him to see how this whole operation was right out in the open. It was a far cry from spy novels and movies where things were done in offshore accounts or passing a suitcase full of money across the table. Instead, the money transfer was entirely public between international finance houses and businesses that by all accounts legally existed.

The money to finance the operation would be legally transferred from a small finance house in Europe or North America to some 'start-up business' in South America that exists only on paper. The infinite means by which money circulates into different currencies across borders and into businesses where prices fluctuate based on negotiations between parties made it virtually impossible to determine a legitimate financial transaction from a transaction with a more nefarious purpose.

"So we have our money and our cover, my dear boy." Cohen retrieved his laptop. "How are we coming with our potential recruits?"

Bobbing his head, Kafka looked at the collection of papers in his hands. "I have certainly got to congratulate you. These are some of the most thoroughly prepared dossiers I have ever seen. The addition of classified reports from all these foreign intelligence agencies is a feat you're gonna have to tell me about one day."

"Tools of the trade and years of experience," Cohen replied with a smirk and twinkle in his eyes.

Kafka chuckled. "Well, I have found some pretty good applicants. You have quite a few well-qualified people and several have extensive histories in this region that guarantee they'll attract attention." Dayan grimaced. "For the others, what I'm reading suggests they're questionable applicants who would be liabilities."

"So what then?" Cohen leaned back on the couch waiting for an answer he hoped would be some kind of good news.

Kafka did not disappoint. "I have about six applicants here that meet all the key requirements and have a low enough profile they should not attract unwanted attention. In addition, and this is important, they don't have rap sheets that make me nervous about questionable loyalties or security breaches."

"We're probably going to need more than six," Cohen said with a quiver of nervousness in his voice.

"I agree. Luckily, I think I have some operators in mind who can cover our bases." Kafka rose and poured himself some water. "I have some guys I know from the American army, and a few more I know from back home who are no longer with the IDF and won't compromise Israel. I have worked with these guys in the past and trust them for the more dangerous field work."

Cohen nodded, "If you have them, I have no objections as long as they don't compromise the mission."

Nouri al'Marak Surriman ambled along the walkway in the park. He admired the Paraguayan artistic architecture and landscaping, the well-carved marble structures, the flowing, brightly colored flower gardens, and lush islands of trees planted throughout the ocean of grassy fields. Not wishing to attract attention, Surriman chose conservative apparel — tan slacks, white collared shirt, and brown sports coat. In a place frequented by young lovers and tourists, it wouldn't be practical to be running about in jogging clothes or anything that denoted a man from the lower class of society.

Exactly as instructed, he discovered a small wooden bench with a Farsi inscription carved into it. Comically, the inscription was a quote from Ishmali Hassan, the founding leader of the ancient order of Islamic killers known as the Hashishins. The inscription read: *Any problem can be solved through education or assassination.* Looking about carefully he took solace that his handlers had chosen a location in the more secluded part of the park — a promise of fewer people and more privacy. It was a comforting sign that he was working with professionals. In the past he had endured the dangers brought about by those ignorant of the espionage world. It was something that made him grateful for such luxuries.

Taking his camera with a telephoto lens, he placed it up to his eye to look as if he were photographing the area. In reality, he was surveying the area for any onlookers possibly interested in his activities. His cover in Paraguay was that of a professional photographer representing a magazine that covered the beauty of South America. It provided him with a great cover story and enabled him to move freely about with few questions asked.

Moving a few steps every couple of seconds, he nonchalantly managed to scan the entire circumference of his location. He found such powerful optics enabled him to catch the teams trying to hide far off amongst the bushes waiting for him to make a move. When he was comfortable that he was not under the scope of any prying eyes, he coolly walked from the bench to the nearest tree. Again, true to his instructions, he noticed an area of disturbed dirt just under the bushes next to the tree. A few seconds of digging with his hand had uncovered a black plastic bag which contained a small disposable cell phone.

It was precisely 1800hrs when the phone rang. Flipping it open, Surriman answered, "Am I speaking to Porthos?"

For a second, there was no one on the other end of the phone, then a deep, slow voice responded. "I presume that I am speaking to Rascal?"

By the sound of the man's accent, he was Iranian. Surriman realized this was not a Hezbollah mission; it was Iranian intelligence. "You are," he responded.

There was a deep sigh that was easily heard over the phone. "You have followed your first instructions well."

"Thank you," Surriman's reply was somewhat ambivalent.

"Good. From where you are, proceed to the Hotel Cordoza and wait. We will call you again at precisely 1900hrs." The man didn't wait for Surriman to reply before the phone went silent.

Surriman pocketed the phone and stepped onto the sidewalk to hail a cab. A small blue cab pulled up to the curb. A plump driver with a curly, black wig poked his pear-shaped head out the window. "Where to, Sẽnor?" The cab driver shot the Arab a big grin revealing a disgusting view of missing teeth and the yellow, decaying remnants of what did remain.

Regarding the man for a moment, Surriman concluded the cab would do and promptly slid into the back seat. "Hotel Cordoza."

"Si, señor." As the cab driver left the curb, Surriman peered out the window for any tell-tale signs of a surveillance team. He saw none, meaning he was safe or the team watching him was very good.

Surriman took note of his surroundings. The cab was cleaner than expected after seeing the owner. It was still well used, but all the necessary equipment and documentation was present. Even the radio chirped continuously with the voice of a female dispatcher, who sounded like a large, middle-aged woman. He kept close track of the cars around him watching which vehicles followed despite numerous turns and lane changes. For any potential suspects, he casually marked down the make of the vehicles and license plate numbers to have them checked out at a later time. To his relief, however, he found no patterns during the ride and was reasonably sure he was not being followed.

Twenty minutes later, the cab arrived at the front entrance of the Hotel Cordoza. Jumping out of the backseat, Surriman bent down to hand the driver his money. The driver made a comment in Spanish wishing the Arab a good time while in Paraguay and drove off. The time was 1830hrs. With thirty minutes to wait before his next call, Surriman decided it was wiser not to draw attention to himself by wandering around outside and headed inside. It was a high-class hotel that catered to the upper elite of society. The driveway was three lanes with a high volume of traffic passing through. The large, polished double doors leading inside were manned by two ushers dressed in military-like uniforms.

Inside, Surriman was happy to see a small bar. He passed polished tables surrounded by leather armchairs occupied by a diverse cast of patrons before getting to the bar. There were gauchos dressed in cowboy attire with boots and Stetson hats alongside city professionals with sports jackets, white collared shirts with the top buttons left open, and crisp light colored slacks. The bar itself was deserted except for two individuals. The bartender, a tall slender woman with dark, mocha skin, was making the rounds from one patron to the next. The girl could have easily been a model with her long, shimmering black hair hanging straight down her back and the toned and well-proportioned figure of an athlete. The gray slacks, black leather vest, and black leather high heeled boots added to her stylish image.

Approaching the Arab, who had moved to the far corner of the bar, she gave him a sultry look. "And what will it be for you, Sẽnor? Or should I say, Sahib?" She gave him a slight bow in a comical fashion denoting the way a woman in a Muslim harem would have addressed her master.

Surriman was amused by the gesture. "I'm afraid you have me mixed up with the North Africans and the Turks. They are the ones who took their harem customs seriously. My people were more concerned with the multiple wives."

The woman smiled back. "Oh, I'm afraid you have me there. I'm not sure I would handle matrimony and housework as much as I would the wilder sexual life of a harem."

"Depends on the harem and the man," Surriman said.

"Some of those young sultans and aristocrats from the remote deserts have no imagination in that area. And some of those old farts from the cities of the Persian Gulf and Mediterranean can be really kinky."

The woman giggled as she knelt down to fetch a bottle of Scotch from under the counter. "Well, give me the experienced old men any day. They're more interesting than boys." She rose back up. "So what will you break your religious rules with tonight? I'm betting a whiskey or a gin. You seem the type."

Shaking his head, he frowned as if contemplating his choices. "I'm afraid there is no challenging my religion tonight. I just want a club soda and ice."

The woman gave a mocking 'tsk' at his lack of adventurism and reached for a glass and filled it with club soda and ice. Handing it over she winked, told him it was on the house, and returned to tending her other patrons. Surriman retreated to a far table, settled into a leather chair, and glanced at his watch. The time was 1840hrs; he had twenty minutes to wait. Scanning the room, no one was within earshot nor was he close to anyone who looked like they would make too much noise or cause a distraction.

To his relief, no one entering after him made any attempt to seat themselves within his proximity. If he was being tailed, it was a given that an operative from a surveillance team would try to interject themselves within listening distance. For the next several minutes he sipped his drink and casually looked about the area. At 1853hrs he stood up, leaving his drink.

At 1857hrs Surriman strode straight out the hotel onto the main walkway. He patiently watched the wider surroundings, pretending he was taking in the scenery. Still, no one was watching him.

His phone rang. Flipping it open he spoke quietly into the receiver, "Porthos?"

"You are at the hotel?" the voice asked.

"Yes, and I don't believe I am being followed," Surriman replied.

"Leave the hotel and walk three blocks to Mangata Street, turn left and continue walking until you come to a small deli. Wait at the corner for my next call."

He was aware of what was going on. His new masters weren't going to take his word that he was not compromised. He was going to be sent on a goose chase. Pre-staged operatives watching from fixed locations could observe for themselves if a detail was tracking him. If this went according to his previous experiences, he would go to three or four arbitrary locations. If at any time someone was spotted shadowing him, he would either receive a call with only a single spoken word 'abort', or he would get to his next ordered location and, after an hour or two of waiting, conclude he had been compromised, and his handlers had simply left.

Surriman began on foot toward his next location. He walked down the sidewalk enjoying the mildly warm evening and the scenery offered by the city. He appreciated seeing the small number of passersby: mostly young couples enjoying the evening as young girls walked by held in the arms of their lovers. The few sketch artists and street performers lining the sidewalk added nicely to the picture. It had been a long time since he had been to such a pleasant city. Even longer since he had been to a place that wasn't a war zone. It was refreshing to just enjoy the serenity of the moment.

Arriving at Mangata Street, Surriman turned left. The small deli was in plain view. The street was less populated and, judging by the small family shops and a consistent clientele of older looking people lining the street, it wasn't likely to be a highly frequented area. It would be much harder for a surveillance detail to follow him and maintain cover.

This proved his handlers were not novices. Surriman got to the porch of the deli and waited. There was a group of old men congregated around a small table in the center of the establishment drinking beer. He dropped onto a small stool outside the deli and opened a newspaper he had picked up earlier.

He caught sight of two men out of the corner of his eye watching him. They were rough looking and certainly of Mestizo ethnicity. They stood in the shadows at the entrance of a nearby alley.

Surriman dismissed the possibility they would be part of the Iranian's surveillance detail. Their intelligence service used hired operatives from the local talent to augment their network. They would, however, use professionals who knew how to be discrete, not a couple of low-life men like these two. Tattoo laden, greasy, and out of place for the neighborhood, they made no secret of their existence. They were most likely muggers looking for a potential score.

Surriman was not concerned with being mugged. He knew he could make short work of them. The problem was they were close enough that they could close in on him before he could make his escape. That meant he would have to fight them in public and draw unwanted attention to himself — something his handlers would definitely not appreciate.

Making the decision to test the hoodlum's resolve, Surriman rose to his feet and began walking. He could see the two men emerge from the alley and move in a direction loosely paralleling his own. Still, not wanting to make a scene he casually turned in a different direction.

In a pile of garbage stacked against the wall, he found a long metal rod. He looked up at the two men coming toward him. Surriman met their gaze with a look of indifference as he tapped the metallic rod against the wall. The loud clanking sound and his inviting look stopped both of them cold. They paused for several seconds, shifting their gaze from Surriman's face to the potentially lethal weapon he held ready and withdrew back into the alley.

His phone rang. Whoever was monitoring him was being thorough. He flipped open the phone to answer.

"Rascal." It was the same voice.

"Porthos."

"You had a little trouble, did you?" The voice asked in a way that suggested they already knew the answer.

"Nothing serious."

"We appreciate the discrete way you handled the matter," Porthos replied.

"No problem."

"Take a cab and go to the Plaza de' Condon. The small water fountain is quite beautiful, and the statue of the little girl has something for you." Click.

Pocketing his phone and rolling up his paper, Surriman casually made his way back to the main road hailing a taxi.

Another beaten blue cab pulled up alongside the curb. An elderly man poked his head out and asked, "Where to?"

Surriman thought for a moment before answering. He directed the driver to a building complex a few blocks from the Plaza. If he was being followed, he wanted to add a few more complications. Slipping into the back seat directly behind the driver, Surriman leaned back. If this was a game orchestrated by his handlers, he decided he was going to take a break from his normal vigilance and simply enjoy the ride.

The cab pulled into a parking lot directly across from the building complex. If the driver was an informant, Surriman would give him the wrong impression as to his destination. He leaped from the cab and walked across the street to the complex before the cab driver pulled away with another fair.

He headed toward the Plaza. The Plaza was in a quiet setting with a few old men leaning against the giant marble fountain and some young lovers enjoying the romantic scenery. With one hand in his pocket and the other clutching the newspaper, Surriman walked casually across the walkway looking like a sightseer. When he reached the statue of a small girl wearing a sundress and chasing butterflies, Surriman did not approach it immediately. He took a seat on a nearby bench scanning the area a few times to see if anyone was paying him any attention. When he was satisfied no one was watching, he slowly stood and walked to the statue. Lowering himself as if to get a better look at the architecture, he slid his hand across her stone arm down to her leg and finally noticed a crack at the base of the copper disk she stood upon. Sliding his fingers into the crack, he felt paper, a small package. It took a little finesse to dislodge it and deftly tuck the package between the folds of his newspaper.

He stood and walked away.

Reasonably sure he was out of view, he took a knee and unwrapped the paper. After retrieving the new phone, he threw his old phone in the bushes. There was a phone number taped to the new phone with two small triangles written over the first digit—one pointing up, one pointing down. This was a simple code. After the international and local code, the first digit was to be counted two digits up from the one written; the next digit was to be counted one down…and so on for the whole number.

Dialing the number he decoded, he waited. It was less than two rings before he heard someone answer. Soon he heard the familiar voice. "Good, you found the phone; so far you have not been followed by anyone as far we can tell."

Surriman rubbed his forehead. "By that, I am assuming that my test for the evening has come to an end?"

He heard a sigh, then said, "One more. Walk across the street, turn south and start walking until you come to the end of the road." Click.

Surriman stood up. Turning south, a collection of small shops and street vendors dominated the landscape, artful, in contrast to the marble structures and stone buildings housing the financial and political power in the country. Though he hated admitting it to himself, South America was his home. Home was not the deserts of the Persian Gulf or the Mediterranean as he had been told his whole life.

At the end of the street, a trio of young men huddled around a blue sedan—wild, young Latino men out on the town taking a moment to smoke and enjoy a drink. Surriman, not wanting to look suspicious, leaned against the corner of a nearby building and read his paper. Within minutes, one of the young Latinos approached and uttered the word 'Rascal'. The young man kept his distance but took note of any reaction. When their eyes met, and it was clear that the 'Rascal' comment was meant for him, Surriman responded with a softly asked 'Porthos?'

The Latino produced a pack of cigarettes which he offered to the Arab. Surriman declined the offer but beckoned the Latino to join him. Sitting, the Latino turned to his compatriots and gave them a nod indicating he had found their contact.

"Rascal?" The Latino asked again, one last request for confirmation.

"I am," Surriman replied looking directly at the Latino. "And I, again, presume you are Porthos."

The young man looked relieved. Surriman took a minute to study him. His face was almost heart-shaped topped by a well-groomed crop of short, oily black hair combed back tightly into a knot affixed at the nape of his neck with the sides of his head shaved. His white collared shirt hung loosely over an athletic frame and was draped over a pair of faded blue jeans, and he was wearing Timberland boots.

Surriman took a breath, "So now what?"

The young man said, "I take you to the one to whom you are to report."

"What is your role in this?"

"You know the answer to that question," the Latino replied. "I am nothing more than a hired man who does jobs like this for those who pay for it."

Surriman rolled up his paper. "So, do we go now, or do you wish to continue with further pleasantries for appearance sake?"

The Latino looked around again. "I think the pleasantries are unnecessary. No one is watching or seems to care. So let us get off the street."

This was clearly not the young man's first time handling such an operation. Surriman and his guide rose from their seats and crossed to the waiting car. By now the Latino's two compatriots were in the front seat with the engine running. Jumping into the back, Surriman and his new friend settled in as the car pulled from the curb and started down the street.

CHAPTER 8

Major Semir Ali Essouri found himself continually rubbing his face as he poured over the documents in front of him. He was an administrator with a penchant for bookkeeping and records. His colleagues affectionately referred to him as the "man of details". He didn't look at all the professional soldier when he was dressed in his casual business attire — tan slacks and a sports jacket with a loosely opened collared shirt. He wore this attire with disdain in contrast to his military fatigues in which he felt the most comfortable. It would be hard for anyone to imagine that this little bookkeeper had seen combat in Bosnia after the fall of Yugoslavia, both episodes of the Chechen war against the Russians, and was an acting participant in the most recent Lebanese-Israeli war of 2006.

His concentration was broken by the sound of a knock at his office door. "Yes?" he tried not to growl.

A voice, muffled by the partially opened door, replied, "A car pulled up, sir. It is our men returning with your contact."

Essouri collected his thoughts which were still focused

on his volumes of paperwork. "Have him brought directly to my office when they get here."

"Yes, sir," the voice replied.

Returning his attention to the documents scattered about his desk, Essouri nearly lost track of time when he heard another knock at the door. "Come in!" The door opened and a man of medium build and thinning hair entered. Behind him was a tall, athletic young man. The first man, whose sweat soaked, vanilla shirt reeked of body odor and cigarettes, motioned to the young man behind him intending to make an introduction. He was stopped by the young man who opened with a single word, 'Porthos?' His eye contact and focus was directed at the small man behind the desk. Essouri fixed his attention on the young man and responded with a single word, 'Rascal?'

The young man nodded. Essouri waved his hand signaling the subordinate to leave. The subordinate moved past the young man and slid out the door leaving the men known as Rascal and Porthos alone.

Neither spoke for a moment as the Major took his time eyeing the young Arab as if making some last minute observations for a final decision. Then, with a single hand gesture, he motioned the young man to sit. The young man slipped into a small metal chair directly across from the older man who continued his assessment.

"So you are the man chosen for this assignment," Essouri finally spoke. Pulling a small laptop from a locked drawer, he began to read. "Nouri al'Marak Surriman, born in a remote area of Northern Argentina, a swath of rather lawless territories involving Paraguay and Brazil known as the Iron Triangle. Recruited at eighteen into the Hezbollah, first in their political wing and later into the military wing. You volunteered for action in 2006 when Israel invaded Lebanon and later stayed with a unit from the Beka Valley carrying out across border insertions into Israel. When the civil war broke out in Syria, you went in with volunteer units to support the Assad regime. Your skill at small war commando operations eventually led to you being recruited into a special program run jointly by Pasdaran and VEVAK for enhanced external covert and intelligence operations against enemies of the true Islamic path."

Essouri stopped and looked up to assess the young man. Surriman's facial expression indicated he was in agreement with what had been read. The major continued, "You excelled in your training and aptitude for raw survival intelligence, excelled in your ability to think quickly and adapt to changing environments, and have shown a remarkable talent for intelligence in the area of field operations."

"Thank you, sir," Surriman responded not knowing what more to say.

Essouri continued, "This brings us to now, and why you are here. Iran is about to undertake one of its biggest, most daring missions ever, and you are going to be part of it."

Surriman said nothing. His eyes were fixed on the small, older man waiting to hear more.

Rising from his chair the Major began to walk around his office. "Our mission is to bring down the government in Uruguay and install one that will be friendlier to Iranian interests here in the Western Hemisphere. Where you fit into this plan will be helping establish a military force that will accomplish this goal." Essouri waited a few moments to let the Arab absorb the information he was being given before continuing.

"As it stands now, we will approach this operation in a

series of stages. The first will be to initiate a wave of left-wing terror campaigns aimed at creating hysteria and culminating in the assumption that the current president of the country is involved. After we create an atmosphere of instability, the intent is to sweep in with a champion from the political right-wing who will swoop in with a force of patriots and assume control of the country. While we already have someone working on setting up the network and all necessary components to carry out the left-wing insurgency, you will be our man on the ground doing all the necessary preparation in establishing the right-wing force needed to ultimately take over the country. You will be responsible for setting up training facilities, recruiting forces, organizing logistical support, training them, and preparing all the groundwork for execution of the mission."

Surriman absorbed the information. "If I may, sir. By the way you describe this plan, it sounds as if I will have to build everything from the ground up."

The Major had made a complete lap around the perimeter of his office before coming back to his desk and sinking into his chair. "Yes, that is your assignment. The purpose of this mission is for Iran to be as hands off as possible without any direct involvement. Otherwise, we risk giving the Americans an excuse to intervene militarily and destroy everything. For this reason, we need you to work quietly to make this all appear as domestically developed as possible. This means using your old connections in the Triangle to procure support in the form of weapons and other logistics that will have to be purchased off the black market. This is something I presume you can do?"

"Yes, I can."

"You will have to find a way to recruit people, move

them to the training facilities, and organize them. We will need weekly reports on their progress. As they develop, we will give you more thorough details regarding the specifics on how they will be infiltrated then be utilized in seizing the country."

"If I may?" Surriman opened. "I can only see this plan being successful in an urban operation. Yet the way you are describing my role, it sounds as if you want me to develop this operation in remote, rural, or, *jungle*, environments?"

The Major nibbled his lower lip as he processed Surriman's comments. "We have to be discrete, so we may have to build town replicas of essential facilities in the jungle."

Surriman interrupted again. "The point is that I can recruit impoverished peasants and mercenaries from former guerrilla armies throughout the continent but, in the end, their experience is still going to be in the jungles and countryside. Inevitably, we will need people who have experience operating in cities and urban environments."

Essouri pressed his fingers to his chin as he contemplated the young Arab's observations. "We can build urban warfare models if necessary, especially if we utilize some of the old mining camps that have been abandoned. However, you make a good point about recruits. They will need urban fighting experience."

Realizing the Iranian had limited experience in the realm of street warfare, Surriman took some liberty. "We can recruit from two key sources."

Essouri leaned back, his index and thumb still firmly molded against his chin, "Go on."

"Recruit instructors from two worlds: former police from one of the more developed locations in South America such as Buenos Aires and Rio de Janeiro, and some of the fighters returning fresh from the conflict in Syria. The fighters can give a more combat directed touch to their training. These men can train and organize your main corps of operatives — your shock troopers can take control of the city, the main streets, and operate against any dissension. The other groups should be trained in a more advanced setting. These fighters should be your Special Forces urban commandos. They should be the advanced group who can take and control all key locations such as Parliament, the President's offices, and offices for intelligence or military general staff."

Essouri was impressed with Surriman's wisdom developed well beyond his years. "This is all quite good. I must say your perception is brilliant. Where can we get such skill on the market here in South America?"

"It is just a matter of finding the right broker to reach out to the right contacts. Several South American born fighters serving in Lebanon and Syria have considerable experience. Have them discharged from service and sent home. This way you can bring them back with a viable reason that will not raise suspicion with the US. They won't be acting as operatives of Hezbollah or Iran but of South America. You can also use them in the actual force you're trying to set up. They will probably prove more reliable than whatever mercenaries you manage to find if they know they are operating in the greater interest of Islam."

The young Arab had presented a great solution to what could have been a serious issue. Essouri said, "So this brings us to the setup." Unrolling a large document onto the top of his desk, Essouri revealed a large scale map of an area encompassing land around the Argentinian/Brazilian border.

At first glance, the land appeared to be in a remote,

mountainous, jungle environment. "Here is where you will be operating." Essouri pointed out the property his commander had recently purchased from the Cuban front company. "You will be in a place with very limited contact with the outside world. With some intense use of camouflage, we should be able to protect the mission from any satellite or aerial surveillance that might prove cumbersome. You will also have limited radio and cyber communications capability to minimize any possible signal interception."

"I'm assuming we will communicate through runners and intermediaries?"

"Correct. Remember, this entire mission depends on concealing any connection to the Iranian government. We will use intermediaries to communicate for added protection."

"What about the *left wing* opposition you intend to create?" Surriman asked. "What involvement will I have in that?"

"None. You will manage a separate operation entirely. Someone else is responsible for setting up and directing that operation. You will have the necessary information to eliminate them when the time is right — only that — so there won't be a complication."

"So, they're not going to be hired guns that can be paid off?" Surriman shook his head, disappointed. "A little cold-blooded, if I may."

Essouri shrugged. "I wish they could simply be paid off. But either mercenaries or manipulated believers will still be a group in this country with guns and a penchant for mayhem. Besides, to legitimize our new Uruguay hero, we have to show that he has neutralized the terrorists and can protect his people."

Surriman understood the Iranian's logic and the need — all very Machiavellian. Still, he didn't approve of leading people through this kind of charade.

The two men discussed further points. Everything was being set into motion perfectly.

CHAPTER 9

Kafka Dayan was sweltering in the back seat of the cheap taxi as it idled through the narrow streets of Bogotá. He had established weeks earlier he was not disposed to tropical weather. If he was not so beholden to the old Mossad spy, he would have divested himself from this mission altogether based on the climate alone. The driver, a heavyset man of gigantic proportions, swayed awkwardly in the driver's seat as he listened to salsa music on the radio. That was bad enough, but when the driver attempted to add to the festivities by singing, Kafka was sure he had discovered a new torture method for interrogation.

The car, and by extension the torment, finally came to a stop. Trying not to look desperate to escape, Kafka exited the car as casually as he could while still exhibiting the speed of a soldier deploying from a vehicle in combat. Outside he found himself standing in front of a small, two-story building on an obscure street corner. The only clue he was at the right location was a small wooden sign in Spanish on the front door: *Guardian Angel Intelligence.*

Paying the driver, Kafka walked toward the building. As

he neared it, he realized the building was far more than it seemed. His operational instincts alerted him at once to a well-hidden but strategically placed camera system. Small and barely visible, the cameras would be easily overlooked by someone taking the building at face value. He approached cautiously, his senses becoming even more heightened. The windows were in cheap glass frames but covered with a strong layer of blast-proof glass of near armor strength.

It was obvious the apparently cheap structure was actually a well-protected fortress. Dayan pressed the rusted and broken appearing doorbell. He then placed his hands up against the wall. Looking up to where he was sure another camera lay hidden, he made certain they could get a good look at his face. He held the pose for several minutes, even though it felt like hours before the battered, metal door cracked open. Seconds later a young woman, looking to be in her late teens or early twenties, emerged from the darkness. She said nothing. Taking her time to look the man up and down, she focused her gaze on his clothes.

"I'm carrying," Dayan spoke up realizing what the girl was trying to assess. "One in my belt behind me, the other under my armpit just under my shirt."

The girl seemed satisfied with his answer and opened the beaten screen door to let him in. Motioning with her head for the Israeli to follow her, she walked back inside. Obeying her, Dayan followed. The lights were low leaving the inside barely visible to someone whose vision had not adjusted. If he was going to be ambushed, now would be the ideal time. Strangely, the girl stopped and stood against the wall watching him. Minutes later his eyes began to adjust to the darkened environment, and he could make out his surroundings. The inside corridors were vastly different from the building's exterior. He found both he and the girl to be in a thick glass holding cell constructed of the same blast-proof material he had seen on the outside windows. If someone did breach the front door, they would find themselves unable to get very far.

"Are your eyes adjusted?" the girl asked in a quiet voice.

Dayan was surprised. She had been waiting for his vision to adjust this whole time. "Ye…yes, they are."

With a nod, the girl lowered her head toward a small electronic device. A green laser illuminated the small corner of the room for a brief few seconds before a second door of the holding area slid open allowing passage to the rest of the building. The girl stepped through and motioned silently for the Israeli to follow.

With his eyesight adjusted, he was able to get a better look at his silent hostess. She was a beautiful, young woman with a perfectly contoured, hourglass figure neatly fitting into a snug, gray business suit that captured every bit of her features. Her hair, a glistening raven black, was tied into a tight bun behind her head. Like the rest of the building, she was out of place with both the neighborhood and the outside cover.

Suddenly, he was walking on nice carpet and viewing thick, concrete walls while going down a long, narrow corridor. This was a virtual death trap for any team of attackers. They would be huddled together with no cover and surrounded by concrete walls that would create a wave of ricochets for any bullets fired in these tight confines. At the end of the hall, he noticed that the corners had been smoothed out to provide excellent fighting positions for anyone defending the location. This building would not be a good location to attack even for the most skilled commandos. Dayan could appreciate the security measures. This environment was more what he had expected both tactically and professionally. It was truly an impressive site.

The young woman led the Israeli to a small door to the left. Punching in a code, she stood back as the sound of an electric lock detaching echoed. Opening the door, the two made their way up a narrow flight of stairs leading to the second floor and another thick wooden door. They found themselves entering a business-oriented setting. Expensive oriental carpeting covered the floor, and the walls were no longer gray concrete blocks but polished dark oak paneling. Lights were suspended from the ceiling in perfect alignment as they illuminated the walkways. This was a sharp contrast from the fortified defense position below.

Motioning the Israeli to the waiting room, the girl turned and looked at Dayan. "Please wait here, sir." Her English was smooth and refined — not broken or accented. It was obvious she was a native speaker of both tongues. Dayan took a seat on one of the four leather chairs circling the polished oak table.

The girl said nothing as she quietly disappeared. The waiting room was bare; there was no reading material or anything to make a person the least bit comfortable. It didn't take Dayan long to realize another miniature camera was hidden in the upper corner of the room allowing someone to observe him. Apparently, the entire setup of the waiting room was a subliminal test to give the observers an idea of what to expect with either a client or potential threat.

After several minutes, the young girl returned to get him. Leading him down the hall they arrived at a large room with a long meeting table in the center. The girl beckoned him to take a seat in one of the chairs surrounding the large table. Dayan sat and watched as she disappeared. This time, however, he didn't wait long before another woman dressed in a gray pantsuit entered from a door on the other side of the room. Except for a slight age difference, she was an almost perfect copy of the young girl who had been leading him through the building. Her hair was even pulled back in a similar fashion — a tight bun atop her head.

"Mr. Herron?" She asked as she came to the chair directly across from him and sat down. "I trust you have been well taken care of?"

"Indeed," Dayan responded, "your assistant has been most accommodating."

"She is a professional," the woman replied implying he was not to mention her again.

Placing a leather writing pad on the table, she opened it up exposing a pristine white notepad and expensive black writing pens. Leaning back in her chair, the woman assessed the man sitting across the table. "I'm Alyssa Rios, the CEO of Guardian Angel Intelligence, better known as GAI. Now, what exactly is it that you require, 'Mr. Herron?' A name which I presume is an alias."

"It is," Dayan replied as he sat back in his seat. "I have to admit this setup is not what I expected from the neighborhood or, for that matter, your combat zone on the lower floor."

"In my business one has to be able to account for several realities; the reality that when you provide intelligence and covert operational services, it is wise to keep a low profile and not make yourself easy to find or watch. This neighborhood is rundown but with a very deep-rooted community. This makes it hard for someone from the outside not to be noticed, and a narrow winding roadway makes mobile signal collection very difficult.

"As far as the palatial corporate setup you now see, the clients who have the connections and go to the lengths you did to acquire my services are not your local street vendor or low-end racketeer. They have powerful interests with very serious concerns. They wouldn't give several million dollars worth of business to someone who looked like they were a detective from a cheap novel or a sweaty, head-chopping mercenary. The professional environment is what people with money expect to see and with whom they expect to deal."

"Then I am impressed," Dayan stated as he rubbed his chin.

The woman remained expressionless. "As far as your interest in the lower floor, it is really just a reasonable precaution. Again, in my business, those who you work against are not always inclined to use legal methods to resolve their problems with people like me. I just like to know that more extreme responses can be mitigated. And since you were so quick to realize the tactical implications as well as notice my hidden cameras so easily, I can only deduce your own professional experience is in the tactical arts possibly from police or military special operations. You are giving your cover away, Mr. Herron."

Waving his hand in a casual gesture the Israeli shrugged. "You wouldn't be worth the business we are offering you if you couldn't figure out something so rudimentary. After all, I'd have to be someone with experience in that type of world to be involved in affairs such as this."

"So let us get down to business." Alyssa Rios slipped one of her pens from its holding sleeve and readied herself to take notes. "I was not given very much information, only that some interested parties from the Middle East required extensive intelligence and possibly operational support against another party also from the Middle-East."

"That is a good understanding of the affair." Dayan chose his words carefully. "We are a political consortium, operating independently of any foreign powers, interested in working against some rival interests that are looking to set up a network here in South America."

Alyssa Rios said nothing only lowering her eyes briefly to jot down notes. Dayan continued, "Our ultimate goal is to identify their operations, all operatives they have, and where they are headquartering their networks. Basically, we need to employ an already established intelligence network to help work against our 'competitors' to identify, engage, and neutralize the threat."

Rios rolled the pen between her fingers as she contemplated the Israeli's explanation. "Who is this threat you are worried about and tell me why you can't use your own assets already in the country?"

Dayan moved uncomfortably in his chair as he contemplated how to explain this to her. "What difference would it make? It's no different from what you are normally up against judging by your security precautions. If we are willing to pay you several million dollars for your services, such risks should be a normal occupational hazard."

Rios leaned back in her seat with her arms folded and stared directly at the Israeli. "Mr. Herron, let me be frank. Security precautions only work so far. The real protection in my field is having the instincts and wherewithal to know when to walk away from a job. I can easily assume what government you are in defacto working for. I wouldn't want to risk hatred from the kind of people you are working against. I either have a good understanding of what I'm getting into, or I can happily show you the door."

The woman held firm. Dayan realized his only option and responded. "We are combating what we believe to be a rogue element of the Iranian Pasdaran, better known as the Revolutionary Guard, who are trying to develop a network and extend their secret war to this side of the world." He looked at the woman who, with pen pressed to her lips, seemed to be listening intently. He continued, "I represent an interest of a similar nature. I belong to a rogue element that intends to neutralize this effort and whatever operation they intend to execute."

"The Revolutionary Guard, huh?" Rios shook her head and muttered something in Spanish. She gave a discerning look at the man across from her. "You are asking for a very tall order. One that I could possibly turn down; that I probably should turn down..." She stopped and looked at the Israeli. She studied him carefully.

Dayan let the woman collect her thoughts. "But you won't, will you?" he challenged.

"No, I won't. However, let us be clear, 'Mr. Herron'. I will support you with intelligence. I will support you with logistics. But neither I nor any of my people will be involved in any 'activities' or operations you take on as part of your war. Use your own people for that." Her eyes were focused and unassailable as she eyed Kafka. The message was received.

Dayan opened the side of his black sports jacket enough to show her he was reaching into the side pocket. Slowly, he produced a small black memory stick which he slid across the table.

Picking it up, Rios examined it for a moment before the

young assistant entered the meeting room. She retrieved the memory stick from her employer along with some instructions delivered in Spanish. The young assistant vanished out the door as quietly as she entered.

Rios returned her attention to the Israeli. "So, I can assume that tactical actions will be carried out in this little affair?"

Dayan nodded. "A lot of things will probably be carried out that the authorities, in general, will not take kindly to."

"How extensive do you imagine this operation will be?" Rios began jotting notes.

Dayan noted her scribbling was in the form of no language he could recognize. "Are you actually writing this down?"

"I'm writing in a code I developed and perfected myself. No one else knows it," she answered reassuringly. "I find it a far more secure means of passing information than a computer, email, or iPad that can be hacked. Where you are concerned, this code prevents viable information from being understood if my files were hacked or stolen. Please continue."

"We assume that we may be operating extensively across international borders and in large metropolitan areas."

Rios said nothing as she jotted down the notes. Dayan continued, "The only information we have is on the memory stick I just gave you."

"It will be reviewed and returned to you," she replied.

"Thank you."

"Well then, I suspect you need me to build you an information system that allows you to capture the intent of your adversary and the support to carry out neutralization measures against them."

"That is precisely what we need," Dayan said as he tapped his fingers on the table, which Rios found extremely annoying.

The young assistant returned moments later with a laptop computer in her hands. Placing it in front of her employer she opened the screen. Waving her hand at her assistant, the two ladies began to speak in a language far different from any familiar Spanish dialect. Turning her attention to the laptop, Rios read slowly as her assistant directed her to portions she wanted to point out. Dayan said nothing as he studied the facial expressions the ladies displayed as they reviewed whatever information was capturing their attention.

It seemed like hours, though it had only been a few minutes, when the room went awkwardly silent before Alyssa Rios looked up and stared the Israeli directly in the eye. "Ali Anwar al Qalmini!" She looked the Israeli up and down. "From what my assistant could gather in her research, we are being asked to collect information against one of Iran's most formidable covert operators." She paused for a moment collecting her thoughts. "You're asking a lot of us. Iranian Intelligence is very well connected in South America in all the worst places. Cartels, dictator regimes, and even a large enclave of ethnic Lebanese throughout some very lawless geographic locations; they have ties to them all."

Kafka Dayan listened but was puzzled. "Forgive me, but I thought your business was in navigating such waters and with such clients. Why would this be any different?"

Rios pursed her lips as she looked down at the table. Waving her hand, she dismissed her assistant who turned and exited the meeting room as silently as she had entered. Looking at the Israeli, Rios folded her hands. "This is my business which is why I can tell what I would be getting into, who I would most likely be dealing with, and know the reach and capabilities they possess. Collecting information on criminal groups relegated to a certain country or city is one thing, corporate espionage and investigations are something else. Each situation has its own risks, and they can be mitigated with planning. However, you're talking about well-connected and very dangerous networks that can easily find out who is spying on them if my people were discovered during this operation."

Dayan acknowledged the woman's concerns. He could also sense she was being somewhat disingenuous. "I understand your concerns. My own experiences with such people and their extensions make me well able to understand your apprehension. Yet, I would guess you are no stranger to such threats, and I doubt this would be your first time working against them."

Rios said nothing as she gazed back at the screen and then the Israeli. "Yes, you're right. I have on occasion provided services for and against such powerful entities. But it was a huge risk and had to be handled delicately."

Raising his hands Dayan beamed. "That is exactly what my people are looking for as well. We want this handled with a light touch and a lot of discretion."

"No, you don't." Rios regained control of the conversation with a sharp interruption. "Allow me to be direct. Discretion is not what I feel when I am speaking to someone like you. Everything I see tells me you're a commando in Special Operations and not a professional spy. That you were sent to be the contact, tells me this mission of yours is going to involve a lot of noise and quite easily cause a lot of blowbacks. My firm and those I would employ could wind up suffering, so do not presume to give me assurances that you will not be able to honor."

Gnawing at his lip Dayan contemplated his next words carefully. "So, what guarantee would put you at ease?"

Rios sighed as she leaned back in her chair. "I'll get you your information. I'll track your people and get the intelligence you need. But if you get out of hand or attempt to carry out an operation that could compromise my people and not clear it with me first, I will consider our business at an end."

"Of course, under the circumstances, I find such conditions perfectly acceptable."

"Very well," Rios replied. "Then let our business begin. I'll start looking for your Iranian and identify who he is employing."

CHAPTER 10

The Contessa Selena de Alvarez relaxed as she enjoyed the breathtaking view of the lushly vegetated countryside from the back seat of her limousine. The upscale community located just south of Caracas, Venezuela was a picture of manicured ranch estates with imported Kentucky bluegrass lining the sporadically placed islands of exotic trees. The wood fencing enclosed pastures where magnificent horses, mostly imported Arabians, pranced about freely. It was all a reminder of her own family estate in Spain.

For the last several weeks, she had been around circles of sweaty Iranian soldiers, low-end dives, overrated universities, obnoxious left-wing militants, and unwashed jungle mercenaries. She found the thought of meeting those who shared her own higher class of breeding and culture refreshing. The limousine drove off the main road and started up the white chalky, graveled driveway leading to a very imposing ranch house. This mansion was an impressive structure standing several stories high with castle-like balconies on each floor. The design allowed the homeowner to project a commanding force. Several smaller houses were connected to the structure adding to the intimidating image.

The limousine rolled slowly around the circular driveway stopping in front of the house. A man emerged from the front door and approached the back door of the vehicle. Attired in a light blue suit, he was in sharp contrast to the surrounding ranch houses and gauchos sporting blue jeans and T-shirts.

The man was well spoken and polished. Opening the door of the limo he gave her a slight bow. "Contessa de'Alvarez, you honor us with your presence. The Patron is upstairs and would be very honored if you would join him for lunch."

Unbuckling her seatbelt, she dipped her head to the man. "I will happily accept the Patron's gracious invitation." She moved to slide out of the car as the man extended his hand to aid her. Accepting the hand gracefully, she exited the backseat. Closing the door behind her, the man gently placed one hand on her back while guiding her to the front door with the other.

As the two walked, the Contessa made note of the subtle security features. The portico and the various corners were covered with small, unobtrusively placed video cameras. Judging by what was visible, she assumed they were high pixel-grade cameras with a variable view. They were likely wireless with a connection to a central database and power grid. This system would be very difficult to neutralize. In addition physical security features circled the house: grass mounds were bunker fighting positions where armed men could be deployed in the event of an attack. The TV dish was actually a satellite receiver probably capable of connecting to anywhere.

As she entered the house, she was impressed by the artful way the South American cowboy motif blended with classical European design. Walking on the smooth oak flooring, the two arrived at an elevator located in the center of the house. Entering it, the man typed in a code and floor number and the elevator promptly rose. At the third floor, the elevator door opened. The two stepped out onto another oak walkway. Again, the Contessa took note of the surroundings: an open lounge of plush chairs, couches, and a small, well-stocked mini-bar. They passed a set of thick wooden doors guarding the entrance to a meeting room. It was cast in a more traditional design with a long table surrounded by Victorian-era leather armchairs. The walls were lined with paintings depicting various battles from the Renaissance period.

It was obvious the Patron reserved this floor for his business while maintaining another room to accommodate clients or parties. In this case, the Patron had apparently decided that the Contessa was a client who would enjoy an outdoor setting and a good meal while discussing business. The more conservative types preferred the formal meeting room, and the wild gangster types enjoyed business over hard drinks, loud music, and the company of pretty Latinas in tight dresses sliding around on their laps.

Her escort moved past her and reached for the door leading outside. Giving him a smile of gratitude, she walked through it. Finding herself on the porch, she saw a long glass table with outdoor patio chairs arranged around it. At the far end, an aged, rather portly man was seated comfortably as he puffed on a cigar while enjoying the pleasant view.

Don Diego Francisco del' Meduriso was an energetic figure even at sixty-five, well groomed with a neat crop of salt and pepper hair and a roundish face. A charming man of wealth, class, and good breeding, known to be a brilliant negotiator and businessman, he had survived many changes over the years. He managed to come out even more prosperous by dealing with the American rage against drug cartels, communist rebels looking to eliminate capitalist competition in the black market, and superpowers with a political agenda that did not include him.

Turning his attention to the young lady, he smiled a sincerely gracious smile as he stubbed out the remains of his cigar. "Ah, my dear Selena, you truly honor me with your presence." His voice was smooth and pleasant.

"My dear Patron, I am honored you would see me," the Contessa replied as she walked over to him. Her movements were that of a confident, sophisticated woman at home in the current environment. The Patron looked at the young lady dressed in a dark business jacket and a matching skirt that hugged her frame nicely. Her long legs were encased in stockings, and she wore heels that showed off her toned calves. She had a curvaceous body, seductive sensuality, and powerful presence.

Her golden hair was tightly secured in a bun that glistened in the sunlight. Don Diego Francisco del' Meduriso looked upon her not with any sense of lust but with a mixture of respect and paternalistic pride. He had known her father years before as a well-respected officer in the Spanish Army and later as a deputy foreign minister. He could remember this young woman as an energetic teenager who enjoyed all the adventures South America had to offer a girl of her stature and position. Even then, she had an interest in the region's politics, economy, and quietly discussed the intrigues that dominated South American society.

Now she was even more beautiful but no longer following her father to important meetings. She was a businesswoman conducting her own negotiations and making her own way in the world. For this reason, Don Meduriso was eager for this meeting. He wanted to see how well the diplomat's daughter was handling the world of business.

Taking a seat directly across from Don Meduriso, the Contessa smiled pleasantly. "Don Meduriso, you are still the distinguished figure I remembered as a child." She extended her ungloved hand which the old man gently took and lightly kissed.

"My dear Contessa, the honor *and* pleasure is all mine. But you came to see me for business, not pleasure."

She crossed her legs and faced the old Don. "I have a business venture for you. One I'm sure you will find quite lucrative."

"Go on," the Don said, intrigued. He folded his hands.

"I'm representing a, shall we say, syndicate of a sort, that is planning to operate here rather extensively in the near future. They will require a continuous supply of armaments."

"I see," the Don said. "What kind of syndicate, my dear?"

The Contessa feigned a look of surprise at the old Don's question. "Sẽnor, of all people, you should understand discretion is most important in these matters for both you and the client."

He smiled with affection. "Your shock is endearing, and I agree to a point. But one in my business survives by knowledge and calculating the odds. That includes knowing enough about customers to understand what type of trouble they bring, and what it will look like when it comes. So, while I don't require names, blueprints, and other detailed information, I won't even begin to discuss this deal until I know what I'm getting myself into." Nothing changed except a hint of menace to his tone. "Who are they, what is their agenda, and how extensive is this group?"

"Very well," the Contessa relented. "I'm working with a group of leftist revolutionaries from Uruguay. You already know the story. They have grievances with the government and believe it is controlled by oligarchs. They feel the situation warrants an armed insurrection. Politics as usual for South America."

"In Uruguay?" The Don was taken aback. "It has a solid democratic system and is one of the more prosperous and better-run countries in this part of the world."

The Contessa looked at him with confusion. "Throwbacks to the old Tupamaros complain about the current state when really they want to relive the old days of their youth. However, in this case, they have managed to attract enough popularity among the countryside peasants and committed college radicals to create an underground movement of some formidability."

Don stared out over the view he enjoyed. He thought carefully as he processed the young woman's proposal.

"In truth," the Countess searched for the hole that would allow the Don to accept the risks, "while I fully anticipate violence across the country for quite some time, I don't see it going anywhere or gaining any real traction with the people."

"Then why bother with them at all? You have never struck me as the political type."

"Because they are very well funded and will be for a

considerable amount of time," she said. "I'm not a supporter. I'm a business agent who can obtain what they don't have access to. I intend to be well paid for it. Even hardened communists respect the need to engage in capitalism in order to achieve their goals."

The Don studied the young Contessa. He could sense she was not telling him the whole truth. However, he believed she had given him enough information to be satisfied that his participation would be safe enough. "Good. The risk sounds right. I don't see any uncontrollable repercussions for me. What will you require?"

"Mostly small arms and explosives, an assortment for both urban and rural operations. I need equipment that is functional and generic. For rural areas, I would need a compliment of AKM types, preferably North Korea 68 models. They are loosely distributed by the People's Republic and are largely untraceable because they've been used in various revolutions. The assumption would be that any Western intelligence service would look to either Cuba or another rebel group to act as a benefactor for my clients — possibly even the Koreans themselves. After all, appearances this early are everything.

"If this is not achievable, I would settle for Eastern European stock that can also be easily explained, such as Romanian WASR models or Ukrainian brands. However, the North Korean brands can fire rockets without the aid of an added grenade launcher. I also need a sizable consignment of hand grenades; specifically, western military grade, not the Chinese or Eastern European products you generally offer."

"Hand grenades?" Don Meduriso asked. "My dear little Contessa, I can easily provide the proper grenade launchers for more upgraded weapons, and I can offer a consignment of RPGs still fresh in their case."

The Contessa hesitated for a moment as she mentally ran through her shopping list. "I will need both. They will be conducting both urban and rural operations. And I am anticipating that while the countryside will be impossible for security forces to lock up, movement of weapons can flow more easily. The urban strategy will require greater emphasis on smaller, more concealable weapons."

The Contessa's strategic logic was sound. But her intentions were focused on her real mission. She had to plan for the dual wishes of her employer — first set up a threatening left-wing terror network to create the havoc and panic required for the desired environment, then be able to eliminate the network upon completion of their service. That meant limiting their access to heavier weapons systems that might make the second part of her mission needlessly complicated.

"For urban operations, the requirements will be more specific: AKM-74, short or collapsible stock, and close quarter weapons like the Russian and Ukrainian naval infantry use. Again, we don't want to use weapons that would be hard to explain. If Uzi 9mm's are easier to obtain, I would accept those. I will also need a consignment of close proximity weapons, preferably Scorpion Cz's, .22 and .32 caliber, for assassinations and operations that can be easily dispatched afterward, plus a variety of explosives with a minimal amount of Semtex. This type could be something obtained from another terrorist group."

Impressed, the Don listened quietly as the Contessa rounded out her requirements with sound knowledge of her subject. When she finished, he sighed, "I will have to look into the arrangements needed to meet these requirements. I will be in touch within the week with a price. We will then discuss a negotiated route."

The Contessa leaned closer, close enough for her light perfume to drift into the Don's personal space. "Thank you, Don Meduriso. I appreciate doing business with you."

"The pleasure is all mine, Contessa Selena de Alvarez." He gently took her hand and kissed it again.

She rose from her seat and started to walk away, then turned back to the old Don. "Before I go, I have one more request."

CHAPTER 11

Buenos Aires was cool for this time of year. An uncomfortable chill permeated the air. Micha Cohen found the weather beneficial. It allowed him to wear his thick, black coat, which concealed the Makarov pistol tucked in his waist. It wasn't his preferred firearm, but it was cheap and easily disposable.

The Jewish Community Center was something right out of the middle-ages. It was three-story building consisting of gray stone and mortar with menacing looking windows protected by thick steel bars. Cohen thought the only thing missing was a moat and an invading army of Vikings. He half expected to see archers posted on the roof.

Ascending the concrete steps, Cohen pushed through the large steel doors guarding the entrance. He found himself in an entryway with light red carpeting and beaten wood paneling. There was a mixed aroma of traditional Jewish cooking, burned cigar tobacco, and aftershave. Down the hall, he could hear singing.

Leaving his coat and Fedora on, Cohen moved carefully down the hall. He entered a spacious main room filled with several circular tables on one side and rows of chairs on the other. The chairs were filled with people whose attention was focused on a round, elderly man belting out an opera-like tune in a deep baritone. He wasn't Pavarotti, but for this local group, he was good.

It wasn't long before the old spy was approached by two young men who eyed him suspiciously. The men were in their early twenties, both well-built and athletic, dressed identically in tan slacks and black T-shirts and wore red armbands on their right biceps, indicating they were part of some Jewish youth defense group.

"Sir, may we help you?" The larger of the two youths asked as they came within a few feet of Cohen.

Behind them, Cohen saw another three members watching from a distance, ready to come to the aid of their comrades if needed. Cohen suspected he was being screened.

"I'm looking for your Rabbi," Micha said, showing his hands. "That is, of course, if Abraham Kovinski is still the local Rabbi here."

The first two youths looked at each other. The smaller one walked away. As he left, one of the three holding back moved up to take his place.

Situations like this were never good. Young toughs like these were the type to punch first and think rationally later. Worse, if they searched him and found the illegal gun he was carrying, the beating would be the least of his worries.

"What is all this?" a gravelly, accented voice called out and broke the growing tension. A large, heavyset man with a long, thick beard waddled slowly across the floor, followed closely by the youth sent to find him.

"Rabbi, do you know this man?" the large, young guard asked in refined Spanish.

The old man sighed, "Yes, unfortunately, I do know him. And as much as I would enjoy watching him die, he is one of us."

The old man's Spanish was broken but passable. His features and accent were unmistakably Eastern European. He took his time closing the distance to Cohen, then took more time to look Cohen up and down before speaking. "I know you are not here at the behest of the Homeland, so don't try to fool me."

Cohen stared back at the Rabbi. "Good to see you too, Abraham."

By now the other youths, who were maintaining their distance, stepped forward to join the discussion. The bigger one, the one that had initiated contact, was quick to pick up on the Rabbi's statement about the Homeland. His interest was sparked. "Homeland, Rabbi? Do you mean he works for Israel?"

Abraham Kovinski turned to the young gentlemen now gathered around him. "Thank you for your diligence, but he is no threat to us. Now, I need to speak to him privately, if you please."

The young men who had been ready to kill their unknown guest and drop his body in a dumpster, were now beaming, believing they were looking at a real Israeli katsa. Cohen felt like Mick Jagger at a rock concert.

Rabbi Kovinski shook his head at the whole scene. He took Cohen by the arm, mumbled something about 'youth being too easily impressed these days,' and led his visitor away from the gathering crowd. "Come, you old *kike!*" he growled as he pushed clear of the bodies. "We'll talk in my office,"

The young men followed them like a pack of mesmerized

groupies chasing a celebrity. Kovinski managed to evade them with well-practiced skills pushing the Israeli into an office down the hall and slamming the door shut. Outside, they heard moans and protests, and the old Rabbi waved his hand in exasperation.

"Start talking," the Rabbi turned to Cohen in irritation. "And don't give me any of your nonsensical spy jargon and broken explanations."

Cohen placed his Fedora at the edge of the Rabbi's beaten, metal desk and sat in an equally weathered chair that creaked under his weight. "I'm here on the Holy Land's business..."

"Don't!" Kovinski said coldly. "I know that's untrue. Try again and this time, my friend, if there is any slight-of-hand, you're leaving."

The determined look on the old Rabbi's face was unmistakable. "All right, I am initiating a mission of my own, and I need your help."

Kovinski changed his demeanor as he sunk slowly onto the small tweed sofa. "Hmph," he scowled.

Cohen updated the Rabbi on the Iranians, the possible threat in South America, and the lack of support from the Mossad. When he finished the briefing, the old Rabbi chewed his lip, absorbing the information.

"I know we've had our differences, Abraham, even going back to being kids in Russia. Though I have no official status, I need help."

Kovinski folded his hands, let out a raspy breath. "What, exactly, do you require?"

Cohen felt a sense of relief. "I know you are connected to the Jewish vigilante and criminal groups in Argentina and other parts of South America. I need to know if you have gotten wind of any suspicious activities or persons who have shown up mysteriously. You also keep tabs on the local Lebanese population in the Triangle in the border areas."

Kovinski gently ran his finger across his lip brushing his gnarled mustache. "Give me a few days. I have a few sources that might know something."

"Thank you, Abraham," Cohen said as he rose.

The Rabbi rose with him. "I will need to be discrete. If some of these young Jewish radicals find out about this, they will insist on taking matters into their own hands and start a rampage."

"You're right," Cohen agreed. "Those young men outside seem a little too eager for a fight."

"Them? They call themselves the *Guardians of Israel.* I figure it keeps them off the streets and out of gangs but, as you point out, they would love to start the Arab-Israeli war over here if they could. I would ask that you don't encourage them. They may start attacking the homes and businesses of the local Lebanese community thinking they're striking a blow for the cause."

"I'll keep that in mind. Again, thank you, Abraham." Cohen caught the Rabbi's bicep.

"Take care of yourself Micha."

Micha nodded and the two men parted.

CHAPTER 12

Ali Anwar al Qalmini looked out from the windowed terrace of the coastal house he had retained as his headquarters. At the moment, the spectacular view from this location was a much-needed distraction from the hours he had spent scrutinizing the records bought from the Cuban. It had all started to become a blur of ink and paper. A glass of water and a cool breeze from outside was a godsend. The spectacle of glistening water glowing from the reflection of the city's evening lights illuminated the coastline and made a hauntingly beautiful scene.

His serenity was interrupted by a voice coming from inside the room. Turning, Qalmini found himself confronted by his subordinates — Majors Rashid al' Akim and Semir Ali Essouri. Qalmini nodded before gulping down the last of his water. Both men looked where their commander had established a workspace for himself on the wide, granite coffee table in front of the couch. A collection of papers were grouped in a series of folders meant to serve as de facto dividers for their commander's strange organizational process.

If the estate was not so well guarded by elite al Quds soldiers patrolling the area, tech agents on loan from the Iranian Ministry of State Security conducting regular electronic sweeps, and the three-member household staff from Qalmini's personal household in Iran, one would view the display as a flagrant security violation.

"Sir, we just came to brief you on our latest progress," Major Essouri began.

Qalmini stepped off the terrace and returned to the living room. "What is our status?"

Essouri looked at his commander. "We have our man. He has been briefed and activated for this mission."

"You have met him directly?" Qalmini asked.

"Yes sir," Essouri responded.

Qalmini placed his empty glass on a nearby counter. "Will he be up to the task you defined for him?"

Essouri nodded. "His name is Nouri al'Marak Surriman. He not only meets all our requirements, but he has a very keen mind. He actually brought up a few key points we should strongly consider."

Qalmini's eyes peaked at his subordinate's statement. "Such as?"

Essouri watched his commander and Akim, who was off to the side. Both men looked interested. "He points out the lack of adequate facilities to train for urban maneuvers despite this being an urban-oriented operation."

Essouri stopped and observed the facial responses from his colleagues as they processed what he said. After a few seconds, they looked back at the small major. "This is very revealing." Qalmini checked with Akim who nodded in agreement.

Feeling he had a receptive audience, Essouri proceeded.

"I have done some research to resolve this problem." He reached into his leather satchel. By now the other two men had sunk into adjacent chairs. Producing a manila folder, Essouri continued. "There's an abandoned mining town only a few kilometers south of our recently purchased property in Brazil. It was well established before the mine went broke and everyone moved out. A thorough reconnaissance of the location revealed a developed infrastructure with several on-site buildings and other facilities that mimic our target location fairly well." Essouri opened his folder which contained blueprints, sketches, and both aerial and on-site photographs. As usual, the little major had been thorough in his research.

Qalmini looked over the documents presented to him. Assessing the information, he looked back at his subordinate. "I see the benefit, however, can we sustain a force of trainees for a period of time with the current internal infrastructure, or will we have to plan for additional logistical support?"

"We can use the existing infrastructure," Essouri answered. "The water still functions. It ties into a nearby lake and river as its source. For electrical, our needs can be met with the use of a decent sized generator. Together it should greatly minimize our outside logistical concerns."

Qalmini pondered the information. Akim shrugged. Qalmini conceded that Essouri was right, and he had come up with a remedy. "Good, your solution is sound, Major. However, use our established methods of obtaining the land and for any services needed to establish it. Contact our Cuban friend and work the deal through Bolivar Investments."

Both majors gave a slight groan at the order. "Sir, Mendoza is a mercenary, and I consider him an utter security risk," Essouri said.

"He's right," Akim agreed. "That man could easily compromise the whole mission if someone offered him the right price."

Qalmini sighed as he studied both of his men. "This mission is a waltz across a tightrope any way we look at it. As much as I'm inclined to agree with your opinion, I see the only alternative is to have an Iranian company assume the part of purchasing land and services which would leave us open to greater exposure and risk."

"Of course, you're right," Essouri sighed as he considered his commander's comments.

"At this point, he already knows more than I'm comfortable with but eliminating him would bring the Cubans down on us which would be even more dangerous," Qalmini continued. "Realizing the stakes, I am assessing every move, taking only the most necessary actions and using the most feasible precautions to mitigate our exposure." Checking to see that both his men were in agreement, Qalmini placed reassuring hands on both their shoulders. "Make contact and secure the land, time is of the essence."

Reaching for his cellular phone inside his coat, Essouri dialed a number and began speaking in Spanish to the contact on the other end of the line. Mendoza never spoke directly to his contacts in these matters but inserted an intermediary to deal with the Iranians. When a deal or instructions were discussed, Mendoza presided over the business affairs that provided the official cover.

While this conversation was taking place, Qalmini

returned to his workspace where his collection of papers was scattered. Akim followed closely to observe for himself. "These are the files the Cuban gave you?" the large Persian asked as he eyed the piles.

"Yes," Qalmini replied. "These are all the possible candidates for the next phase of our operation."

Akim looked closer at the material. There were dossiers filled with facts and reviews with recent photographs attached. From what he could tell, the information suggested that all the dossiers were for men who were sitting members of the Uruguay Parliament. "What do you think?"

Qalmini rubbed his eyes. "So far I have narrowed the focus down to these three men as suitable contenders for our purpose." He reached down and scooped up a collection of documents spread-out like a fan and handed them to Akim.

Akim browsed the information. There were dossiers of three senior politicians — all members of the opposition right-wing National Party. "These men?"

"Those three have the position, the notoriety, and the right connections to make them the most viable candidates for our purpose."

"And our other purpose?"

Qalmini sat in the closest chair. "That was a somewhat greater challenge, but I think I have *a* suitable candidate."

Akim dropped the dossiers as his commander handed him another one. It was only one person. Akim carefully read the information and placed the dossier back onto the desk. He looked back at his commander. "You're right, he could possibly do. He could also be a threat."

Qalmini agreed. "For what we are asking, the necessary qualifications make our choices slim. Either way, we only have the ability to approach someone once before we become compromised."

Akim looked down at the dossier he had just discarded and sighed. He read the name at the top of the file very carefully — *Oskar Vlak Straudner.*

CHAPTER 13

The Ronin Establishment was everything a regular guy not looking for a fight or a lot of flash could enjoy. On the corner between two main streets of Bogotá, Colombia, it was a mid-level operation. It catered to revisiting foreigners and expats who appreciated a quiet night of drinking and socializing. Its low profile and conservative setting was the best hub for someone to conduct business of a mercenary kind.

The proprietor was a man by the name of Ian 'Plucker' Ferry, known for his extensive friendships among the soldiering world and, to a lesser extent, his previous affiliations in the Loyalist Volunteer Force in Northern Ireland. This was where a person went if he was looking to buy weapons or find men for a privatized war or operation.

Kafka Dayan stepped through the glass and wood double doors and entered the main corridor. The glass doors offered a distorted image to anyone looking from the outside in. From the inside, one had an unhindered view of the streets.

In the main room, Dayan casually assessed his situation. From outside, the bar had been misleading. It looked like a small corner establishment between two buildings. Once inside, the bar expanded — stealing space from the neighboring buildings — to form two large areas for drinking. A two-step drop led to these areas from the main room. This arrangement further hindered anyone trying to gain information by loitering outside. It was obvious the bar was designed to be an assassin's nightmare and to weather attacks should another revolution or drug war break out.

Moving to the bar, Dayan found a seat along the wall. It was only seconds before a dark-skinned Negress with braided locks and ornamental jewelry approached him to take his order. The tiny gold ring protruding from her nose was impossible to ignore.

"Sẽnor!" she called abruptly, breaking the Israeli from his semi-trance. "Your drink?" She looked at him in exasperation.

"Beer, please…anything German," Kafka said, caught off guard. The woman turned and walked away.

Rubbing his forehead and cursing himself for the awkward moment, Kafka decided to focus on a different subject. The crowd was an expected assortment of people for a place like this. Several customers wore crumpled suits — businessmen nursing a high-end glass of bourbon, rum, or American whiskey while they chatted among themselves about the day's business. A few foreign expatriates mixed with this group sporting tall mugs of beer. By the brands, Kafka assume most of the expats were from Eastern Europe. The remainder of the patrons consisted of a few leather-jacketed motorcycle types and some retirees.

The Negress returned with a tall bottle and a decorative coaster. Placing it in front of him she stepped back. "Anything else, Sẽnor?"

"No, thank you." She left the Israeli to his own thoughts.

Cohen had told him that the Ronin Establishment was one of the few places still catering to the old-fashioned world of private market intrigues. The soldiers-for-hire, ex-spies — now rogue operatives — and black-market business types who twenty years ago were so common among the capital cities of Europe and North America were now endangered species. They were known to view this place as their last refuge.

Cohen, deciding that the veteran commando would be better in this element than him, had dispatched Kafka to fulfill the next phase of the operation. The first sip of beer was smooth with a strong taste. He usually enjoyed his libations after the completion of a mission, but under these circumstances, that seemed out of place.

A small, well-built, muscular man appeared from a doorway behind the counter. His mustache was neat and well-trimmed which mixed nicely with his gleaming, bald head and milk-white complexion. It was Ian Ferry — or 'Plūcker' to his old comrades in Northern Ireland or 'Ulster', which he preferred. The Israeli reminded himself to remember he was addressing a former Loyalist.

Plūcker greeted the men around the counter like a politician addressing his constituents. Making the rounds, the Irishman shook hands with some whom he addressed by their first name, a couple others were apprised of the latest bits of news from previous business or discussions they had had with the proprietor. Finally, at the end of the counter, Plūcker found himself eye to eye with a dark-skinned man of Arab extraction. "Long way from Israel ain't ya boyo." He spoke in English as opposed to the Spanish he had been using with the other patrons.

In his own accented tone, Kafka responded. "What makes you think I'm from Israel?"

Plücker looked amused. "Well, you're hardly Spanish, and the way you treat that beer — like it's perfectly normal — an Arab Muslim would have acted like he was committing a sin. A less religious type would have acted like it was his first time out and was doing something exciting because of the sinfulness and criminality of it all. So, you're not Muslim. I'd wager you are Jewish, which likely means Israeli."

Kafka was impressed with the Irishman's deductive abilities. "You would be right. You are either a first-rate psychic or your skills no doubt would serve well in espionage work."

"I imagine so," the barkeep laughed, "but that's not really my bag. I'm assuming it's not yours either. You strike me more like the operational type."

"I'm sorry?" Kafka was taken aback by the Irishman's statement.

Plūcker Ferry turned to attend to his inventory, then leaned toward the Israeli ready to further the discussion or end it based on the patron's wishes. Kafka chose to pursue the subject. "What are you talking about?"

Plūcker faced the Israeli bending down to meet him at eye level. "Don't play me for a fool, boy. I see the toned physique of someone who exercises long and hard on a near-daily basis. Before walking in here you moved around outside. You were casing the place like a professional operator planning a mission, and you've been scanning the folks in my establishment either collecting intelligence, sizing up the threat level, or pursuing a target."

Plūcker was good. "Oh, I admit your skills are first-rate;

no one really caught ya. I only noticed because I've been around the game long enough to observe the pros. You have too many tells of a seasoned soldier, one who has seen action — a good deal of it. But you could hardly be mistaken for a professional spy. That said, you must be here on business for the state and someone here is the intended target or you're here to hire out on the free circuit, in which case I'm assuming it's your first time."

Kafka's jaw might have dropped had he had less self control. Was he that obvious? He did not know how to respond. The Irishman had him completely figured out. "Wonderful fantasy, my friend." Kafka tried to downplay the bartender's assessment. "You're partially right. I am Israeli, and I did a few years of military service. But I hardly think I would qualify for the professional soldier type with my administration skills."

A sly look appeared on Plücker's face. He didn't believe the Israeli but had no wish to expose him. Kafka only wanted to maintain his cover. "All right, me boy," the Irishman met the Israeli's eyes. "So, I'll let ya go with that bullshit story. And, I'll put the word out you're a fucking spy looking to collect on those working the market."

Kafka was beside himself. The Irish barman had him cornered again. He needed to recruit mercenaries, and this guy was looking to wreck his chances. With few options, Kafka tried to play out his hand. "Well, do what you like, but why is this such a big deal to you?"

Plūcker leaned back and let his eyes wander toward the ceiling as he searched for his next words. "Well, let me just say I have a few years in the game myself, and I've seen your type many times before. Either you're lookin' to get into trouble, or you're trouble lookin' for a place to land. I'll not have you interfering with friends of mine."

Kafka lowered his gaze toward his drink. "Or, I am exactly as advertised, as my cousin in the US loves to say, and your tough guy routine should be practiced on someone else."

The Irishman leaned in closer, a twinkle in his eye. "Well, there's one more reason I'd be inclined to assume ya are a professional in these matters. Mr. Cohen told me an athletic-looking Israeli would be coming through my doors in the next few days. Said the fella would go by the name Kafka Dayan."

Kafka's eyes widened. The Irishman pulled away and chuckled. "Micha and I go back to my earlier less mindful days. He had a problem and asked if I could help. Wants me to facilitate a few meetings and help get the word out to some folks you be thinkin' about for your mission."

Still bewildered by what just happened, Kafka composed himself before answering. "Ya-yes, I would like that very much."

Plūcker stood up and surveyed the room to see how his Negress was managing things on the floor. When he was satisfied she was in control and there were no obvious issues, he turned his focus back to Kafka. "Make your way slowly to the washroom and from there go where you're told." Plūcker sauntered into his backroom.

Following his instructions, Kafka drained the last of his beer, dropped some pesos on the counter, and rose from his seat to head to the toilet. Looping around the bar, he managed to snake his way through a small corridor that led to a narrow hallway. He was less than a meter from the door marked *Men's Room* when he was stopped by a young man who emerged from a steel door on the opposite side. "Sẽnor Jew?" The young man asked.

A little put off by the cover name, Kafka nodded his head. The boy motioned for him to follow. The Israeli followed him through the steel door. The young man navigated through a labyrinth of hallways and storerooms of various expensive liquors and finally into an office. Plūcker Ferry sat behind an aged desk covered in piles of papers and ornaments.

The room was large, doubling as a conference room for meetings as well as the boss's office. The lights were assorted lamps, wall lights, and overhead tracks. The conference room consisted of several long tables and rolling office chairs that could be arranged to fit the occasion. It was a room where one could discuss business of a private nature with relative security.

"I figure you can conduct your business in here," the Irishman said. He rose from his desk to meet the Israeli. "I have the place swept for bugs before every meeting; it's done by a very reputable specialist. I also have the walls lined with metal and wiring that ensures someone trying to listen from outside will have a bloody hard time getting anything viable, especially since I pay some of the local brawlers to keep the back streets clear for me."

"Thank you," the Israeli replied.

"Micha said you would have a list of specific qualifications you worked up as to what you will be needin' for this mission."

"I have some names that I'd like to run by you to see if they're active and still worthwhile."

The Irishman rubbed his thumb against his chin. "I'll put the word out in the next few days through the barkeeps and message takers. In my experience, it will take two or three weeks for the professionals to start comin' around."

"That's faster than what I expected." Kafka looked back at Plūcker. "What do you mean, before the professionals come around?"

Plūcker grinned, "I've been at this game awhile me boy. The talkers will jump on any rumor or offer of a job without question. The truly experienced vets will wait, check it out, and ask around before they step forward. They'll make contact with me informally to see what you're goin' on about and what you're offering pay-wise for the work. I would recommend five thousand a week. Anything less and you'll turn off the professionals."

The Israeli didn't like being involved in something he knew little about. "So, in the meantime…we wait."

"Give me your names and let me do some reachin' out. I'll let you know when we start to get some responses. For the most part, these boys stay tuned to the mercenary community and, knowin' their fitness for duty will be pretty easy to check. As a precaution, assume if I have six names for you, figure that three won't be viable. Factor in guys who are retired, fallen to the drink, or burnt out.

"I'll make the first contact. The less you're seen by the first prospects, the less of a security breach you risk. After all, I can shake these boys pretty easily if they don't make the grade. You only make a target for yourself and bring unwanted exposure. Another word of advice. In addition to informants and criminals, this world you're about to enter collects a lot of intrigue junkies. They come in the form of journalists who love to rub shoulders with your type and are always lookin' for some secret war or covert operation they can expose and report on. Know that they'll be a bigger problem than the local security boys around here."

"What will you tell them?" Kafka asked.

"They'll know they're being recruited but not what for." The Irishman looked at the Israeli before continuing. "They'll be briefed as needed. They know the money is real and the job adventurous and quite possibly illegal. Again, the true professionals will ask the right questions to know if the job is being run by pros, or if it's just a bunch of wankers slumming in the merc world for kicks."

Kafka realized nothing more was going to be accomplished today. He handed the number of one of his disposable phones to the Irishman and bid him goodbye.

CHAPTER 14

The first busload of recruits was inspiring.

The Contessa Selena de Alvarez watched from a distance the collection of would-be revolutionaries descending the warped steps at the backs of the old school buses. To her amazement, they were far above her expectations. She assumed she was going to see an assortment of misfits, wishful adventurers, and psychopaths. Instead, she saw a cast of clean-cut kids, nicely, though not expensively dressed, with a look of true believers sold on the idea of social revolution. The professor turned out to be a wise choice as a recruiter.

The Contessa had arranged with the professor to collect the recruits at a farmer's market near the Argentina border. They were dressed as if on a camping trip enjoying the woods. Any policeman or onlooker would assume the kids were exploring the countryside. The villagers, happy for the business this number of college kids brought, would assume the same. That they all gathered into a caravan of buses solidified this answer in their minds.

Checkpoints were avoided by using a honeycomb of prereconnoitered roadways that were hardly ever secured by the overstretched border patrol of either country. With the help of Argentinian gauchos, who on occasion smuggled people and product into and out of Uruguay, the recruits disembarked from their buses when the roads became impassable. The large number of recruits were able to bypass security surveillance and any record of their movement across borders by trekking several miles through seldom used goat trails known only to the wild-living gauchos. The Contessa had ensured the gauchos provided plenty of pack animals and water for the hike. After all, the urban rich kids were not hardened cowmen and probably not as resilient to the rugged conditions.

Crossing into Argentina, the recruits were brought to a designated assembly point where a convoy of buses waited ready to pick up the much-relieved recruits. Finally, arriving midday at the training camp, they disembarked and adjusted their eyes to the brightness of the sun.

It took them only a few minutes before they were acclimated to their new surroundings; the thick forest, the abandoned mining camp, and deserted mining town were seen in the distance. Most of their attention was focused on the rough looking figures clad in military battle dress standing off to the side. Their expressions were hard and unmoving. If any one of the recent arrivals thought they were going to summer camp or something fun, it vanished with the sight of those men. This bit of intimidation was designed to get the young radicals in the right frame of mind.

The Contessa had recruited her trainers from the ranks of the Colombian National Liberation Army — better known in the southern world as the ELN. The ELN was a Communist rebel group residing in the shadow of the larger, better known Revolutionary Armed Forces of Colombia or FARC, and was certainly as capable and just as lethal. They were perfect for training a raw army of guerrillas. Unlike the FARC, which was founded by and comprised almost exclusively of impoverished rural peasants and Indians with poor education, the ELN was an organization composed of leftist clergymen and intellectuals of both higher education and certainly higher breeding.

She had wisely concluded that as products of wealth, privilege, and breeding, the recruits would not mix well nor have any respect for those of the lower classes who could hardly read or write let alone be able to grasp any serious intellectual concepts. Despite the rantings against classism, well-groomed and educated social elites would never take Colombian peasants and rural Indians seriously as mentors.

The lead instructor, Venzuelo Zamora, looked far older than his thirty-one years. Marching past the young students, he looked them over carefully. Then, in a gruff and gravelly voice, he called for their attention. "All eyes on me now!!!" he shouted.

Everyone went silent as the recruits turned in unison to the ominous figure now standing before them. Zamora stared at them coldly. "You are here to liberate your country from the clutches of the capitalists and the impostors who have betrayed you and the ideals they presume to represent!"

The crowd of recruits cheered in unison. Zamora had been a revolutionary long enough to know how to motivate adherents. He counted thirty in this batch and was aware that by tomorrow another truck full of recruits would be arriving. He expected nearly eighty recruits in total. Like the Contessa, he was pleased they were not the collection of misfits he had initially anticipated. Instead, he saw a batch of athletic and prepared adherents to a cause.

The Contessa observed the spectacle through her binoculars. She had not intended to stay long and would certainly not mingle with future terrorists who could identify her later. Once she was confident Zamora had taken control, she planned to depart to initiate the next phase of the operation.

She had known Zamora through her connections with the Spanish intelligence services that still had active missions in South America. He was respected by the Basque Separatists who had worked with him on joint operations and who had helped recruit him for this mission. She had also learned from her contacts in the European arms trafficking world that he and a few others had become disillusioned with the conflict in Colombia and the feuds with the FARC over territory. The narcotics trafficking to finance the war had begun to supersede all other aspects of the movement. The intensified efforts by the Colombian military had worked to nearly decimate the ELN's hard-fought efforts. By offering a good price for men looking to get out of the revolution business, she now had her instructors.

The Contessa arranged the travel of the former revolutionaries into Argentina through negotiations with the Cali Cartel. Over the years they had developed an additional business as a professional logistics network for various black-market ventures that needed to bypass troublesome international borders and security officials.

Zamora wasted no time breaking the recruits into ranks and assigning them instructors. Line by line the recruits were led away to begin several weeks of training.

"They look like a solid lot," said a voice with a strong Irish brogue.

Sitting across from her, a medium-sized man with a muscular frame and a bushy crop of sandy blond hair attended to his stout beer.

Martin Derry observed the ELN instructors directing the trainees. He leaned back in his wooden chair. "Fuck sake, it's hot as bullocks around these parts," he sighed as he wiped the beads of sweat from his brow.

"I'm glad you approve," the Contessa said, lowering her binoculars. "I would hate for you to have a pack of students you found undesirable."

Her Spanish flavored English was sensual, almost erotic. The Irishman had to resist the urge to make sexual overtures. She was way above the class of a poor Irishman from the farming country of County Armagh.

"So now we begin our next phase, Mr. Derry. I hope you are capable." She rose from her seat and gave him a look out of the corner of her eye that suggested she was expecting an answer.

"I am. Everything is in place, so we should be able to hit most of our objectives." Derry again wiped collected beads of sweat from his forehead and sipped his beer. Martin Derry had been a member of the Real Irish Republican Army — one of the breakaway groups that formed after the signing of the Good Friday Peace Accords that essentially ended the near thirty-some year conflict in Northern Ireland.

Much like Zamora, he had become disillusioned with the *good fight* and decided to try his hand in the free market. Through friends in the Basque Separatists, he had been placed in touch with a Spanish aristocrat looking for professionals with his expertise. His job was to bridge the void of knowledge the ELN instructors couldn't provide — training advanced urban warfare tactics to these recruits and the directing of 'phase 2' that the Contessa had been planning.

The Contessa watched as the truck drove out of the facility. The recruits were marched off to their barracks. Comfortable that Zamora and his men had control of the situation, she bid farewell to Derry, who replied with a slight wave of his hand and started out of the building. "In two days' time, Mr. Derry, I expect you at our appointed location. Will that be sufficient to finish up any last-minute complications?"

Turning his head, Derry said, "More than ample time, madam. Everything is ready, and I perceive no foreseeable problems."

"Good. Until then." With those last words, the Contessa departed.

CHAPTER 15

Despite being a vehicle of far superior design and construction than the aged, cheaply built army jeeps he had used for patrolling around Syria, Nouri al'Marak Surriman found the drive down the severely weathered dirt road nauseating. It was ironic he had be born and raised in this country and still found traveling in it physically difficult. The Land Rover traversed the dips and near lake-size puddles. The driver, a young man in his early twenties, kept a wide, toothy grin on his face the entire time. He even found the nerve to play tour guide when coming across something he found exciting to talk about. Nouri couldn't decide whether his driver was being a smart ass, knowingly adding to his suffering, or was sincerely oblivious to his passenger's discomfort.

Before the situation became serious, the vehicle pulled onto an even worse dirt trail and within minutes the hellish ride ended. To his relief, Surriman found they had stopped just outside a village — the sign guarding the entryway was ominous; a forewarning. After the Spanish verbiage of *painful endings to trespassers,* a lengthier message was written in some Middle Eastern foreign scribble. The writing, as far as Surriman could tell, offered a few Koranic edicts to those going farther.

Studying the driver, whose toothy grin had been replaced with a look of hesitation, Surriman nodded calmly letting him know his job was done. Exiting the Land Rover, Surriman started walking. At the edge of the village, two men suddenly appeared from behind the shrubs. Dressed in a strange combination of civilian work clothes and military fatigues, they looked like a picturesque image of South American guerrillas. The Soviet-style Kalashnikov rifles slung across their backs would have solidified that assumption for any stranger. To Surriman, they were all too familiar.

The two guerrillas viewed the man before them. His tan slacks and vanilla colored shirt were not the apparel of a local from the mountains. Despite the clothes, shorter hair and shaved face, they recognized the man before them. They smiled, and with an assault-like lunge, fell onto the man with exuberance. "Long time, brother," the older of the two men said affectionately.

"Too long! Much, much too long?" Surriman responded with equal enthusiasm.

Stepping back, the three old friends exchanged a few more words before heading toward the village. To his relief, the small Lebanese settlement had hardly changed. It was still a collection of tin-roofed shacks lined up almost side by side with open pit stone fireplaces. Some of the houses were larger, some even had a second story, while others were only one room.

Thick canopies of forest vegetation provided excellent protection from anyone trying to watch them from overhead. The three men talked as they walked proudly down the dirt road cutting through the village. Various people happily greeted the long-gone youth who had run off to fight for the old country and the Shia cause in Syria. It was the perfect family reunion Nouri al'Marak Surriman had hoped for. He did not want to be overwhelmed by joyous family and friends, but he also hoped he would not be ignored as a runaway.

A few miles past the village they arrived at a makeshift factory. There, small oven-like smelters of clay and rock roared angrily with flames, as tables holding an assortment of parts, both metal and wood lay before them.

Atop the ovens were big clay caps covering the exhaust holes attached to large clay smokestacks that led underground. Surriman found it interesting that the stacks were dug several feet deep and led to a river several miles away from where the smoke exited under water. Not only did it keep the operation protected by not exposing clouds of smoke for reconnaissance aircraft to see, it also protected the true size of their operation.

It would have been disconcerting for anyone to know that hidden beneath the thick vegetation beyond the façade of remote, backward villages was a massive operation for replicating weapons. The handmade furnaces and workshops provided the Lebanese immigrants and their offspring the ability to develop near-perfect replicas of varying weapons from AK-47s of Soviet military grade to SKS assault rifles and Rocket Propelled Grenade Launchers to exact specifications of the 7 and 7D models.

What would have been more shocking was the near perfect models of American M-4 compacted automatic rifles and some Fabrique National machine guns they created. Aside from the Arabic writing on the side of the magazine weld, they were perfect copies of the American military weapons.

The village had been making quite a handsome profit manufacturing and selling weapons to various criminal and rebel groups that had no external connections to obtain combat weapons. Luckily, these villages were most discriminating with whom they chose to conduct business. They had gone largely unnoticed by the outside world allowing them a great deal of anonymity.

This situation also created a great deal of confusion for the governments of the region who were apt to assume their criminal networks and guerrilla bands were being supplied by phantom weapons suppliers or some hostile foreign government. Surriman thought it strange how the intelligence agencies of the world spent so much money and time looking to the industrial world to track the flow of illegal weapons when the biggest producers were not even on their radar. The two old friends led Surriman through the workshops.

He was endlessly greeted by longtime friends and relatives who would quickly exchange pleasantries and embrace him before continuing their work. Entering the center of the operation, the two old friends brought Surriman to a formidable, bear-like figure of a man standing before a large wooden shack. At almost six foot seven, Basham al Allimuri was a giant with a most commanding presence. Far from using physical intimidation, his smart management and astute business sense had advanced him to the level of the village chief. Dressed in a similar fashion to the two men that flanked Surriman, Allimuri had the salt n pepper, thick bushy beard of a mountain guerrilla leader.

"Salam a lakem," the elderly man said quietly.

Surriman looked up at the approaching figure and replied, "Wha lakem salam."

Allimuri smiled through his thick crop of facial hair. Surriman gave a bow of respect to the older man. "It has been a long time," he said as he rose.

"It has," the older man replied. "You have fought for God. I commend you for that. You bring nobility to your people."

Somewhat embarrassed, Surriman gave a gesture toward the older man in gratitude. "My service is not yet complete, which is why I am here."

The older man cocked his head as he waited to hear more.

Alyssa Rios knew the murky world of espionage and the dark alleys it led to. Having graduated Purdue with degrees in Political Science and International Relations, she later obtained a law degree from San Diego University and was recruited into the Drug Enforcement Administration. She spent the next 10 years navigating the mean streets of the various cities of South and Central America that hosted the most powerful narcotic cartels.

Though she had proven quite an effective operative, she found the DEA was not to her liking. Bureaucratic thinking and Anglo-Saxon colleagues dominated the culture. The work was tedious and often counter-productive. The targets and direction of the agency were driven more by the need for political expedience than serious beneficial gain. She also felt she was treated more like a potential spy than a respected co-worker. When she got wind of a joke circulating through the department about Latino agents being referred to as *Escobar's Secret Task Force,* she had had enough and quit.

With her knowledge of South American politics and business combined with her expertise in covert operations and espionage, the most logical choice was simple, and Guardian Angel Intelligence was born. She found steady work with the numerous businessmen looking to ensure that possible business partners or business deals were not fraudulent or connected to the cartels. Reformists looking to know what politicians in their country were corrupt, or just politicians looking to know who their enemies were in Parliament also provided a steady amount of work.

She discovered her old friends in the DEA were actually keeping tabs on her for a time wondering if her talents were providing support to any criminal networks. When the DEA determined she was not involved with criminal networks, she was approached by one of her former superiors who intimated that she had a patriotic duty to her old country. Her old bosses felt she at least owed a debt to the agency to run missions as a front for them.

A polite refusal ended any relationship she had with the man she had once called her boss and with her old comrades. Now, she was her own boss and liking it. From time to time, however, she would have informal and indirect approaches made to her when a US agency was in need of information.

Mulling over the information splashed across her computer screen, she rolled one of her expensive pens between her fingers as she read. Her thoughts were mixed with grave concerns over her recent findings and the instinctive excitement the espionage agent felt over the intrigue of what she was seeing.

Her desk communicator rang, and she heard the soft voice of her assistant telling her Mr. Herron was in the office for their scheduled meeting. Thanking her assistant, she clicked the communicator off and slid out of her seat. Picking up the leather notepad and packet that had been assembled for the meeting, she went to meet her Middle-Eastern client.

She entered the room where they had first met. The Israeli was dressed in a sports jacket, gray cotton slacks, and a white buttoned-downed shirt that hung loosely from his shoulders. She figured this was his uniform.

Exchanging pleasantries, they took their seats. Her leather pad and packets were directly in front of her as she looked the man squarely in the eye. She opened the conversation with, "I have found some things out over the last few weeks regarding your person of interest." She had Dayan's full attention. "It was not easy, and we only captured what we did by sheer luck."

Opening her leather notepad she produced a picture of a well-groomed man of obvious Latin origins dressed in an expensive tailored suit coming out of what looked like an office building. The man was of medium height and looked to be in his late forties to mid-fifties.

"His name is Elloy Mendoza. Officially, he is CEO of Bolivar Investments & Acquisitions, a prominent financial operation headquartered out of Buenos Aires, Argentina. He has investment and business interests across South America. That's the official story. In reality, Sẽnor Mendoza is a high ranking operative with the General Intelligence Directorate, better known as DGI, the Cuban intelligence service."

Dayan acknowledged the information. Sensing no questions, Rios continued. "His name has come up from time to time in other investigations of mine. You could say he is something of a competitor. He sells his connections, both business and intelligence, as a side business. I bring him to your attention because several weeks ago, shortly after the recorded arrival of your Iranian in Buenos Aires, Bolivar Investments & Acquisitions conducted a sizable business transaction for an Iranian company. This company happens to be a distant subsidiary of the Gorb Corporation, a corporation known to be controlled by the Iranian Revolutionary Guard. It purchased several parcels of real estate from Bolivar Investments for what we can determine was far above its current valuation — almost three times the price of similar property."

"A business transaction of another kind," the Israeli retorted.

"Yes," Rios agreed. "That is what I and my people have determined, except for some of these properties." She removed the leather pad and grabbed the packets sitting underneath it. She handed them to Dayan. "These properties, upon further observation, appear different."

She stopped speaking long enough for the Israeli to review the information in front of him. When he got to the maps and overhead pictures, he examined them further before placing everything on the table returning his attention to Rios. "Unlike the others, the prices on these properties were negotiated for quite some time before a price was agreed upon. Even more interesting was that there was not an immediate agreement on the properties themselves. I was able to obtain correspondence whereby several other properties were discussed and dismissed before deciding on these specific locations. I found some interesting highlights: these properties skirt the borders of both Argentina and Brazil.

They are far out of the way from any modernized urban center, and they are all locations of what was once either a town or a mining camp sight."

"In other words, the perfect location for training a combat force," Kafka reviewed the overhead photos with greater scrutiny.

Rios pointed out additional highlights, then allowed her client time to digest her findings.

It took several minutes of silence for Dayan to review everything. Rios sat back in her seat ready to answer questions once they were posed.

Kafka Dayan raised his head as if he was coming up for air after being underwater. His facial expression showed he had questions but had not quite formulated them yet. His eyes explored the walls and ceiling as if looking for the answer from some alternate source. "What do you know about these locations?"

"Not much outside of what I have already told you," Rios said anticipating the question. "I have few resources in that region, so I have to work slowly. When I have something of note, I will contact you."

"By *work slowly* what do you mean?" the Israeli asked.

"Provided you agree that these are areas of interest, I will establish the means to collect intelligence around the described locations to see what is going on."

"They are," Dayan replied with enthusiasm. "However, you said *around* the locations."

Lowering her eyes with a gentle air of feminine mystery and professional reserve, Rios sighed. "As we discussed before, there are limits to what I will involve myself in. I will investigate the situation and see what further information develops. However, if there is any need for internal penetration into these locations, and I deem it too dangerous for my people, it will have to be done by your people."

Dayan could not argue with the woman's position. She was protecting her people in a fight that was only hers because of monetary reasons. Her demand was realistic and fair as far as he understood it. He agreed to her position. "If it proves to be what you fear, I will accept that my people should take the greater risks."

"I thank you for understanding," Rios replied.

With business concluded, Dayan received a USB stick containing all the documents and information and took his leave.

CHAPTER 16

Oskar Vlak Straudner was a man of ambition. Though he often tried to convince himself his actions were in the national interest, somehow the *national interest* always conveniently coincided with his own interests either financially or politically. He was a member of the long-established Partido Nacional or National Party — Uruguay's leading right-wing political party. From a rather inauspicious beginning, he had clawed his way up through the ranks of the Chamber of Deputies, Uruguay's lower house of Parliament. Though he held no formal rank within the party's infrastructure or in the Chamber, he had managed to amass a sizable base of silent power and influence making him a dominant force.

Straudner was a product of long-established wealth from the sugar plantations of the Caribbean his ancestors had established upon emigrating from Germany in the mid-eighteenth century. In later years, their children would build on the family fortune with a succession of wise and highly lucrative business ventures that cemented the family's connections and political influence in other parts of the world. In the late 1950s, with the gradual rise of the communists throughout the islands and other parts of South America, the Straudner family relocated to their stronghold in Uruguay.

In the new country, the elder members of the family decided their mission lay in combating the communist menace seeking to destroy a world the family had spent generations building. Through the military and politics, the family ensured that Uruguay would not follow paths similar to Cuba and other countries they had once seen as allies.

A graduate of the best European boarding schools as well as Oxford and the London School of Economics, Straudner was a product of the finest education and the highest breeding. Coupled with the business experience he acquired through the family's vast international holdings, he was easily one of the most worldly and experienced politicians in the Chamber.

Resting on the leather seat of his limousine, Oskar Straudner occupied himself with the collection of documents loosely assembled on a small drop-down table before him. The documents were copies of the leading Uruguay newspapers as well as an assortment of reports from various government departments that fell under his committee responsibilities and a few that did not.

Rolling a Rocky Patel cigar between his fingers, he perused a letter from the French Ambassador. What had come to be almost habitual, the ambassador was citing a list of policies France took issue with. As was the custom, the Europeans felt the need to lecture the politicians of South America about the way to run a country. For Straudner and many of his colleagues, it had become apparent that Western Europe still viewed the the countries in Western Hemisphere as their colonies. Though Straudner felt the recent letter would be best used as toilet paper, he still gave it the attention the ambassador felt it deserved. The young politician understood all too well how badly the Europeans took it when the advice of older and 'wiser' countries was not heeded or, at least, given strong consideration. As usual, a quick read before conferring with fellow politicians about the best way to placate the ambassador was routine.

A buzz broke his attention. A small red light flashed. It was the driver's way of letting Straudner know they were within minutes of their destination. With a sigh, the politician collected his documents and filed them in his leather satchel. Moments later the door opened, and he was greeted by a tall, muscular figure dressed in a gray suit and wearing sunglasses.

Monti, his driver, looked like a hit man from a 'B' movie. Still, he possessed two things Oskar Straudner valued highly — his loyalty and discretion. Monti had witnessed too many of the politician's more secretive and morally questionable affairs over the years and was stalwart in maintaining his master's privacy. This particular meeting was one of these affairs.

Monti parked the car at the private end of a paid parking area wedged between groups of high-rise buildings. He could easily explain himself to any colleagues who might see him — a surveillance team or security force doing routine probes or hired agents from one of his several enemies.

After checking the immediate vicinity for possible threats or observers, Monti bow respectfully to Straudner. The driver partially closed the door calmly indicating a potential threat. A short distance away, a young, romantic couple headed for their car. As the couple neared the limousine, they were joined by another man who appeared to be about the same age.

Monti reached casually for his .45 caliber automatic. Straudner likewise leaned back and gently fingered the shotgun under the seat. Luckily for Straudner, most assassins were accustomed to a target being helpless after disposing of the protective detail. In this case, Monti might pose an immediate deterrent, but the aggressors would find the true battle inside the backseat.

Without an upward glance, the young trio continued past the limo and out onto the main road. The driver waited a few more seconds, then opened the door. Straudner emerged from the backseat, straightened himself and with a quick nod to his driver started walking.

Leaving the parking lot, Straudner turned south. He was dressed casually in his cream-colored sports jacket, tan slacks, and a white collared shirt, blending well as he strolled the influential areas of Buenos Aires. He wasn't a trained operative by any means, but in the years of playing backroom politics, he had acquired an instinct and taste for intrigue. He stopped every so often to look at window merchandise. The reflection from the windows gave him the ability to observe anyone behind him. He had found this tactic most useful when being tailed by dubious figures.

He had passed three different shops along his randomly chosen trail, taking a moment to catch any suspicious movement. When he was satisfied he was not being followed, he went directly to a small watchmaker's shop tucked neatly into a corner along a small side street. Entering the shop he was met by a kindly old man of near-walrus proportions who lurched out of a chair far too small for his frame and shuffled over to the young politician standing in his doorway.

"Ah, Sẽnor Straudner," the kindly old man opened with grace and charm. "It is always so good to see you."

Placing a hand on the old man's bicep, the young politician looked at him with the affection a child would give a grandparent. "It is always an honor to see you Herr Laudman."

The old man nodded back happily. Straudner changed from an affectionate to a more serious look. "Herr Laudman, forgive me my abruptness, but have my guests arrived?"

The old watchmaker, with a more serious expression, replied, "They arrived 15 minutes ago. As you instructed, I have accommodated them accordingly."

"Good. What is your assessment of them? Did they give you any reason for concern?"

The old watchmaker shrugged. "They are not assassins and have no intention of killing or threatening you. However, all of them are definitely professionals, and you would be wise to be cautious regarding anything you say or accept."

"You have the room monitored?"

"As always," Laudman replied. Waving his hand, the watchmaker led the politician behind his counter through a labyrinth of small tables and workstations where employees busily worked, ending at a nondescript, weathered door in the corner. Laudman lumbered slowly down a narrow, wooden stairway. Reaching the bottom, the two men continued down what looked like an old secret passage for the underground resistance. Given Laudman's background, Straudner often wondered if it wasn't originally used for that purpose.

CHAPTER 17

Before arriving in Argentina, Ulbrict Laudman had served as a devoted servant to the People's State of East Germany in the secret intelligence organization known as the Stasi. His career began in the mid-seventies working in the foreign office in operations focused largely on the Scandinavian countries. His penchant for languages and his aptitude for intelligence and paramilitary work led him to be transferred into the then growing special operations department. He spent the final decade of his career working overseas in Africa and South America augmenting the Soviet para-military and covert missions.

When the cold war ended and East Germany ceased to exist, Laudman found himself confronted with two serious dilemmas: he was suddenly out of a job, and with all he had done throughout the eighties, he had become a target. Several NATO countries wanted him to answer for his crimes.

Desperate to escape and with few options, he landed in the most unlikely of places. Eyren Straudner, Oskar's uncle, was at one time a target for assassination by Laudman.

Eyren, a most forgiving man, recognized that the former Stasi officer had acted on orders when attempting to kill him, and an espionage expert with his vast experience could be useful.

As a committed communist, Laudman would have found an executive position in a large corporation utterly distasteful, especially if it was with a powerful bourgeoisie family of deep-rooted old money. Eyren offered the watch shop which was far more acceptable to the old Marxist. It provided Straudner with a quiet and unassuming place to conduct discrete affairs protected by a professional spy.

Laudman had access to several additional rooms in his small shop that were ostensibly used for private showings and quiet auctioning of highly expensive antique watches to wealthy collectors — at least that was the official story. In reality, some of the 'auction' spaces were set up with anti-bugging equipment, security cameras, and hidden escape exits. The Straudner family did not use the watch shop often, but they infused Laudman's business with funding to ensure he could afford the latest in security systems in the event they were needed.

Before entering the meeting, Straudner wanted to observe who he was about to meet. The watchmaker led him to a small two-way mirror. Pulling back the curtain the two men found themselves looking into what could have been an old English drinking parlor. Nicely arranged furniture could accommodate one big meeting or several smaller ones going on at once. Three people — two men who appeared to be of Middle Eastern extraction, military types by the watchmaker's assessment, and a woman who was fair, elegant, and definitely of European old money — occupied the room.

The two Middle Easterners sat adjacent to each other on

separate couches while the young woman moved around the room sipping a glass of wine, admiring the various art pieces on the walls and the displays of artifacts scattered among the tables. Both men observed the trio for several minutes before they were satisfied there was no obvious threat.

Still, the politician had concerns and ordered Laudman to take *the necessary precautions.* Obediently, the watchmaker disappeared behind a corner. Straudner walked down a separate corridor leading to a solid oak door.

Taking a minute to straighten his clothes and fix his hair, he was looking quite professional when he strode through the door. His entrance was received with mild interest. The two Middle Eastern gentlemen maintained their seats on the couches, and the young woman took only a slight look at Straudner before resuming her interest in the room's decorations.

As a veteran politician, Straudner was neither insulted nor intimidated by this behavior. Assuming this was either a tactic of people determined not to be cowed or professionals unimpressed with a small country politician, Straudner played his role accordingly. He was interested to see where this little act was going.

Moving to a table housing the libations, he picked up a small glass and a bottle of Tennessee Wild Turkey. Pouring himself a drink, his attention was broken by a feminine voice. "Thank you for taking time from your schedule to meet us, Herr Straudner." He looked up to meet the woman's gaze. She was an alluring beauty dressed in a dark black jacket and a knee-length skirt tailored perfectly to fit her figure.

"We realize you are taking a significant risk by your very presence here," she continued. "If it were not such an exceptional chance for you and your family to benefit greatly, we would not even consider putting you at such a risk."

"But you have, and here we are," Straudner replied neither amused nor taken in by the young woman's attempt at charm and flattery.

Realizing the politician was unaffected by placations to his ego, the young woman became more serious. "Let me get right to the point. I am Selena de Alvarez. I represent a *concern* that has growing interests in South America. Interests that greatly involve your country." She turned her focus to the two Middle Easterners. The larger of the two gave an approving nod for her to continue.

It was apparent to Straudner that she had been chosen to conduct the negotiations, but the Middle Eastern gentlemen, particularly the larger of the two, was clearly in charge. He said nothing letting the young woman continue. "Your country would be ideal for a larger picture strategy, which makes it imperative we have powerful allies."

The politician settled in a nearby leather chair continuing to nurse his drink. Selena de Alvarez continued, "For that, we would like to enlist your support in our endeavor."

"And what support would that be?" Straudner took a sip of his drink.

"To help us change the controlling powers," she said gently, almost casually.

Straudner stopped focusing on his whiskey. He slowly placed his glass on a nearby table and was now looking squarely at the young woman's face. At this point, his mind was a battleground between his survival instinct telling him to end the meeting at once and his ambition for advancement and power that told him to stay. The next words spoken by anyone other than him would determine which side won.

"I realize what I'm proposing is quite an unusual concept. Under normal circumstances your most logical reaction would be to bolt for the door," she added. "However, if you understand the picture, I think you will find such a notion is not wholly unreasonable. Since you control the environment we are discussing, you really have nothing to lose by hearing us out. And why pass up an opportunity to build your family's legacy?"

Straudner waved his hand for her to continue. She described the general plan of creating a destabilizing wave of communist terrorism that would eliminate any challengers and produce the political environment needed to justify the emergence of a powerful leader. She explained the plan to eliminate the left-wing radicals with an equally developed right-wing opposition that would *materialize* to combat the threat and help pacify the country outside the use of government forces. She avoided discussing the weaknesses that could threaten the plan but was not so vague that her briefing sounded like an exotic conspiracy theory.

Colonel Qalmini watched in silence. Turning his gaze every so often to his compatriot, Major Essouri, he checked on how he thought the negotiations were going. The small major indicated a positive assessment of the Contessa's handling of the situation.

Qalmini had fretted about his decision to bring the Contessa into this part of the operation. She was supposed to handle the left-wing aspect only. Involving her in too many fields served, in his mind, to expose them to unnecessary risk. Let not the left hand know the actions of the right was how he wanted to manage this mission. A woman who is supposed to be an operative to their phony communist menace should not be in the company or exposed to the intended icon of the opposition they were proposing to build.

It was a risky decision, but one he felt he had to make given the significant roll Straudner played in the whole operation. With such an important recruitment, he understood the necessity of having the overture made by someone who the politician could relate to. An old money Spanish aristocrat seemed a far better fit than an Iranian soldier.

The Contessa had finished explaining the broad plan and the role of placing Straudner at the head of an authoritarian regime. For several minutes the room remained silent as Straudner pondered the information. He picked up his drink and, finishing the last drops of the golden liquid, rose from his chair and turned squarely to look at the two other gentlemen who had remained conveniently quiet throughout the meeting. "Who exactly wishes to do this?"

The two Iranians rose from their seats. Essouri remained silent as Qalmini now took the lead. The Contessa slowly took a seat off to the side. "We are a consortium if you will. A consortium that represents the Islamic State of Iran."

"So this is an Iranian backed operation," Straudner said. "I didn't think it could be al Qaeda or ISIS."

"No," replied Qalmini. "We are not involved with either. What we are is a country that desperately needs allies in the Western Hemisphere. If it means we have to create one, then that is what we must do."

Straudner was now pacing. "What would this *ally* be expected to do for Iran?"

"We would like to expand our trade and private sector investments for the most part. Also, a strong pact allowing for a military partnership, training, and operations would be ideal," Qalmini chose his words carefully.

"Military?" The young politician looked back at the Iranian. "That is my biggest concern. Military alliances with America's chief adversary these days have a way of making one's presidency short-lived and unpopular."

"This is why we work behind the scenes," Qalmini interjected. "We understand the risk of raising the American's wrath. That is exactly why we are tailoring this to look like an entirely organic regime change within Uruguay with no real outside help."

"The Americans are hardly concerned with the politics of most of South America when their hands are full dealing with the Middle East, Russia, and China," the Contessa interjected. "As long as all is done discretely, you should have no difficulties. Given the high echelons of power in Washington DC are littered with old men nostalgic for the Cold War days, the idea that you're ridding them of a communist menace would endear you to them."

"So what military arrangement would you be looking for?" Straudner asked.

Qalmini again took the floor. "To have some security in having a base of operation in South America would be of great value — some bases, military advisors, and logistics support."

Straudner said nothing for several minutes. He had been given a serious offer to consider. He didn't like the idea of having military ties to such a country as Iran, but the idea of having a lifetime presidency over Uruguay was enticing.

"To further sweeten the pot," the Contessa spoke again. "I would point out that Iran has strong economic ties to the emerging and established economies of the Middle-East and the former Soviet Union. Such ties could help establish your popularity among the economic powers in your country after such a culture shock."

Straudner thought the offer was appealing while at the same time dangerous. If this was a trick or if the plan failed in any way, he alone was left to answer for all of it. Still, the idea of assuming the presidency for life without any challenge seemed impossible to pass up.

"Why would I not assume you're lying? More importantly, what would you expect of me in orchestrating this little operation? As I see it, my involvement in any way leaves me open to great risk, a risk you may choose to exploit. I would like to hear what role I would play in executing this coup of yours. In the end, if I don't feel comfortable with the plan, you may assume my participation will not happen."

Essouri was incredulous, as he tried to use his eyes to protest such a notion. Qalmini faced his subordinate and allowed his eyes to drift in the direction of the politician. His meaning was clear. They had no choice. Straudner had proven to be more astute than they had assumed.

The Contessa was fixing herself a drink. She realized the Iranians had decided to acquiesce to Straudner's demand, and she gave them a nod.

Qalmini turned to face the politician. "When the time comes, you will present the face of legitimacy to our *cause.* When the wave of left-wing terrorism becomes too ominous, you will call for law and order. At which point, a faction from the security forces will rise to heed your call and take to the streets imposing order. At the same time, a right-wing militia will emerge to support your cause. They will pour into the countryside and cities attacking the terrorist strongholds and eliminating the menace."

"Militia?" Straudner perked. "Do elaborate on that."

"We are in the process of building a force designed to augment your military in securing the country." Qalmini explained. "It will also provide a good scapegoat for you when accusations of murder and mayhem arise from the activist community. As a militia, you have deniability when they eliminate the guerrillas and their bases leaving no real loose ends. You can point out that you have no control over marauders who will just as quickly disappear once the threat subsides."

Straudner rotated his glass slowly between his fingers. "You mentioned support from security forces. You have recruited officers within the police, military, and intelligence worlds?"

"No, that is also where your services come in," Qalmini moved slowly toward Straudner. "You see part of our concern is our inability to independently recruit from these circles without taking a serious risk. It would be more advantageous for all of us if you recruited those elements."

Straudner chuckled lightly. "You really are investing a lot in the notion that I will be a party to your plan. You want me to recruit fellow conspirators and risk exposure to myself?"

"Think of it as mutual security," the Contessa added. "As my colleagues have observed, they would be at grave risk of discovery if they attempted to build the coup from inside the security ranks. However, you not taking the lead at this level leads you open to equal threat. If you do not secure your own base of power for this operation, then you will be entrusting the entirety of your position to those loyal and beholden to a foreign power. This would reduce you to a puppet. If you recruit from the police, military, and intelligence community, this will secure your position."

The Contessa was appealing and articulate as she addressed the politician. If anything, she had spoken the words that firmly captured him. Turning his attention back on the Iranian, Straudner sipped his drink before speaking. "So, if I do this, you put the operation together, and I recruit the force to ensure my control of this country after you eliminate all those who could pose a threat. What, then, is to stop me from simply reneging on our arrangement? Severing ties with North America's number one enemy could only serve my greater interest?"

Qalmini slowly dropped into a chair sitting across from him. He looked the politician in the eye. "You could do that. It would be the politically logical thing to do. Yet, please remember that the force that removed your terrorist menace will have been put together and directed by us. In addition, the Hezbollah network, which we have extremely good relations with, has quite an extensive network here in South America. It would be bad for Uruguay's savior from left-wing terrorism to suddenly be caught between right-wing extremists and Islamic radicals who are both well trained and well supported."

Straudner smiled. A begrudging look of admiration crossed his face. The Iranian was no fool or amateur. Satisfied that the plan was good, the politician rose to his feet and raised his glass, "Well gentlemen, and my lady, I'm in."

"Good," Qalmini smiled. A sense of relief rushed through him. "We will begin the preparations at once. Expect the first phase of our operation to commence within the next two weeks. They will be directed at politically strategic targets.

This should help eliminate any threats to you and give you a legitimate concern to begin recruiting."

"I can accept that," Straudner said coolly.

The trio filed out the door with Qalmini leading and the Contessa in the rear. Straudner returned to his seat contemplating what had just transpired when Laudman entered.

"It looks as though I have made a deal," Straudner announced. He watched the old man.

"I assume risk mitigation will be unnecessary, sir?" The watchmaker asked, remaining stoic.

"You are correct," Straudner replied. "It looks as though I have found the moment that secures my contributions to my family's greatness." Lowering his glass to a table, the politician stared out across the room.

CHAPTER 18

Ian 'Plūcker' Ferry had stayed true to his word. The men meeting in the room at the back of the Ronin Club looked every bit like the tough professionals with the years of hardened experience he promised. The muscle-bound action seekers covered in military-like tattoos were absent. The individuals present were low key types — intent on not drawing attention to themselves — staying cognizant of the world around them. Almost everyone on his invitation list was present. Kafka was pleasantly surprised as he looked at the filled seats. Plūcker stood off to the side and allowed the Israeli time to observe the applicants.

Finally, turning to the big Irishman, Kafka spoke. "So, can I get your opinion? Are these men solid?"

Plūcker nodded. "I've known these boys for a long time. I know their histories, their personalities, and their aptitudes. I filtered out the lads who might prove questionable. Every man in here is trustworthy. They'll respect the secrecy of this operation even if they don't get hired. The question now is: what do you need, and who meets those requirements?"

Kafka shook his head, "Well, let's begin."

"You can use my office for privacy," Plūcker offered.

"Thanks," Kafka said and started for the office. Behind him, the Irishman bark out instructions to the applicants, preparing them for the recruitment process.

Rabbi Abraham Kovinski sat directly across from his old childhood friend. Micha Cohen looked sullen. It was obvious neither man was bearing any pleasant news. Kovinski started first. "Well, I went off the assumption that if the Iranians were trying to carry out an operation of any sizable proportion, it would be a sure bet they would try to enlist the aid of the local population. By that I mean, the Shia Muslim communities, primarily the Lebanese conclaves in the Triangle region who spill across Brazil, Argentina, and Paraguay. It would give them the best flexibility.

"Since the death of Imad Mughnivah, Hezbollah and by extension Iran, have lost their contact here. Which means, they would need someone from this region, someone who is a native of these Lebanese communities, to bridge that gap. So, we focused on young men who had left home to go fight in the Syrian conflict against the Sunnis.

"We were looking to see who was coming home under mysterious circumstances. After we ruled out severe injuries, we focused on those who just came home. Many returned to their families and seemed to have no further movement outside their normal work routine, so we discarded them. Then we followed those who came home and seemed to be holding off returning to their previous lives. From there we examined these individuals closer, tapping our contacts in the Middle East for information. What we found boiled down to these three names."

The Rabbi pulled a folder from his desk and handed the list to the old spy. Cohen took the folder and looked at the photographs and hastily typed dossiers on three individuals.

Kovinski continued, "These three not only served in Syria fighting for the Assad regime, they also served with distinction. Each had been selected by Iranian intelligence at various times to be flown to Tehran where they presumably received advanced Special Forces training. When they returned to Syria, after several months having simply disappeared, they were assigned to special operations units focusing on clandestine warfare behind enemy lines. If anyone would be approached to carry out this mission, it would have to be one of these three."

Flipping through the photographs, Cohen only glanced at the reports, figuring he had heard all he needed to know from the Rabbi. He raised his head to face the Rabbi when he finished with the last name on the list. "What are they doing now?"

"Well, the first one has seemingly been inactive. He works at a small bakery in Montevideo and hasn't broken his pattern in several weeks. My people think he's clean."

The Rabbi looked at the katsa waiting for a response. There was none. "The second man has been a little more interesting. He has been making contact with known radicals and Hezbollah types, but he's having trouble adjusting to civilian life and trying to get back to the war in Syria. He is a suspect, but it's unlikely he's the man you are looking for."

The Rabbi paused waiting to elaborate if needed. Again, the katsa remained silent, his eyes focused on the documents in his hand. "This brings us to the final and most likely suspect, *Nouri al'Marak Surriman*."

Cohen's gaze focused on the picture of the young Lebanese expat, and Kovinski took it as a sign to continue. "Again, all things considered, he has had a most interesting life. Since returning from Syria, he has been making a series of trips all around the region: Montevideo, Paraguay and, most recently, a trip into the Arab Triangle where we lost him. However, the Lebanese villages in those parts are known for surviving on illicit activity including smuggling and arms trafficking."

At that point, Micha Cohen lifted his eyes from the documents and stared directly at the old Rabbi, his attention now undivided. Kovinski continued, "We weren't able to verify who exactly he saw or on what business. Yet everything seems to point to him being the person laying the groundwork for whatever operation the Iranians have planned."

"He is making all the right moves," Cohen concurred. "What do you have on his contacts in the cities?"

"Nothing yet," the Rabbi replied. "Whoever his contact is, he has apparently been given his marching orders already and has been carrying them out. Don't worry though, he's on my watch, and my people are keeping close tabs on him. When he comes down the mountain, we'll be on him and anyone he attempts to meet."

Not knowing how to take the Rabbi's words, the katsa handed a folder to the Rabbi. "I would also appreciate your input on this man, Elloy Mendoza." Cohen said. "Somehow he plays an essential roll in this. From what my sources tell me, he's Cuban Intelligence."

Kovinski frowned. "That means it could get extremely

tricky if we should have to deal with him. Neither you nor Israel can have any part in any action against him."

"Exactly, but he's still a player in this operation, and we may need your assistance."

Kovinski checked the file. "We will, I promise you."

"Thank you." Micha was humbled by the risk the Rabbi was taking, especially with the tenuous history the two had shared.

As the two men talked, both were unaware of the young girl quietly hovering against the door, her broom tilted against the door frame beside her. She listened patiently as the conversation inside the office progressed. On a small piece of paper, she scribbled notes. Her last note was the name, *Elloy Mendoza.*

The conversation ended. Deciding she had what she had been sent to get, she quickly stuffed the note paper under her sweater, reclaimed her broom and swept unobtrusively toward an exit. To her relief, she had cleared the main corridor just before Rabbi Kovinski and the other man walked out.

Kafka Dayan's head swam. It had been a long day of interviews, and he felt his instincts slipping as he listened to one applicant after another. Luckily, Plūcker had already filtered out the obvious undesirables and idiots, leaving a cast of experienced professionals to choose from. It had been hours and his applicants ranged from former commandos from the Royal British Marines, former French Legionnaires slumming, members of various South American rebel and counter-rebel groups looking to branch out on their own and enjoy a paying gig and, surprisingly, some former soldiers from regional militaries looking for better than what they had gotten in their previous organizations.

Fortunately, most of the men met his criteria and pay scale. The few who didn't seem disinterested in work that was more focused on commando operations than a long-term war. The prospect of better job security that comes with a long-term campaign was more appealing to professional guerrillas and guerrilla fighters. Commando jobs usually lasted for only a few weeks to a few months. These jobs did not appeal to those who lived with the uncertainty of going from conflict by conflict. Their preference saved Dayan a lot of awkward dismissals. Those who stayed had a reasonable balance of urban and rural battlefields experience.

His new force consisted of nine men, mostly former soldiers from various parts of the world with a few coming from Latin American guerrilla groups. He wrote all their names down in his notebook along with his remarks regarding experience and abilities that caught his attention as well as any personal observations. For Kafka, being a soldier with considerable experience with militaries around the world, it was relatively easy to separate fact from fiction when it came to those who tried to puff up their resumes or lie outright about their experience.

Dispatching the recruits, Dayan directed them to meet back at Plūcker's office in three days. He figured this would be long enough to brief Cohen, obtain instructions, and not go so long that his newly recruited team would get bored and start looking for work elsewhere. It also would give him time to figure out how he was going to organize them. The men departed with promises to return at the end of the week.

Plūcker and Dayan were left alone in the backroom. Their privacy was short lived as the young Negress cracked open the side door to alert her employer that one of his rowdier patrons was picking a fight with some people. Promising to be out quickly, the burly Irishman dismissed the girl with a wave before turning to Dayan. "I can work on gettin' ya equipment and arms but, unless you're willin' to settle, it will be a few weeks before I can get quality goods."

Dayan frowned. "Until I speak to Mr. Cohen and get instructions, a timeline is out of the question. In the meantime, I can already see from the information I have what the mission is going to look like, so I can draw up a list tonight of what I'll need. Look to obtain high grade but keep an eye out for more immediate supplies in case we have to move faster than anticipated. In any case, we need to be as discreet as possible, so try to balance quality with equipment commonly used in this region. We have to bear in mind that whatever we use has to be hard to trace if any are captured. If the equipment is too sophisticated, it will be easy for our enemy to track it back to our supplier and then back to us."

"Right." Plūcker went to handle the trouble outside as Dayan quietly deliberated. He had a lot to prepare and had only passed the first hurdle.

CHAPTER 19

Martin Derry slid his finger across the skin of his other hand. It was a calming technique he had learned years ago — something to do against the tension when out on a mission. Observing the majestic lights of the Hotel Castrana Casino from afar, the Irish mercenary leaned back against his seat. He conducted a series of actions—licking his lips, cracking his jaw, clacking his teeth. These actions were all very annoying to the Colombian sitting in the driver's seat trying hard to ignore his passenger.

Parked off the road, the two men waited. Derry had wanted to ensure mass attendance before the next phase of the operation. The Colombian, a professional of the mercenary craft himself, appreciated the Irishman's concept, however, the litany of nervous habits was difficult to ignore. Keeping his eyes fixed on the lavish hotel, he told himself if his cohort began whistling *Oh Danny Boy,* this operation would be over.

Derry scanned the parking lot of the hotel through a pair of binoculars, then followed up surveilling the entrance. The long line of well-dressed businessmen accompanied by their female companions and flanked by assistants and, in some cases, bodyguards walked in a parade-like fashion toward the main doors.

"It's time," Derry said to his driver who instantly turned the ignition. The car, a sleek black BMW, glided forward pulling onto the main street. The vehicle rode somewhat low in the back leaving the Colombian to wonder if it was attracting too much attention. The Irishman seemed wholly unconcerned and stoic.

Luckily, the roads this hour were only mildly busy — not enough to make driving difficult but enough to not become a spectacle. Turning into the long driveway leading to the hotel, the Colombian skillfully maneuvered the car around the large lagoon-like fountain in front. He kept the car slow but fast enough to avoid suspicion. Rounding the fountain, the car edged off into the turn leading to the parking lot. The lot was packed with expensive cars — everything from high fashion Lamborghinis and Porches to classic American vehicles like vintage Camaros, Mustangs, and GTOs.

Even though he considered himself a committed soldier of the people and the working class, the Colombian couldn't help but feel a sense of remorse at the crime he was about to commit against these beautiful vehicles — their wealthy owners were a different matter entirely.

"How much time do we have?" the driver asked as he cruised through the parking lot pretending to look for a parking space.

"Our ride will be here in ten minutes," Derry said checking his cheap imitation watch.

At the edge of the parking lot closest to the building, the

Colombian turned and proceeded to back the BMW toward the hotel. As expected there were no attendants managing the parking operation, and the only security was focused on the casino. Derry smiled at how easy it had been. Exiting the car, the two men casually looked around to ensure there were no potential witnesses or alarm sounders nearby. Confident they went unnoticed, the Irishman gave his accomplice a nod.

Once back in the driver's seat, the Colombian grabbed a small transistor and, after punching in a few numbers, pressed a button for activation. Tucking it under the driver's seat, he closed the door after manually locking it. He dared not press the electrical lock.

It wasn't long before a small, white van pulled up next to them and came to a halt. Recognizing the two men in front, Derry and the Colombian walked over to the slider door and quickly hopped in. The door was barely shut when the van took off. Both men nearly fell over from the jerk of the vehicle. The van driver was not as cautious about attracting attention as Derry and the Colombian had been. Circling the fountain, the van nearly hit a couple of hotel ushers standing on the road. At the end of the circular drive, the van screamed out onto the main road almost crashing into a delivery truck in the process.

On the main street, Derry pulled a phone from his jacket. It was a cheap throw away that flipped open, however, it served his purpose well enough. Punching in a few numbers, the Irishman took a breath before he pressed the send button. He looked across at his accomplice — the Colombian's eyes were indifferent.

A second later, the explosion was thunderous. Even from

their distance, the rumble from the ground was powerful. "Oh shit!" one of the men sitting up front exclaimed. "There's a big fucking smoke cloud in the air from that bomb of yours."

"It's a start," the Irishman shrugged as he righted himself and settled into his seat. "I don't normally like using TM-500, but it's what my old friends in the CIRA were willing to sell. It's really a hell of an effective plastic explosive."

"Rich fagots," the Colombian murmured with a morbid joy.

Ramon Caldoza never had a moment's rest in his job. As head of the research staff for the Partido National in the Chamber of Deputies, his phone was always ringing, or he was rushing from one dire meeting to another handling financial issues. The sight of his car in the parking lot was an image he equated to the light guiding him to heaven. It was a symbol that his day was finally over. There were no last-minute meetings, no emergency projects, and no political intrigue he had to circumnavigate. His day was done.

With his briefcase in hand, his tie loosened, and the top button of his shirt undone, he wondered what meal his cook had prepared for his evening dinner, or what new home design project his wife wished him to undertake. He had had a day full of the same erratic debacles he would again have to traverse tomorrow. But for now, he was free.

He had just managed to get the door of his car open when a voice caught his attention, "Sẽnor Caldoza."

Spinning around, the bureaucrat found himself staring at

a small masked figure dressed in dark clothes. It took Caldoza only moments to realize he was in danger. But it was too late. A loud crack echoed in the evening silence. The bureaucrat felt a sharp pain in his stomach. He lowered his chin and saw blood splattering his white shirt. Stepping back, he gasped as his mind raced to understand what was going on. A loud collection of clicking sounds caused him to refocus on his assailant who was now joined by two other masked and blackened figures. They were all armed with small machine guns.

Not an expert in the field of weapons, he was unaware the guns were Vz Scorpions, a Yugoslavian made compact sub-machine gun, and for several decades, a choice weapon of European terrorist groups. Now lined up in a de facto-like firing squad, the terrorists aimed their weapons toward the bureaucrat.

"Wh-Why are you doing this?" Caldoza cried out with a full measure of confusion and terror.

"Because you are an enemy of the people," one of the masked figures replied, further terrifying Caldoza, who realized his life was about to end.

The 32 caliber gunshots sounded like so many small firecrackers going off in rapid succession. Caldoza's body nearly exploded with all the metal penetrating his flesh at once. It was only a few seconds, but the execution seemed like hours to both the victim and the killers.

With the weapons emptied and the night now silent, the old bureaucrat choked up a pool of blood and gasped a few more breaths before his lifeless corpse slid to the ground.

The Legislative Palace was the house of the Uruguay Chamber of Deputies and the center of the country's national politics. It was a rather unassuming compound of brick in a somewhat grayish brown color. It lay atop a slight hill giving a hint of authority to all who passed by. Yet, like so many significant buildings within insignificant countries, this structure was lightly guarded, only a few watchmen to dissuade trespassers.

A small van slowed a little way from the palace. Pulling off to the side of the road, the van came to a stop as the driver turned off the lights but kept the engine running. To those passing by, it looked like a parked vehicle. Only a slight amount of exhaust and the dull rhythm of the engine indicated otherwise.

Leaning against his seat to avoid a silhouette, the driver observed the legislative structure. His eyes were fixed and stoic. He was a professional who had developed an ability to maintain indifference while in the field. In the back seat, two other members of his team were quietly preparing themselves. A man and a woman both dressed in black tactical military attire were opening a set of cases. Within seconds they were holding Rocket Propelled Grenade Launcher 7D caliber — a common weapon used by insurgents against US forces in Iraq. The driver thought to himself, "If it's good enough to kill Yankee soldiers, it's good enough for this."

His attention was diverted from the weapon by the approach of two figures walking toward the car. To anyone else, they were a normal couple coming home from the local bar. Nearing the vehicle on the passenger side, the man and woman came up to a door. The window was already rolled down. The driver was waiting for them.

The meeting was quick. The couple reported the results

of their reconnaissance of the facility and the immediate surroundings. They finished with an equally fast update on the most likely escape routes. The couple then strolled down the road.

"Get ready," the driver quietly ordered his cohorts. Hearing the sound of the rocket being screwed into the launcher tube, the female confirmed they were ready. The driver thrust the vehicle into drive and turned on his lights. As he pulled the van onto the road, he heard the woman curse as she unlatched the back doors. Now, held shut by just her hands, they were ready. The roads were largely empty except for a few late night drivers — perfect for an easy escape.

Arriving at the target area, the driver began to slow the van. "Be ready," he ordered. A few feet farther he gave the command to attack. The male subordinate, armed with the RPG, bolted out the back doors past his female partner. The driver didn't stop, he only took his foot off the gas and allowed the van to idle forward to clear the distance between him and his operative. The backblast from the weapon would be intense and far-reaching. The vehicle needed to be a good distance away to avoid getting scorched. Jogging a few paces, the operative stopped and took a stance positioning himself and his weapon. With stone cold calm, the man took aim at the parliamentary structure, drew a quick breath and pulled the trigger. The rocket fired from its launching tube with tremendous force. The backblast was powerful and intense.

The shooter was another experienced professional — he didn't stop or freeze to watch the results. He dashed for the van with all the speed of an Olympic sprinter. He quickly handed the firing tube to his female accomplice and jumped into the back of the moving vehicle. The doors were barely shut behind him before the driver pressed the gas and the vehicle sped down the road. From his side mirror, the driver took note of the thunderous fireball and gigantic cloud of smoke. The mission was a success.

CHAPTER 20

Nouri al'Marak Surriman stood quietly by the small black pickup parked off the side of the road outside a small Brazilian village a few miles from the Uruguay border. At a glance, he was just a guy enjoying the pleasant night with the aid of a cold beer. This would only work in Surriman's interest this evening. He couldn't afford to have any nosey countryside police pulling him over to ask questions. It would be hard to respond convincingly.

Major Rashid al' Akim remained in the bushes. An obvious foreigner with limited Spanish, the objective was to keep his exposure in the operation limited. He preferred to let the young Hezbollah operative engage with any potential troublemakers, but they agreed he should be armed. In the event Surriman was approached by someone who was intent on being difficult, the Major could take more direct action. He cradled an American military-grade M-4 short stocked carbine rifle fixed with a silencer. This was a replica from Surriman's family village that would help create confusion if killing became necessary.

In the few hours the two men had been working with

each other, they had managed to develop a bizarre symmetry of respect and disdain. The seasoned soldier of the Revolutionary Guard had observed the Lebanese operative and decided he was skilled in the art of espionage and the shadow world of covert operations. However, he also saw a contemptable disciple of the religion — comfortable living in big cities, a cosmopolitan life filled with sinful decadence. It was somewhat irritating to hear the young Muslim so easily discuss the selections of wine and his all too frequent sexual liaisons.

By contrast, Surriman saw the elder Iranian operative as a wise, resourceful operator who could size up a situation and adapt accordingly. He was also, by the Hezbollah operator's assessment, rough and largely unsophisticated. The Iranian was a field soldier who was definitely more at home in a war zone base camp than a metropolitan community and would have a heart attack if he missed evening prayers.

Neither man spoke as they waited in the dark. Surriman leaned up against the hood of the pickup as he took a deep breath of the jungle atmosphere. Behind him, he could hear the bear-like Iranian as he nestled down into the grass resting his large frame against the truck. They had been there for two hours. The timeframe had been left open to compensate for any complications.

In the distance, Surriman caught sight of headlights. Major Akim must have recognized something, too. Surriman could feel the shifting of the big man's body against the truck as he struggled to stand up. Not wishing to be hasty, both men maintained their positions; Surriman leaned against the hood of his truck pretending to nurse a beer; Akim hunkered in the shadows with his weapon aimed and ready for action.

They had used this routine twice this evening with previous vehicles. First, a local priest asked if the young Arab was having any trouble. Next, a couple of attractive Brazilian girls tried to pick up the handsome guy with the beer. Both were easily dismissed with a few polite words.

The headlights became brighter as a vehicle approached. Surriman rolled the head of his small glass bottle between his fingers. If they ran into any hostiles, Surriman would fall to the ground and retrieve an automatic pistol taped under the vehicle, clearing a path to allow Akim to initiate an engagement.

A few meters away the shadowy vehicle slowed. Surriman held steady. The driver of the weathered gray Land Rover gradually maneuvered his vehicle until the side was less than a meter from him. The window was already rolled down as the Land Rover came to a halt. From the shadows a voice spoke up, "Pardon Sẽnor, do you have any cigarettes?"

The question caught Surriman's attention as well as the attention of the Iranian in the shadows. Gripping his weapon firmly, Surriman replied, "I have Marlboros, will that suffice?"

The driver was silent for a few seconds, and Surriman prepared to fall onto his back.

Then the driver said, "I'm sorry, I prefer Turkish brands, but I'll accept Camels if you only have American types."

Surriman's eyes lit up. "Then I'm afraid I cannot help you. We are at an impasse."

There were another few seconds of silence. Then the driver's door opened followed by the passenger door. Surriman was confronting a tall, slender figure with a long, bushy beard. The passenger came around and the Arab was looking at a slightly younger man with a crop of curly hair and a few days' facial growth that was barely noticeable in the darkness.

"Keppa?" Surriman asked the taller man.

"I am," he replied. "And you are Nouri?"

"Correct."

The conversation that took place between the two men over cigarettes was obviously a pre-designated code. The significant pieces of the conversation were particular word choices. Passwords could be obtained by hostiles who kidnap or try to impersonate an operative. They threaten one operative to give up his end of the password or accompany the operative to the meeting threatening to kill him if he does not comply.

The initial request for cigarettes opened the exchange. The reply that he only had Marlboros was the instigation. Surriman's specific use of the word *suffice* was the alert for the other side that a code had been initiated. If Surriman had ended his sentence with any other word than suffice, the driver would have realized his contact had been compromised or was the wrong man.

The driver responding to the initial statement about liking Turkish brands stated he recognized the code initiation. Had he opened his response with a sentence about *camels,* Surriman would know the driver was an imposter. He was listening for word placement about Camel cigarettes. Had the driver not specified American *types* rather than *brands,* the passenger would be identified as hostile.

A person can be threatened to give up a password with a gun to their head. Trying to warn a person under such circumstances is difficult, but the code is crucial to protecting the other side.

Keppa leaned over to embrace the shorter Hezbollah operative. "Nouri, I have heard many good things about your exploits in the Holy Land."

"Thank you," Surriman replied. "I actually miss home and, believe it or not, these fucking mountains."

Waving his hand at the man with curly hair, Keppa said excitedly, "Let me introduce you to Avi, my cousin."

Avi was reserved but pleasant as he extended a nod to the man he only knew as Nouri. Surriman returned the acknowledgment with a nod of his own.

Surriman beckoned Akim. The burly figure lumbered through the foliage like an animal. He finally join the others with his M-4 held loosely at his side. Pleasantries were kept to a minimum as Surriman made quick introductions. People working in covert operations were safer knowing no more than is necessary.

Surriman and Akim hurried back to their vehicle. With a click of the ignition, the engine roared to life. Keppa swung a U-turn, and soon both vehicles were hurrying down the road at a swift but acceptable speed careful not to attract attention. After driving about five kilometers, the Land Rover pulled onto a partially overgrown trail. Surriman slowly navigated the car through the shrubbery and grass fields. It seemed to take forever, although it had only been a few minutes. The Land Rover stopped directly in front of a long semi-circle of headlights.

Surriman headed toward the center vehicle and came to a halt. With the engine running and the headlights on, both men stepped out of the car. The collection of headlights from the other vehicles outlined a sizable group gathered around the other vehicles.

Keppa and Avi joined them. Even in the darkness, Surriman could make out Keppa's toothy grin.

"We had good luck in our recruitment," Keppa opened excitedly. "All are from the Lebanese villages in the areas of Argentina and Paraguay so language shouldn't be a problem. They are all hard, rugged types who exist in the back-country and are accustomed to hard living and, when necessary, will break the law."

Akim said nothing as he tried to size up the collection of bodies around him, but it was nearly impossible to do this in the dark.

"How many were you able to recruit?" Surriman asked.

"Nearly five hundred," Avi replied in almost a whisper. "It is what you asked for but, again, we tried to meet our standards while being discrete. We have a hundred in this lot; next week we will have a hundred more. Not so few you can't begin working with them, but not so many we can't manage the transport."

"Well, let's collect them and move them to the base camp," Akim interjected. "We should be able to move as one single convoy. Surriman will divide forces with your friends here. You lead, and I'll ride with the others taking the rear position so we don't lose anyone. We can't afford to have a bunch of Spanish speaking Arabs wandering up and down the roads here."

The three Arabs nodded in agreement. Soon everyone piled into vehicles. Surriman and Avi were in the lead pickup with Keppa and Major Akim following in the Land Rover. The convoy rolled out through the darkened trails.

In the ghost-like quiet, the convoy's passing was a secret except for one person — a young man dressed in the clothes of a local peasant. He was crouched down and peering through a powerful camera with an infrared lens that allowed him to take clear pictures without flashes. Next to him was a small collection of goats watched over by a small but attentive Australian sheepdog. If noticed or approached, he could quickly explain that he had been tracking down strays from his herd.

When the convoy disappeared behind a security gate, the trucks came to a halt in one long line just outside a small make-shift campsite. Surriman leaped from his car and began directing traffic. When he was finished, a row of ten large military-style hauling trucks stood parked in front of him.

He was soon joined by Major Akim and Keppa.

"Assemble your men," Akim commanded.

At once Keppa reached under his shirt and produced a small radio. Speaking into the transmitter, he uttered a few short commands. Moments later the back of several of the trucks began to shake. Within seconds more silhouettes emerged from the back and scrambled to the front of the vehicle.

Like drill sergeants, Keppa and Avi started shouting commands loudly as they began directing the shadows into a formation. Their verbiage was a strange variation between Spanish and Arabic, but the figures were soon arranged into a recognizable organization.

Akim and Surriman approached the formation. Keppa turned giving them a nod and stepped to the side. Acknowledging he now had the floor, Surriman stood before the shadows and spoke in the Spanish flavored Arabic adopted in the South American Lebanese communities. His discussion centered on a rough plan for seizing control from anti-religious communists and creating a place in the Western Hemisphere that would be friendly to the Arab cause. In addition to fighting for God and their freedom, they stood to earn a lot of money at the completion of this crusade. For men from the world of black markets, the latter raised a special excitement.

His speech served as a motivator for the men who had traveled several miles through jungle backroads. He stood back and Akim took the stage. In his gruff baritone, he explained the order of the operation. His oration was quick and to the point. When he was finished, he turned back to Surriman who gave orders directing everyone to their barracks.

Micha Cohen could feel the cool leather of the armchair through his cotton slacks and a buttoned shirt. He watched while Kafka paced endlessly across the Oriental rug. He had spent the last hour reviewing documents and allowing Kafka to give him an update on his recruitment efforts. Now the old katsa listened as the young operative detailed his assessment of the situation.

"So far we seem to have what we need. However, I'm still not sure what our target is," Kafka said as he waved his hands to emphasize his point. "Do we take out this Surriman character? Do we want to kidnap the Iranian and get him to talk to this Cuban intelligence asshole still in play or is he inconsequential? I mean right now it seems like we are in limbo. If we make a wrong move, we will tip our hand and the enemy will be onto us. If we don't move and try to figure out their operation, everything we are working toward could go for nothing, and they will accomplish what they're after…whatever the fuck that is."

Cohen folded his hands together and rubbed his chin with his thumbs. "I don't believe our situation is dire. Whatever they are planning, it is elaborate and going to take some time to accomplish. From what we have on their timeline, it is unlikely it will come to fruition anytime in the next month or so."

Kafka stopped pacing and was looking intensely at the old man. Cohen continued. "Right now, they are still building their plan like we are. So focus on that. We already know the locations they are likely preparing. As for intelligence, you're right. If we move too fast, we risk being discovered and exposed. So, we will gather intelligence slowly through the sources we have cultivated. When the time is right, we will consider riskier options. In the meantime, we shouldn't be impatient."

Kafka knew the old spy was correct. Realizing the point had been made, the katsa resumed reviewing the list sitting in his lap. "This is the estimated equipment you require?"

"Based on what I can make of the current situation, yes. However, if the situation changes, how hard or long would it take to obtain additional equipment?"

Cohen considered the list. "Until I fill this order and test the available contacts, I cannot say for sure. However, from what I see on this list, I assume you foresee eventually attacking these base camps?"

"Right now, that is where I see the focus of the mission," Kafka replied. "However, we are still planning around several unknown variables. The best thing to do right now is to get a close-up of what they are doing."

"Well, just make sure you understand this operation may

change considerably as information comes in. Don't get too focused on *bush wars* for this." The katsa waved his finger in a warning gesture.

The young commando shook his head. "I have no intention of doing anything like that. But I do believe we need to consider a reconnaissance." Placing his finger on the map he directed his superior to a thin blue squiggly line. "Everything else is too risky. The fences are well covered by surveillance cameras, and I can tell you that these boys are professionals and smart enough to be running regular patrols. We would end up engaging with them and ruin any element of surprise." Kafka looked up to see that Cohen was following him intently. Kafka continued, "However, the river that runs alongside their camp is largely outside their camp area; therefore, they are more limited in the security they can place on it. I can have my team move up from there and infiltrate more easily."

The katsa wanted to tell his subordinate that he was thinking as if he was in the West Bank or Lebanon, but his own evaluation agreed with Kafka's. It was their only option at this stage.

CHAPTER 21

Oskar Straudner basked in the moment. Resting on the sumptuous couch at the elite Excalibur Club, he watched news reports of the recent wave of terrorist attacks across Montevideo, the capital city of Uruguay. The anchorman, a polished looking young man, explained the horrors of the situation with a controlled reverence.

Nursing a glass of Kentucky bourbon, a delighted Straudner listened as a police commander spoke of a new age of radicalism sweeping across the country. *Communist menace* was the term repeatedly used by the police commander and parroted by every supposed expert commentator who could get in front of a camera. All excitedly recounted the radicalism while trying to downplay concerns about a return to the old days of the Tupamaros' right-wing vigilantism.

Straudner eyed the men he had gathered for evening drinks. They bore expressions of deep concern. It was exactly the response he had hoped for. He had strategically gathered representatives from the various agencies and organizations that comprised the Uruguay security and intelligence community. The older, seasoned veterans weren't quite agency directors or department heads, but they were high ranking members who knew how the system worked and had considerable influence.

Straudner planned to have them gathered at this moment in an informal setting. It was a setting in which he was able to make casual overtures to test his assessments and the mood of the very people he would need for his power bid. As he predicted, they all grimaced nervously as they listened to the ongoing reports, reminding them about the violence of the old days and those dreaded horrors.

When he felt the mood was right, Straudner casually interjected, "If this proves to be a long-term trend, will it lead to a possible right-wing backlash?"

His question had been appropriately timed, and the looks on the faces of his guests grew even graver. One colonel with Ejencino National, the Uruguay army, gently bit his thumb as he pondered the politician's question. "I don't know. I-I don't think it's as serious as the old days when Soviet and Cuban support heightened the dangers." The colonel was trying to convince himself this was not the beginning of another bloody surge of political radicalism — a return to the Tupamaros, the urban violence, and the equally violent military responses from overzealous commanders.

Glancing around the room it was clear to Straudner that all his guests were harboring similar attempts of diluted rationalization.

"But what if it is?" the politician questioned as he calmly sipped his drink.

His comment was well placed. The collection of guests were again taken aback, their latent fears resurging.

"We can't be sure this is not some random chain of

events," a long-serving deputy in the Ministry of Interior interrupted. "We are definitely being hasty."

As if playing a game of chess, Straudner, ever the master politician, made his move. "One of the country's most noted hotels was just blown up killing several and wounding several more of our most important citizenry." The politician was now looking around the room with a cold, discerning eye toward everyone in his little circle. "They just assassinated a long-term political figure right outside his office in an obviously planned attack."

His gaze focused on one of the men in deep thought. "I can only wonder what is in store since we are obviously dealing with what is a well-organized and equipped movement. Or maybe, just maybe, it is a series of actions by individuals who all in a single moment in time decided to carry out well planned and resourced attacks."

When Straudner was sure he had tempered the mood well enough, he made his key move that would either solidify a base of support for his future plans or end his campaign right there. "I'm curious. Has the president called any emergency meetings over this?"

The men unanimously shook their heads, a look of revelation and concern written across their faces. The politician continued, "Umm, I certainly hope he's not having romantic reminiscences of his youth as a revolutionary clouding his judgment." The comment was sarcastic, but it had its intended impact.

Venzuelo Zamora could hardly contain the exuberance

elicited by the pools of recruits. The combination of being on the verge of graduation from the rough training camp and the news of the strikes made by the *revolution* had instilled the camp with a powerful surge of jubilation.

The recruits were further energized by the arrival of their equipment. Over the course of their training, they had been using an assortment of cold war era weapons: antiquated, well-used Kalashnikov 47 and FN FAL assault rifles for the field portion, Makarov automatic pistols and Uzi compact sub-machine guns for the urban fighting, plus German PZF-44 grenade launchers and Soviet RGD-5 grenades. The grenades had come from a stash of Chinese armaments.

To her delight, Don Meduriso had filled most of the Contessa's requests. However, to her dismay, the grenades were cold war Chinese stock instead of American which caused problems. For instance, simply pulling the string that fell from the bottom of the throwing stick after being unscrewed would be easier to master than the more complex models. Zamora, ever the soldier, quickly rejected them because of their short and often unreliable fuses. That they could explode anywhere between a second to five seconds after string activation made them more dangerous than beneficial.

The arrival of crates by trucks hauling machine parts bound for a factory in a nearby city created quite a stir. A quick detour to drop off the *additional cargo* filled everyone with excitement and a sense of true accomplishment. Breaking open the crates generated a loud cheer.

The Contessa had proven her logistical brilliance. The trick was negotiating the line between equipment needed to be effective in their operations and not providing equipment so sophisticated that outside patronage from another nation-state became obvious. The equipment was better than the antiquated material the students had been using but were still old and dated enough that any intelligence agency would assume some black-market dealer or guerrilla band in need of money was peddling the arms from some crooked military or paramilitary outfit in South America.

Don Diego Francisco del' Meduriso had proven most discriminating in the collection of weapons he had made available for this operation. He had delivered the North Korean military grade AK-47 68 models she had asked for initially. The Don had also obtained short stock Rumanian WASR model AKMs as opposed to the Russian and Ukrainian models originally sought. Though not as well designed as the AK-47, the Rumanian models were highly regarded on the world market. They were also more easily explained in the hands of South American terrorists. Rumanian laxity for arms exports and controls and the long-established black market in the Baltics was convenient for countries to disavow any direct involvement. This left the door open for suspicions and conjectures that would never amount to any real verifiable facts.

The arsenal also included a small consignment of Semtex plastic explosives and some reasonably modern era Russian made detonator charges. The rest of the shipment was comprised of palenite nitroglycerine — a much more easily obtainable explosive that would raise fewer questions and be less easily traced. Czech made Scorpion CZ .32 caliber and Israeli made Uzis, still somewhat popular among drug cartel shooters, were included. The old model CZ had proven an effective killing device on numerous occasions throughout its history, so the Contessa and her employers figured they didn't need to mess with the proven classics.

Almost like children opening presents on Christmas, the newly trained recruits looked on excitedly as the boxes produced the brand new equipment. If at any time they had thought they were playing a game, it all vanished at that moment. The training was nearly over, and they were about to become revolutionaries. They would surely be remembered in the mold of the gallant, passionate fighters they had only read about in the history books. For good measure, Zamora had taken the step of lining the walls of the students' barracks with pictures of such memorable icons as Che Guevara, Manuel Marlunda, and Mono Jojoy along with others famous for *peasant revolts* in the area. The result had the psychological effect of conditioning their mindsets. They were about to fight the passionate revolution they had only heard or read about.

Martin Derry leaned back in a wicker chair nursing a small glass of some sort of alcoholic beverage produced by the locals. He watched the recruits take the weapons. He nodded with a sense of accomplishment. In the last few weeks, the Irishman had been quite busy between carrying out the *revolution* in Montevideo and training the recruits in urban warfare.

Watching the Contessa walk toward him, the Irishman declined to stand up. Instead, he offered her a small bottle of whatever he was currently drinking. He wrinkled his nose. He didn't like the indigenous brew very much. With a wave, she politely declined. Derry set his glass aside and turned to his employer.

"They look quite good," she opened. "Will they be able to operate at the high level you have set in the last few weeks of your campaign?" She was referring to the recent attacks Derry had conducted at the casino, Parliament, and the assassination of the political strategist. At the same time, he had also bombed a police precinct, the headquarters of a major South American bank, and assassinated the CEO of one of Uruguay's largest shipping firms.

"They won't have to." The Irishman responded after swallowing another gulp of his libation. "By now everyone is on full alert and expecting an attack. That means the next stage will be multiple attacks and smaller targets forcing them to have to spread their resources thinner and pointing out the true vulnerability of their situation."

The Contessa nodded. She was impressed with his plan. She had obviously chosen well by recruiting Mr. Derry. Despite his hard features and working-class demeanor, he was every bit the man he was reputed to be. He was a tough, an intelligent operator, and a good strategist.

"So, what is the next step?" the Contessa pressed.

"Divide them up with the bulk staying in the countryside and send a third to the city. We will carry out a series of small attacks in key locations designed to get the general masses nervous: mid-size businesses, police stations, and middle-class neighborhoods. When you get the middle and upper classes in a state of unrest, it will force some drastic action. About the time they start sewing up the city and cracking down on the ghettos and working districts, which is a natural reaction to assume the poor are the culprits, then it will be time for the countryside to erupt into wild violence. Violence, by my good Colombian friends, will be directed against the plantation owners and security elements."

"Long-term, the wealthy of the country will be in a state of panic and looking for extreme responses to all the violence," the Contessa stated as she evaluated the plan laid out by the Irish mercenary.

CHAPTER 22

The Guardians of Israel were huddled in a tight little circle at the far end of the local coffee shop a few blocks from the Jewish center. Solomon Cabriza Gold, a tall young man with broad shoulders, sat at the center — the recognized leader of their group. With all eyes on him, he was hunched with his chin resting on the bridge created by his folded hands and stabilized by his elbows nestled into the meat of his thighs. His attention was fixed on Myra, the young girl who had smuggled the information on Elloy Mendoza from the Rabbi's office.

"Are you sure?" His voice was cold and deep, intimidating.

Myra examined the man interrogating her. He was well proportioned with sculpted biceps that protruded from under his tight-fitting black T-shirt. His face was like a chiseled picture set on an oval-shaped canvas. Solomon Gold could easily have been a model with his good looks, but just as easily, he could be an enforcer for a crime family with the way he could look at someone and completely intimidate them.

She tried hard to avoid his ice-cold gaze. "I am positive. I was right outside the door listening." She was struggling to keep from hyperventilating as she felt her nerves start to give way. "The katsa specifically mentioned this man." She pointed to the small piece of paper on which she had written the name. It was now clenched in Gold's fists. Gold told the Rabbi the danger Mendoza posed, the importance of finding him, and, "Apparently, he is in league with the Iranians," he added.

Gold took his gaze off the nervous young girl and began looking at the young men gathered around him. They were in their late teens and early twenties, athletically built, and best of all, they were hungry for a fight. They now had a chance to aid the Jewish cause and fight the enemy of their people.

"He's right here in Buenos Aires, and we can get him," Gold said with the deliberate purpose of opening a dialogue.

"He is a target that's within our means to take out for Israel!" another young man exclaimed.

The group enthusiastically agreed. They finally had the mission their group had been seeking.

All eyes returned to Gold, anxiously anticipating his decision. Dismissing Myra with a wave, everyone waited for her to leave. Action was called for, and it was now a conversation for men. After she left the room, Gold turned to the assembled group. "A katsa, an agent of Israel, considers this man a threat. What's more, he is a threat from Iran! The katsa may have to move quietly to do something about this Cuban, but we do not!"

The attendants were all now on the edge of their seats as they fed off their leader's energy.

"I will not let those fucking terrorists kill or threaten

more Jewish lives, especially here in our own home. We will not let another community center be bombed, and we will not mourn our loved ones again! I say we kill this Mendoza bastard ourselves and strike a blow against Iran."

As he predicted, his speech met with thunderous applause as the men pounded their fists against their seats.

Major Essouri could not deny being impressed. Looking through the small window of what served as Akim's office, he watched the Lebanese recruits maneuver around a series of obstacles on the course, while others moved through the various buildings practicing for urban warfare. Though they were residents of small mountain villages, they negotiated the buildings of the training site almost like professionals.

"A few battalions of men such as these," the small Iranian shook his head as he turned and started toward his larger colleague, "and we could invade this country, coup d'état be damned."

Akim was already settled comfortably in a worn roller chair that had been inexplicably procured for his office. Folding his hands under his chin, he looked at his colleague then stared out the window. "They are turning into a crack team of soldiers all right. I wait with excitement to test them out."

Essouri shoved his hands in his pockets. "We seem to be building a fine army. Honestly, the idea of working with that rather despicable character we plan to put into power does not sit well with me."

"But we need him nonetheless," a voice interjected in

accented Farsi. Both men turned to see Nouri al'Marak Surriman standing in the doorway. Dressed in his usual attire — tan slacks, and a white cotton shirt — he contrasted greatly with the camouflage adorned Iranians, especially since he was now sporting a white Panama hat.

Surriman stepped into Akim's office. "I just came back from my visit to the village."

"Do you have an update on the status of our weapons?" Akim asked.

Grabbing a wooden chair and flipping it around, Surriman sank down into it, resting his arms over the back. "They have over half the order finished, I have inspected the finished arsenal stock and tested a few random pieces myself. They look and operate like the real thing."

Both Iranians cracked smiles and rejoiced at the news. "So, is there any question of the variety?" Essouri asked trying to contain his excitement.

Taking a deep breath, Surriman shook his head. "Not so far. The short stock M-4's look like perfect replicas of the American variety. The short barrel compact AKMS-74s could just as easily have come from the Russian army. Presuming that most of the operation would be centered in built-up urban areas, Surriman and his handlers wanted to keep the majority of the rifles at 5.56 caliber. In the early stages, we had trouble with lettering. The first batch contained Spanish markings. The second was in Arabic. It took a third batch to finally get the English markings and Russian cyrillics on them. Having no experienced translators, I had to work to overcome that hurdle."

"And now?" Major Akim asked impatiently.

Surriman raised his eyes and looked from one side to the

other. "Everything is good. The weapons will all look like they came directly from a US arsenal or Russian factory directly to you."

Both Iranians breathed a sigh of relief. "Did you bring a specimen back for our review?" Akim asked.

"No," Surriman replied. "An American made military assault rifle was not something I was going to risk taking across the border. It would have been dangerous enough if it was an obvious surplus from the cold war, but an honest and experienced border guard would be guaranteed to report modernized armaments to domestic intelligence. So, no, I didn't. But I do understand your need for personal verification. That is why I arranged for the first shipment to arrive early, so you can conduct your own tests. If you discover any problems, we can rectify them before the next shipment is sent."

"How did you manage that?" Essouri asked.

"The first shipment will be small," Surriman said. "Thirty-to-forty weapons consisting of samples of all the types specified. If the weapons meet your approval, the second shipment will be larger. Because I can vouch for the quality, the rest will be stockpiled with markings and specific identifiers left off so we can make the markings we need. If you have problems with more than the markings, I have already taken the precaution of reaching out to a few other neighboring villages that also specialize in this industry. I don't like risking a security breach, but they will be able to make up the time and keep the supply on schedule."

Essouri and Akim glanced at each other. They had recruited the right man for this mission.

Surriman eyed the two Iranians. "I'm presuming we are ready to start coordinating the next step?"

The two majors looked at each other for a moment, and Essouri replied, "We start preparing now for the movement portion of the plan."

CHAPTER 23

The two young radicals displayed a mixture of feelings ranging from giddy excitement at their first opportunity to act for the revolution, to dismay that it didn't present the hoped-for challenge. The police station was little more than a group of small adobe and wood buildings built closely together. The structures had been joined to create a single building by making a few carpentry adjustments. Aside from a metal chain-link fence, the building had little security.

Carefully, they drove closer. Their vehicle, a white Toyota van, hardly looked ominous as it continued along the road adjacent to the police compound. Based on their intelligence, the security and vigilance were lax if not to say non-existent. The front of the gate was completely open without any guards posted. Driving slowly past the compound there were only three older, pot-bellied policemen standing outside having a smoke.

"Are you ready Marcia?" the male radical asked his partner.

Marcia took a deep breath. "Yes," she whispered. Her

weak response left her partner feeling somewhat skeptical. But this late, both his question and reservations were completely irrelevant.

"Right there," Marcia pointed as the van neared a gentle rise by some bushes. The van was already moving slow enough to not make anyone suspicious. Seizing the small bag Marcia had sitting on the floor between her legs, she opened the passenger side door and leaped out into the night. The van pressed on at the same slow speed.

Darkness was the perfect cover. Dressed entirely in black, her presence went completely unnoticed as she slowly crawled up behind the berm. Once safely behind her cover, she opened her bag and pulled out WASR Rumanian made AK-47 long-barrel assault rifle. Resting the weapon against the berm, she reached into her bag again and produced two fully charged banana magazines. Tucking one magazine in her belt, with the open end covered by her black sweatshirt, she carefully felt for the magazine slot of her rifle. The sweat dripping from her brow didn't help as she struggled to not give herself away while carefully working in the darkness. '*I have done this before*,' she told herself, trying to remain calm.

Finally, she felt the magazine slide into the housing and heard the slight click locking it into place. An immense sense of relief flowed over her. She crawled her way up the berm until she could peek over the top and see the police barracks not more than fifty meters away. Placing her rifle into a firing position, she sighted on the light hanging over the door. The steel sights were not ideal for night shooting, but scopes could easily lose their zero with rough movement. She had not really mastered their use.

Luckily, two of the three pot-bellied cops were still standing out front which gave her a good reference point.

Aligning the front sight post with the rear aperture, she sighted on one of the cops.

Meanwhile, her partner pulled off the road stopping short of the tree line. Exiting the vehicle, he rounded the side and inched into a darkened corner. A passerby would simply assume he was a driver relieving himself. He calmly viewed the police barracks. The side closest to him had a fenced-in perimeter where a few patrol vehicles were kept locked up. Deciding all was well, the man edged to the back of his van. Cracking open one of the doors, he slid out a long, blue canvas bundle. Slipping back to the side of the vehicle, he laid the canvas down and began unrolling it. Soon he was looking at the outline of a rocket-propelled grenade launcher. Unwrapping another small canvas bundle, he produced a small rocket.

He fixed the rocket into place. When it was adjusted correctly, he stepped several feet away from his vehicle. He had seen and felt the back blast of a rocket enough times to be leery and was able to find enough darkened space to ensure he would not be immediately noticed. Taking careful aim, he sighted in the weapon. Because he was looking at a broad target, he was not too concerned with precision. Lowering slowly to one knee, he steadied himself and fired.

The jolt of the rocket was strong, but not nearly as strong as the fury of the back blast. The raging heat and sheer force created an overwhelming sensation. He watched as the rocket spiraled wildly toward its target. Moments later, the side of the police station exploded in a giant fireball.

Leaping to his feet, he quickly ran back to his vehicle. The blast created its intended effect. Inside, one could hear the shouts of men crying out in Spanish as they struggled to understand what was going on and to carry out orders to evacuate the building.

Marcia was waiting when the front doors of the station burst open, discharging a flood of policemen and administrators scrambling to escape. Crowded together and in a frenzy, they were oblivious when rounds of gunfire from across the way tore into them.

Marcia still had the porch lights to guide her, but it was the incessant cries of the evacuating people that she focused on. Careful not to overexert, she fired four to five round bursts maneuvering her weapon a few centimeters side to side to better capture the changing patterns. She had finished with her first thirty round magazine and was in the process of reloading when someone shouted. "My God! They are dead! They are dead!"

Marcia realized her targets had been noticed.

More shouts came.

"We are being shot at!"

"Where are the shots coming from?"

"I don't know! I think from across the road!"

Deciding it was better to hold off for the moment, Marcia waited quietly. Her wait was not long. Soon she heard gunfire coming from a different direction. As planned, her accomplice had begun redirecting their attention. The police, confused and scared, were hard pressed to know what to do, and the screams continued.

When the shooting stopped, and the police focused on the tree line away from her, Marcia began shooting again. The shouts and the blurry outline of silhouettes were enough. Using four to five round bursts again to conserve her ammunition, she finished the magazine and slid backward. By now, the police had scattered, dashing into the barracks or running down the road taking their chances that they were not surrounded.

It was difficult to see how many they had killed, but the point had been made. The micro terrain helped her stay out of sight while she carefully maneuvered her way to the road in the direction her accomplice had gone. The sound of his occasional gunfire guided her to his location. She could still hear the terrified screams of the frantic people as they ran around in a chaotic frenzy.

The revolution was on.

He was impressed. That was what Kafka Dayan thought the first time he glanced at all the information Guardian Angel Intelligence had presented to him. Alyssa Rios had sat erect in her cushioned chair directly across from him and passed him a wealth of additional information. She had pictures of convoys — mysterious trucks moving in the dark hours of the morning — and meticulous notes documenting timelines of vehicle movements, activities, and other pertinent information taken by her surveillance team.

Rios and her operatives had certainly earned their money. Now sitting back in Ian 'Plūcker' Ferry's office, Dayan poured over the intelligence reports scattered across the table. Along with him were the three men he had tagged to be his team leaders: Darren Ripley, a former member of the Royal British Marines Special Boat Service (SBS) and the naval equivalent to the army's better known Special Air Service (SAS); Klaas Vanderhook, a former sergeant with the Korps Mariners, the Dutch Marine Commandos; and finally Oskar Perez, a native of Paraguay who had cut his teeth in the French Foreign Legion as part of the elite 2nd R de Rep Parachute Battalion working in the urban warfare company.

Though not a marine by training, Perez was a seasoned para-commando with local connections in the region and a grounded understanding of both the customs and the language — greatly needed attributes for the locations they were going to operate in. With the number of South American mercenaries that had been recruited for this job, it would have caused dissension to have just Europeans and Middle Easterners in leadership positions.

Dayan took the time to give a briefing discussing the general overview of the mission and a more detailed explanation of his accepted team leaders.

One report taken by an operative disguising himself as a goat herder rounding up stray goats was close enough to walk along the fence line. He discovered that small video cameras were placed at intervals of fifty meters in areas that offered sparse shrubbery and a clear field of view. Further recces established that where foliage and other collections of debris and rocks were denser, the camera placement narrowed to fifteen meters. The report went on to point out that the cameras were older models — they had physical cable hard-wired from the camera leading to a command post that housed the monitors and recording devices.

The fence itself was a two-layer system: first, a basic chain link fence to keep out the annoying herdsmen or curious peasants. Directly behind it was a more complicated structure of concertina wire spirals stacked on top of each other matching the height of the chain-link fence. An array of little coin-like disks dangled from arbitrary strands that would provide loud, continuous jingling. This noise would alert security personnel in the area and cause more complications for an infiltration team that might attempt to slip through. The presence of the disks also alerted Dayan and his mercenaries that security patrols were most likely just out of sight, posing another serious problem. The agent's report of a silhouette lurking in the tree line of the property was another concern.

"Were your people able to obtain information regarding any armed security that might be patrolling the vicinity?" Darren Ripley asked in his rough Welsh accent.

"I asked about that, and our source made it clear trying to get that information would go beyond her limits for this operation," Dayan responded. His eyes were still fixed on a trio of enlarged pictures. "That is an intelligence gap we are going to have to fill ourselves."

"Not a very cozy thought," Ripley replied.

"True. That is significant information we need," Klaas Vanderhook added in his heavy accent.

Dayan rubbed his jaw as he glanced at the photos. "We'll have to do a recce to get a better look."

"The trouble is how to look without raising the enemy's awareness of our existence?" Perez spoke up. Ripley and Vanderhook both nodded in agreement. "I mean, if we go in blind, we may walk right into their trap."

"It seems we have to consider some kind of probe recce that gives us what we need without too much risk." Dayan was now walking slowly around the table as if expecting to find his answer within the collection of scattered documents. "As I see it, the best answer is the river."

"It looks possible," Ripley responded checking the sizeable waterway on the map. "It would be the hardest to monitor, especially if we insert underwater."

Perez spoke up. "The problem is, without knowing their

security layout, we run a couple of risks. We could walk right into their operation and get caught by a professional security team. Or we could end up making our presence known. Either way, we risk having them find out someone is onto them."

"It's definitely a risk," Dayan responded, "but one we need to take. Whatever additional intel we do obtain would still be uncertain. It wouldn't include security teams and other hidden features we can't see from the outside."

"True," Ripley agreed. "The only way to gain anything viable at this point is looking at it from the inside. That means a waterborne insertion."

They all nodded, even the young Perez. The plan had been hatched.

CHAPTER 24

Elloy Mendoza's head was swimming. It had been an exhausting day filled with both business and state affairs. For business, he had skillfully negotiated the joint venture of an Argentine shipping company and a Chilean manufacturing company. For the state, he had a grueling go-around with his superiors in Havana, dealing again with some wild and, he thought, idiotic scheme.

Resting in the back seat of his limousine, he rubbed his head. His assistant, the Mortician, sat up front with the chauffeur as they traversed the narrow streets.

Deciding the troubles of the world would not be solved right now, the Cuban reached for the rolled-up newspaper resting on the small worktop in front of him. It was the Spanish translated copy of a prominent business journal from Europe. The reported good news for South American business seemed to make the previous issues of the morning a distant memory.

CRRRRASH! The impact against the front of the car would have been powerful enough to send all the occupants flying if their seatbelts had not been fastened. The car was almost thrown off the road, but the driver's competence at the steering wheel prevented a disastrous accident. Mendoza regained his faculties quickly as he looked around and started to growl. Both the driver and the Mortician were still caught in a daze from the shock of the sudden impact.

The driver was regaining his focus when he looked up and watched as a sizeable metal object dropped onto the hood of the car severely cracking the front windshield. He had little time to think before he noticed several individuals wearing jumpsuits and masks approaching. He saw the Mortician solely regaining his own faculties and could hear Mendoza snarling with demands to know what the hell was going on.

The driver returned his gaze toward his window just in time to see one of the suited figures walking toward the car with a gun held tightly in both hands. It still didn't register before the figure raised his weapon and fired. The explosive blast of the handgun shattered the window, sounding like a cannon. The Mortician felt the shards of glass as they pelted him. Shielding himself, he turned and caught a glimpse of the driver slumped over with half of his head gone.

"Patron!!" He screamed at his master in the backseat. "We are under attack!"

The Mortician, his faculties now working, reached into his coat and produced a .40 Caliber Para-ordinance automatic. Turning, he grabbed for his door. He barely had it open when two of the masked figures materialized and pushed the door back trying to bar his way. With one hand clutching his weapon, the Mortician was only able to use one arm to force his way out. On the other side of the door, he could hear two men arguing. "Shoot him! Fucking shoot him!" They pushed against the door while one of them was fumbling for something in his front pocket.

The Mortician guessed he was reaching for a weapon. Pressing his automatic against the inside of his car door, he fired repeatedly. The sounds were a collection of thunderous booms that echoed loudly inside the car. The bullets tore through the layers of wood paneling, plastic, and metal. Seconds later, the two aggressors were screaming as the bullets ripped through the door.

While neither attacker was hit, the shock caused both to fall back on each other. Seizing the opportunity, the Mortician pushed the door open and started to get out of the car. His only thought was to rescue his employer. Halfway out the door, he heard another loud blast coming from behind him, and he felt something ripping through his body. He looked down and saw a large gaping hole in his stomach. He had no time to think before he felt more bullets. He exited the car only to slump to his knees. His ability to breathe became labored and his energy left him quickly. He could only stare down at the concrete beneath him when he felt the barrel of a gun press against his head and heard the click of a hammer.

In the back seat, Mendoza had managed to free himself from his seatbelt. Scrambling to reach forward, he nearly fell out of his seat. He slipped onto his side as his feet smacked against the car door window. He fumbled under his small worktable scrambling for a small 9 mm automatic pistol. Mendoza was not one to rely entirely on a protective detail. Sliding onto his back, he turned just in time to see several masked figures approaching the car.

The adrenaline and testosterone filled shouts infused the atmosphere around the masked figures. The biggest member of the group approached the backseat with one hand gripping the car handle and the other tightly holding his revolver. With a quick look across the car, the giant received an approving nod from a figure who could only be their leader. With the gun raised to waist level and a group of excited accomplices cheering him on, the giant drew open the door.

As the door swung open, a sound like a firecracker going off erupted. The assassins quickly changed their cheers of excitement to bellows of surprise when they saw the head of their large compatriot explode. Before anyone could react, sounds of a gun firing repeatedly echoed. Soon members of the group were howling in pain as the gunshots hit them.

Mendoza scrambled out of the car still firing his gun wherever he saw anyone with a hood or a mask. He fell onto the street but continued firing while trying to clamber to his feet. By now he realized the assassins were not professionals. They had fallen into complete disarray as they scrambled to avoid the Cuban's unexpected return fire. Seizing the moment, Mendoza threw himself against the back of the car as he edged his way to a standing position.

He felt shards of glass behind him as the bullets were fired from across the car and burst through the side windows. He turned in time to see a masked figure circling from the other side coming toward him. With no hesitation, the Cuban raised his weapon and fired his remaining two shots. The masked figure stopped in his tracks. He reached up with his free hand to feel his chest. Only moments later, streams of dark red poured down the front of his coat.

Mendoza took advantage of the brief pause; his assailants seemed to be in some kind of suspended animation. They were not prepared for the Cuban fighting back. After hitting several of their comrades and dodging past the remaining attackers, he darted down the street and ducked into the first side road he came to. Behind him, he could hear a deep voice trumpeting rallying calls to pursue their quarry. Mendoza realized they would soon be after him.

At the end of the road, he turned and headed left in the direction of what appeared to be an industrial laundry service. Several men and women wearing white uniforms and matching aprons went about their business. They were completely indifferent to the well-dressed man running swiftly toward them. Reaching the edge of the neighboring building, he ducked behind a wall. He took time to catch his breath, recoup his faculties, and slow the adrenaline rushing through his entire body.

He drew a few deep breaths before his mind returned to rational thought. Going over the events, he tried to think who had tried to kill him. Reviewing how they operated — clumsy, disorganized and unsure — they certainly weren't professionals. Their weapons seemed to be an assortment of revolvers and old cold-war-era automatic pistols — Soviet Makarovs and NATO type Berettas.

His thoughts were soon interrupted by his attackers' shouts as they headed into the side road he had used to escape. He peeked out just far enough to see a small group of masked figures gathering at the mouth of the road. Their behavior revealed confusion as to what to do next. Clearly, nothing was going according to their plan. Eventually, one of the figures, who Mendoza presumed to be their leader, began dispersing his group into pairs, as he sent them in various directions. The two-man units moved swiftly to give chase.

One of the teams proceeded in his direction. Mendoza

thought of running into the laundry facility. He quickly discarded the notion, believing the workers would most likely point out his direction to the assassins. Running aimlessly only heightened the possibility that he would inadvertently come upon another team. He considered trying to grab an apron and cap to blend in with the workers, but it would be hard not to notice him in the ostentatious clothes he wore. His last option rested with neutralizing his enemies.

Picking up a large rock, he readied himself as he lifted it to head level. The assassins were so amateurish he was given ample warning as they conversed with each other while approaching. Two figures passed by the corner of the building when the one closest to him felt a powerful blow from a hard, jagged object smash against the side of his head. The Cuban attacked like a savage animal as he again raised his arm and delivered another blow.

The other assassin, taken off guard, stood frozen, unsure of what to do. Mendoza took further advantage by pushing his disoriented victim into the other assassin knocking them both off balance. Meanwhile, he continued delivering blows to the first man who only raised his hand weakly in defense.

Falling to the ground in the stack of human bodies, Mendoza continued to bash the rock into the back of the first assailant's head. By now, a river of blood poured from the man's head as he limply tried to defend himself. At that point, Mendoza changed his focus to the second man. There was a wild look in the eyes of the masked figure as he struggled to free himself from under his immobile partner. He was far from defeated and determined to carry out his mission.

Without hesitation, Mendoza thrust the rock directly into

the face of the second assailant. The rock hit bone and the man screamed in agony. Within seconds, blood poured profusely from the second man's nose and gums. Two more good hits and he was sure the second assailant was finished.

Mendoza wanted to leave but his instincts pressed him to confirm the identity of his attackers. Ripping off the masks of the two figures, Mendoza found himself looking at two young men no more than twenty years of age. Neither looked like a professional soldier or operative. However, what caught the Cuban's attention was the small black, disk-like cap that fell out of one of the masks. Examining it, he was puzzled before he saw a small star-like emblem on a chain around the neck of one of the men. He realized it was the Star of David. The small disk cap in his hand suddenly became recognizable — a Jewish yarmulke!!

Mendoza's mind was awash with confusion and anger wondering why Jews were attacking him but finding an answer was for later. Not wanting to wait for more attackers to show up, he jumped to his feet and raced to the main road where he vanished into a sea of pedestrians.

It was a detour from his normal political strategy. As a rule, Oskar Vlak Straudner preferred soft flattery followed by a strong incentive to sweeten the deal as his initial tactic for bringing allies to his banner. However, due to the time limits and the high stakes involved, he needed to employ an entirely different tact.

For several moments neither he nor the small pear-shaped figure sitting across from him said anything. Nothing needed to be said. Straudner leaned back in his seat rolling an Alec Bradley cigar between his fingers, watching the contorted facial expressions of his guest. He had learned long ago that distressing news tended to be more powerful the longer it was allowed to ferment. In this case, the distressing news came in the form of a file presented by a mysterious German to his guest, Felix Guzman Uraba, a few days before this meeting.

A guarded figure had approached him and produced the small file while he was enjoying lunch at a small delicatessen he frequented. The file before him was an old police record Urbana thought had been destroyed. The man had chosen his location well. He obviously knew it was one of the few places where the union official kept his own company — they would not have any prying eyes to worry about.

Felix Uraba had, for nearly forty years, been a loud and heroic champion of Uruguay labor. He had risen steadily through the ranks of power in the PIT-CNT, Uruguay's labor union federation. He had started out in the seventies as an organizer working his way into the local leadership ranks of the Plenario Intersindical de Trabajadores (PIT) and very quickly became a power at the national level. Eventually, he worked into a quiet but powerful position within the federation where he had promoted himself as a tireless champion for the workers of his country. The real story was entirely different.

Uraba read the first page. He didn't need to read more to know the horribly damaging information that rested within the rest of the pages. Waiting to hear the amount of money he would have to pay or the strike he would have to call off, he was shocked when the mysterious figure gave him a date, time, and location and proceeded to walk away leaving Uraba with the file and the realization that it was a copy.

Now sitting across a table in the darkened room of an obscure hotel, Uraba found himself in the presence of the politico, Oskar Vlak Straudner. Straudner was a man he had fought against before and loathed deeply. The now worried labor official waited in silence. His future was in the politician's hands.

The situation was not lost on Straudner who patiently enjoyed his cigar between sips of Glenlivet. He watched in silence as the union official's complexion became whiter with each passing moment.

"I always considered myself quite the political animal," Straudner finally interjected. But I felt I had limits as to how loathsome I would be willing to go to achieve my goals. However," the politician leaned forward, his gaze cold and serious, "I, at least, never pretended to be what I wasn't."

Uraba's face gleamed with sweat. "You have to understand. The way things were back then, I had no choice...."

"Save it!" the politician snapped. The union official went silent. The powerbroker of Uruguay's union coalition was now just an image of a frightened child. Straudner continued, "All this time I watched as the common people and many of your colleagues looked to you as an icon, a saint of the labor movement. How many times have you shown off the scars on your chest that you got in street brawls with strikebreakers and police?" Straudner paused to wait for an answer — there was none. The union official was a statue at this point. Straudner continued, "It all goes away when everyone learns that your true rise to power came in the eighties when you were an informant for General Gregorio Alvarez Armelino's secret police. Imagine what will happen when so many who lost loved ones to that regime find out it was your information that led to those who came to such a horrible end."

Uraba was by now as white as a sheet with his lips quivering. Straudner continued, "I know, because of my own connections from those days, that you fabricated much of your information in order to get the secret police to eliminate rivals within your movement as well as senior officials. All this was to pave your way into seats of power. Hell, you can read further and see the notations where police didn't believe half of what you were reporting and figured you were exploiting the situation for your own gain. But your interests were aligned with the state — so a win-win at least for you and the police, right?"

The color was returning to Uraba's face, and he began to straighten in his seat. The quiver in his lips was gradually replaced with a smirk. "But, you aren't going to expose me. You want something that I can give you, or you wouldn't have bothered with this elaborately secretive meeting."

Straudner cocked his eye and gave a slight nod of his head to signify a compliment for the Union official's perceptive instincts. A few weeks earlier, Straudner had met with his Iranian contacts. During the meeting, he had taken great measures to impress upon them that South America was not Asia Minor where the military controlled a significant amount of their society and most of the private economy.

To ensure a successful overthrow, several institutions outside of the security forces would have to be enlisted. The power and influence of the PIT-CNT demanded that the operation have a foothold in the hierarchy. Luckily, Straudner knew, from his access to archived information in police files, exactly who to recruit.

CHAPTER 25

Alyssa Rios, the CEO of Guardian Angel Intelligence, was less than enthused to see *'Mr. Herron'* in her office. It was true he, or his 'clients', had paid for her services and paid well. But what she had thus far found for them was unnerving. An experienced professional in the covert world, she knew better than to raise questions. Yet, she also knew a covert operation when she saw one. *Mr. Herron* was hardly a political operative or journalist looking to break some rival or pick up a scoop. Nor was he some random intelligence officer working out of an embassy and using her agency to build his local intelligence base.

She saw the athletic frame seen on so many Special Forces soldier types. He was very direct and explicit in the information he required and suggested methods of collection she had only heard from people who were preparing for a combat mission. It was all too clear that whatever *Mr. Herron* needed her to do, it would involve the potential for great risk to her and her business.

Still, whatever risk there was, she had most likely incurred it already. Now, all she wanted was to finish her business with the Middle-Easterner and wash her hands of whatever she had gotten into.

"Ma'am," *Mr. Herron* began, "I want to thank you for your services. They have been instrumental…" Rios cut him off in mid-sentence.

"*Mr. Herron,*" she spoke with a quiet yet authoritative voice. "I don't wish to know any more than I have to about your business. I feel more comfortable just knowing what information you need and nothing more. I have already, I feel, placed myself and my people at greater risk than I would have preferred."

Kafka Dayan, *Mr. Herron,* nodded in agreement. "What else do you have so far?"

Producing an expensive leather binder, she placed it on the small, glass table that separated them and pushed it toward the Middle-Easterner.

Picking it up, Kafka opened the binder. He found in its contents a well-organized collection of photographs identifying people arriving and leaving the target facility. The rest of the contents included detailed reports from her operatives observing the times and interactions of these individuals. What most captured Kafka's attention was a report noting virtually no communication interception coming into or going out of the area.

Staring at the woman, he had a stunned look on his face. "You tried to intercept communications?"

"Yes," Rios replied abruptly.

"And there was no radio, phone, or computer communications, at all?"

Rios sighed. "We assumed they would have sophisticated means to mask their communications, but even then my people would have been able to capture individual phones or, at least, tell if they were communicating with someone outside. We have heard nothing — as in no technological means of communication is being used."

"So, do we have any idea if they are communicating directly with anyone outside?" Kafka asked hoping for a positive answer.

Rios shook her head. "The best assumption my people have made is that any communication is being made away from this installation. And if it is being done the way I think it is, that works in your favor."

The Israeli perked up.

Rios continued. "We see general vehicle traffic going into and out of the installation at odd times throughout the day. My guess is they keep their schedules vague and unpredictable to complicate any planned ambush. I'm also certain many of these runs are decoys specifically to throw off potential threats. Your targets are not stupid."

The Israeli nodded but had a distraught look on his face.

Rios continued, "Assuming that, we then tried to identify someone going in and out on a daily basis. None of this seems part of the logistics operation."

"And?" Kafka finally spoke.

"So far, we have been unable to complete this. They also vary the types of vehicles they use as well as dressing in plain, civilian clothes that obscure any means to identify authority or position. So, trying to assess who is in authority is difficult. Again, I stress your targets of interest are not fools."

"I agree they are not fools, but they have to communicate somehow," the Israeli said. "And that somewhere is not located in the security of their compound."

"Stop right there!" Rios cut him off. "Whatever you're

thinking, I don't want any part of it. I have been inclined to help you so long as you only wanted information. If we're discussing possibly involving someone's abduction or death, then you and I are done right now."

Realizing his mistake, Kafka lifted his arms in a slightly defensive posture. "Ms. Rios, I promise you that is not my intention. I have understood the rules of our arrangement the entire time and continued to abide by them. You are not being made into an accomplice to any crime. However, I need to know what these people are doing and, within the scope of our agreement, I am thinking of a way to identify them and, hopefully, determine their plans and to whom they are reporting."

Rios sat back in her chair. She looked the Middle-Easterner up and down while quietly assessing her next move. After what seemed like an eternity, she responded. "All right, I'll keep my people on it. But Mr. Herron, if I get this information for you, and it results in some operation where one of these people gets assassinated or kidnapped then assume our business is at an end."

Kafka nodded. "Thank you, Ms. Rios."

Solomon Gold wasn't sure which issue was of more concern. His group, the Guardians of Israel, had messed up so badly and proved their complete incompetence by bungling the first chance they had to prove themselves. Not to mention that Rabbi Kovinski was in a tirade, yelling at him about the jeopardy he may have caused an Israeli intelligence mission thanks to their failed stunt.

The police were currently furiously combing the streets

following up on the trail of clues the group had left behind. He looked at all the members who suffered injuries and were now being treated by some of the ladies who had medical training. He felt a true sense of humiliation.

Despite the first two situations, Gold realized the latter stung the most. He had always considered himself a soldier for Israel, and now he had proven a liability to their mission. Sitting in one of the folding chairs, the words being screamed at him by the irate Rabbi had become a blur over the inner voice calling himself a failure.

"Are you listening, Solomon?" The Rabbi's growl shook him out of his self-absorption.

"Ah, yes…yes of course I am," the young man grasped for words as he saw the reddened face of his mentor staring angrily back at him. "I...I mean we only wanted to help the cause. If Israel couldn't..."

"Israel," the Rabbi growled "has been fighting this war longer than you have years on this Earth. I think they know what they're doing when they operate in the shadows, which is something I cannot say about you!"

"Rabbi, please. We wanted to help," Solomon pleaded.

"You don't help the Jewish cause like this," Kovinski stated more calmly. "You aren't helping by going off like a bunch of vigilantes. You have the police looking for you, and some of your friends are badly injured. The Cuban is going to figure out how you know about him. If anything was left behind, that will place our friends in more danger because they will have lost the element of surprise."

Solomon groaned and leaned back in his chair. Kovinski realized he had said enough. These boys had done their damage and were completely demoralized. Now it was time to try and clean up the tracks that might lead the police back to them. It was also paramount that he contact his old spy friend and inform him of this problem. He stood up to leave.

As he walked out, Solomon's eyes followed him. All that was going through his mind was, *you have to make this right.* The Rabbi disappeared down the hall to his office. Once he was out of the room, Solomon Gold quickly caught the eye of Myra, his earlier informant. Catching her attention, he waved her over. Cautiously, the small girl approached him. In a nervous, quiet manner, she asked, "Yes, Solomon. What is it?"

"I need you to see what the old Rabbi is up to," Gold replied softly.

Myra looked around nervously. "I hate it when you bring me into these things. I'll get into trouble."

The blond, Jewish boy gently patted her hip. "Please, Myra. Friends of both of ours were killed today because of me. Now I need to do something so they will not have died for nothing."

Myra stood silently for several moments looking her friend in the eye. It was clear he was riddled with guilt. Reluctantly, she lowered her eyes and nodded. Turning away, she made for the hallway leading to the Rabbi's office leaving Solomon Gold with the possibility of another chance.

Senior ranking officers of both the military and the police were called to discuss the recent waves of terrorist violence that had seemingly risen from out of nowhere and now threatened the entire country. The state of the meeting was a riot. Manuel Culvera, the Uruguay Minister of Interior, rubbed his head as he tried to conceal his exasperation.

He had tried to bring the meeting to order several times in the hour since it had begun but without success. Representatives of various agencies of Uruguay's security apparatus were in a state bordering hysteria. The public wanted results and, so far, no one had been arrested. The major problem with the raids was they did not even know who to target. The government was at a low point looking completely impotent in the face of this threat.

Culvera was at an impasse. Each time the issue was raised to impose some form of martial law, President Mojica had made it very clear the government would do no such thing. The sixty-five-year-old former lawyer found himself trying to navigate between the unwavering wishes of his president and the fervent demands of his security heads.

"If the government doesn't act now, how long will it be before the forces of the political right respond with their own retaliation? And, will it be against whoever they blame for this?" "We don't know who is to blame, and the retaliation will be against those living in the poorer areas — the peasants and the unionists," cried one officer with the national police.

"Worse, it will gain momentum amongst the working class, and then it will be a full-blown revolution," growled one of the senior army officers who wore the tabs of the Special Forces unit. "Does the president wish to see that happen?"

"Gentlemen, please," Culvera implored. "Of course, the president does not wish for further violence. However, we must remain calm. We cannot take our country back to the dark days of dictators and secret..."

The room was in an uproar over the Minister's words. Again, Culvera found himself rubbing his forehead in exasperation. The military believed they needed to intercede, and the police believed they needed to be allowed to conduct blanket roundups of known left-wing radicals. This last request was easily quelled by the minister's question: *Do we have any evidence these leftists even know who's doing this, let alone if they are doing it themselves?*

The meeting ended much as it had started — loudly and without much resolved — since the president was not about to suspend liberties or declare martial law. The officers exited the meeting clearly disgruntled with the results. One commander, Ernesto Guevero, a long-time commander in the army, walked slowly along the corridor. His mind was awash with concern that the situation was deteriorating. *This is the danger of too much democracy;* he thought to himself. Going through the military ranks, many of his most memorable mentors, like his father, had been supporters of the old regime. A regime of strong leadership serving the country that gave no quarter to the radical and chaotic ideologies of the ignorant masses. Raised on Benito Mussolini's concept *that the masses seldom educated themselves properly on issues of significance and were prone to follow the loudest most erratic leaders as opposed to the most logical,* Guevero saw vindication of his beliefs in the chaos sweeping the country.

Outside the building, the commander reached for his phone. He didn't bother to dial as the number needed was already in his caller history. He pressed the number, and it began to ring. A voice on the other end answered. "I assume by this call, the meeting did not go as you had hoped?"

Guevero hesitated for a few seconds before replying coldly. "No, it did not. I fear you may be right after all Sẽnor Straudner."

CHAPTER 26

For Darren Ripley, the idea of infiltrating a secret compound didn't bother him as much as the idea of doing so via a river of pitch black water. In a way, it reminded him of the treacherous waters he endured at Loch Long in Greenock, Scotland during his selection course for the Special Boat Service. The blackened waters of the eerie looking canal brought bad memories of the ordeals he faced during that period.

Kafka, Oskar Perez, and Klaas Vanderhook could only sympathize. Despite the real-life action these seasoned operators had seen in their lives, it was always the selection course that seemed to produce the most profound memories. Three miles from where the mysterious compound was located, the team pulled their Land Rover near the bank of the canal. Dressed initially in jeans and T-shirts, they could have easily been just a group of guys out enjoying the summer. They even took care to bring lawn chairs and a couple of ice chests — one full of brews — to give that appearance.

The Land Rover came to a stop and immediately everyone jumped out. Two more Land Rovers followed them carrying the rest of their force. The two vehicles stopped in front of the first vehicle. Dressed in similar attire, they quickly joined the operators near the first vehicle.

With everyone assembled, Kafka wasted no time pulling a large map from the passenger side of the front seat. He spread it out over the Land Rover's hood, and everyone listened attentively as he outlined the plan. It was now late-afternoon. Kafka calculated timelines and hours of light for this time of the year. Dusk would be settling into night as everyone reached their positions.

Kafka, Ripley, and Vanderhook would move up the canal in the Klepper Aerius canoe toward the entrance of the camp. At the same time, Perez would move around to the other side of the perimeter where the vegetation was much thicker. Perez would divide the rest of the force into two groups, and they would move toward the camp from different angles.

The purpose of the mission was to conduct their own recce of the site. The information received from Alyssa Rios and her agency had been of critical importance. However, deeper intelligence collection was needed. Kafka, Ripley, and Vanderhook, the two other experienced combat divers, would slide in under cover of night and attempt to recce inside the compound. Meanwhile, Perez and the others would stage themselves at the opposite side of the camp's perimeter. The recce could last no more than a half hour. If they exceeded the time limit or if shooting and alarms were activated, Perez and the others, being more seasoned jungle fighters, would initiate a decoy attack to provide a diversion.

Perez, though largely urban trained, had a fair amount of jungle training from his Legionnaire days. However, he did not have the jungle, combat experience of the men working with him. They drew their proficiency from para-military groups such as the Aguilas Negras (Black Eagles), the successor to the Colombian right-wing United Self-Defense Force of Colombia or AUC. Their resumes boasted years of fighting experience in South American battlefields. Still, the young mercenary was confident he could maintain discipline and control amongst his group.

The meeting ended with a summary brief and a radio check of their communications system. Plūcker had been able to get his hands on HF radio systems. It was late afternoon. Perez and the others jumped back into two Land Rovers and left Kafka, Ripley, and Vanderhook enough time to set up their operation.

Opening the second icebox, they retrieved their tactical kits. Underneath the chairs and beach blankets, they collected their diving equipment. Luckily, Plūcker had come through with even more decent equipment. Granted it wasn't exactly the state of the art equipment the three were accustomed to using. Yet, it was definitely new and still useful for their purposes. The final component was the weapons. They had been tucked neatly in plastic bags inside rubber sheeting underneath the vehicle's undercarriage.

Instead of the TAR or Galil rifles used commonly by Israeli soldiers, they were looking at short stock AKMs and .45 caliber 1911 handguns. Luckily, these were quite new and proved to work very well when tested.

It was near dusk when all the men were kitted up. The Klepper canoe had finally been assembled. Looking at its lightweight wooden frame and canvass and rubber skin, one could question whether it might be safer to commence their journey in a paper boat. Still, the Klepper had a decade's long trusted record for naval commandos the world over.

Fortunately, it had been so widely used for so long by so many of the world's elite forces, it was relatively generic and easily obtainable. The aluminum rudder was a little difficult to handle, but they managed. The team opted to paddle their way in. It was a two-man boat which meant a third man needed to hang along the side. This role fell to Kafka, who still wasn't sure how that happened.

"Mind the crocs and piranha that might be in there," Ripley joked.

"Remember, I have to live through this mission if you want to get paid," Kafka replied as the two men launched the canoe into the water.

Vanderhook followed with rowing paddles in hand. By now they had all blackened their faces and were all decked out in black diving suits, with tactical webbing strung over them. Stowing their weapons, Vanderhook and Ripley got into the craft as Dayan slid into the water and took hold of the rear. The last touch was to lay a grassy covered gilly-suit over the top of their bodies and the canoe to help break up outlines. For someone looking through a surveillance camera, they would appear like nothing more than debris or floating driftwood.

The natural current drifted toward their location, so paddling was not so exhausting. Their concern was the return trip against the current if they had to make a run for it. The sun was setting as the craft floated in the water. The canoe gave them a low center of gravity to further aid in this masking.

Kafka held on behind, his body drifting in the water. Though chilled, the Israeli took solace in the idea that he had endured far colder waters in far worse circumstances during his operational days. He peered through the gilly-suit at the darkening landscape. The soldierly instincts developed from years in combat zones were honed to precision as he looked for any anomalies or human forms moving in the growing darkness.

Even with the cover of a wet-suit, it was impossible not to feel the vegetation and aquatic life rubbing against various parts of his body. Dayan couldn't help but think of the comments Ripley made about the dangerous creatures known to swim in South American waters, and he shuddered each time something fluttered against him.

Neither Vanderhook nor Ripley uttered a word as they paddled. They were careful to keep their strokes slow and the paddles close to the water to prevent attracting attention. They also took care to keep close to the shoreline to avoid being observed. They were less than half a mile from the target's perimeter when the last rays of the sun disappeared below the horizon. The team broke out their night vision optics and continued. The optics displayed a world of lime green outlines and ghost-like creatures roaming around them.

It was the potential for outlines of humans to be detected that concerned the team the most as they neared their destination. Inside, Dayan could feel the mixture of nerves and excitement emerge within his bowels. Although a seasoned operator, natural human responses were still a reality. He felt a touch on his forearm. It was Vanderhook trying to direct his attention to the mesh of wire fencing across the land they were about to pass over and through as they entered the camp. A slight gleam coming from high up in a tree caught Dayan's attention. He easily noticed it due to the lack of any other lighting and the stark contrast it made through the lenses of his optics. As they expected, it was a security camera covering the waterway.

The paddles suddenly stopped dead in the water. Dayan could only assume the other two operators had seen the camera's gleam as well. The craft floated some distance in complete silence before the paddles were taken up again. They could see no further signs of hidden cameras or other electronic devices. The two paddlers directed the craft up against a patch of mud and grass along the shoreline.

Disembarking, Vanderhook and Ripley tactically positioned themselves on the soft earth with Dayan following them from the water. They slowly and quietly pulled their equipment from under the camouflage covering, then handed off the weapons. Condoms had been slipped over the rifle muzzles to protect against mud and debris clogging them, and the 1911s were kept in plastic bags to prevent water damage. With weapons now slung and holstered, the men slipped their night optics into the rubber bagging they kept with them. From the same bags, they retrieved their snorkels and diving masks and placed them on over their faces while lowering the bottom half of their balaclavas to take in the breathing devices. One by one they slipped into the murky waters of the canal.

They estimated they would have to swim nearly three hundred meters downstream from the entry gate before coming within proximity of the campgrounds. Given the odds of patrols, the operators agreed that staying in the water as long as possible gave them the best chance to avoid any conflict. Once all three were in the water, Ripley attached a thin infrared tape along a dangling tree branch just a few feet from the canoe. Hopefully, that would prevent them from overshooting the canoe on the way back. The tape was the most discrete and practical way to mark the location in the darkness.

The three hundred meter swim encompassed an endless labyrinth of thick, underwater vegetation that repeatedly tried to latch on to the divers. All the debris and nocturnal swimming creatures moving about bumping into the team of night invaders made accidents a strong possibility. All three men had undergone extensive training for operating under such conditions. Anyone else would have either drowned or given up and moved to land early in the mission.

Dayan mentally paced off what he roughly calculated was three hundred meters. Reaching back, he tapped the arms of the other two and together they maneuvered toward the shore. Emerging slowly from the water, the three men took a few moments to assess their situation. Dayan had calculated the distance accurately. They saw lights from the campgrounds and heard men barking out orders.

Staying close to the water, the three men moved along the shoreline against the bank carefully scanning the location. There was no wire or any other deterrent along the shoreline. It was obvious that the security concern was an intrusion by land from locals not from water by professionals.

When they were satisfied the area was clear, they signaled each other with a pat on the shoulder. From this point, no form of verbal communication could be used. Operating in the darkness with enemy patrols anywhere and within such close proximity to a populated campsite, talking would be dangerous.

One after another they slid up from the water working their way through the slimy mud along the bank until their hands, at last, touched the grass and twigs. Inching their way slowly onto drier ground, they took up positions against the first micro-terrain that provided concealment. Dayan, the first into position and carefully slid his rifle out from beside his body. Cautiously lifting his body slightly off the ground, he was able to maneuver his weapon enough to bring it up to a firing position. Aiming in the direction of the camp, he scanned the area, traversing slowly from side to side, alert for any movement.

Though it felt like hours, it had only been a few minutes Dayan was alone before he felt Vanderhook come up behind him on the left, then Ripley took up his position on the right. No one moved for several seconds as Ripley and Vanderhook scanned their flanks with their night optics. When they were confident all was clear, they each tapped one of Dayan's feet.

Slowly the trio rose. A hand signal from Dayan had them moving forward. With Dayan taking the lead, followed by Vanderhook with Ripley securing the rear, they moved toward the camp. Their black wet-suits were their only camouflage, so they stayed close to the shrubbery and, when necessary, sunk to a crawl when in the more open areas.

As they neared the camp, shouts and talking became clearer; they could make out actual conversations. To no one's surprise, the conversations resonating from the camp were a mixture of Spanish and Arabic. The Arabic being spoken was in a different accent than the Arabic Dayan had heard around the Mediterranean. Still, the natural way the conversations flowed indicated that these men spoke this Arabic dialect like natives and not as a second language.

The conversations amounted to small talk and joking by random voices shouting back and forth. However, a deep baritone bellowing loudly rose above all other voices and quickly cowed everyone into silence. This voice particularly caught Dayan's attention. This man was not joking or speaking generically. He was giving orders!

Dayan raised his hand with a clenched fist. His signal called for the other two men to freeze in their tracks. It was obvious that neither Ripley nor Vanderhook spoke Arabic. They could only understand the Spanish. They both were ignorant of what was being said by the baritone. However, whatever was being said was by the baritone was enough to stop their team leader in his tracks — it was important. Slowly, the trio sank down on their knees and waited.

The Israeli listened as the baritone continued his monologue. Dayan realized immediately that they were instructions for training that was about to commence. What had caught his attention initially was that the baritone yelled out that they had only one month left before the operation was to be executed. The baritone was giving instructions for securing street blocks and moving on multiple story buildings.

Dayan listened for a few minutes until the order was given for the teams to form up to conduct training. After that, the Israeli lifted his arm. This time his hand was open, and he waved it forward. The three rose from their position and started moving again. Navigating slowly through the shrubs and keeping close to the trees provided concealment as they continued forward.

Occasionally, they stopped in the shrubs when they heard voices. The patrols Dayan was initially concerned about were roving about in the dark. However, they were not professional soldiers. They bantered back and forth then complained about trudging in the dark and running into bushes. From the conversation, it was obvious that no one but the patrol leader had any night vision equipment. This limited their effectiveness and worked to the advantage of the commandos.

Now within sight of the camp, the trio took positions behind a thicket atop a slightly elevated point providing a view of the camp. Ripley and Vanderhook watched the rear and flank while Dayan observed the camp. Inside the site was a military compound. Men, Arab from their looks and speech, were moving about dressed in olive green military fatigues. Most of them were gathered around two old buildings that looked as though they had once been living quarters. The whole compound looked like it had been a mining operation. Now, it appeared it was being used for combat training.

Reaching into his rubber case, Dayan produced a small digital camera. While on this mission, he, like the other two, had left their mobile phones and evidence of their identities behind to prevent the enemy from finding anything. Peering through the camera, he began rapidly snapping shots working his way from one end of the camp to the other. He tried to catch as much as he could in the limited time he had. Raising his wrist, he looked down at the slight glow from his watch. They had less than thirty minutes before Perez and the rest of the team would initiate a diversionary attack if they heard nothing from the trio.

Finishing his second scan with the camera, Kafka stopped to take note of the man he determined was the source of the baritone voice. A large man with a thick beard and bear-like frame was barking orders to the others. Aside from his obvious position of authority, what caught the Israeli's attention was the uniqueness of his accent. He spoke Arab as did the others; however, he had a Persian accent that

Kafka was all too familiar with. He had heard this same accent from the Iranian al'Quds that worked with the Shiite guerrillas he encountered during an operation in Lebanon. The baritone was directing the men as they practiced moving to and then storming the buildings.

The Israeli took several pictures of the baritone before tucking his camera away. Signaling the other two that he was finished, the trio got up slowly and made their way around to the far end of camp's left flank. By now the lighting from the camp was good enough that the commandos had removed their night optics. Sliding into a depression that ran along the first three buildings offering a cover of darkness against the camp lighting, the three inched their way along the buildings. They listened to the sounds and conversations to determine what each structure might be used for.

Then he heard the words coming from the second building. "I need to have these reports and logistics requests drawn up for the commander's review meeting tomorrow." He could only assume this building hosted the leadership of the camp. "In another building the conversation was about soccer, and the words were spoken with the same Persian accented Arabic he had heard from the baritone, and one building was silent.

The Israeli beckoned the other two commandos to follow him to the second structure. At the edge of the depression, Dayan motioned the other two to stay as he stepped closer to the building. Peering inside he saw the office he saw one man who looked like a bookkeeper. He was dressed in cotton slacks and a collared shirt and appeared to be immersed in a mountain of paperwork.

Dayan stood fast as the front door flung open, and the

baritone walked in wedging his way through the door. The two Iranians looked at each other before the larger one spoke. "They're coming along. Still, they don't have much actual experience."

"They are quite receptive to the training, which is better than we initially assumed," replied the smaller man.

The baritone shrugged. "Is that what you are going to tell the commander tomorrow?"

"Of course. I see no other answer. Besides, the timeline only gives us one more month before we proceed with what we have," the smaller man reminded him.

The baritone turned to the door. "Let's get some tea. I'm thirsty."

The smaller man rose from his chair to follow his compatriot out the door. The door shut leaving the office deserted. Dayan signaled the men of his intentions, then slid through the back door. Luckily, it was not very well secured. Inside, he moved to the desk where the smaller Iranian had been working. He glossed over the contents and saw some memory sticks lying off to the side of the laptop the Iranian had been working on. With only a few seconds available, the Israeli made the decision to grab what he could. The information was more vital than discretion. He had stashed the sticks in his bag when the door opened.

Major Semir Ali Essouri stood looking at the figure dressed in a black wet-suit with the face concealed behind a balaclava. The tactical webbing and weapons made the figure an all too recognizable sight. He had seen commandos on missions in Lebanon many times, and he knew at once who or what he was looking at.

In an instant, both experts gave into their natural combat-honed instincts. Essouri reached for the pistol he had tucked in his holster as Dayan pulled the knife from this belt and attacked. It was a scene from an American western. Dayan embraced his adversary like an old friend. He wrapped his arm around of the Iranian's head. The Iranian barely felt his assailant's arm clutched around him before he felt the sensation of the cold, sharp blade entering the back of his head. Dayan struck the brain stem with surgical-like precision.

It was only a second, and Dayan was now holding the dead body of Major Semir Ali Essouri. Gently lowering the corpse to the ground, Dayan closed the door Essouri had come through and headed toward the back. He had just reached the door when he heard creaking from the front. He turned to see the baritone standing in the doorway.

Major Akim glared at the black-suited figure. Out of the corner of his eye, he saw the body of his comrade laying on the floor. His eyes stayed focused on the dark figure. The two men met each other's gazes before Akim instinctively went for his rifle. Dayan jumped out the back in time to avoid a fusillade of gunfire.

"Move now!!" Dayan screamed to his comrades as he flew into the depression. The three men moved quickly. As they raced out of the depression, they saw Major Akim standing in the doorway with his AK-74 at the ready. He scoped the depression and prepared to fire. He was stopped by a quick burst fired by Ripley as he moved to cover the escape.

Akim, taken by surprise, fell to the floor dodging Ripley's bullets. The trio raced to the tree line to make their way back to the river. To their amazement, the gunfire from the training masked their gun battle, ensuring no immediate response. The larger body of the camp had no idea what had just happened.

The three men ran quickly through the shrubbery assuming they had only minutes before their presence became known. They had just cleared the camp and were halfway to the river when they stopped to quickly affix their night optics. They heard a loud cry of someone screaming in Arabic, looked up to see the security patrol fanning out and moving in their direction.

Foregoing the optics, the three stood up and started running when the patrol opened fire. The trio began a relay of cover-by-fire. First, Dayan began shooting to cover Ripley and Vanderhook. The two men ran a few paces stopped and turned to call back to their comrade that they were set. At that moment both men began firing as Dayan turned and ran past them. They continued this relay as they slowly worked their way back to the river. Thankfully, the patrol was still inexperienced in actual combat. The return fire from the trio caused them to lose their focus, and they began firing wildly in the general direction of the invaders. Meanwhile, the seasoned commandos continued to steadily take well-aimed shots, managing to hit one or two with every other burst causing the patrol to slow their pursuit. The commandos were confident they would make it safely back to the water when they received gunfire from a different location.

Major Akim had wasted no time trying to sound the alarm. He knew that time was of the essence and had tracked the infiltrators. He caught the sound of the gunfire exchange and followed it to where his patrol was engaging the invaders. Flanking off to the side, he continued the bursts of gunfire. Assessing the volume of fire and lack of discipline from one side to the steady tactical movements of the smaller group, he aimed for the smaller team and took his shots.

They were close. Immediately Dayan turned to return fire that appeared on his flank. But the Iranian was not a green trainee and was not fazed by the bullets whistling past his head. Instead, he ducked into a cluster of trees and continued firing. At the same time, he began calling out to the patrol. His voice was distinctive and quite familiar to his men. On his orders, he began directing them while continuing to stay on the infiltrators' flanks. The commandos were now being attacked from two different directions.

The commandos remained disciplined as they continued their movement toward the river. They directed their shots based on which side seemed to be closer. Major Akim continued weaving through the trees, staying down, and carefully aiming his fire as he continued shouting orders.

The situation was becoming dire for the commandos. They could see their adversaries slowly boxing them in. It was the sound of the river close by that suddenly gave them hope. They realized they were near their escape route. Their spirits were further lifted when a loud explosion thundered in the distance. The trio realized they had exceeded their time limit, and Perez and the others had initiated their assault.

CHAPTER 27

It had not taken Elloy Mendoza long to find out that the attack on him was the result of his business with the Iranians. It also did not take him long to figure out who had carried it out. The Guardians of Israel was the group that emerged as the likely perpetrators of his near assassination. Yet the question remained — how would these idiot street thugs have obtained intelligence like this?

The way to get an answer was to ask. It was well known in the South American intelligence world that the old Rabbi, Abraham Kovinski, doubled as a well-connected source for Israel. Sending some men to the Buenos Aires Jewish Community Center with guns and a strong penchant toward violent behavior would be the Cuban's scheme to achieve two objectives: find out how the Jews knew about him, and make sure they suffered for their recent antics.

Mendoza's men returned with the news that they had *spoken* to the old Rabbi. Despite cutting off three of his fingers using a pair of scissors, he would not talk. The Rabbi finally opened up when they took the teenage girl named Myra, who worked around the center, and threatened her.

They also found a file listing the sale of land from Bolivar Investments & Acquisitions to an Iranian front company.

Mendoza took great satisfaction from the story when his men regaled him with how the Rabbi was made to watch as they proceeded to violate the terrified young girl before beating her to death after he had cooperated. The Rabbi had been in tears when they sliced his throat and let him bleed out. Mendoza took an even greater interest in the file which he quickly realized could only have come from one competitor: Guardian Angel Intelligence.

Alyssa Rios was not quite nervous, but concerned. Looking at the screen focused on the outside road, she wasn't sure what to make of the white van that had mysteriously parked across the street for seemingly no reason. Her focus was on the screen showing a large, well-dressed man standing at her doorway with an impatient look on his face.

Mr. Vargas, or at least that was the name he was going by, when he introduced himself several days ago over the phone. He was an attorney working for a politician who had concerns about conspiracies within his own party. The job seemed common enough, and she had agreed to a meeting. Now looking at *Mr. Vargas* on her screen, she felt something was not right. This high-priced attorney looked far too athletic and was devoid of nice jewelry. Most of the successful legal people she came across tended to display their wealth and enjoy comfort. The man at her door looked anything but a high-priced attorney. Despite the new suit and haircut, the man's face was rough. He looked more like a professional soldier. What really caught her attention was part of a tattoo that protruded from under the cuff of his shirt.

She had been on edge since hearing from her sources in Brazil about the mysterious attack against the camp the Arab had hired her to watch following the attempted assassination of Elloy Mendoza — another person Mr. Herron was interested in.

She had learned through experience never to assume she was just being paranoid, her senses were too keen for that. Reaching into her desk she produced a mobile phone. It wasn't her business or personal phone; it was to be used for only one thing. Pressing send the phone rang twice before a gravelly voice of a man answered, "Yes?"

Speaking gently Rios answered. "Sẽnor, if you're not busy right now, I would like to come over and discuss hiring you for floral arrangements."

"I'm very busy," the voice replied slightly tense.

"I understand," she replied before the phone went dead.

Pressing a buzzer, Rios waited only seconds before her assistant entered her office. "Yes, ma'am?" the young girl asked quietly.

Rios compressed her lips tightly. "Malia, go put on your sweats," she said quietly.

Malia's eyes widened, and she began to look frightened. The older woman raised her hand slightly. "Don't be unprofessional, my dear."

Malia regained her composure and with a nod turned and headed out the door.

Viewing the security camera where Mr. Vargas was standing, she pressed a small button to speak on the intercom. "Sẽnor, I'm afraid I won't be able to see you today as we had arranged. I apologize for the inconvenience, but something has come up."

The man calling himself *Mr. Vargas* did not move or speak. Instead, he turned a chilling gaze toward the camera. "Let me in, woman."

Rios had by now stripped down to her underwear and was collecting a neatly folded pile of clothes from a nearby closet. It was a futile effort at this point to respond. The intimidating manner only established what she half wanted to believe was paranoia. Still, she answered anyway in the hope it would buy time. "Sẽnor, I do not respond well to threats. If you do not wish to reschedule, then I feel we need not do business." She hurriedly slid on a pair of jeans.

Mr. Vargas said nothing more as he glared into the camera lens. He turned toward the street and sliced his hand across the front of his body. Rios watched her monitors to see what the man was doing. Suddenly, the back doors of the mysterious white van flew open and a flood of figures dressed in tactical gear appeared carrying an arsenal of weapons. Rios watched them cross the street and realized what was about to happen. Mr. Vargas produced a Glock .40 caliber from a holster hidden under his jacket.

She had finished dressing in jeans, sneakers, a gray T-shirt, and a tan-field jacket. Malia returned wearing similar attire. The combination of balancing practical mobility with clothes common to the neighborhood was paramount in these situations. Malia slung a small, green knapsack across her body. It contained essential materials needed for later.

"I sent out the call, Ma'am," the young assistant said. The call was the quick emergency message dispatched to all operatives and contractors of Guardian Angel. Everyone was alerted that the company had been compromised, and they were to break all contact.

"Good," Rios replied as she grabbed her bag. She heard the sound of a door being bashed in. Malia had already activated the additional security doors that were reinforced with steel and would be difficult to penetrate, giving the ladies more time to escape.

Alyssa Rios had just activated the spyware on her computer system which would completely destroy any intelligence collected and all her business records. A loud explosion shook the building. The attackers were using shape charges against the doors. The other security monitors showed the attackers, their faces covered with dark balaclavas, had already begun pouring into the building. They were slowed down by the blast-proof glass box, narrow concrete walls, and thick metal gates that stood in their way.

It was easy to figure they were going to lay waste the door with more explosives. Luckily, the packed conditions meant they would have to go back outside before they could blow the box. The women didn't wait. Walking to the back of the office, Rios moved an old metal cabinet to reveal a small hole in the wall leading to a crawl space. The ladies were just through it when they heard the sound of the second explosion and the tremor that followed.

Downstairs, the man, who had identified himself as Mr. Vargas was following the assault team back into the building. He looked around the compound and found himself hard pressed not to begrudgingly respect his current adversary. A skilled operator with years in the Kaibil (Guatemalan special forces), he found that his professional senses demanded a certain degree of challenge when undertaking a mission. Looking around at the ingenuity of the building's setup, he could admire the forethought and wisdom of the mind that had laid this all out. Only a seasoned operator on a par with him could understand the concepts of such things.

His men discovered the blast-proof box was still intact enough to be a barrier. It took another blast before the attackers could finally press their assault. The darkened corridor made an irritating complication. It wasn't yet dark enough for night vision, but dark enough to make it arduous for the professionals whose eyes had not yet adjusted. They definitely didn't see the infrared laser running only a few inches above the ground across the exit of the hallway. The first aggressor walked over it as he turned and started up the stairs. The second man, walking closely behind him landed right on the point of the beam. A second later the small neighborhood echoed with the sound of another powerful explosion. The corridor was suddenly engulfed in a massive flame that blew swiftly through the entire lower stairs and exited viciously out the front door burning every member of the assault group to near ashes.

Rios and Malia were just exiting the end of the tunnel when they heard the last explosion. They knew the difference between their own deterrent and the explosives used by their attackers. Arriving at a small opening secured by a heavy steel door resembling a submarine hatch, the two ladies worked in unison to twist the securing wheel. Moments later the door opened, and they pushed away the debris and shrubbery masking the exit.

Outside, the two ladies worked to shut the door. They were in an area between properties, surrounded by old fencing. Rios took a second to peek over the fence separating them from the open street. When she was comfortable there were no suspicious people visible, the two women climbed over the fence and started down the street. Malia nervously began to look around but was stopped by her employer who reminded her to keep calm and look casual.

Rios took Malia by the hand and picked up the pace. Knowing what her employer was doing, she attempted to follow her example. Since several explosions had just occurred, they looked like two frantic women trying to get away from apparent trouble. Had the explosion not gone off, they would have been walking along joking and laughing with each other.

At the end of the street, they turned and slowed their pace complaining about the violence in Bogota. A few more blocks and they turned another corner, walked about ten minutes and changed directions again. Around the next corner, there was a small, dumpy man of about seventy selling food to passersby. The two ladies approached slowly. Despite sporting a thick bushy mustache covering everything below his nose, a smile could still be detected as the ladies neared. Three customers were quickly served and dispatched before the old man put up a closed sign on his truck.

Nothing was said as the ladies passed by him and moved into the back of his vehicle. They both took cover in a makeshift kitchen. Outside, the old man carefully broke down his operation. The steel door that served as shading from the tropical sun was lowered to the side and buttoned down. Seconds later the women could feel the change in weight as the dumpy fellow climbed into the driver's seat. The engine roared to life, and they could feel the large barge-like truck pull slowly out of its parked location and begin moving steadily down the road.

Victorio Diego had sold his homemade meals for nearly thirty years. During the time Guardian Angel Intelligence had been established, a certain party, on behalf of Ms. Rios, had given him a monthly stipend of three thousand dollars in cash. The stipend had been greatly appreciated during the slower times and helped him expand his business. The first payment had come with a mobile phone he was never to use but keep on his person at all times. He was made to understand that one day he might receive a call from a woman who would discuss floral arrangements. If so, he was to be ready to provide a means of escape for two women and whoever else might show up. He had seen the woman in question a few times to remind him of their face. He knew without discussion who was slipping into his vehicle. Driving down the road, the old meal vendor peered nervously out his side mirrors and all around as he drove at his steady pace. One hand tightly held the wheel while the second held a .40 caliber revolver.

CHAPTER 28

Kafka Dayan was sprawled out on the long couch in the back office of Plūcker's establishment. Despite the fact that he knew he was being growled at by an irate Micha Cohen, he was concentrating hard on his breathing and too tired to care. Besides, when he did open his eyes to give the old katsa a few moments of his attention, he found the diatribe from the old man a confusing litany of muttering in English, shouting in Arabic and, occasionally, speaking calmly in Hebrew. He figured he wasn't missing anything important. And given the old man hadn't seemed to notice his complete lack of interest, he was certain of it.

Cohen's anger derived from the fact that a mission which was supposed to be a quiet reconnaissance — leaving no trace — turned into an all-out battle. Kafka did regret how the operation turned out. However, unforeseeable problems happening were virtually warfare and intelligence operations 101. The katsa continued railing, and Kafka waited for Cohen to complete his tirade.

At the same time, he peeked over to where Plūcker and his Negress were busily looking over the documents recovered from the mission. Apparently, just like her employer, who doubled as an arms and mercenary broker, she too had a sideline job in the murky world of intrigue. Her eyes darted quickly from side to side as she pored over the contents on her computer screen.

"Anything of value?" Kafka asked as he fought his way to sit up from his sprawled position.

The Negress said nothing, her attention remained fixed on her work. Plūcker's attention was focused on the same screen, and he spoke up. "Well, what we have is a mixture of documents written in both Portuguese and some weird fucking squiggly shit — possibly Arab writing."

Cohen stopped speaking. He was annoyed at how his young operative was so casually dismissing him. He moved over to where the Irishman and the Negress were working. Kafka followed closely behind. Both Israelis looked at the screen. The document displayed was in Portuguese. The Negress spoke up. "This is a report discussing local security, mostly military, and police patrol schedules."

"Really?" Kafka asked.

"Looks like someone in the Brazilian military is feeding reports to these guys. The reports pertain to possible concerns about local security in the area and future military movements that might affect the camp," the Negress continued. Her Spanish was natural and polished. Her ability to flawlessly interpret the Portuguese documents was surprising considering she was supposed to be a barmaid. She continued. "Judging by the detail in these reports, they have someone at high levels in the Brazilian military feeding them this information."

"What do the other documents say?" Cohen interjected. "One is not in Portuguese."

The Negress pulled a list of PDF files. "These, I couldn't read," she said as she placed the cursor at the first listed file and clicked it.

A document flashed onto the screen. The Israelis identified the writing immediately, it was in Farsi.

"You can read that sand nigger shit?" the Irishman blurted out.

"Yes," Kafka replied, his eyes lighting up as he began to read.

"My God!" Cohen exclaimed, his eyes growing wide with surprise. "This is an outline of strategic movements for these forces." The old katsa slowly turned to face the younger Israeli.

Kafka's face was intense. "The opening line states a plan for mobilizing forces into Uruguay."

Beckoning the Negress to scroll down, the Israelis marveled as they began to read more. It was ostensibly a blueprint for taking over a country. Kafka waved his hand in the air looking bewildered. "They can't think a bunch of mercenaries from around South America is going to simply take a country without a serious fight."

"No," Cohen said. "They most certainly have plans to have greased the inside for this. Like any good coup, they need chaos and people on the inside for their operation to have any chance of success."

They were amazed at the elaborate nature of the plan. First, set up a left-wing guerrilla insurgency to shake the current government, then cause instability to pave the way for an eventual military coup.

"They have a whole fucking training camp in Argentina for this," Kafka exclaimed. "They hired an entire mercenary corps. Who the fuck is this Contessa?" A name that appeared in several paragraphs. "She seems to be running this made-up guerrilla force for the Iranians."

"Well, that explains the other properties," Cohen said with a sigh. "Luckily, that means the camp we just infiltrated is hosting the Arab force. This other camp is just a decoy element that apparently is already operational."

"Wait a minute," the Negress suddenly exclaimed. "There has been a lot reported about an outbreak of violence going on in Uruguay. Some left-wing terror group has been waging a violent campaign down there. If I'm hearing you right, you're saying all this activity is fabricated by Iran?"

The Israelis nodded in an almost synchronized manner. "Yes, my dear," Cohen replied. "Apparently, the plan is to create mass violence to justify a military response that would inevitably lead to seizing control of the government. Nothing gives greater support to a military coup from all the right power brokers than a communist menace."

"Here's something," Kafka pointed his finger at the screen. "Operational contact has already been made with domestic allies. You were right, they do have people working from the inside," Kafka continued to read. "Have reached out to elements of the far political right; they have been enlisted."

"We need to see what else we have." Cohen was adamant. The Negress went through a series of other documents. They turned out to be mostly training reports discussing the progress of the Arab forces and a few planned annexes. Then they came across the document they had hoped to find. A document marked: Report on meeting with a domestic contact.

Opening it, they read what was, in fact, a record discussing a meeting to recruit a contact. The report listed no names but did state that the recruited party was political, not military, and holds a position as a member of the Uruguay House of Deputies.

"Well, it's not enough to give us a target," Kafka rubbed his hand across his face with exasperation.

"No," replied Cohen. "But it does give us a trail to follow. A right-wing politician does narrow the field greatly. Not to mention that it will be easier by just looking at who is stoking the flames to take remedial action in light of all this violence."

"Then what?" Kafka asked, still exasperated. "I mean even if we do find out who this guy is, what are we going to do? It sounds like this whole thing is well underway. It's not like we can simply expose this plot by leaking information to the press."

"You're right," Cohen replied. "It means, we kill'em."

Kafka's eyes widened as he stood erect to face the katsa. "Say that to me again." His voice was low and his gaze focused.

Cohen disregarded his operative's glare as he concentrated his attention on the computer. Kafka was adamant. "Say that to me again!" His voice was deep and stern.

Cohen turned his head to see the younger man's face out of the corner of his eye. "When we find out who we're looking for, take it as an automatic that they'll have to be taken out — killed." The katsa spoke as if this conversation were perfectly normal.

It was all the young operator could do to stand there and not stare coldly at the old katsa. The tension in the room was becoming all too apparent. Plūcker tapped the shoulder of the Negress and beckoned her to follow him. Carefully, she rose to her feet.

"This looks like a Heeb thing," Plūcker said, as he and the Negress started for the door. "You boys can read that raghead shit yourselves. We've got a bar to tend to." Plūcker and the Negress were already out the door before he was even finished speaking, leaving the Israelis on their own.

Cohen remained focused on the computer documents. Kafka was now pacing back and forth as if expecting an immediate explanation.

"Run the part about the idea of this assassination concept again," Kafka demanded.

Realizing the subject was not going to end, Cohen turned to face the young commando. "Well, what else did you think we were going to do? Magically find evidence to blackmail them? Besides you've assassinated foreign nationals many times before in foreign lands. Why should this be any different?"

"I killed terrorists, soldiers, and spies. I have never had a mission to eliminate an elected official of a national government halfway around the fucking world," Kafka said incredulously.

Cohen waved him off. "It's Uruguay that we are talking about. You're acting like we're killing someone in England, Russia, or some other major power with a long reach. Last time I checked, Uruguay was not exactly a power player on the international stage."

By now Kafka was beginning to question his own sanity. He started to pace and marveled at the old spy's miraculous calm. "We're still taking on a massive responsibility no matter what country. And I might remind you, all of this is being done entirely without sanction from our government. We are ostensibly mercenaries working in a rogue capacity."

Cohen rubbed his face. He now turned to face the

commando. "Kafka, I understand the gravity of the situation. If we fail anywhere in South America, we will be going away and will never see the sun again. However, I've been at this game for a long time. I've done hundreds of operations on behalf of the Jewish state that, if caught, they would have completely disavowed knowledge of me. So, to hell with this government sanction crap! Now, as to your sanctimonious display about killing South American politicians, kindly remember we're trying to stop perhaps our greatest enemy from gaining a dangerous foothold in the Western Hemisphere. They have the means to spread their influence in our best ally's backyard if they succeed here. So, yes, I'm aware of the ramifications of what I'm asking. However, I am even more aware of the greater ramifications if the Iranians win. Which means we do what we must to see this through."

Kafka still wasn't happy about the idea. But, the old man had made his point. The discussion was over and the research continued.

Ali Anwar al Qalmini rubbed his brow as he puffed feverishly on the fat Meduro wrapped Cao cigar. The bad news seemed to be bombarding him non-stop. First, it was the report of the camp infiltration by this mysterious force that seemed to have raised all hell and simply vanished. Then, there was the report of Elloy Mendoza's campaign to avenge the attempt to assassinate him.

The seasoned covert soldier thought the brash and very public disposal of a popular local Rabbi and a young female volunteer was excessive, bringing attention they could not afford. He had just received a report about the Bogota incident of some obscure private intelligence company that was completely over the top.

"That fucking asshole couldn't have quietly abducted them off the street so we could interrogate them in some remote location. No, he let his God damn Latin machoism get in the way and turned this into a Wild West shootout for the whole world to see!" The Iranian gnawed on the butt of his cigar.

Qalmini glanced up at Major Akim, who was standing at the corner of the big oak desk while Nouri al'Marak Surriman leaned against a near wall. Both were struggling to maintain a professional bearing despite the smoke from their boss's cigar.

"Who do we think did it?" Qalmini asked tapping his fingers against his desk.

"Was it some reconnaissance mission by local police? Guerrillas perhaps?" Akim replied.

"Neither," Surriman interjected. "If the authorities were so sure about us, they would have sent in a full attack force, and we would all be in handcuffs, and they weren't guerrillas. The infiltration team Major Akim engaged with seemed to have planned their insertion into our camp rather well. They bypassed our perimeter by going through the river, our weakest point, and maneuvered past our security patrols to get into our facility. I would also point out that whoever killed Major Essouri did so with precision. That is not something you would see from a jungle guerrilla.

"The *assault* was organized, professional, and well led. The enemy struck the camp before they were even close enough to breach the fence. It was meant as a decoy to distract us from the infiltration team. It was too undermanned to have been any serious threat. To maneuver that skillfully with such good command control, assaulting from two points with good coordination, requires intelligence. But to maintain cover until they had breached our lines does not add up. Could this be part of a bigger mission? My guess is the full attack at the end was a decoy to allow our infiltrators a diversion to escape."

Qalmini thought the young Arab was making sense. "Then we assume professional operators."

Akim said nothing. Surriman replied, "Possible, but I think it's someone else. If they were government, we would be exposed already. Even a foreign power, if they knew about us, would have shut us down at once or pressured the Brazilians to do it, and we're still in operation. We have someone else involved who has been onto us for a while. From the look of it, they don't really know what our intentions are yet. Hence, their need for taking such a risk in trying to obtain documents as opposed to just gathering intelligence through observation."

Qalmini discarded his cigar and opened a window — his subordinates appreciated the change. He sat back in his chair as he rubbed his tongue over his teeth. "Then it's a safe assumption we are perhaps dealing with an independent group of what, vigilantes? If so, our Cuban friend just attacked the best avenues we had for tracking them down. It appears this Rabbi in Buenos Aires and the intelligence firm in Bogota were most likely the means by which these new adversaries discovered us, or what they were able to find on us. Now, where do we go from here?"

CHAPTER 29

Oskar Straudner slowly rolled the fat Monte Cristo between his lips as he stood over his computer looking at the news report splashed across the screen. The headlines were all focused on the terrible bombing at the union rally in downtown Montevideo — the assassination of Elonzo Mazzina, the president of the PIT-CNT, the massacre of his entire entourage, and several hundred other deaths involving nearly a thousand people.

Things could not have been better, he thought reading the details with a sense of jubilation. Laudman had executed the operation perfectly. The overall objective was to create the appearance of a right-wing movement emerging as a response to the outbreak of left-wing terrorism, paving the way for new leadership in the labor movement.

Recent meetings of the Ministry of Interior resulted in a hardline refusal by the administration to take stiffer measures against the terrorists. Straudner had guessed this would happen. Some right-wing vigilante mayhem was required to create all-around panic. The Iranians had deferred to his better grasp of the political situation.

Straudner had begun planning months in advance — after his first meeting with his new foreign backers. He had sent Laudman to ply his trade, organizing all the necessary preparations. In truth, he would have carried out the operation whether the Iranians agreed or not, knowing that a response to the terrorism would be needed to get the whole country on edge. This planned response helped secure his own power base for when the coup was actually executed. Nevertheless, it was still wise to let his backers believe they were holding all the control.

He reviewed the mission in his head. Laudman had recruited his operatives from intelligence and military units in Mexico and Guatemala. These organizations tended to do side work for various criminal organizations and, occasionally, other foreign powers. The van was placed at the rally, weighted down heavily with dynamite. The bombing was planned using a high-grade Semtex. It had exploded close to the edge of the tightly packed crowd. Reviewing the day's activities in his home office, Straudner settled back onto his cool leather couch savoring his success.

The old Stasi had pointed out that the success of an operation lay in the skill of hiding behind simplicity. The explosive used was dynamite. It had been stolen from local mines and construction sites. After all, to be too organized, professional, and sophisticated, would seem suspicious and defeat the intended purpose. The operatives hired for the assassination team on Mazzina had carried out their mission with brutal efficiency. Then all the participants involved had been quickly and quietly whisked out of the country on a waiting cargo ship heading for somewhere in Central America; the same way they had been brought into the country. There was no record of entering or exiting — no trace for anyone to investigate.

The next part of the plan was to bring the hysteria of these attacks to a boil. That came in two forms: first, a note attached to the knife that was grotesquely plunged into the eye of Sẽnor Mazzina, which when translated into English read: Soldiers of Retribution. This alone had the media of Uruguay and, by extension, neighboring countries, in a frenzy discussing who this group was. Second, was the sudden and mysterious arrival of a manifesto that was presumably from this group to the Chamber of Deputies. In it, the group claimed responsibility for the attacks against the PIT-CNT. They called it a reprisal for the outbreak of violence by the left-wing terrorists that had gone unchecked. The attacks against the unions were for their *quiet* support of this radicalism. In it, they promised that if the government, led by a former Tupamaro continued to *protect* these terrorists, the citizens would handle the reprisal themselves.

The Manifesto had been composed almost entirely by Straudner. He had taken the step to specifically not dispatch the manifesto to the leadership of his own National Party. He felt it would look too suspicious to some and too politically partisan for others. Instead, the manifesto found its way into the hands of Hecktor Ramon, the leading figure of the more moderate and politically influential Colorado Party. Placed in such a compromising spot, Ramon had to make his discovery known. Now it was causing virtual panic amongst the lawmakers.

Straudner basked in his own self-adulation over his brilliance. He had come from a meeting earlier where he played his part of concerned politician well while inwardly relishing the fallout as his colleagues deliberated nervously over how to handle the situation. The Soldiers of Retribution group had carried out two massively devastating and very public attacks. The politicians were now beside themselves trying to explain where they had failed. Had they been too slow in forcing a stronger military and police responses? Should they have authorized the suspension of civil liberties to more easily curtail the movement of these radicals? Aside from interjecting a few of his own concerns to add to the fervor, Straudner was content to sit back, play his role, and watch the results of his plan unfold. He was aware that in the end, it was going to go as he had planned.

Now, back at his mansion relaxing in the comforts of his private office, he entertained himself by watching the clouds of grayish-blue smoke rise from the tip of his cigar. The clouds danced about in a hauntingly beautiful display of ghostly images before vanishing into the atmosphere. His mind was awash with visions of what the future would look like once he was in control.

Under his leadership, he intended to create a bastion of power that would make Uruguay a serious player in the Western Hemisphere. His contacts with the soon-to-be reigning hegemon in the Middle-East would prove to be a most valuable ally — far beyond their current support. His intention was to milk them for their connections beyond his current borders helping him negotiate the way to the most favorable trade deals with numerous overseas nations. He even intended to exploit Iran's relations with Pakistan, a mercenary state, when it came to selling nuclear technology. The ambitious politician would leave a legacy of greatness in his stead. This legacy would more than make up for the carnage and destruction he had thus far orchestrated.

Solomon Gold's attempt to do something in the service of the Jewish State had not only ended in embarrassing failure, but now the old man, Rabbi Abraham Kovinski, was dead. This was very sobering not just to him but to the members of the Guardians of Israel who sat around wallowing in mixed feelings of remorse, guilt, and helplessness.

The true rallying cry that had them all gathered quietly at the far end of the Jewish Community Center was the thought of little Myra. She hadn't even wanted to be involved in this. They had bullied her into it. Now, she was dead along with the Rabbi. What lingered in their minds was the image of her when she had been found. It was Gold and some of the others who had walked in on the ghastly display left by Mendoza's men. The Rabbi had been torched and carved up, but the corpse of the little teenage volunteer with her face bruised to a dark black, her panties ripped off, and the pool of blood that had formed from between her legs made it all too apparent what savagery had befallen her.

It was a vision none of them could get out of their heads. The Guardians had done this to her when they failed to kill the Cuban. He had been allowed to retaliate. This was an act that had to see justice done. Not justice by the police but justice directly from the Old Testament.

None were as hurt as Gold. He had been the leader, the instigator, the one who had pushed Myra into this. As he sat ruminating, his mind was on one thing — he would make this right. The fight for the Jewish cause must still be fought, but Elloy Mendoza was going to die.

CHAPTER 30

It had been a long and excruciating process going through the plethora of documents seized at the camp. Somehow, between the Israelis, Plūcker, and the Negress, they managed to discover a trove of information — a treasure of regional news sources from around lower South America. There was a flood of stories discussing the rash of violence plaguing the tiny country of Uruguay.

Sitting in the back office of Plūcker's bar, Kafka and the old katsa were beside themselves. The information outlined a broad and intricate plot. From the sources acquired, it was obvious this operation was already well underway. The situation was made even more disturbing by the recent reports about the assassination of Rabbi Kovinski and the attack on Guardian Angel Intelligence. It was too convenient to think the two incidents were disconnected from the current operation. So, the question remained — what to do next?

Cohen sat somberly in his chair contemplating their next move. Plūcker and Kafka reread some of the reports and documents in an attempt to glean some gem that would give them a lead. It was obvious the enemy had established themselves and were carrying out their operation. Furthermore, their chief intelligence sources had virtually been eliminated, most likely by the Iranians. They were flying blind and, more than likely, had targets on their backs. The elephant in the room that no one asked about but was on all their minds was: *How badly had they been exposed?*

"As I see it," the old katsa broke the silence as he rose to his feet and began pacing. "We have to assume the Iranians know someone is on to them. We left no trace of who we are with the GAI, and I would argue that Kovinski would have never cooperated. If anything, he would have given misleading information to the enemy."

"We don't know what was obtained at GAI headquarters," Kafka interjected, as he lay sprawled across a nearby couch. "Ms. Rios has no loyalty to us but was very protective of her people. She wouldn't hesitate to give up information on us if a gun was put to her head. Especially, if she blames us for putting her in this situation." The commando rubbed his forehead. "Realistically, even if she didn't give up anything, we still don't know what was salvaged from the raid on her office. I know they have me on at least one and possibly more high definition security cameras. For all we know, Rios, as a precaution, might have been tailing us too. And, if those files exist...?"

"Well, nobody's here right now," Plūcker interrupted. "It's a safe bet they haven't found too much. And given what I've heard about the degree of wreckage, it's doubtful they'll really find anything."

"Plūcker's right. We have to assume that since we're in the same city, they would have been here by now if they had anything, so we also should assume we are safe enough to continue our operation," Cohen added. Plūcker wore a contemplative frown. Kafka, tapped his thumbs across his chest and staring up at the ceiling. Realizing the old man's gaze demanded a response, Kafka finally rolled his head to look at Cohen and gave a reluctant nod of approval. His people were on board to continue the mission.

"What's our next step?" Kafka asked. He untangled himself from the cushion, slid off the couch, and stood up.

Cohen, at the same time, sunk back into his chair. "I have documents and proof of our initial fear that we have an Iranian presence and mission. We can send this to our embassies in South America. However, it's all too general, and diplomatic pressure takes time, especially if we have to wait for the Israel Foreign Ministry to be briefed, decide on a course of action, and issue instructions. Even then, it would be doubtful our country alone would have the clout to affect any positive outcome. We can't assume any other countries would be inclined to move on this issue.

"So, we're back to dealing with this situation ourselves scenario," Kafka cut in with clear exasperation, "which ultimately means some highly illegal and totally unsanctioned missions into a sovereign nation and possibly killing political figures."

"I understand your concern, lad," Plūcker sympathized. "But, sometimes nasty things have to be done for the good of the cause. I mean back during the Troubles in Ulster when I was with the LVF, we often had to take unpleasant actions for the right outcome."

"Spare me your Loyalist rationalization for how you justified it," Kafka was adamant. "It's the same rationalization every terrorist uses when they do heinous things. And that's what these are, heinous actions. I'm not a terrorist. I'm a soldier, and I like having boundaries when I operate."

"You killed plenty of people during your service for Sheyret 13," Cohen interjected. "I killed terrorists. I killed enemy soldiers. I killed hostiles in a complex battlefield, but I kept it to hostiles. I didn't go around killing politicians because they were crooked. I just don't like playing God."

"What would you suggest then?" The old katsa asked quietly, open to alternate suggestions. Everyone in the room knew there were none.

Despite his evangelizing, Kafka realized that as well. Walking around the room, he clicked his teeth and made a full circle before speaking. "The problem that we have is to identify our chief targets. We don't know if the Iranians reached out to numerous people or just one who is possibly building a network on their own. It means the difference between eliminating a few over several."

"I doubt the Iranians recruited more than one," Cohen spoke up. "They would not risk exposure trying to recruit and build a network. This is not the Middle-East. It is not familiar territory where they have had years of established connections. They are operating in a largely foreign world and must tread lightly. It makes sense they would conduct studies and target a person with great care. They would have to keep their recruitment small and pointed. Either they would carefully choose a single individual with influence in all the right spots to obtain the needed outcome or, at the most, a very small handful of people.

Kafka thumped his hands against his chest. "In the end, we don't know. Until we figure out who Iran's chief guy is, we can't investigate him to get the whole picture."

"Perhaps we might," Plūcker interrupted.

The Israelis turned to face the Irishman, who was eyeing a printout from an Uruguay newspaper. Plūcker raised the article he'd seen. "I've been noticing a pattern here. It would seem that certain demands have been voiced for the Uruguay president to declare some form of Martial Law."

"That would be expected, considering the panic created from all the violence," Cohen replied.

"True," the Irishman continued. "But, I've kinda been noticing, when I read some of these articles, one name keeps appearing in favor of this action. He is a member of their Parliament. His name is Oskar Straudner. Apparently, he's a member of the Partido Nacional or National Party — the country's leading rightwing political party."

No one said anything for several moments. Plūcker broke the silence. "Given what we know so far, our boy seems to look like a pretty good fit."

"Well let's not jump to conclusions," Kafka said hesitantly. "I don't want to start grasping at straws."

"Straws are all we have right now," Cohen replied. "What do we know of this Mr. Straudner?"

Plūcker shrugged his shoulders and went to his computer typing in the name. The computer screen was covered with the politician's articles, reports, and speeches. As the three men gathered around the computer, they began pointing out random articles.

Oskar Straudner was definitely becoming more interesting as they continued to read. A biography and other documents were also posted: the fortune the man controlled, his international business dealings and, most importantly, his long-established government connections. Particularly interesting were his connections with the country's security elements.

Plūcker leaned back in his chair. "All right, if we have

nothing else to go on, I'd say he's our best lead. If I were a cop and this was a crime novel..."

Kafka was leaning against the wall. "This leaves us with a new problem. We don't have Rabbi Kovinski to tap into anymore. And with GAI apparently out of business, we don't have any intelligence assets."

"Can we perhaps find Ms. Rios?" Cohen said to the young commando. "I mean her office may be gone but not her network."

"We don't even know if she's alive after that attack," Kafka responded incredulously. "If she is alive, she's in hiding and probably not in business anymore. Or, if she is, seeing how we were most likely the cause of her current situation, she is probably not going to be inclined to want anything to do with us."

"In the absence of any other options, Cohen shrugged, we have to try."

"I'll make inquiries," Plūcker offered. "My connections on the Bogota streets are better than most state intelligence services. If she's alive, I can most likely find her. But after that, convincing her to help is going to be your problem."

The Israelis agreed. It was their only viable option.

CHAPTER 31

The recent bombings in Montevideo stirred a dangerous amount of anxiety in the country. Qalmini read the latest news articles online discussing the state of hysteria with a sense of accomplishment. The pressure on President Jose Mojica was becoming intense. Things were falling into place.

Tapping his fingers on his desk, he looked up to see Major Akim standing attentively on the other side. The large man had been quie[illegible] waiting for some acknowledgment from his comma[illegible]

"The ten[illegible] n Uruguay is reaching a boiling point," Qal[illegible] "Now, the question is where are we with the mob[illegible] ur troops?"

Akim clear[illegible] at before speaking. "Our recruits have responded well to training. They are ready to be mobilized upon order."

"Logistics and transportation?" Qalmini asked. "That was being coordinated by Major Essouri. Now that he's gone, what problems will we have?"

"None," Akim replied. "His death was unfortunate. However, he had planned everything out and made all the necessary preparations beforehand. Our young Arab, Surriman, is doing all the groundwork to prepare for the mobilization and housing of our troops. He has arranged contacts to obtain various types of hauling trucks that will meet our people across the border in Uruguay."

"Our troops will be driven to Montevideo in small, informal convoys and dropped off in warehouses in the parts of the city closest to strategic areas. During the last few months, we have been slowly and discretely provisioning the locations with all the necessary materials to support the men until it is time to mobilize."

"No one is suspicious of the large numbers of hygiene supplies and bedding being moved to these locations?" Qalmini asked.

"The materials are being purchased by our import-export front companies. Everyone we deal with assumes we are going to move the merchandise across borders or overseas. So nothing will appear out of the ordinary."

"And our elements will be sent to the countryside?" Qalmini tapped his fingers.

The Major continued. "The forces will be somewhat smaller, so we can move them to old farmhouses. Many who inherited small family farms with no real economic future were happy to sell and didn't ask many questions. We were able to buy them very cheaply. The support materials will be dropped off by trucks. They will have manifests to take the material to supposed mining camps."

Qalmini nodded his approval. "We need to have our people in place so when our *friend* instigates his takeover, we'll be ready." He looked down at his computer screen. "I don't trust our friend, and I want to make sure we are in a strong position, so he'll have to deal with us and honor our agreement whether he wants to or not."

Professor Raphael Patrica hated grading papers. Like most academics, he found it both time consuming and tedious. After so many papers on the same general subject, it was monotonous. He often wondered, after about the fifth paper, if there were any original thoughts left. They all tended to say the same thing over and over again. In his mind, he joked to himself, *could they make the cheating less obvious by using a different scammer.* He knew better, yet the lack of originality was depressing nonetheless.

"Ah'hem." His thoughts were interrupted by a manufactured cough. He looked up to see the woman he had met many months ago. He knew her only by the name 'Reina'. The Contessa Selena de Alvarez glided forward into the professor's office. It didn't surprise her in the least that nothing had changed since her last visit.

With eyes widened, as if seeing some mystical deity before him, the professor rose excitedly to his feet. "My dear, it is so good to see you!" He started to come around from behind his desk, but stopped short when she raised her hand in protest.

"Please Sẽnor," the woman he knew only as Reina said. "My feet are tired; can we please sit?"

"Oh..oh, yes, of course we can," the professor replied, moving back behind his desk and sinking into his familiar chair. He was somewhat puzzled by the sight of a plastic bag clutched in the woman's hands. He hadn't failed to notice it or the wonderful aroma coming from it.

The Contessa was aware the professor was eyeing her bag. She said nothing as she moved to take a seat in one of the guest chairs on the other side of the desk. The look of jubilation in his eyes told her all. "I have been so pleased with your work," the professor spoke up almost immediately. "The revolution seems to be in full swing." His voice lowered as he grew concerned over prying ears.

"Yes, it is. I and the revolution owe you a great debt for helping us set it up," the Contessa replied quietly as she watched the professor. His eyes were wild with the youthful excitement he remembered from his revolutionary days. "We are gaining momentum."

"I see it. I see it all the time. Students here are constantly discussing the rebels. The newspapers are writing about our exploits," the professor said. A slight drop of perspiration slipped off his head. He was in his element — the revolution, the intrigue. "Police have asked around trying to acquire information that could help identify the rebels. They asked me, and I said nothing. I acted like I was as surprised by the rebellion as anyone else."

"You are a good fighter, Sẽnor Patrica," the Contessa replied, again in her quiet voice. "I came here to discuss plans for expanding the revolution and beginning further recruitment."

"The rebellion has gained many supporters, the professor said. I have been cognizant of the need for potential recruits. You see, I anticipated that we would be having this meeting someday." Like last time, the young woman was dressed in a gray T-shirt, jeans, and cowboy boots; attire that drew no real attention. She'd be seen as just a student meeting with her teacher.

"Well, I'm glad you have been so diligent." The Contessa

picked up her plastic bag and set it on top of the desk. "I thought our meeting would look less suspicious if we were enjoying a casual meal together."

The professor watched as she removed the plastic bag and revealed two plastic containers. The aroma was strong. "I hope you like Thai food," she said as she handed one of the two containers to the professor.

"Thank you, I haven't eaten all day," he said as he popped open the container and began devouring the tasty collection of meats, vegetables, and noodles. He was particularly taken by the strong taste of curry and savored each bite. "How many recruits do you need for this next wave?" the professor asked between mouthfuls.

Sitting in her seat and crossing her legs, she replied. "We're keeping the numbers small, maybe twenty."

The professor gave her a bewildered look. "Only twenty. I could find you almost a hundred at this point."

The Contessa shook her head. "No, we don't need that many or the attention that comes with transporting a larger number, especially, since there are more prying eyes than before."

"Oh, yes, of course. You are entirely correct," the professor replied, embarrassed that he came across looking like such a novice in a world in which he should be familiar. "We must maintain security and discretion at all times."

The Contessa nodded slowly. The professor began to feel a stiffness in both his neck and face. Thinking it was a kink, he attempted to move his head to limber up. The stiffness persisted becoming even more painful. Soon his arms and legs began to spasm. Feeling more embarrassed than concerned, he fought to get his body under control. The muscles across his entire body began to tighten all at once.

He looked across the desk at the woman who calmly sat watching him. Seeing her calm demeanor, he wondered if the painful contractions were all in his mind.

The professor slid from his chair onto the floor where he thrashed around like a fish. Casually rising to her feet, the Contessa, in her calm and tactful manner, walked over and slowly closed the door. She returned to see the professor's body contorted and his back arched. His eyes were wide open, and his face had turned a dark shade of blue, as he began to succumb to asphyxiation. The muscles around his larynx prevented him from calling out for help. A few minutes later, the professor was a corpse on the floor.

Observing his body, the Contessa felt a professional sense of satisfaction with her work. The food had been laced with Strychnine, a powerful neurological toxin. The poison is derived from a plant resembling mandarin oranges that is grown in tropical environments. Their blossoms, every bit as lethal, have an odor that resembles curry power. She had mixed a large number of ground blossoms in the curry rich meal before bringing it to the meeting.

Satisfied he was dead, the Contessa calmly set about picking up the plastic containers and stuffing them back in her bag. She walked to the door and slipped out of the professor's office. It was so late on a Friday afternoon, the campus was nearly deserted. No one would find his body until next week.

CHAPTER 32

Alyssa Rios shuddered at the knock on her door. Glancing at Malia, who looked petrified, she reached for her gun and held it tightly to her body. She angled the weapon in the direction of the entryway. For a moment, there was silence. Both women stayed focused on the door thinking it might have been a person with a wrong address. Then the knocking resumed, this time harder and with the confidence of one who knew they were in the right location.

Malia's employer clutched her firearm tightly in the tactical pose she had learned years ago at Quantico. She had used this pose many times in her law enforcement career. With no side windows to see who was at the door, the two women could only wait. The pounding continued loud and hard. The person outside had no intention of leaving.

Finally, a woman, who looked to be in her late forties emerged from an upstairs room and quickly came down the staircase. Rushing to the other women, she whispered, "Sẽnor Genti is in position across the street."

Rios sighed with relief at the news. Sẽnor Esteban Genti was a former sniper with the Colombian army. He had seen action many times, both in the jungles fighting guerrillas and in the city, when he was a part of joint counter-narcotics operations with the US. As a side business, he took money under the table to ply his trade and provide additional security for legitimate business people who were threatened by the country's more violent criminal elements. Holding a small mobile phone, the older woman handed it to Rios.

"Esteban, are you there?" She asked nervously.

"Yes, Sẽnora," replied the man. "I have your knocker in my sights. Stay to his left when you engage him. I'll watch for your signal."

Feeling a sense of assurance, Rios started toward the door. Carefully, she wrapped a hand towel around her gun. If it were an enemy, the towel would mask the gun, so her attacker wouldn't try to take away her only protection. If attacked, she could use her gun and shoot him while he was on top of her.

The banging continued loud and hard. Rios approached the door. Behind her, Malia and the older woman followed, each having acquired some instrument to use as a weapon. Positioning herself to the left as instructed, she prepared to open the door. The two other women had taken up defensive positions in a corner off to the other side.

With a deep breath to calm her nerves, Rios reached for the knob and opened the door wide. With her gun, wrapped in the towel, she was prepared. With the door flung open, there in the doorway was the man she knew as *Mr. Herron.*

Standing her ground, the seasoned, former drug enforcement agent studied the man before her. *How did he find her? What was he here for? Could he have been the one who sent the attackers to her office, because she had become a loose end?* These questions raced through her mind as she quickly made an assessment.

Realizing what was going on, Dayan stood still and maintained a casual manner. He was cognizant of the fact she was deliberately avoiding being lined up with his frame. It could only mean a sniper had positioned himself across the street and possibly had him in his sights. Looking down at the towel clutched tightly to the woman's body, he assumed she had a gun. In any case, he was fully aware he was the one in danger if he made the wrong move.

Watching Mr. Herron, who had extended his arms and pressed his hands against the sides of the door frame leaving his jacket open to show he had no gun within easy reach. Rios was satisfied she was not in immediate danger. Keeping her gun on him, she mouthed to Genti, *"it's OK."*

"May I come in?" The Israeli asked quietly.

Rios stepped back into the house, keeping a good distance between her and Herron. Entering slowly, the Israeli was quick to notice the two other women standing off to the side. Both women were clutching pieces of furniture they obviously intended to use as weapons if needed. They looked terrified at the thought of possibly having to take any action.

"I'm shutting the door now," Dayan said. His hands were still up and away from his body. "If that's alright with you."

Rios nodded. Turning slightly, the Israeli pushed the door closed quietly. He turned back to face the former head of what had been GAI. Her posture had not changed. Her weapon was still fixed on him, and her expression was one of grave suspicion.

"How did you find me?" Rios snapped.

"You're not the only intelligence service I employ," the Israeli responded.

"Why are you here?"

Dayan lowered his arms. "I still need your services."

The woman glared at him. "My business is in shambles. My office is now rubble. Someone sent professional killers after me, and somehow, I think it has something to do with you. Or maybe those killers were sent by you. Are we loose ends you now need to clean up?"

"I didn't send any killers," the Israeli replied quietly. He was keenly aware that the other two women stood ready to pounce on him at any moment. "And if those who attacked your office were because of me, then I'm sorry. I can offer some compensation."

Rios said nothing. She stood looking the man over trying to analyze the situation. Finally, she spoke. "What sort of help do you still need?" Her attention was slightly diverted by the shocked look from the other two women — they looked as if their boss had just lost her mind.

Dayan sighed. "I need you to spy on someone — a politician in Uruguay."

"I'm on the run right now. She was exasperated. "How do you expect me to complete such an assignment?"

"You have built a good business in a risky line of work," the Israeli replied. "A line of work that requires flexibility and adaptability. Your networks are still in existence, and I doubt you just discarded your lists of contacts."

"Suppose you're right," Rios said. "Why would I continue to work for you? Part of being flexible is also knowing when to walk away. And, everything says I should walk."

"I agree. I would tell you that you should point to the

door and tell me to leave at once. However, you're going to need seed money, and I'm willing to pay a great deal for what I'm asking — one and a half million US."

Rios glared at *Mr. Herron* for what seemed like forever. "You have that kind of money to just throw around?"

The Israeli chuckled. "You know I do. I have paid you hundreds of thousands so far for your services. As desperate as I am right now, and for the quality of work you have delivered, I believe it would not be unreasonable."

"How do I know you were not the one who tried to have me and my people killed in the first place?"

"How do you know the attack on your office had anything to do with me?" Dayan replied, maintaining his calm demeanor despite the hostility surrounding him. "My other resources allowed me to find you here in your safe house. I would have had the resources and certainly an easier time to kill you here."

With another sigh, the former law enforcement officer lowered her weapon. Whether he was the cause that led to the attack or whether he was the one who initiated it was now irrelevant. If a veteran operator had the means to send skilled assassins the first time, he could have easily sent them again to her less guarded safe house.

"Who's the politician? She relented. "And it's two million US or use your other sources."

The Israeli smiled. "Deal. The name is Oskar Vlak Straudner."

CHAPTER 33

Straudner sat comfortably on the leather sofa in his private meeting chambers within his safeguarded Buenos Aires watch store. Directly across from him, sitting awkwardly on a similar piece of furniture, was Ali Anwar al Qalmini.

The two men looked at each other in stone silence — as if locked in some testosterone induced battle of wills. It was anything but that. This was the meeting to finalize all the arrangements and planning. Everything had led up to this moment. Everything accomplished thus far had laid the foundation. The two men enjoyed an unspoken recognition of the magnitude of what was about to be discussed.

The Iranian was the first to break the silence, while the politician nursed a shot of single batch bourbon. "We have our militias ready. They will be deployed to strategic positions throughout Uruguay. It will be done slowly and methodically to avoid raising any attention. When the time is right, and you announce your takeover, they will be deployed in your support."

"I see," Straudner replied, uncertain.

The Iranian let his statement hang in the air until the

politician seemed ready to hear more, at which point Qalmini continued. "We can place a trained force of around 4,000 men in the country to ensure a stabilized transfer of power. They will have resources to sustain them for a period of several days. Now, sir, where are you with the government backing."

Straudner took a sip of his bourbon before responding. "Well, it took some doing. The leaders of our security forces were not inclined to challenge the president or interfere with the civilian government. However, in light of recent events — attacks on the unions and the killing of the labor coalition president and his entourage, I have seen greater support among the echelons. They seem to like my idea of taking more aggressive action to combat the utter lawlessness plaguing our country and are falling in behind me."

"So, we can expect strong support from the military and police?"

The politician smiled as he downed the last drops of his drink. "You certainly can. I have already been at a meeting where we discussed plans for the takeover. I have officers in the major military and police installations ready to move to assert command on my signal. I also have key officers ready to move in and arrest all political leaders who could pose a threat. In addition, I have trusted associates within the most financially connected of Uruguay's elite society. In light of the attacks, they have given me their unspoken blessing which is sufficient for our purposes.

When the time comes, I will announce the call for martial law in the halls of the Chambers. Upon that announcement, all forces standing by will mobilize and begin seizing control of the key installations. That is when your militia should move."

"And how will you explain the militia to your conspirators?" Qalmini asked as he reached for a pitcher of water that had been provided for him.

"My fellow *patriots* have been informed that elements sympathetic to our cause have been organizing their own self-defense groups to combat the guerrillas. I have explained that I have reached out to the leadership of these groups for their support in establishing control."

"And the commanders have accepted this?" The Iranian asked, surprised.

"Our military and police forces are small," Straudner replied. "The 2,000 man force we have deployed to missions overseas makes them even smaller. We have less than 3,000 ground troops currently available. Even for a country as small as Uruguay, that would be insufficient to maintain order. The self-defense forces would help augment our forces."

"Besides, the commanders realize they'll have enough trouble with just subduing the protests and rounding up the leftists. They would rather not be confronting an already armed group of vigilantes who are technically pursuing the same goals. Moreover, as I have established myself as the only liaison, they will have to accept this significant militia force; it will secure my position as the guaranteed chief executive of this country."

The Iranian was impressed with the politician and his operation. "This leaves one other issue: the force that carried out the recent attacks against the labor organizations — a supposed response to the leftist insurgency. I imagine you have some acquaintance with The Soldiers of Retribution organization?"

"Possibly," the politician raised his eyebrows. "They

operate at my discretion in a way and can stand down or be called up as needed."

Straudner wasn't going to tell the Iranian that the whole organization was entirely fictitious, and all the supposed members had already been ushered out of the country.

When dealing with a dubious ally, the politician had learned it was always better to have a card to play, even if the card really didn't exist. As far as the Iranian was concerned, Straudner had an embedded private army of his own to call upon.

Straudner continued. "I will also tell you that my men will retain control of the military bases. They know not to let the self-defense forces in. That includes our offices of intelligence and operational planning. I have connections inside the unions. They understand they are not to create any labor problems or protests during this operation unless I give instructions to do so. So, if you think you're going to take over key locations of infrastructure support or government buildings and start dictating terms, I will bring this country's economy to a halt."

By now Qalmini was angrily tapping his fingers against the table as he listened to the politician lay out his own additional plans. The Iranian had anticipated this, though he still felt somewhat annoyed at the idea. "Don't forget, sir. We'll have our own force both in town and locking down the countryside. If you think you're going to just kick us out, I would advise you to tread lightly."

Waving his hand and displaying a self-satisfied grin on his face, the politician replied. "I don't. I am fully aware that you will have a force well established in my country when this is over. I can only assume that that force will grow in the months following the takeover. I have no intention of reneging on our agreement. However, I will not be your puppet and will maintain my autonomy. We will have the ability to ruin each other if we attempt to betray one another. Our strength will be in our unity. Neither side will have overwhelming control. You'll have your foothold in South America, and I won't be able to get rid of you even if I wanted to. I, however, will plot my country's direction without an overbearing Iran."

Indeed, the politician had thought this out well, and the terms seemed reasonable enough. "All right, Qalmini said. So long as we get what we need, and that is in the works as we speak." Qalmini pointed his finger warningly in Straudner's direction. Straudner merely replied with a nod and a knowing smile on his face.

"My other concern is what is to be done about our leftist insurgency?" Straudner reached over a small table where a large, polished oak humidor sat. Opening it, he pulled out a short Montecristo and proceeded to clip the top and light it. He offered the Iranian a cigar which Qalmini declined with a flick of his hand. The politician continued, "We have to bring their campaign to a quick and successful end."

"I agree." For the first time, Qalmini sat back in his seat. "Preparations are already in place to terminate their existence before the coup is executed. That way, they will not be a nuisance. We'll have a decoy force that can be decisively eliminated by your security forces, so the credit will go to you."

Straudner took a puff. "Good. I have to show something to the power brokers and the elites to get them behind me."

"I know," Qalmini replied. "We planned for this."

"Another thing we need to discuss," Straudner said. "Something has to be done about our current president. He must be eliminated to create the necessary confusion and opening for my assured ascendance to the presidency."

"He stays out in that little chicken farm on the outskirts of the capital with his lover," Qalmini said.

"Yes, and even in all this turmoil, he has refused protection. Killing him is not the problem. It's who will do it? It can't be one of our people. That would only make him a martyr and build a movement against me."

This was nothing to the Iranian. "We have people affiliated with the guerrillas who can get this done. The guerrillas will ultimately take the blame and give you even more credibility."

Straudner raised his hand with the cigar in it and gave a half-hearted salute to the Iranian. His smile had mutated from a slight smirk to a sinister expression.

Outside, unbeknownst to either man, a small vending truck sat across the street from the watch shop. A dumpy, little man distributed food to a collection of office workers on their lunch break, while his partner, a small middle-aged woman pretended to tend the grill. Meanwhile, a hidden monitor showed images of the watchmaker's store and transmitting from a small camera was a recording everything going on at the front entrance.

CHAPTER 34

It was nearly dark when Elloy Mendoza walked out the front doors of his offices at Bolivar Investments & Acquisitions. His mind was on several things: his recent business dealings conducted for his cover as a businessman, communiques from Cuba — they were still not convinced the assault on him was somehow just an attack gone wrong by local hoodlums as he had originally reported — and an update on the Iranians who were getting ready to execute their operation. Wearily, he descended the polished, white marble steps of his headquarters. Flanking him on each side was an entourage of bodyguards.

Since the earlier attack, he had quit taking chances and had started employing a consignment of former and off-duty police to shadow him. It was risky, given his assortment of illicit business dealings, to have so many ears listening to him. However, he decided that the would-be killers he had previously encountered were still lurking around waiting to take their next shot, especially given the way he had exacted his retribution on the Rabbi and the young girl. It was either a good means of intimidation or an escalation of the war.

The Cuban wanted no more overt violence drawing attention to him. Surrounding himself with police or former police ensured him the hoodlums would be deterred from any further attacks — at least for the time being.

In a small café, a little way down the street, Micha Cohen sat enjoying a small espresso as he watched the Cuban descend the stairs of the building and walk over to a row of polished black cars. The old katsa took a sip as he watched Mendoza slip into the back of a classic looking limousine. The small army of suited figures flanking him filed into the rest of the vehicles. Within seconds, the convoy pulled onto the main street and passed the café where the katsa was relaxing.

Cohen calmly watched the vehicles go by. He continued to sip his espresso while picking up a copy of the local paper as he was considering what his next move was going to be. Mendoza was clearly the eyes and ears of the Iranian operation. The old spy wanted to assassinate him. Not just as a tactical measure to cripple the Iranian intelligence flow, but as retribution for killing Rabbi Kovinski. He knew vengeance was never a good thing to pursue in the world of intrigue. It was often costly in its execution and fruitless in its resolve. In his experience, revenge-driven thinking tended to be clouded and dangerous.

As much as Cohen wanted to liquidate the Cuban, his instincts insisted he kidnap him and pump him for information. The real problem was how to find out to what degree the Iranians knew of his existence. What had they found from their move on Kovinski and the community center? To what degree were they now aware of him and his office,

Kafka, and Plūcker? They had found out enough to discover Ms. Rios and were moving quickly to neutralize her. And why was there such an overt attack against her office when they could have discretely abducted her off the street or kept her under surveillance to see who she was meeting? Nothing was adding up, and the old spy didn't like what was developing.

Sitting at the table, he was contemplating what options he still had at his disposal. His thoughts were interrupted by the appearance of a tall, young man standing directly over him. The young man was wearing a tight-fitting T-shirt that enhanced his muscular physic giving him a rather threatening persona. His facial expression was one of bitter intensity.

Solomon Cabriza Gold looked down at the older man, who was quietly enjoying a drink. By all accounts, he was just another person on the streets of Buenos Aires. Even though it had been only a brief encounter, the young man recognized the man sitting at the table. He was the Israeli who had wandered into the community center looking for the Rabbi — he was the Mossad man.

"I want to speak with you," the young man spoke more as a command than a request.

Seeing the muscles tighten on the young man's body, Cohen decided it was wiser to invite the young man to have a seat rather than try to shoo him away. "How may I help you?" Cohen asked with innocent politeness.

Wasting no time, the young man slipped into the seat across from the foreigner and said, "I want in."

"What do you mean?" Cohen replied.

"I know who you are, katsa. I know why you are here,

and I don't wish to have my time wasted on games. I want in!" The young man growled.

Waving his hand and shaking his head with annoyance, Cohen tried to reject the young upstart. "I have no time for this!" he snapped. "Leave me alone! I have no idea what you are talking about."

"Elloy Mendoza," Gold snarled. "You are interested in him. Israel is interested in him, and I am very interested in him!"

The Israeli waved his hand, again, in an attempt to dismiss the young man. He was cut short by the young Argentinian who said quietly. "I was there the day Rabbi Kovinski received you. I also had friends outside his office when you and the Rabbi discussed threats to the Jewish people. I saw the files you and the Rabbi discussed regarding Elloy Mendoza. He is a Cuban spy who is helping someone who is against Israel."

By now Cohen realized two other tough-looking young men had come up behind him and taken seats at a nearby table. It was obvious from the nod given by the Argentinian to them that they were together.

"My friends also recognized you from that day sir," Gold added.

The old spy was aware that any further attempts to deflect the young toughs would be pointless. He also decided that as angry as the young men obviously were, a continued denial would only result in heightening their tempers and risking unwanted attention for him. Besides they already knew enough.

CHAPTER 35

The Contessa Selena de Alvarez sat enjoying the nighttime South American atmosphere. The sounds of nocturnal creatures, the light rustling of bushes from the gentle breeze blowing through them, and the dimmed landscape in the haunting beauty of the pale blue moonlight all seemed to mesmerize her. She had always felt at home in South America. It was unfortunate that when her business was complete, she would need to leave quickly. Part of surviving in her business was knowing how to move and when to leave before clients started to think of you as a liability. For the Contessa, that time was quickly approaching.

She heard the sound of thrashing in the bushes that was alien to the pattern she had been enjoying all evening. It was the sound of a person moving in the foliage behind her. Venzuelo Zamora was soon standing next to her. His breath was hard, not from any physical exertion, but from the emotional pressure he was feeling.

"It's a job. Don't forget that," the Contessa said coldly as if reading the mercenary's thoughts. She was well aware of his current ailment. Though she had thought to offer something consoling or even share a mutual regret, she could find none. Nor did she wish to divert him from his job.

"I still don't have to like it," Zamora replied with a twinge of bitterness in his voice.

Taking a sip from her bottle of water, the Contessa replied. "You stopped being a revolutionary before you took our money. You came to work for me because you decided to stop hiding behind the façade of being a revolutionary and admit what you really are." Her tone, like her manner, was neither cold nor impassioned. Instead, it was indifferent, as if offering advice from a mentor to a novice. "And what you are is a mercenary who trained people you knew were going to end like this."

"It's that simple?" the mercenary retorted with indignation.

"It's that simple," the Contessa replied ignoring the implications of his tone. "So now, you will carry out what needs to be done. And you will let what's about to happen, happen."

"My men are already assembled and ready to move out tonight to the rendezvous point," Zamora said with a grimace. "The rebels have all been collected at the camp except the Irishman's team which is still in the city."

"Is there any suspicion?" the Contessa asked in the same unconcerned tone.

"No," Zamora replied. "They understand that they have all been gathered to be briefed on the next phase of our operation, receive instructions for their targets, and celebrate their achievements for the revolution. As you ordered, we even distributed quantities of beer to ensure they will not be very alert."

Their attention was diverted by a sudden flash of lights.

In the distance, the double glare of headlights was visible as a vehicle crested the rise on the dirt road leading toward the camp. The first vehicle was immediately followed by another set of headlights and another in what seemed like an endless pattern.

The Contessa noticed Zamora's jaw tightened even in the darkness.

"I took the liberty of making alternative arrangements, so you and your men won't have to do the act yourself," the Contessa spoke calmly.

The mercenary shook his head. He wasn't thankful for the surprise he was witnessing. He was happy that his employer didn't feel the need to press the issue or assume any gratitude from him. She, instead, remained quietly sipping her water.

The vehicles were now passing by in rapid succession. They were hauling trucks, not unlike the ones commonly seen on the roads loaded with goods from some farmer or local merchant. There were about ten in all by the mercenary's rough count. They continued past the Contessa and Zamora heading toward the campsite.

"You should take your men and go now," the Contessa said. Her continually calm demeanor was proving somewhat unnerving to Zamora.

"Who are they?" he asked looking at the trucks driving by.

"A word of advice. If you have any future prospects in this business," the Contessa responded, "don't ask questions you don't need the answer to."

Acknowledging her advice, the mercenary gave her a nod and headed back into the bushes. He and his men had staged themselves across the foliage along a weeded jeep trail that led into the interior and eventually to a collection of roads that would take them to their extraction point. Before he left, the mercenary turned to view the darkened silhouette of his now-former employer. "I'm still interested in future employment should you have need of me."

The Contessa didn't reply, and Zamora, having nothing further to say, disappeared into the bushes. She didn't have to say it. She would have a use for his services in her later dealings. He was worth the money paid to him.

Emil Zacha had been a long time operative of Argentina's feared Intelligence Secretariat (SI), the dreaded secret police. They conducted extensive surveillance domestically and, at times, took more direct action against the government's more troublesome dissidents. This was a responsibility that Zacha had carried out on numerous occasions. President Christina Kirchner had decided to disband the SI and, in 2015, replace it with a more accountable organization. The intelligence officer found himself, one of many who had served the more shadowy missions of the state, unemployed and out on the streets.

He put himself on the open market to ply the skills he had honed so well for his government. When he was approached by a refined young woman of foreign origins about a job eliminating a group of left-wing terrorists operating in the northern Argentina countryside, his answer was an immediate, 'yes'.

Flush with a sizeable amount of seed money, Zacha reached out to connections he had established long ago among the feared Los Monos (The Monkeys). It was a gang that virtually ruled the underworld of the major city of Rosario. Through their stranglehold on the drug trade, they maintained extensive connections with criminal networks throughout the country. It wasn't long before the old protector of the state had assembled a small army of experienced killers from various rural gangs near the target training camp. Armed with grid coordinates, a well-documented pictorial biography, mapping of the camp, and a sizeable force, Zacha, set out to combat the terrorists he had spent his career protecting.

Arriving at the predetermined location, the trucks pulled into a loose line. The vehicles were barely stopped before the covers in the back flew open and menacing-looking men were leaping out onto the ground. Their weapons were an assortment of old M-16s and AK-47s mixed with newer MP models and a few HK sub-machine guns. It was easy to assume the gangs were using their personal arsenals for this job.

Following at a distance was a small, unobtrusive little white Toyota pickup. It stopped some distance from the collection of criminals. The passenger door was flung open and out stepped a figure of medium build, approaching middle-age, dressed in a pair of white cotton slacks and matching jacket. Emil Zacha looked around and within seconds caught sight of a figure waiting just at the edge of the tree line.

Seeing her operative in the distance, the Contessa moved into the open and caught his attention. Understanding her need for discretion, the intelligence officer waved to his driver to stay in the truck as he approached his employer.

"Everything is set?" The Contessa opened the conversation.

Zacha nodded, as he removed his straw hat showing his receding hairline. "The men are grouping up now and will begin within the next ten minutes." The intelligence officer acted with the reserved professionalism of one all too familiar with these sorts of activities.

"Good. Everyone is gathered down there and are totally unsuspecting of anything," the Contessa replied quietly. "Now, if you will forgive me, I will take my leave. A woman shouldn't be around the type of men you've brought."

That wasn't her real reason, and Zacha knew it. She had organized the dirty work to be done, and he was here to do it. But she was also right. The men he had with him were criminals who enjoyed violence and were completely indiscriminate in the way they carried it out. She was wise not to be present. With a nod of approval, the young woman took her leave, vanishing into the shrubbery.

Returning to the pickup, Zacha met the driver who was exiting the vehicle. Felix Augusto had cut his teeth as a tough and efficient street soldier for Los Monos. He had, at one time, been a trusted lieutenant of Claudio 'El Pajaro' Contero, before Claudio was assassinated in a bar in 2013. Zacha needed to ensure his collected gunmen would be well led and controlled for this attack. He thought no one would be better than the tall, wiry gunman with a thick mane of long, curly black hair.

"We'll get started soon," the young man said quietly. "You'll probably want to wait here."

Zacha said nothing — a nod of approval was his only reply. The young man did not look like a professional killer. He wore a simple T-shirt, a pair of jeans, and cowboy boots. At a glance, he was the image of a typical gaucho one would see working a ranch, not a man, who by age thirty, had killed well over a dozen people.

The intelligence operative leaned against the hood of the truck and started to fan himself with his hat. The young gunman walked toward the trucks to the waiting gunmen now assembled for action. Like his employer, Zacha wanted no witnesses to his involvement when the killings occurred. Felix was the only one who knew of his participation and even he knew the intelligence officer only by the name Eduardo. It would be easy to disappear after the attack, which would look like right-wing thugs retaliating against communist guerrillas. It was an all too common story in this part of the world.

Zacha watched as the young gunman took control of the motley group. Within minutes, they were organized into teams that were quickly fanning out into the tree lines encompassing the perimeter of the camp. It was only minutes, but the tension made it feel like hours, if not years. Zacha chuckled at the thought that no matter how many times he carried out such actions, the tension building in anticipation always happened.

His thoughts were interrupted by the thunderous barrage of gunfire going off in a coordinated chorus. The barrage was soon followed by the responding choir of terrified, blood-curdling screams of both men and women. The tension eased as the attack proceeded with violent precision. It wasn't the killing that bothered the intelligence operative. He had done his fair share in his time and had a strong disdain for leftist radicals of all types. He felt a sense of justice rather than remorse. His concern was the same as all those who operated in such service for the state — the fear of one day being held to account by those he once hunted. Of course, there were also those who, in safer times, felt a need to question the actions of those protecting the society they enjoyed.

The gunfire was now becoming sporadic, and Zacha realized the gunmen had moved from the tree line and were now entering the camp. Despite the powerful echoing of the gunfire, the occasional desperate screams could still be heard very clearly.

Felix Augusto directed his men like a general commanding troops on a battlefield. He kept half his force hunkered in the cover of the tree line to protect the high ground overlooking the campsite. The rest of his force had moved from the bush line into the camp. Under cover of their comrades above, they began moving from building to building, clearing out any survivors. The first two structures, a two-story building and an office hut, remained silent as the assassins moved in and later came out without incident. But when the men entered the third structure, in seconds, it was ablaze with gunfire.

From inside, his men were calling for back-up. They had apparently come across survivors who had obtained weapons and were now mounting a defense. More men from the ground team were about to enter when Augusto called for them to fall back. The command was repeated and his men poured from the building into the yard. Augusto commanded them to take positions surrounding the structure and motioned one of the men to his side to take the small metal box sitting next to him.

Grabbing the box, the underling raced down the hill to where the other attackers were positioning themselves. The men quickly opened the box to see a neatly packed collection of grenades. "Give them hell!" Augusto hollered to the men who had received the parcel. Soon, men from the ground forces were running up and lobbing the small round explosives through every window opening in the building. It was only seconds before the walls of the wooden building were torn apart by the fury of grenade blasts exploding in rapid succession.

It wasn't long before people were frantically running out of the building. The shock of the blasts and the heavy smoke and debris had taken the young terrorists by surprise. A few of them fired wildly trying to mount some sort of defense. The gunfire from the experienced assassins swiftly cut them down.

Satisfied they had killed the last of the resistance, the gunmen rushed into the building. With no more complications, they set about checking the rest of the buildings. They found no survivors.

CHAPTER 36

Was it luck or just good intelligence analysis?

Kafka looked over the collection of documents and pictures scattered around the table. Alyssa Rios and her organization had proven their abilities yet again. The information he had received was both thorough and well documented.

The old man had, apparently, been right on his first guess. Oskar Vlak Straudner was the most likely suspect for Iran's operation. The documents were a series of detailed reports discussing the man who, as Kafka was coming to realize, was proving to be an ever-greater mystery. On the surface, he was a politician, who publicly appeared to be humble regarding his career. He didn't hold any official leadership titles in the Chambers and, for the most part, didn't seem to enjoy any serious popularity among the large base of the populace or political movements. Yet behind closed doors, he was known to be a powerbroker within the halls of Uruguay's legislative institutions.

According to reports marked, *off the record*. He was his party's chief negotiator when it came to *backroom* deal-making. Known to be ruthless, maniacal, and calculating, Straudner often demonstrated his ability to successively push his party's agenda. Many senior ranking political leaders owed their positions to his shrewd tactics. Yet somehow, he was able to operate in a way that kept him out of the spotlight allowing him to move freely without garnering attention.

The reports discussed Straudner's long-established relations with components of the country's intelligence and security elements. Much like his political dealings, nothing seemed to be out of the ordinary. He held memberships at exclusive clubs that catered to the elite of the government's power base including high ranking officers of the police and military. However, beyond the innocent veneer was a litany of reports of shadowy dealings. Straudner had forged strong unofficial relations with the country's security forces. He helped them gain more concessions when struggling with the staunchly anti-military leftist elements of the legislature. In return, the intelligence institutions were quite helpful collecting information on his enemies. The reports further documented rumors that suggested elements within the security echelons may have provided more direct services for the politician.

Regarding his finances, Straudner presided over a vast fortune of old money that was spread over both formal and shadowy business dealings throughout the continent. He owned plantations and held silent ownership in a series of financial investment firms that catered to handling large sums of foreign capital being invested in South America. He also seemed to have his hands in international shipping as well as silent ventures in real-estate. In all, he controlled a large, wide-spread, but secretive, organization.

Straudner was also known to be active in a diverse array of less legitimate business ventures. Outside of Uruguay, he was involved in smuggling. Those activities included oil bought from Islamic radicals, timber illegally harvested, and the occasional selling of weapon components and machine parts to UN-sanctioned countries.

What proved the most interesting factor was the shared interest the politician had with a small watchmaker's shop in Buenos Aries. They found that Mr. Straudner was accustomed to conducting a lot of business in the Argentinian city. He often found time to visit the little shop. At first, it was a location documented by the agent tailing him. Then when the excessive number of hours spent there was revealed, the surveillance team took a greater interest in the shop. When an agent ventured inside to see what was so interesting, he was quick to discover that the politician was nowhere to be found.

A more elaborate surveillance mission was set up to monitor his dealings in the place. It became even more remarkable when the surveillance team attempted to break into the shop one evening to wire it for audio. Entering through the back, they found the door was secured with an expensive security lock that was nearly impossible to breach. Attempting to go through the front, they were shocked to find a camera surveillance system hidden along the outline of the storefront. On closer observation, they found a system that was more often seen in highly secured facilities.

Attempting to enter the building during working hours, they slipped surreptitiously into the back areas to plant listening devices in a couple of offices. When they tried to activate the receivers, they were listening to static that seemed to originate from a strong jamming device. As documented in the report, they found themselves fighting through a state of the art security system seen only in well-protected government facilities or used by large private intelligence firms. The surveillance team eventually had to reduce their operation to photographs taken from outside the building.

The photos offered in Ms. Rios' report contained images of both Straudner and the Iranian operations commander, Ali Anwar al Qalmini, arriving in this obscure place at roughly the same time. The two men were photographed entering and leaving the premises, during which time it was noted they were in the shop at the same time for a period of three hours. Rios had meticulously documented times of people entering and leaving the establishment. She reviewed the report before sending it to her client, and knowing of the Iranian, she had filtered out all other photographs of obvious customers on legitimate business.

Not much more was discovered regarding the politician's activities inside. A note on the report explained that the windows were of a fine tint that obscured any visual observations. Even using high definition cameras, the tint prevented them from capturing anything inside the premise. It was an interesting discovery. It all seemed like a very costly and unnecessary security addition for a simple watchmaker's shop. It caught Dayan's attention as it had captured the attention of the surveillance team. It was enough to solidify the politician as Iran's agent. But it still didn't offer any crucial details needed for planning. However, it was definitely clear the little watch shop was something more than it purported to be. It also solidified Straudner as their target.

Kafka finished reading the report. Plūcker had been

sitting by quietly listening. "He could be your man, or he could be the go-between for the man you really want, as I see it."

"He has to be our man."

"Everything you just read to me says he's a man who hides in the shadows," the Irishman pointed out. "Doesn't seem like the type to risk himself on such things."

"True," Kafka ran his tongue across his teeth. "But, he does crave power. And in a case where he can assume complete control and not have to work with the bureaucracy, I think he would jump at the chance. Besides, given the degree this man goes to for secrecy, he operates like a trained spy. The way he covers his tracks and shields himself — I mean for God sakes, a highly protected watch shop? You do all sorts of business, like me, and you don't have nearly the sophisticated security this place has. And, by all accounts, he doesn't even seem to have any ownership in it. He is a virtual ghost."

Plūcker folded his arms, deep in thought. "Well, that leaves us two scenarios. Either Mr. Straudner is the man that has been selected by Iran for their little takeover, or he is the man Iran recruited to prop someone else up to take over power. In any case, you're right, the man seems to be deeply involved in this."

"The question to answer: What's to be done about it?"

The Irishman unfolded his arms. "You need more to work with. That's what needs to be done. You can't move only knowing this guy's involved. He is or is not the brains of this operation. And, if he's just a middleman, then we have to know who's on the other side."

Kafka agreed.

The Irishman asked, "Why don't we try to focus on the Iranians?"

Kafka perked up as he gave Plūcker a bemused look.

Plūcker continued. "I mean, it sorta dawned on me that we're looking to chase a man on his home turf. Here's your Mr. Straudner, who has been playing the game of intrigue and has set up a pretty secure means of transacting business. That places you on unequal footing. However, the Iranians have been here only as long as you have. As I see it, the boys pulling this off are staying clear of their government's established networks. That means they're operating with the same drawbacks and circumstances as you. For the time being, you might have better luck reviewing your person's intelligence reports on the Iranians rather than on Mr. Straudner."

CHAPTER 37

Qalmini rubbed his forefinger gently across his lips as he reviewed the newspaper. With a feeling of satisfaction, he read of the *termination* of the leftist guerrilla camp operating in northern Argentina. He was particularly elated at how the newspaper account blamed the attack on the right-wing Para militarists, who had discovered the operation and attacked in retribution for the attacks in Uruguay. It was an entirely believable story. One that alleviated any concerns about complicated inquiries.

He thought the Contessa was a true master of her trade. She had organized the operation completely and disposed of it neatly.

He was even happier that the Contessa had arranged for a small force of guerrillas to be moved to Montevideo for a hypothetical new urban operation. At the final meeting with the young Contessa, he had articulated a need to ensure that a few would survive the camp liquidation so they could be eliminated by the police in a very public raid.

The Uruguay police desperately needed something to show for their aggressive tactics. They needed to promote them as being effective in their efforts to combat the terrorists and bring stability back to the country. After all, dictatorships are most popular when they prove their effectiveness against chaos and bloodshed. It wouldn't do to say the guerrillas were stopped purely by the efforts of right-wing paramilitarists.

He had received a report from Major Akim earlier in which he explained the preparation of their forces. Their equipment had arrived as planned, and their training had progressed on schedule.

Such news came at a most convenient time. That news was in conjunction with the recent meetings with Mr. Straudner, who had reported favorable results in preparing for the takeover. So far, the timeline was being met perfectly.

Sitting back in his chair, the Iranian folded his hands behind his head. Things were coming together despite the recent inconvenience of the mysterious infiltrators and Sẽnor Mendoza's irrational antics. This was news he desperately needed.

The infiltrators had been on his mind since the incident, but nothing appeared to have compromised the operation. He was aware that there was still some shadowy force lurking, keeping tabs on his project.

Who were they? Why had they not reported his operation to the police? Why had there not been any further attacks? These questions needed answering.

So far, all he knew was a group of street thugs had clumsily tried to kill Elloy Mendoza and Guardian Angel, a private intelligence firm had been feeding information to this mystery force. And, thanks to Mendoza's irrational response, any attempt to find out the identity of the client was now lost.

This situation was made worse by the sudden killing of some obscure Rabbi in Buenos Aires who was somehow mixed up in this. Again, finding out to what extent he was involved died when the Cuban's henchmen killed him.

This left Qalmini with nothing but theories and assumptions and no real targets. If it is the Israelis, why have their embassies not leaked this information to force the hand of the involved countries? Was it some group of local Jewish vigilantes who somehow caught on to his operation?

No, the way the report from Major Akim read, it was clear that the camp infiltrators were too skilled and too sophisticated to be some group of amateurs. Regardless, the situation was clear. This mystery force was still at large and possessed resources that made them gravely detrimental. It was imperative that this group be neutralized. Without knowledge of who they were and how they were connected, they remained a serious threat.

Earlier the Iranian had diplomatically explained his concerns to Mendoza. Now that Mendoza felt vindicated by his revenge, he was open to approaching the situation more rationally. The two men discussed the problem, and Mendoza concluded, after things had been explained, that mercenaries had been most likely employed to aid in this operation.

The Cuban left, promising to reach out to his contacts in the black-market world to see what he could find out. As a professional courtesy, he had offered to do this with no charge for the extra service. Had he demanded additional compensation, Qalmini would have probably killed him right in his office.

It did give the Iranian comfort to hear that some options were still available to find this threat. Although his trust in the Cuban had never been strong, after the recent fiascos, it was gone entirely. It was the realization that without Mendoza, he would be forced to reach out to his country's established intelligence network in the region. Doing so would expose Iran to the dangers of being connected to this mission.

Still, Mendoza was a problematic resource at best and a possible liability at worst. The current situation offered nothing in the way of a good option.

Then, he realized he had another avenue at his disposal. When Major Akim made contact again, Qalmini requested to see Nouri al'Marak Surriman.

Solomon Gold didn't exactly trust the Israeli spy, but he realized he had no one else to go to for information. The story he had gotten from the older man seemed reasonable, especially since it coincided with the young man's concept of typical Middle Eastern plots. He expected a bombing of some sort or possibly an assassination — this was close enough.

Micha Cohen was used to being in complex situations. Being accosted on the streets by some group of hostiles was nothing particularly new to him. It didn't, however, negate the fact that he was surrounded by a group of toughs demanding answers and threatening to bring unnecessary exposure. Since it appeared these young toughs already had a certain degree of understanding regarding the situation, it made them a dangerous liability. He wasn't about to give a group of wild hoodlums the truth and risk them going off on a tangent creating further complications. They had already caused problems with their initial botched assassination attempt. And it was clear they wanted revenge for the Rabbi and the young girl.

Treading lightly, Cohen explained that the Cuban was in the business of selling guns to Arab radicals residing in the communities of Paraguay, Argentina, and Brazil. He told them Iran was recruiting for an Arab network within the Lebanon communities and were Shia in their religious affiliations.

It wasn't the complete truth, but it was close enough to at least track with whatever information these young hoodlums might already have. He kept Uruguay and the possible coup plot out of the discussion. It was better to give the young men something that they could act on without raising any further problems, especially if it meant taking a swipe at some of the local Arabs who tended to side with Iran or hated Israel. It was much better if they terrorized local shop vendors than try to get involved way over their heads.

Despite his rookie introduction into the world of intrigue, Gold was certain the Israeli spy was not being completely forthcoming. He sensed the older man was trying to placate him and his group. Still, the explanation given did match the scant bit of information they had been able to gain from Myra and the Rabbi.

It didn't matter. The young radicals demanded they be part of whatever the Israeli and his team were doing against this menace. It was no longer just about helping the Jewish cause. These boys had greatly respected the Rabbi, they had all grown up with the girl, and both had just perished brutally in this secret war. They had the right to exact their own justice.

It placed Cohen in a terrible position given they were

ready to expose his presence if he didn't. The meeting ended with the katsa being permitted to leave, and Gold feeling dubious about the whole matter.

In the end, both parties agreed to meet in three days at a location of the Israelis choosing. Here they would jointly prepare for the next operation.

Leaving the meeting feeling anxious, Cohen wondered if he could have played the situation any better. At some personal level, he wasn't sure he wanted to. If these young men were itching for a fight, perhaps they could prove useful within a limited scope. In either case, they were involved in his mission now, or they would compromise it further.

It was better to keep them close.

It was called the Sunset Glory — a sizeable yacht of three levels and nearly forty feet in length. It was one of two yachts Straudner owned, the other was a hundred and fifty feet resembling a small cruise ship. The Sunset Glory was capable of being controlled by a single man. For someone like the secretive Mr. Straudner, it was his choice for discrete meetings with guests.

Normally, there were numerous places the politician used to avoid undue attention. In this case, he let slip that he had to suddenly cancel a regular golf game because of a call from his government office. That phone had been successfully bugged by Rios's people.

The golf game was a usual gathering of some very important people. It was not something a man like Straudner liked to miss. To suddenly decide to go boating seemed out of character.

Rios had passed this information on to Kafka with a notation explaining her suspicions. Kafka liked that Rios had caught this change. In the absence of direct information, this was a break that could possibly pan out.

Taking a trip to the marina where the yacht was anchored, Kafka, Darren Ripley, and Klaas Vanderhook meandered about as tourists enjoying the coastal scenery. It was no surprise to any of them to find the Sunset Glory located in an isolated area offering greater privacy for those willing to pay for it.

They were also not at all surprised to find that the yacht maintained a full-time security detail. The guards were casually dressed, though obviously in tactical clothing, and their muscular physiques indicated they were ex-military or police. The way they carried themselves made it easy to peg them as having served in special tactical units.

After a quick reconnaissance, the three decided the only way to get aboard the ship was through the water. The difficulty was working in the daylight giving them a very narrow timeline. The only positive they had was that the politician was casting off sometime early the next day.

That evening, three men along with Oskar Perez, found themselves intently waiting in a small boat piloted by an elderly fisherman just outside the waters of the marina.

The old man, distantly related to Perez, calmly navigated the craft. He stayed vigilant in the darkness just outside the waters of the marina. The small boat looked like it was something out of the last century and was easy to justify using a bare minimum of working lights. This allowed ample darkness to mask the tactically dressed commandos riding in the bow. The old man was proving a skilled sailor as he maneuvered the waterways purely by instinct.

When they came to the point they estimated to be parallel with the yacht's location, the three commandos donned their scuba gear and dropped into the water. Once again they had foregone their tanks in favor of snorkels. With no serious security on the water aside from a boat watchman, there was no need to bring more gear than necessary.

The real problem would be on the docks where the professional security team was on guard.

In the pitch blackness, the three kept their heads above water as they swam a hundred meters into the marina. The plan was to navigate by the string of lights outlining the marina and submerge just before reaching the docks keeping all movements below water to prevent making any noise. In a pool, a hundred meters would have been easy, but the current and waves were strong enough to cause difficulty as they fought to stay on course. Making it even more taxing was the need to keep their strokes entirely underwater.

Arriving at the edge of the docks felt like a grand achievement. Tired and feeling their muscles ache, they once again resisted the urge to verbally express their aggravation. The professional instincts that came with years of performing such duties prevailed.

Only a few feet ahead, lights adorning the dock's perimeter glimmered across the water in a beautiful display. It also revealed everything to anyone observing the water.

Kafka broke off from his companions heading for the yacht while Ripley and Vanderhook circled the far end. If there was trouble, they were his response team. Submerging himself just below the surface, Kafka kicked with his fins and began moving forward.

The isolation of the craft protected it from surface-based infiltration but made it easier to penetrate from the water. Spared the virtual maze found at most marinas, it was not difficult for Kafka to estimate the direction and distance to his target. He had completed many night operations during his days with Shayret 13 that were vastly more complex.

Nearing his target location, Kafka slowly lifted his head from the water just high enough to see. The yacht was a short distance away. Luckily, it rode low in the water presenting several access points from which to sneak on board.

There were three men attentively patrolling the docks. It was apparent Mr. Straudner was deeply concerned about security and those threatening him. It was also apparent he was even more concerned about having anyone on board that could witness his activities. There were no cameras and no patrolling guards on the yacht. It was also obvious that Straudner never thought about the possibility of a threat approaching from the sea.

Swimming to the bow of the ship, Kafka held onto an available railing and waited. This time the confines of the marina controlled the degree of force that he had felt out on the open sea. In the darkness, he could make out the illuminated watch hands and ticks denoting the time was 2330hrs. His men had ten more minutes before they would execute the next phase of this mission.

From his position, Kafka could hear the guards on the other side. They spoke very little, but from what he could make out, the discussion was all business related. The guards definitely were professionals. It was now 0000hrs and time was getting close.

The Israeli prepared himself accordingly. He would have a limited window of time and couldn't afford to hesitate.

Suddenly a loud high-pitched scream whistled loudly in the air. On cue, Kafka quickly pulled himself onto the ship.

Listening for the guards, he could tell they were acting as intended. They didn't move to investigate the noise — they remained at their post. But the scream had fulfilled its purpose by masking the sound of Kafka sliding onto the yacht. His prearranged route placed him on the opposite side of the dock and allowed the higher structure of the craft to conceal him from the security team on the other side.

The scream stopped; silence returned.

As planned, Vanderhook and Ripley were on the far end of the docks. At the prescribed time, they would detonate a loud firecracker to mask their comrade's activity. Anyone would presume a firecracker would be just an innocent bit of fun by the less mature members of the marina's yachting club. It could be easily explained and would prevent concern of something nefarious.

The guards discussed what they had heard. As predicted, they expressed irritation as opposed to alarm. They concluded it was some idiot rich kids messing around and returned to their posts.

Keeping low and cognizant of the shadows, Kafka slipped around the base of the ladder well leading up to the bridge. Having no plans to work from, Kafka was navigating slowly in the dark feeling his way. He had brought a pair of night vision optics but wanted to wait until he was below deck and away from the guards before turning them on. Once past the ladder well, he moved slowly toward what he presumed would be the entrance to the lower deck.

He was dressed in his black wet-suit. It was not his first choice of apparel for a highly delicate mission. Normally, he would have chosen the more practical fatigues that allowed greater mobility. However, under the circumstances, fatigues would have taken too long to dry and would be noisy as he moved.

His hand felt the brass doorknob, then the wood, and finally the space between door and door jam. Taking a minute, the Israeli looked around. His natural night vision had, by now, adjusted enough that he could make out the general outline of his surroundings.

The outside patio had a small table with some chairs and looked like a spot where one would spend a great deal of time if they were lounging. The easy answer would be any business conducted would probably be done there.

Kafka hoped he was guessing correctly since he had no wish to remain on the yacht any longer than necessary. However, logic dictated that with so little prior intelligence regarding Mr. Straudner's habits and routine on board, it was a serious gamble to assume.

The possibility of creating any noise loud enough to alert the guards didn't sit well with an intruder armed only with a small .22 caliber Berretta. He needed to check the entirety of the ship and place bugs in all areas that might be used for discussing business. Kafka clinched his teeth and slowly proceeded to turn the knob. He actually hoped the door would be locked, and he would have to make do with the outside table area. Somewhat to his dismay, the door opened. Gently, he widened the opening while he silently prayed to God there wouldn't be any loud creaking.

God was listening as the wooden door opened almost without a sound. Not wanting to press his luck, the Israeli opened it only a few inches before he attempted to slowly slide his way inside. Jamming a small wedge of cloth between the door and frame to keep it in place, he began moving. His wet-suit was restrictive and did not aid his gymnastic-like movements, but it did allow him to move with a degree of silence.

He reached inside and immediately felt the first step in a staircase. Carefully sliding through the space between the door and the jam, he felt his way from one stair step to another. At about the fifth step, his hand touched what he determined to be solid ground. By then his body was completely through the entrance.

Continuing down until his body was on the floor, Kafka slipped on his night optics from his waterproof bag. Turning them on, they illuminated a lavish dining room. One side hosted what looked like a well-stocked mini-bar with a neat seating arrangement. The other side offered a long, plush couch and a couple of equally comfortable-looking chairs. A long glass dining table in the center could seat a half dozen people.

It was obvious this was the best place to discuss business. Deciding the mini bar would presumably be the natural gathering point, he started for it. To his dismay, Kafka discovered there was a hardwood floor. To prevent any sound from creaking boards, he decided he would make less noise if he slid slowly across the floor. He began moving toward the bar, one hand after the other. He began to feel like a trained seal in an aquatic show. He even entertained the thought that if he was discovered, the humiliation would be worse than the bullets fired at him.

At the edge of the bar, he reached into his bag and pulled a small plastic container from a side pocket. Unclicking it, he produced a small rectangular object. Removing the adhesive strip, he felt the underlining of the bar and stuck it in just underneath the lip.

Deciding it was in the best place he was going to find quickly, he began sliding back toward the staircase. Then he moved to the door, removed his optics, and returned them to his bag.

Listening for a few moments, he could hear the guards still moving around on the docks.

Confident he was safe, he slid back through the door. Removing the cloth, he closed it cautiously. His heart raced, but he was able to maintain control with a succession of quick short breaths.

Kafka glanced quickly at his watch. It was 0030hrs. His men had instructions to move back to the fishing boat at 0045hrs if they didn't hear any shooting.

Continuing toward the table outside, Kafka stayed close to the deck. He was still shielded from the guards by a declining bulkhead that lined up with the outside ladder well. The wall lowered as it neared the deck causing greater exposure from the docks. Only the shadows presented the Israeli any protection. At the base of the table, Kafka clutched one of the small listening devices in one hand. Carefully he felt around until he found the lip of the table. To his dismay, he found the table was glass. His only other option was to reach for the nearest chair. Finding it made of a hard plastic, he felt around until he had an area that might work. He slipped the object in place.

Sliding back the way he had come, Kafka continued crawling, keeping his eyes fixed in the direction of the guards. When he was back behind the wall and moving along the walkway surrounding the yacht, he rose to his feet. Feeling for the railing he took hold and slowly went over the side, dropping very quietly into the water. Once completely submerged, he released his hands and slid into the murky darkness. He was relieved. With all the luck he must have used tonight, he could see this all ending with a shark attacking him on the way back.

CHAPTER 38

The rebels were anxious as they roamed about the confines of the warehouse like wild and caged animals. Due to their situation, their actions were entirely justifiable. Some paced as others loaded magazines, looked over weapons, and studied maps of the city, and pictures of future targets.

The urban force of the leftist-guerrillas had been on edge following recent attacks. In the last three weeks, they had successfully bombed a post-office and two banks, assassinated a police commander, and nearly succeeded in killing the mayor of the upscale Pocitos barrio.

As predicted, the police responded with a heavy hand aimed at the working-class areas and college campuses. The results had been as expected. The campuses had been set ablaze with student protests turning into all-out gang brawls against riot police.

Several poorer barrios had exploded into violence as police used more heavy-handed tactics aimed at flushing out supporters. However, because of the rebels' selective recruitment and their already established networks of logistical support, the police found nothing. It was as if they were dealing with ghosts.

Both the police and the military had suffered devastating losses and public embarrassment. Powerful elements from among the country's elite demanded some type of response. In desperation and anger, government security forces lashed out at the most likely suspects, the colleges and the poor.

The country was on fire.

The young radicals felt the fervor of revolution. Their excitement was further fueled by the recent instructions they had received. Their IRA advisor and strategist had called together the various teams operating around Montevideo. This was a strange departure from the established policies of keeping operational teams compartmentalized. The operatives complied but were somewhat confused. Everyone stopped questioning this change after being told there would be a meeting to readjust their police response strategy.

Now, gathered together in a dismal warehouse, they waited in anticipation. Only an hour ago, they had received a message that their instructor would be running late. He had been detained by last minute complications and would arrive shortly. By now, the entire facility was in a tense state and on heightened alert.

The Irishman, Martin Derry, had still not shown up. Police were setting up surprise roadblocks to conduct vehicle checks. Many wanted to go, but they were held back by the more disciplined adherents who insisted they all remain together. Documents and caches of weapons were everywhere, and everyone had taken a serious risk to be here. But if they left now, they weren't sure they'd get the chance to meet again.

BOOM!

An explosion. The thunderous blast shook the whole structure, the noise and concussive shock nearly paralyzing them. A thick cloud of smoke quickly filled the room. The blinding fog caused a powerful burning sensation. Though ringing ears, they heard the big steel door being smashed open, followed by the sound of boots running across the floor.

Instantly, everyone knew what was happening. The Policía Nacional de Uruguay, Uruguay's national police, swarmed into the warehouse decked out in black tactical fatigues, body armor, and gas masks. With M-4 carbines held in the tactical ready position, they moved to engage the radicals.

The paralytic state of the guerrillas lasted only a few seconds. Their defensive senses kicked in quickly, and they were running for their weapons. The smoke still clogging the air made it nearly impossible to see.

Choking and blinded, the guerrillas somehow managed to mount a resistance. Many of the radicals grabbed weapons, firing in the general direction of the black swarm rushing through the door.

Receiving fire, the already tense police returned their own well-aimed fusillade as they moved across the room, engaging their quarry. The building erupted into a wild gunfight as the two elements clashed with each other. The guerrillas continued to put up a fight, but smoke, shock, and surprise had taken their toll.

The police fanned out in a line with the men alternating shooters to create cover as they approached the guerrillas. Aside from the Spartan collection of tables and chairs provided for the evening's meeting, the warehouse was empty, offering no cover. Well-aimed shots by the police led to one radical after another being cut down.

Fueled by a toxic mixture of adrenaline and anger, the police were in no mood to show mercy to the animals who had murdered their friends and colleagues while terrorizing their country.

Army commander Ernesto Guevero had received intelligence from a source only hours earlier. An individual, unknown but possessing detailed information about the guerrillas, made contact with his office. Describing himself as a *concerned citizen,* this individual had an in-depth knowledge of the guerrilla operation.

Normally, Guevero would have demanded a thorough vetting of such a source, but the desperation and the utter lack of any other information on the guerrillas forced Guevero's hand. He forwarded the information to the police who, desperate for a break on the terrorists, wasted no time assembling and mobilizing their forces.

Finding themselves embroiled in an all-out gun battle with a well-armed group, the police could only presume they had finally caught the leftist-phantoms who had been terrorizing the entire country. Outside, the police leadership gathered around the hastily erected command post. They listened nervously to the massive exchange of gunfire and the erratic yelling of the engaged police screaming over the radio. One of the senior officers was dutifully monitoring a phone set up to go directly to the presidential palace. He continually briefed members at the highest levels of authority who were anxiously standing by for every detail of the operation.

In back of the nominal perimeter, crowds of onlookers began to form. Behind them, the vans and trucks carrying the logos of the various news stations appeared.

It was apparent to everyone huddled within the makeshift command center that this was going to be a highly contentious situation. It wasn't long before the media vehicles parked, and the area was littered with cameramen followed by polished looking reporters. Other onlookers were a mixture of excited gawkers and angry protesters. All of them were intent on being as difficult as possible.

Inside, the operation turned into an all-out war as the two sides fired a hail of bullets at each other. Even though the radicals fought with AK models that carried the larger caliber 7.62 rounds, and the police were using M-4 models with the smaller 5.56 rounds, the radicals were quickly being routed by the better trained, better-prepared police.

With literally nothing to use for cover, the radicals fell in large numbers. The operation was turning into a bloodbath.

The bewildered guerrillas were frantic and, although they were intoxicated with adrenaline, they could only fall back and keep shooting as the black-suited figures quickly overran their ranks.

In a last desperate act, one of the guerrillas dropped to the ground and turned over. Fumbling with her jacket pocket, she managed to produce one of the grenades she had been given at the training camp. Unscrewing the cap from the bottom of the wooden stick, she let the cap drop as a string slithered across the palm of her hand.

She could feel the steps of the advancing tactical figures as they pounded toward her. Holding the string tightly, she curled up until she felt a powerful hand grabbing her shoulder. With a hard tug, she rolled over to face a masked figure kneeling over her. The figure didn't notice the object clutched in her hand. Within a second the sound of gunfire was muted by the thunderous blast.

Fragments of the grenade fired off in all directions. Those not caught in the immediate blast were caught in the following blanket of sharp fragments that tore into their bodies like so many throwing knives.

Martin Derry could hear the gunfire in the distance. Rubbing his head, he sighed quietly as he listened. His absence at the warehouse had been by design. The young Spanish Contessa, who retained his services, had explained that it was time for the operation to end. His instructions were to gather the remaining members of the group — those who had been dispatched to operate in the city and have them housed collectively in a location that would prove easy for the police to raid.

She also explained that the meeting was to be a break from protocol and have both an assortment of weapons and documents that the police could obtain. Knowing the whole time this was the inevitable end, the Irishman had planned this moment well.

The explosion of the grenade, a sound he had heard so many times before, seemed to paralyze the people around him. He was not surprised to see the younger people in shock and stopped cold by the frightening sound. The older generation, those who remembered the horrible violence of the 1970s, remained indomitable, displaying only a look of disappointment. Their displeasure was not for the fighting going on just a few blocks away. It was the worry that the brief decades they had enjoyed peace and safety was about to vanish.

It was the same look he had seen when he was an operator in Ireland. The younger crowds, not used to fighting, jumped in fear at the sounds of gunfire and occasional bombs. The older generations, who had lived so long with the violence, merely responded as they had been conditioned, going about their day's business as if nothing had happened.

His watch read 2330hrs; the shooting was dying down. The shots still being heard were overwhelmingly 5.56's, the caliber used by the police. One could only surmise that the guerrillas were losing and dying in large numbers. The heavy firefight lasting so long told the Irishman enough. He had been in several such fights over the years, and he was all too familiar with how they ended. The Contessa's demands were being carried out exactly as she wished. What was once the fearsome guerrilla army waging war against the *capitalist oppressors* was now a bloody pile of corpses.

Derry waited silently to board a cargo freighter that would take him home. He had mixed feelings. He had set up his own students — kids he had spent months training. Kids he had led in several operations against the police and the powers that be. Now he was standing by listening to the final shots of their last stand.

His other feelings, those of the professional mercenary, were that this wasn't his war. His only reason for being associated with these people was that he was being paid.

Either way, the point was moot. This was his last thought on the matter.

He snapped up his P-coat and walked the gangplank

onto the vessel. His job was completed, and he had confirmation of his payment being made to his bank account.

Illana Muricia had made it a practice to enjoy her afternoons at the coffee shop. Unlike many of her college associates, she avoided the trendy places catering to the latest fads. She found tranquility and peace in the small little shop frequented by old retirees. The old men who had served out their careers in the police force or the military and had not succumbed to an over-fondness for adult beverages.

She found comfort in dealing with men who approached her with a fatherly, paternalistic demeanor and seemed at home with their natural manliness. The younger men seemed too caught up with being *tortured artists* and whining about being *misunderstood* which she considered nothing more than annoying bullshit.

However, this afternoon, Muricia found the shop nearly empty except for the shopkeeper and a couple of his close friends. It was not unusual. It was a time when most of the men enjoyed fishing. She expected them to wander in later, either with tales of catching *the big one* or muttering about their bait betraying them, and she found their stories amusing.

The quiet shop gave her time to enjoy reading. Settling into a small table with her coffee and lime cake, she peered out the large glass window overlooking the street. She reached into her canvass bag to pull out a beaten paperback. It was a Spanish copy of Jack Kerouac's *Dharma.* She began reading while enjoying sips of her coffee.

She became aware of a young woman who casually

entered the establishment and stared at the counter. Even though she continued reading, she kept an eye on unfamiliar people. When the woman took a seat opposite from her, Illana Muricia didn't bother to raise her head or exhibit the slightest curiosity.

"Illana Muricia, I presume?" The woman opened with a somewhat friendly but still direct manner.

Muricia lifted her eyes slightly to meet the woman's gaze. The woman was beautiful and had a great figure. Despite the fact she hid her golden hair by tying it up and covered her body with a loose-fitting T-shirt under an even looser sweater, it was obvious this was not the woman's natural look or choice of apparel. However, she did wear it well, and a casual observer would assume she was a college student.

The woman waited for a response; there was none. Muricia continued watching the stranger before her. The woman cracked a smile of satisfaction.

Muricia finally responded in an unamused tone. "You came here to find me."

"Yes, I did," the golden-haired woman responded, her smile growing wider. "I've been watching you for a while."

Muricia lowered her eyes to focus on her book. "I know. I saw you observing me from across the street. You waited until I sat down to come in here. What I find so interesting is that you could have caught me on the street. Instead, you chose to follow me to this place. Then you came in here to make your presence known. I was assuming you would have ordered a drink and found some excuse to casually talk to me."

The golden-haired woman was impressed. Especially since the young lady before her continued to seem unamused by all the intrigues. "Illana Muricia, you are the daughter of a very successful and wealthy corporate lawyer who deals with an international clientele. You currently attend an Uruguay university but have graduated from elite boarding schools in France and Spain. You are intending to transfer to the London School of Economics. In between semesters you clerk for your father and accompany him on his business trips around the world."

The college student maintained her stoic expression, still unmoved by the woman before her. The golden-haired lady continued, "What I find most intriguing about you is the relationship you have with your uncle. Your father's brother has enjoyed a rather illustrious career in the army. He has, in his own right, developed an impressive international resume with missions all around the world. In fact, he and your father have, on occasion, worked together in the service of not so legitimate clients for not so legal business."

Muricia's focus remained on her book. "I'm a little unsure what I'm expected to do at this point? Is this the part where I'm supposed to start acting concerned about something or become angry and behave in an undignified fashion over such accusations?"

By now, the golden-haired woman was becoming quite impressed with the young woman before her. She was unflinching in her behavior. She didn't act like a spoiled brat by shrieking and whining. Nor was she the slightest bit intimidated by the amount of knowledge the mysterious woman was displaying. "No, this is the part where I offer you a job."

Throwing her book on the table, with an exasperated look on her face, Muricia was now irritated at the unwanted companion. "What makes you think I'm looking for a job, especially, with a woman who follows me around, sits down at my table uninvited and proceeds to try to intimidate me with my own biography?"

"I can offer you something you can't get in your current position. A chance to break out on your own with a career and prospects for your own business," the golden-haired woman replied.

The college student said nothing. She studied her visitor's face looking momentarily confused. The mysterious woman continued, "You are intelligent, observant, street-wise, and worldly. But, you are a woman in a man's world. Your father tortures you with the highest education, experience in the world of business, world travel experiences and yet, like many fathers in our world, they still see us as their little princesses being groomed to marry a prince. You know that your father, like your uncle, has given you a taste of a world you can thrive in. But in the end, they will still only let you be an intern with expectations that you become someone's wife."

"And what are you after?" Muricia looked both confused and interested.

"I don't expect you to just trust a perfect stranger who is wearing a disguise and accosts you in your favorite place," the golden-haired woman smiled. "I am the Contessa Selena de Alvarez. The name should mean nothing to you. I was able to find out a lot about you through your father and uncle's business dealings. No doubt you have the means to vet me.

"I am looking for a *right-hand man,* so to speak for my business, which at present, is expanding. I'm not in an industry that allows me to place want ads and set up interviews. I have to rely on my own recruitment."

Muricia tapped her fingers on the table. Seeing that a response was not forthcoming, the Contessa reached into the small purse she carried and produced a small paper card. She slid it across the table toward the college student.

"This is the place I'm currently staying in Montevideo," the Contessa said pleasantly. "I will be there until tomorrow evening. If you are interested in charting your own course, I look forward to continuing this discussion in a more dignified setting. Otherwise, when I leave to catch my flight, my offer and interest in you expires."

Rising from the table, the mysterious woman casually turned and made her way out the door.

Muricia looked at the card now in her hand. Crossing the street, the Contessa began walking away confident she had found the candidate to become her second in command.

CHAPTER 39

The fishing trawler bobbing pleasantly along rolled with the ocean waves that rippled against it. For the three commandos, it was quite enjoyable to be in a boat on the water soaking up the warm sun rather than having to prepare for a mission.

The same could not be said for Micha Cohen, who was concerned about receptions from the transmitter. The commandos had been outside the marina for over an hour and heard nothing from the bugs Kafka had placed on Straudner's yacht. It was equally irritating for the katza to watch his operatives lounge about in nothing but their jeans. Shirtless and barefoot, the three men lounged in lawn chairs, nursing bottles of beer, and fiddling with fishing rods brought to the operation. Earlier they had been attentive in assisting the old fisherman who owned the boat with casting his netting into the water. As it turned out, all three found common ground in growing up with families who earned their living as fishermen.

"Just remember, this isn't your real job," Cohen scolded

the young men who were having too much fun reliving their childhoods.

Just then, the transmitter came alive with the sound of men talking. "At least we got the right ship," Dayan spoke up with a sense of triumph.

"Or, this is going to turn out to be a bunch of fat investor types, who we get to hear lie about their sex lives," Cohen snapped back as he placed his ear close to the transmitter.

The reception was good, but it was obvious the conversation was being held outside. Between the sound of the wind and the changing proximity of people walking around, it was difficult to make out what was being said or how many were present.

The fishing boat went silent as everyone strove to listen. Finally, voices became more coherent when someone, they guessed to be Straudner, announced they were taking off. Excitedly, like a commander preparing his troops for war, Cohen leaped to his feet and began issuing orders.

First, he instructed the old fisherman to prepare to move. Then, turning his attention to his three commandos, he barked orders for them to raise the net and get their shirts on immediately. All three responded with a salute and the appropriate response expected from their navy origins.

The katza was annoyed to find himself being compared to Captain Blye in Dutch, Hebrew, and English. However, their retorts failed to deter him, as he continued issuing orders to his less than enthusiastic crew.

The old fisherman signaled to the others that he saw a large ship exiting the marina. Everyone looked to see a sleek yacht moving toward open water. It was the yacht Dayan had infiltrated only a few nights before. As the ship emerged out onto the open sea, it made a gradual turn to the left and started in a northwesterly direction.

Dayan felt vindicated when the yacht turned enough to reveal the name Sunset Glory on the back. His vindication was further strengthened by the conversation coming across the transmitter. The voices briefly broached the subject of a government takeover.

Continuing to snap orders, Cohen commanded the fisherman to follow the yacht. By now, the commandos had hoisted the netting back into the boat and prepared everything to move. Luckily, the fishing boat was part of a collection of five or six other such crafts and was some distance away. Fishing boats were a commonality in these waters and generally looked the same to other boaters. It made them a great choice for this type of surveillance work. However, the type of people they were pursuing was not inclined to ignore a single fishing boat if it kept showing up in the vicinity as the yacht.

The Sunset Glory moved at a swift pace and was gaining distance quickly. Looking through his binoculars, Dayan saw the man whose picture he had studied so carefully over the last few weeks. It was the politician, Oskar Straudner, at the helm. Continuing his visual recce, Dayan was able to catch a good look at the few guests on board.

Beckoning the katza with an urgent wave, Dayan was extremely excited. Joining Dayan, the old spy took up the binoculars and focused in the direction pointed out to him. Within seconds his eyes widened when he saw the all too familiar image of Ali Anwar al Qalmini.

Cohen promptly demanded the craft get underway. The fisherman did as ordered but grimaced — aggravated at being given commands on his own boat. At one point, the commandos considered how they were going to keep the two older men from killing each other as tempers flared.

With the netting and other components stowed aboard, the motor revved and the fishing boat started to move faster. Snaking its way out of the cluster of vessels used for concealment, it progressed rapidly into the open water.

The yacht, by this time, was also moving quickly, becoming a speck in the distance. Thankfully, the transmitter was still receiving fragments of the conversation not masked by the sounds of the waves crashing against the ship's hull or the wind cutting against its aft. With Straudner steering, it was hoped that the important business was not being transacted at the moment, and the ship would be stopped when they finally started discussing their plans.

For an old, beaten up fishing vessel, the craft moved at a deceptively fast pace. It could not quite equal the yacht it pursued, but the fisherman managed to keep the yacht in sight.

It was almost an hour later, and the chase continued. The yacht made a few unpredictable turns — a clear attempt to thwart any tagalongs. Nevertheless, the old fisherman proved to be extremely adept at this business and was able to navigate well enough not to be noticed.

Some 12 miles out, the yacht came to a stop. Now, well into international waters and better protected from prying eyes, the ship's occupants felt safe to speak more freely. The sounds of the wind and waves had died down considerably, and the conversation coming across the transmitter was much clearer.

The fisherman cut his own engines, and the commandos

immediately cast the large fishing net into the water and set up everything to appear like they were fisherman looking for a new spot.

Cohen was now glued to the transmitter while Dayan moved inside and began looking through his binoculars to try to get a better look at the ship's occupants. The distance was too great, and he could only make out enough to know they were still monitoring the right ship.

Returning outside, Dayan caught what seemed like the beginning of a conversation. The transmitter was picking up a much better signal. The yacht's occupants had ceased moving about and seemed to be settled around an outside table.

"We are all set," began an accented voice they presumed was Qalmini's. "Our forces can gradually begin moving across the border into Uruguay. They will first set up in the staging locations established in the city. Then, they will move to locations in the countryside where we presume resistance is most likely to emerge."

"The riots on campus and in the poorer sections of the city have given the appearance of a country out of control," a polished, more refined voice, thought to be Straudner's replied. "Since the leftist guerrillas have been dispatched, they will keep the fire alive. My supporters in the wealthier areas and among the security services are already calling on me to assert authority and bring order to chaos. Since the police have been heavy-handed in dealing with rioters, it has only stoked the fires. I intend to *reluctantly* call for martial law and assume control of the country in the following month."

"The first wave of your support militia will be on the

road in a few days," the accented voice added. "They'll move across the border in numbers of fifty to a hundred. Once crossed, they'll be met by smaller hauling trucks that can move them in numbers of ten to twenty. Slowly, we should be able to insert our people into position. But, I still don't want my men lingering too long where the prospect of unexpected trouble becomes more real."

Straudner's voice took over the conversation. "Assume at the beginning of next month, I will announce my call for a military takeover, suspension of parliamentary proceedings and courts. The only problem will be Mojica, our current president. It wouldn't do to assume control of the country while the current president is still in place. Arresting him will only erode the legitimacy of my ascension and give opposition and pesky outsiders like the UN a reason to interfere. He will have to be dealt with."

"That can be arranged," Qalmini replied. "Let me know when he will be at his home the evening prior, and he will meet his end at the hands of leftist radicals. It has been my experience that killing a man on his little chicken farm will produce a more beneficial reaction than killing him in his castle where he looks like a fallen king. It truly helps to erode the opposition when they have killed a true man of the people."

"Good," Straudner was again speaking. "My people, whom I have gathered into my inner circle, have already begun moving into place. The military and police barracks in and around the city will be placed on alert upon my speech to the populace. Regarding political opponents and other individuals who could be perceived as threats, I would prefer the militia you are furnishing to deal with them.

Arresting legitimate politicians and journalists would not endear our cause to the greater numbers in the country. It would be better if they were rounded up and eliminated by non-government entities. I will have the military attending to the riots and restoring order."

Qalmini responded, "That is reasonable. With the president gone, and our combined forces firmly controlling the city and the countryside, how long do you think it will take to quell the opposition?"

"Quell, is not the word I would use," Straudner spoke up. "The opposition I was concerned about is gone, and the rabble I'm dealing with now is so disorganized they will not be much of a threat once dealt with properly. We just need to apply pressure and move quickly to make sure no base exists for a resistance to form. My concern will be what else this *patriotic militia* is going to take control of."

Cohen and the commandos listened in near shock as the plan unfolded. The coup was moving faster than they had anticipated. As the transmitter continued relaying Straudner's and Qalmini's plans, Cohen ruminated, Dayan bit his lip, and the fishing boat began to feel like a mortuary.

After an hour, the conversation finally ended. The two men were heard leaving the table and a few minutes later they heard the sound of the yacht's engine purring to life. In the distance, they could see the yacht begin to move.

At first, Ripley wanted to catch up with them on the open water and eliminate them when they were the most vulnerable. Dayan cautioned against this plan, pointing out they didn't have the necessary equipment. In addition, they may have heard more than two voices originally and hadn't gotten a good look at who was actually on board the yacht. It would have been a dangerous gamble to try something with so many variables working against them.

Ripley reluctantly agreed, as did Cohen and Vanderhook. They had what they'd come for. Oskar Straudner was their target, and he was the key figure in the Iranian's plan. The question now was what was their next step?

CHAPTER 40

Zamora listened from his vantage point to the combination of his people speaking to each other and the random shots fired when they found a survivor. The Colombian nodded with satisfaction. His training had paid off. The natural, instinctive disdain he held for any government soldiers made the killings feel more like vindication than murder.

The assaulters had been eager to engage the military after they had heard about the attacks carried out by the Soldiers of Retribution — a retaliatory group. These terror attacks were carried out against the workers of Uruguay, the people Zamora's students were fighting for. What made it worse were articles from recently formed underground newspaper asserting that this new vigilante group was an instrument created by the army to inflict retribution and intimidation.

When the recruits at the camp were given this information, they were livid and demanded revenge. What was not known to anyone was that the mysterious underground newspaper was being bankrolled from secret accounts controlled by a foreign business interest under Selena de Alvarez.

Alyssa Rios shuddered at the knock on her door. Glancing at Malia, who had a look of horror on her face, she reached for her gun and held it tightly to her body. She angled the weapon in the direction of the entryway. For a moment, there was silence. Both women stayed focused on the door thinking it might have been a person with a wrong address. Then the knocking resumed, this time harder and with the confidence of one who knew they were in the right location.

Malia looked at her employer, who was clutching her firearm tightly in the tactical pose she had learned years ago at Quantico. She had used this pose many times in her law enforcement career. With no side windows to see who was at the door, the two women could only wait. The pounding continued, loud and hard. The person outside had no intention of leaving.

Finally, a woman, who looked to be in her late forties emerged from an upstairs room and quickly came down the staircase. Rushing to the other women, she whispered. "Sẽnor Genti is in position across the street."

Rios sighed with relief at the news. Sẽnor Esteban Genti was a former sniper with the Colombian army. He had seen action many times, both in the jungles fighting guerrillas and in the city, when he was a part of joint counter-narcotics operations with the US. As a side business, he took money under the table to ply his trade and provide additional security for legitimate business people who were threatened by the country's more violent criminal elements. Holding a small mobile phone, the older woman handed it to Rios.

"Esteban, are you there?" She asked nervously.

"Yes, Sẽnora," replied the man. "I have your knocker in my sights. Stay to his left when you engage him. I'll watch for your signal."

Feeling a sense of assurance, Rios walked toward the door. Carefully, she wrapped a hand towel around her gun. If it were an attacker, the towel would mask the gun. He wouldn't notice the gun immediately and try to take away her only protection. This way, she still had a chance. If attacked, she could use her gun and shoot him while he was on top of her.

The person continued to bang loud and hard. Rios approached the door. Behind her, Malia and the older woman followed, each having acquired some instrument to use as a weapon. Positioning herself to the left, as instructed, she prepared to open the door. The two other women had taken up defensive positions in a corner on the other side.

With a deep breath to calm her nerves, Rios reached for the knob and, with a twist, opened it wide. With her gun, wrapped in the towel, she was prepared. With the door flung open, the man she knew as *Mr. Herron* stood outside.

Standing her ground, the veteran former drug enforcement agent studied the man before her. *How did he find her? What was he here for? Could he have been the one who sent the attackers to her office? Was she a loose end?* These questions raced through her mind as she quickly analyzed the situation.

Realizing what was going on, Dayan stood still and maintained a casual manner. He was cognizant of the fact she was deliberately avoiding being lined up with his frame. It could only mean a sniper had positioned himself across the street and possibly had his sights on him. Looking down at the towel clutched tightly to the woman's body, he figured she had a gun. In any case, he was fully aware he was the one in danger if he made the wrong move.

Watching Mr. Herron, who had extended his arms and pressed his hands against the sides of the door frame leaving his jacket open to show he had no gun within easy reach, Rios was satisfied she was not in immediate danger. Keeping her gun on him, she nodded to Genti that it was okay.

"May I come in?" The Israeli asked quietly.

Nodding her head, Rios stepped back into the house, keeping a good distance between her and Herron. Entering slowly, the Israeli was noticed the two other women standing off to the side. Both women were clutching pieces of furniture they obviously intended to use as weapons if needed. They looked horrified at the thought of possibly having to do so.

"I'm shutting the door now," Dayan said. His hands were still up and away from his body. "If that's all right with you."

Rios nodded. Turning slightly, the Israeli pushed the door closed quietly. He turned back to face the former head of what had been GAI. Her posture had not changed. Her weapon was still fixed on him, and her expression was one of grave suspicion.

"How did you find me?" Rios snapped.

"You're not the only intelligence service I employ for my purposes," the Israeli responded.

"Why are you here?" Rios snapped again.

Dayan lowered his arms. "I still need your services."

The woman glared at him with hatred. "My business is in shambles. My office is now rubble. Someone sent professional killers after me. And somehow, I think it has something to do with you. Or maybe those killers were sent by you. Are we loose ends you now need to clean up?"

"I didn't send any killers," the Israeli replied quietly. He was acutely aware that the other two women still stood ready to pounce on him at any moment. "And if those who attacked your office were because of me, then I'm sorry. I can offer some compensation."

Rios said nothing. She stood looking the man over trying to analyze the situation. Finally, she spoke. "What sort of help do you still need?" Her attention was slightly diverted by the shocked look from the other two women — they looked as if their boss had just lost her mind.

Dayan sighed. "I need you to spy on someone — a politician in Uruguay."

This time Rios gave the Israeli an irritated look. "I'm on the run right now. How do you expect me to complete such an assignment?"

"You have built a good business in a risky line of work," the Israeli replied. "A line of work that requires flexibility and adaptability. Your networks are still in existence, and I doubt you discarded your lists of contacts."

"Suppose you're right," Rios said. "Why would I continue to work for you? Part of being flexible is also knowing when to walk away. And, everything says I should walk."

Dayan nodded. "I agree. I would tell you that you should point to the door and tell me to leave at once. However, you're going to need seed money, and I'm willing to pay a great deal for what I'm asking — one and a half million US."

Rios said nothing. She glared at *Mr. Herron* for what

seemed like forever. "You have that kind of money to throw around?"

The Israeli chuckled. "You know I do. I have paid you hundreds of thousands so far for your services. As desperate as I am right now, and for the quality of the work you have delivered, I believe it would not be unreasonable."

"How do I know you were not the one who tried to have me and my people killed in the first place?" Rios continued to glare bitterly.

"How do you know the attack on your office had anything to do with me?" Dayan replied, maintaining his calm demeanor, despite the hostility surrounding him. "My other resources allowed me to find you here in your safe house. I would have had the resources and certainly an easier time to kill you here."

With another sigh, the former law enforcement officer lowered her weapon. Whether the Arabic-looking man was the cause that led to the attack or whether he was the one who initiated it was now irrelevant. If a veteran operator had the means to send skilled assassins the first time, he could have easily sent them again to her less guarded safe house.

Nodding her head, Rios looked the man over one last time. "Who's the politician? And it's two million US or use your other sources."

The Israeli smiled. "Deal. The name is Oskar Vlak Straudner."

With a slight nod, Surriman raised his eyes and looked from one side to the other. "Now everything is fine. The weapons will all look like they came directly from a U.S. arsenal or Russian factory directly to you."

Both Iranians sighed a breath of relief. "Did you bring a specimen back for our review?" Akim asked.

"No," Surriman replied. "An American made military assault rifle was not something I was going to risk-taking across the border. It was dangerous enough if it was an obvious surplus from the cold war. But modernized armaments were guaranteed to be reported to domestic intelligence if discovered by an honest and experienced border guard. So, no, I didn't. But I do understand your need for personal verification. Which is why I arranged the first shipment early — early enough so that you can conduct your own tests. If you discover any problems, we can rectify them before the next shipment comes."

"How did you manage that?" Essouri asked.

Waving his hand as if gathering his words Surriman replied. "The first shipment will be small. Thirty-to-forty weapons consisting of samples of all the types specified. If the weapons meet your approval, then the second shipment will be larger. Because I can vouch for the quality, the rest will be stockpiled with markings and specific identifiers left off so we can make the necessary markings. If you have problems with more than the markings, I have already taken the precaution of reaching out to a few other neighboring villages that also specialize in this industry. I don't like risking a greater chance of a security breach, but they will be able to make up the time and keep the supply on schedule."

Essouri and Akim glanced at each other. It was apparent they had recruited the right man for this mission. Surriman pressed further into the spine of the chair as he slowly eyed the two Iranians. "The next step? I'm presuming we are ready to start coordinating it?"

The two majors looked at each other for a moment and gave a mutual nod to the other. "We start preparing now for the movement portion of the plan," Essouri replied.

CHAPTER 41

The Ronin Club looked almost deserted. Obviously, mid-afternoon was not the best time for the establishment. All the better, thought Nouri al' Marak Surriman as he watched from an alley across the way. On orders from Qalmini, he had been sent to Bogota to check up on a private intelligence firm that had been spying on them. The firm, through some debacle not explained to him, had gone up in smoke. The question of who they were working for still lingered.

Surriman figured that someone wouldn't pay for that kind of intelligence unless they were planning something in response. He also believed that if they were using the resources of a private intelligence agency as opposed to a government intelligence organization, they were working outside of any government authority. It was a safe assumption that they were working through the black market to operate.

With nothing else to go on, he also assumed it was a safe guess that the people who had attacked the training camp a few weeks ago were, most likely, the same people who hired the intelligence firm. Since the attack and infiltration were done by people with extensive military training, this was an easy deduction for the Arab. These mysterious people threatening their operation had to have used mercenaries. Since this was not the type of business for legitimate private companies, the only possible avenue one could use to recruit such professionals was through an old-fashioned merc broker.

Prevailing upon his friends to tap into their contacts around the city, it wasn't long before one name came to his attention — Ian Ferry or 'Plūcker' as he was called. Talking up several freelancers, Surriman learned that the Irishman had indeed been doing some recruiting only a few months earlier for some undisclosed job. Ian had been tight-lipped about who he was recruiting for, but the rumor was he had been working for some Middle-Eastern type. Several of the young guys looking for some exciting work hoped the Arab/Israeli stuff was finding its way to Colombia and would provide employment in an upcoming covert war. Surriman was sure he had found his avenue to locate their secret enemy.

Surriman found that such *Middle-Eastern* types had been seen coming and going quite often over the last few months and were taken directly to the back rooms upon arrival. It was too coincidental — he had to be on the right track. Realizing this Irishman was no kid off the block and would likely be cognizant of any suspicious-looking characters, the Arab chose to bide his time for a few days and watch the man's establishment from a distance. His hopes were to catch sight of the types of men coming in or going out. After several days of watching without any luck, he decided to apply more direct means.

Keppa and Avi joined him for this expedition. He sent them to hire some local muscle for assistance. With their connections to the Bogota underworld, they soon returned with a couple of guys who were known to do freelance assassinations for the cartels. Directing them to case the place, Surriman was impressed when they returned with good, viable intelligence regarding the overlay of the premise. Their detail was exceptional, and their assessment of the Irishman and his staff was quite well done. They even noted that their target seemed to catch onto them relatively early. Both men cautioned their current employer not to send them in again unless the intention was more than reconnaissance.

Reviewing the information from the Colombians and from his own observations, Surriman hashed out his plan of attack. Standing across the street, the Arab casually sauntered toward the doors of the Ronin Club. Opening the door carefully, he stepped inside. Just as it had been described by his Colombians, the place looked like something out a spy novel. Aside from a few elderly looking pensioner types sitting at a table in a far-off corner, the bar was deserted. Taking a seat at the edge of the bar, he waited. It wasn't long before the Irishman walked over to him. An immediate glare denoted the barkeep's suspicions.

"What will ya have, sir?" Plūcker asked in his deep Fenian brogue.

"Just a beer, thanks," Surriman replied, nonchalantly. Ignoring the Irishman, he focused his attention on a bowl of peanuts an arm's length away. The Irishman's obvious, assessing gaze was not lost on him.

Reaching for a long glass mug, the Irishman tipped it under one of the tap nozzles. The sound of the tap gurgled as the liquid poured into the glass. Seconds later, Surriman was staring at a mug filled with a gold-colored brew.

Plūcker had known the man for only a few minutes and determined he was of Middle-Eastern descent and no run of the mill patron. This man had seen action and lots of it. Most likely, he was a special operations type by the way he carried himself. Not wanting to engage in any conversation with the stranger, he turned and started to walk away.

"Ah, one more thing," the Arab, waved him down again.

The Irishman turned to face the customer. "I'm looking for work, and I was wondering who's hiring around here?"

Shaking his head slowly, Plūcker responded. "For someone with your skills, there is not much available right now."

"I haven't told you my skills," the Arab replied with a smile painted across his face.

Plūcker licked his lips. "Oh, boyo, you've told me plenty. I can tell by your looks, your casual demeanor, and the way you sized me up just now. You're fresh off a battlefield. My guess, commin' home from the war over in the desert lands, Iraq or Syria, maybe. You approached this place slow and cautious. And, you scoped this establishment out before sitting down — as if you wanted to see the resistance you'd be up against if there was trouble. My guess is you already have work in the field you're lookin' for."

"Possibly. Then you might be a little paranoid from years fighting in the streets of Belfast, or was it Portadown? Then again, it could be from too much swimming in the pool of sharks around here," the Arab replied a look of arrogant amusement on his face.

The Irishman was sure the Arab was no kid off the block. Just as he was equally sure he didn't like him. Moving closer to the unwanted patron, Plūcker assumed a more intimidating pose. He also looked closely to see if he could note any potential weapons on the man. He couldn't see any.

Surriman maintained his calm demeanor even as the barkeep neared him. Slowly reaching into his inside jacket pocket, he pulled out his cell phone. Pressing on the plastic coating, he looked to catch a text message he just received. It was from Keppa informing him that they were in position. Placing the phone back in his pocket, he looked back at the figure towering over him.

"I think you'd better leave now," the Irishman said in a low authoritative voice.

Unintimidated, the Arab glanced back at the barkeep. "I haven't finished my drink or my business."

At that moment, the tension was interrupted by the sound of a loud bang echoing from the back of the bar. For a few brief seconds, Plūcker was distracted. Realizing something was happening, he turned his back on the Arab. He started to unfold his arms with the intent to attack. Suddenly, he was stopped by the sound of two loud explosions going off in rapid succession. He noticed the Arab had one hand under the counter from which a plume of gray smoke began to emerge. He unexpectedly detected the smell he had become all too familiar with over the years — the odor that came from ignited gunpowder. Lowering his head, he saw his white apron turning red with his blood. Lifting his head, he saw the Arab slide out of his chair and step back. In his hand, he held a gun. It was a gray, Sig model .45 caliber.

Assuming that the Irishman would have noticed the weapon hidden under his jacket, Surriman had moved his weapon to his belt at the small of his back. When the Irishman's back was turned, Surriman carefully slipped the gun in the bend of his knee to make it more accessible when the Irishman was distracted.

Coming to his senses, Plūcker realized there were gunshots going off in the back room. He began to fear for his waitress, who had been working there.

"Friends of mine," Surriman interrupted his thoughts, "just clearing the backrooms while I keep you busy here."

Plūcker began to feel the pain of his wounds, and they were excruciating. He looked over at the Arab and started for him. But the sight of the raised gun pointed in his direction stopped him cold.

Surriman took a quick glance over at the two pensioners. They were cowering in the corner, their heads turned, hoping not to be seen as potential witnesses to the violence. Confident they were no threat, he focused on the barkeep, who was hunched over in pain. "All right, I had hoped not to involve you in this business. But I'm pressed for time. I need to know who you have been recruiting mercenaries for."

"I-I don't know..." Plūcker tried to speak but he was cut off.

"Please don't give me that shit," the Arab said calmly. "If I believed that, I wouldn't be here. Start again."

"Go to hell! Argh," Plūcker attempted to speak.

His tough words this time met with another explosive sound of a gunshot. This time the bullet was fired through his shoulder.

"This macho shit is getting old," Surriman said, still keeping a cool demeanor. "While I have never enjoyed torture or needless killing, I honestly can't say that I feel too guilty about torturing you. My understanding is that you were with Billy Wright and his Loyalist Volunteer Force when they broke with their parent UVF."

Plūcker grunted bitterly but gave no response. Surriman continued, "I wouldn't speak with pride either. Your concept of war was to unleash unbridled terror upon Irish Catholics in the hopes they'd come forward and give up the local IRA in your area. How many innocents died because of your mere suspicions? People who just wanted to live their lives in peace, and you sucked them into your violence?"

"We were soldiers fighting a war!" The Irishman growled bitterly.

Surriman smirked. "That's what they all say in the end, isn't it? It was a war, you wouldn't understand. Well, I have seen war and a lot of it. I still saw my enemy by what they did on the battlefield, not what religious or ethnic group they belonged to. I never deliberately killed those who were simply caught in a conflict they'd rather not be a part of."

The pain was faster in coming as the Irishman's shoulder was now feeling like it was on fire. Surriman moved up against the wall to prevent anyone from sneaking up on him or getting a view of his victim. He also had a better view of the room and a clear view to the outside. He heard the movement of his men as they made their way to him.

"Again, who were you recruiting for a few months ago?" Surriman asked. "And your tough guy shit is going to make things worse for you, I promise."

Plūcker was no longer replying to his tormentor. He began to heave deep breaths in between gritting his teeth in agony. At that moment, the back doors flew open and out came Avi with one of his Colombians in tow.

"We found some stuff," Avi said as he met his boss's eyes. "They have documents and dossiers on some of our people. These guys have definitely been investigating us. What's more, they have documents that were clearly stolen from us — reports, timelines."

"Anything giving us a clue to who it is we're dealing with?" Surriman asked somberly.

Avi shrugged. "We haven't had a chance to look through everything thoroughly."

Surriman said nothing. He pointed his finger at the Irishman where he knelt on the floor. With a nod, Avi waved at the Colombian to deal with the barkeep. As ordered, the Colombian walked over to the injured man. Producing a menacing-looking knife, he wasted no time as he jabbed it deep into the Irishman's cheek.

Plūcker howled in pain, as he fought to remove the painful object from the side of his face. With one arm wounded and his strength greatly diminished from loss of blood, he was too weak to fight. The Colombian easily overpowered him while continuing to dig the knife ever deeper.

Surriman watched the event before him with a look of indifference. His experience had taught him that torture could lead to praying on the conscience or be easily enjoyed as payback if not regarded entirely as a tool. He had seen so much barbarity in Iraq and Syria. It had not been lost on him how easily men could get out of control wanting to exact vengeance for their friends and comrades. In doing so, they became embroiled in their own personal affairs and forgot the purpose of the exercise. He had also seen the same thing with those of a supposed more timid nature decrying humanitarian morality when the information was desperately needed. How many had Surriman seen die because civil methods of interrogation were ineffective and untimely? No, for him torture had to be a tool with a purpose. That purpose must be at the forefront of the mission at all times.

"All right. All right. I'll talk," Plūcker gasped out. Blood was oozing from the side of his face like a red waterfall. "It was some joker named Mujeeb. Don't think that's his real name, but he's the one who hired me. Said he was lookin' for some top-notch soldiers for hire. The way he was talkin', I figured it was some revolution lookin' to flare up somewhere," Plūcker looked up to see a resigned face from the Arab looking back at him. The expression sent a message of disbelief.

"Keep trying," Surriman replied. His voice was calm and reserved. "You chose a foreign name. That means you already know that we did not find you randomly. We have a pretty good idea who hired you. Let's try again."

The Colombian began twisting the knife, creating excruciating pain for the Irishman. With teeth gritted, Plūcker remained still.

"I understand the professional courtesy," the Arab spoke up. "You're a broker of troops on the black market. Men, professional soldiers, trust you and your word in this murky business you're enmeshed in. I'm not asking for their names. I am asking just for the names of those who are employing them. If you're hoping that you'll bleed out before we get really nasty, understand something. I've worked with all sorts of battle wounds under much worse conditions than here. I can and will keep you alive, if necessary."

Surriman walked over to where the barkeep was kept kneeling. Extending his hand, he gripped the man's wounded shoulder. The additional pain was too much for the Irishman, and he began to wail.

"I don't relish this," the Arab said softly. "I don't see this as your war. But, you have become involved in it, and I will do what I must for my side. Please know this. Even if I have to extend these methods to that young waitress who does so much for you, I will."

"Micha Cohen!" Plūcker finally cried out — his weakness now discovered.

"Good," Surriman replied. "I believe you; keep talking."

Pale-faced, with bullets of sweat running down his forehead mixing with the reddish pool of blood-forming across his shirt, the Irishman conceded defeat. "He's a rogue Israeli spy who's mounting a war against the Iranians here in South America."

"Not good enough," Surriman countered. "If that were true, he has much bigger and more visible targets that would debilitate Iran's overall presence in this region. No, he targeted our mission specifically."

"He knows about Uruguay," Plūcker managed to hiss out, as he felt himself getting colder. "They know about the overthrow."

Surriman gnashed his teeth. "This Micha Cohen. If he is a spy, he wouldn't have had the commando training that infiltrated the camp. Who's leading his assault operations?"

"Kafka Dayan," the Irishman said. This time with genuine tears in his eyes. The weight of his betrayal was heavy on him. "He's an Israeli soldier; a commando Cohen uses for missions. He leads the mercenary force they have."

Surriman maintained his composure. "How do you contact them?"

Taking another deep breath, Plūcker fought to get the words out. "He shows up and works out of here when he's in town."

The Arab thought to ask more questions. But, looking at

the pale figure slowly sinking to the floor, he concluded that further interrogation was pointless. Reaching into the Irishman's clothes, Surriman eventually found the man's phone. Handing it to Avi, he instructed him to have all the numbers checked and go into the office to search for any disposable phones. Pulling the knife from the Irishman's cheek, Surriman rolled the weakened man's head over and, with precision, launched the sharpened steel directly into the man's brain stem. A quick jerk and the Irishman was dead.

Standing up, the Arab looked over at the two pensioners. They had stayed true to their unspoken deal, keeping their attention averted from the violent business. Deciding to keep his part of the deal, Surriman left the same way he had come in. It was not a professional move, but killing innocents was not something he liked doing.

Surriman, Keppa, and the Colombian debriefed each other in one backroom before progressing to the other backroom offices. There, they grabbed all the documents they could lay their hands on. Exiting out their initial entry point, it was only a few minutes before they returned to the bar, each carrying fuel containers. The original plan had been to blow up this enemy headquarters with explosives. However, it was deemed too risky moving around Bogota with an explosive device. It was an unnecessary risk trying to obtain a device in such unfamiliar waters as Colombia. Burning the place to the ground would accomplish the same results with fewer complications.

The Negress watched from the small opening in the rafters as the assailants drenched the back office of the establishment with gasoline. Having worked in various capacities for her boss, she had developed and rehearsed an escape plan that one day would become necessary. She watched as they set a room ablaze and made their exit. When she was sure they were gone for good, she quickly slid out from her hiding place and made her way to the floor. The flames were spreading wildly through the lake of fuel that floated around the office.

Leaping from one table to the next and inching along the walls, she choked as the smoke grew thicker and more suffocating. Fumbling clumsily, she felt around until she caught the edge of the door jam. Sliding further, she almost missed the steel doorknobs. With a turn, she flung open the doors and quickly slipped through to what she hoped was the outside.

Her first desperate gulp of air was refreshing — like water to a parched man. There was still smoke in the air, but the fire had not yet completely spread. Quickly, the Negress raced down the hall to where a decrepit looking door lay partially hidden behind a pile of boxes. The boxes appeared full and heavy, but she threw them off to the side with ease. Reaching into her pocket, she produced a set of keys. Frantically, she sorted through them until she found a small, round one. Sliding it into the lock, she turned the key and flung the door wide open.

The room was a little cubbyhole of storage space. At a glance, it looked like nothing more than accumulated junk. However, a small metallic box neatly tucked between a box of forgotten clothes and some old bar equipment caught her eye. Grabbing it, she wasted no time as she darted back toward the bar. Already the smoke in the room was becoming thicker. In the brief time it had taken her to retrieve the box, the temperature of the room had risen dramatically.

She was relieved to see the entire place was now deserted. At that point, she knew it was too early to come out of hiding. It was certainly too dangerous to go outside — not knowing if the killers might still be in the vicinity. But the fire was rapidly gaining. She could feel the heat, smell the choking odor, and hear the crackly sound of the flames that were turning the building into a hellish inferno.

Tucking the box under her arm she made for the most direct escape route — the main doors. Thrusting the thick barriers open, her instincts warned her to prepare for danger on the other side. From what she had seen, these killers were professionals. They were not the type to be easily intimidated or inclined to leave loose ends. The feeling of the afternoon sun coupled with the relief of fresh air was welcome. Her eyes darted from side to side as she scanned the streets and buildings around her. She did not stop to collect herself or assess her surroundings. Her legs kept moving swiftly as she continued to run. At that point, all she knew was that professionals had attacked her place of work and now she needed to be somewhere to hide and get off the streets.

Surriman stood on the street just out of sight. He watched as the young Negress ran the opposite way. Behind him were the rest of his team waiting for his next order. No one said anything. When she had gone some distance, he dispatched the two Colombians to follow her. They took off at a fast-paced walk keeping their distance but keeping her in sight.

From his previous reconnaissance of the bar, Surriman knew the Negress was inside. Given other gathered information, he presumed she was much more than a barmaid. She had skillfully hidden from them during the attack, and she was well versed in her employer's business affairs. When it became apparent Plūcker wasn't going to cooperate, his plan was to coax the barmaid out and see who she went running to. The Arab assumed that if these Israelis were important enough for Plūcker to suffer severe torture, it would be likely his assistant would try to make contact with them.

Instructing Avi to report back to their base camp with the retrieved documents and an account of what happened, Surriman sent Keppa to recruit more men. He cautioned Keppa to prepare for the men who were likely to be professionals and be sure to recruit only the best, most experienced men he could find and offer them $250,000 apiece. It was expensive, but the work was guaranteed to be dangerous.

The Arab was confident that, if his assumptions proved right, the results would be an inevitable bloodbath.

CHAPTER 42

Dayan didn't like it. Even though he had expressed this opinion several times, he was expressing it again. He knew it was fractious to continue arguing, but the situation went against all his professional instincts and training. Now, he and Micha Cohen were sitting on a bench in a barn-like structure in the middle of a park just outside of Buenos Aires.

"Cheer up," Cohen ordered. "Initially they wanted to have this meeting in the back corner of some low lit bar."

"Where someone following them could slip in unobserved and watch us meet," Dayan scoffed with irritation.

"Have you taken the necessary precautions?" the katza asked, as he buttoned up his coat.

Dayan leaned back against the wall and shoved his hands deep into his pockets. "The guys and I came out last night and recced the area. We found all possible ambush points, decent sniper positions, and checked for spots that might make good observation posts. I have four teams out there manning the posts that give overhead surveillance to this spot. If this is a setup, we'll be protected."

"From what I've seen so far, these little shits don't seem that intelligent," Cohen replied incredulously. "Still, open stupidity best hides quiet deception."

Dayan had only heard of the Guardians of Israel and the assassination attempt on Elloy Mendoza a few days ago. He thought their actions stupid and was angered by the danger the hoodlums had placed everyone in. Additional explanations had been provided, and now the two Israelis had to risk meeting them. The idea of having to sit down with the people whose actions had resulted in so many detrimental repercussions had nearly sent the commando into a rage. His first thought had been to ignore the street brawlers altogether. When Cohen explained that they knew too much, and there was a good possibility they would do something else to jeopardize their mission, the commando's next consideration was to kill them the moment they showed up. Cohen's diplomacy prevailed.

A voice came over the tiny microphone in Dayan's ear. It was Oskar Perez alerting him to the arrival of two men walking up the road in the direction of the barn. Acknowledging the message, Dayan unzipped the tan field coat he was wearing to give himself better access to his firearm — a 9mm Glock. Normally, for an outdoor engagement, he would have preferred a .40 caliber model, but this was not a mission where he entered expecting a gunfight. This was a meeting that could remain peaceful. He had been led to believe these were not professional operatives, but local hoodlums. If a gunfight was to take place, he figured he would be laying down a barrage of fire to cover an escape. Consequently, he went for magazine capacity over caliber size as the more practical option.

Two figures appeared at the other end of the barn; they stopped at the entry.

"Shalom," called one of the figures. The two Israelis gave each other questioning looks.

"Shalom, as well," Cohen replied. "I'm assuming we all know each other, so can we get down to business?"

"We meet in the middle," the figure commanded.

"No," Dayan chimed in, his bitterness thinly veiled. "We're good where we're at."

For what seemed like forever, no one from either side moved or spoke. It was only when the two Israelis began walking away that the two figures started walking toward them.

When the two figures were close, Dayan stepped back to maintain some distance. They were both strong, muscular looking men. Dayan wanted to stay well out of arm's reach in case things turned violent. Both men looked to be in their early twenties, possibly even younger.

Cohen approached the young men. He gave a slight nod of recognition to the larger of the two. Dayan kept his eyes fixed on both of them but stayed within grabbing distance of the katsa.

"Good day, Mr. Gold," Cohen opened the discussion with a mild pleasantry.

Gold and his cohort said nothing but kept their eyes and facial expressions cold and hard. They were clearly trying to look the part of hardened professionals in front of the two Israeli operatives.

"We want to be involved in your operation," Mr. Gold announced.

"Well," Cohen replied, "since we all know who everyone is, there is no point in trying to be evasive and play stupid."

"And, you are who exactly?" Dayan asked.

Gold turned to face the younger of the two Israelis. "We are the Guardians of Israel. We fight to defend Zionism and the Jewish people."

"Defend us? How? In South America?" the commando asked sarcastically.

Gold and his cohort both glanced back at him with annoyance. They turned to face the katsa, whom they concluded was in charge. "We are both fighting the same war against Elloy Mendoza and whoever he is working with. My organization is extensive in this country, and we can lend you a hand."

"Hand at what?" Dayan asked, exasperated. "Like you handled trying to kill the Cuban in the first place — fucking it up badly from what I've heard. And then, thanks to you, letting him and those he works with know we exist. So, how do you see yourselves helping?"

"We fight for a cause and defend the Jewish people," Gold's cohort blurted out as he glared at the commando.

Dayan shook his head and smirked, which only angered the younger men more. "How? Bar brawls with guys over anti-Semitic remarks and gang fights with Nazi assholes in the streets?"

The cohort spit back. "Like you, we are warriors fighting for a cause."

"Really," Dayan was now bordering on belligerent. "Try infiltrating the Bekka Valley sometime."

"All right!" Cohen interceded, as he regained control of the meeting. "I realize tempers are high. This is not a good time for anyone. Please, can we keep this civil?"

When everyone had composed themselves, Cohen opened the discussion again. "What exactly are you after? I know you said you wanted to be part of our operation. But to what extent? My subordinate here may not have much in the way of diplomatic skills, but he does make a point. We are not chasing skinheads or brawling in the streets. We are dealing with some well-connected professionals."

"We can handle ourselves," Again, Gold tried to display an image of the tough professional.

"You say this," the katsa replied. "But your actions so far have not proven this. Your previous attempt to kill the Cuban only complicated matters for us."

Gold nodded. "We've had setbacks. But even the Mossad has messed up in the field. I don't think you can judge us too harshly. With the help of professionals like yourselves, I'm sure we will get better."

"We aren't military advisors," Cohen said gently. "We're just some guys you think a little too highly of."

Gold shook his head, and his cohort bit his lip. Neither of them believed the old man. "Look, we know about you. We know Rabbi Kovinski died because he was doing something for you. This is our home and, if there is an enemy to Israel here, then they are an enemy to us, as well. I know we are fighting someone more dangerous than what we're used to. And, I know you two have to be skilled operators. If you can help us, we can help you. We have lost people too because of this situation, and we're going to be a part of this regardless. We don't need your permission."

The looks of both Israelis turned cold. Not the 'hard and cold' persona the two young toughs were trying to project. No, it was the deadly stare of two veteran killers. At that point, Gold realized he had gone too far. These two men could just as easily kill him and his friend. He didn't like to think Jews would kill other Jews, but the old man was right

— he and his gang had only dreamed of this kind of fight. They had never dealt with the real thing, until now.

No one said anything for several seconds. Dayan looked the two young men over until Gold finally broke the chilling silence. "Look." Gold ran a hand across his close-shaven scalp. "When they killed the Rabbi, they also killed a young girl."

"We know," Cohen responded in more sympathetic tone.

Gold continued, "What you don't know is that the only reason she was there that day was because of me. She was the one who crept into the Rabbi's office and gave us the documents that let us know to go after Mendoza. She wouldn't have even been working that day except we wanted to have another chance at these guys and pushed her to keep spying on the Rabbi. She was trying to help us get more information." Gold and his cohort were now looking more distressed than tough. "She wasn't just killed. They violated her and beat her until you couldn't even recognize her. She was just an innocent kid from our community trying to help us out. She didn't even want to spy on him or get involved. But, we all grew up together, and she knew how important this was to us."

Dayan pursed his lips. Neither he nor the katsa knew how to respond. The professional answer would have been that's how it works in this business — get over it and move on. God only knew how many friends and people they had grown up with that they had watched die back in Israel.

However, the human answer was that they had lost one of their own, an innocent. They had lost her in a horrible way and felt responsible. "What was her name?" Dayan asked. His tone was quiet and soft, revealing a sincere sign of sympathy.

"Myra," the cohort replied, in a similar tone. "She was only nineteen. All she wanted was to get accepted into the cooking school and be happy working in a restaurant. She didn't deserve what happened to her."

Dayan looked over at the katsa, who met his gaze. Then turning back to the two young men, he responded. "As it happens, Mendoza is on our list, and we intend on taking him out."

Cohen walked over to the commando and in a hushed breath asked, "Are we sure about this?"

"Are we sure it's good to cast them adrift and worry about what they'll do on their own, if they don't work with us," Dayan replied in a similar whisper. "Besides, thanks to Mendoza, we have lost our intelligence organ. And now that the Iranians have a line on us, we have to cripple their intelligence organ as well if we want to succeed."

Cohen pursed his lips. "We don't need to have trouble with the Cubans, and we will have trouble if we do this."

Dayan placed a hand on the katsa's shoulder. "We already have trouble with the Cuban. He's going to continue his rampage and continue aiding the Iranians. Given he already thinks Israeli intelligence sent these guys after him, the rest is a moot point." The katsa offered a hesitant nod of agreement.

Dayan turned back to the young men who, by now, were once again trying to look the part of experienced veterans. "Provided we can trust you, and you remember this is about the mission and not revenge, we can use your help." The young men perked up, their attention was completely undivided. Dayan continued, "He has bodyguards, and he knows we're after him. He's a really hard target now. So, we have to take our time to develop intelligence and a plan. If you have people who can be discrete, we need surveillance on him. We need to know his routine. We need to know the number of men he keeps in his entourage. I want this done slowly, methodically, and with precision when we take our shot."

The young men were nodding, both trying hard to mask their excitement. "I can give you that," Gold replied, his face still stern.

Dayan continued, "Try to learn what you can about his security detail, and what type of weapons they keep, both on them and inside their vehicles. If we have to deal with them, I want to know what we will be up against. And again, I don't want any adventure seekers. I don't need any more telegraphing of our moves so that he knows we're coming. Use only your most disciplined guys. And remember I only want intelligence. The action will come later."

The meeting ended on a friendlier note as the two groups parted company. Cohen looked back at Dayan, "I have my reservations."

Dayan nodded. "As do I, but at least, they won't be on our blind side anymore. I think the thought of actually doing something worthwhile will keep them in line. Besides, I meant what I told you. Our intelligence network is blown. We need to blind the Iranians as well. It makes killing Mendoza an operational necessity."

The Contessa was not the least bit surprised when she saw Illana Muricia being led into the parlor of her house by one of the casually dressed men she employed for her security detail. He led the young lady over to a couch before crossing to a corner awaiting further instructions.

"That will be all, thank you," the Contessa said, casually waving the man off. With military precision, he turned sharply and disappeared out the way he came, leaving the two ladies alone.

The Contessa took a moment to study the young lady sitting before her. Illana Muricia was dressed in informal business attire — a pale blue pantsuit, slacks, and a matching vest over a light blue blouse with the top buttons left undone. It was professional, yet restrained. Ms. Muricia had clearly come with the intention of taking the job offer seriously.

"Might I offer you a drink?" the Contessa inquired as she walked over to the mini-bar located in the far corner of the room. It was out of the way but positioned so she had a full view of the room and the outside driveway leading up to the house.

"No, thank you, I'm fine," Muricia replied, crossing her legs and assuming a more assertive pose.

"Then let me get down to business," the Contessa continued as she poured herself a small glass of gin. "You're here, and I assume that you have inquired about me and know who and what I am."

Muricia nodded. "My sources say you are a business-woman doing quite well in a rather *intriguing* field. You are expanding your business with a global clientele from what I understand. What I don't understand is why you are interested in me?"

With a glass in hand, the Contessa returned and took a seat across from her guest. "As you said, my business interests are growing and not just regionally. As for my interest in you, you have traveled extensively and have a great deal of experience in business — both legal and illegal. Two qualities I need. And, as you know, my dealings are not all legal. Our previous meetings had the greatest impact on me, however. You didn't just mindlessly drink up everything your *illustrious* professor espoused, nor did you simply dismiss it out of protest. In the coffee shop, I, a complete stranger, began citing your biography, and you didn't even flinch. In my business, I need someone who is not easily intimidated nor is a mindless follower."

Muricia looked around. The room was well decorated and clearly maintained by professional cleaners. "I still don't see how I would be of much use to you. You reside in a world where I think a more viable male candidate would be found among our military ranks."

The Contessa smiled as she brought the crystal glass to her lips. Lightly sipping her libation, she eyed the young woman. "You are right. I am a woman operating in what is definitely a man's world, as it should be. As a rule, women are too sensitive and feminine for this kind of work. I consider myself an anomaly. But, as to your question, why not a soldier or someone from the intelligence world? Why not, above all, a man? Well, to be honest, a man would be more beneficial. He would also have the same attitude as most men. That I would better serve in his bed than as his employer. Once they had knowledge of my operation, I would have to worry about them taking over. After all, machoism thrives among this community. Both subordinates and clients tend to see me more as a mistress than someone in the business."

Muricia cocked her head to one side and gave the

Contessa a sly look. "And you think I won't do the same if given the chance?"

The Contessa nodded. "Oh, I'm sure you would, given the chance. But, it won't be as easy for you. I don't think you would ever be happy taking the reins from someone else's creation. I think your ego would demand you branch out on your own and create something for yourself. In the meantime, you'll dutifully carry out my orders and bide your time learning the ropes and gaining experience. During this time, you'll prove of great benefit to me."

"You're quite sure I'm going to take your offer," Muricia said as she cocked her head a little further.

"You came," the Contessa replied. "You already know what you're getting yourself into. You would have ended our associations at once if you weren't interested. So, I have already made arrangements for our departure. We leave tonight at 2230hrs. There is no need to bring anything. We'll see to your wardrobe and any other needs at our destination."

Muricia was slightly put off by the Contessa's arrogant, self-assured attitude. She almost wanted to say no to the offer and leave just to prove the woman wrong, but she was intrigued. She had completed her classes, and she had nothing to lose. There was nothing exciting waiting for her. Besides, the woman before her was in her early twenties and had already managed to accomplish so much. She couldn't help but respect her.

"All right," she replied as she uncrossed her legs and rose to her feet. "I just have one question. If we agree that I'm not a special forces soldier, some covert operative, or a career criminal, and I can't stand up to pee, what was the allure that brought you to seek me out?"

The Contessa took another sip of her drink. "I'll respond by asking a question of my own. Why, when we met in the coffee shop for the first time, were you not the least bit intimidated by a complete stranger knowing such details about you? Most people your age would have been frightened. You just brushed it off."

Muricia realized she would not get an answer until she replied. "Ask around, browse the internet. In the end, it's not a magic trick when you can figure out how easily someone could do a little research. If you had meant me harm, you would have accosted me at any number of more discrete locations. A coffee shop that I regularly frequent with friends, where people could easily watch us, wouldn't have been the best place to choose if you had intended to be more threatening. Only in a bad spy movie would someone try something that stupid."

The Contessa nodded, clearly impressed and answered Muricia's question, "Because you have natural instincts for this life you are about to enter."

Muricia said nothing more as she turned to leave. She was just about out of the room when the Contessa called to her. "Bring nothing but your passport and some money. Your old life is over. Any other needs you have will be provided."

CHAPTER 43

It was sheer luck.

That was Dayan's thought when he recognized the distinct voice on the recording.

Figuring it was far too risky to retrieve them, they had kept the receiving devices on Straudner's yacht. Even with few intelligence assets left to work with, Cohen decided to keep the operation in place in the hopes something might develop. Offered a considerable sum, Alyssa Rios had reluctantly kept up surveillance on the politician. Not long afterward, they caught Straudner on his office phone discussing the time he was planning to take the *Sunset Glory* out again.

Oskar Perez was able to enlist the services of the old fisherman for that day. True to his word, Straudner was on his yacht. This time he was in the dining room which made his conversation clearer. The sound of glasses clinking and liquid being poured came in quite well. He was speaking to someone, who remained nameless, and whose voice was unfamiliar.

"I realize your concerns," Straudner snapped indignantly.

"I'm just saying that we must seize the moment before a revolution breaks out," replied the mystery man nervously. "The campuses are in mutiny; the poorer districts are rioting."

"Yes, yes, I have read the same reports and watched the same footage on the news. However, my dear sir, we must bide our time. If we do not have the full support of the right backers, then this will all be for nothing. Our move to save the country will fall apart."

"Those bastard oligarchs!" The mystery man cried bitterly. "Too busy worrying about their next polo match than the welfare of their nation."

"They have their interests, and we must respect that they can't be expected to just up and move at our demand. As an oligarch myself, I understand their concerns. The military has a bad habit of overreacting and making rash decisions when they take control. They'll come around when they see the same things you and I see. Besides you, yourself, have pointed out we still have some finer points of the plan to work out before we initiate anything."

"Just minor points," the mystery man said in a calmer voice. "Nothing we can't work out in the field."

"Patience," Straudner commanded quietly. "When we move, it will be with a united front."

"Just so," the mystery man said.

"The meeting to finalize our plan will be at the Saratoga Manor on Saturday, two weeks from now, at 1800hrs," Straudner said calmly but sternly.

"The others will be there. I will see to it." The mystery man said with a tone of reluctance. "The Saratoga Manor though? Such a location is so visible. Won't it raise suspicion, if the politicians find out?"

"Not at all. It will be the perfect cover; it will be Colonel Rega's birthday party. We'll have it at his estate, and everyone will assume we're just celebrating," the politician replied. "I will, in the meantime, work to convince our friends the oligarchs that this needs to happen. I'm sure by the next meeting we will have them on board with our plan."

"And if you don't?" The mystery man asked. Again, his tone was nervous and unsure.

"Then Uruguay falls to anarchy," Straudner replied.

The conversation came to an end. Dayan and Perez looked at each other with both excitement and bewilderment — unsure what to do next. They waited for a time, continuing to listen. The conversation had ended with the mystery man apparently departing leaving the politician alone. Then, they heard him making a call.

"Romaros," Straudner said elatedly. "Everything is on track. We'll have our little get together. I just finalized the arrangements with our friends in the army. You just be sure to invite your friends in the police department. We are going to ensure everything is set for the celebration." Again, the politician had taken care to be careful with his words and not use any incriminating statements. However, his message was clear. This meeting was going to be a gathering of all the conspirators in one room. At last, Dayan thought, they had everyone in one place. They had finally achieved their target. The next step was planning the mission.

The message Dayan received was strange and disconcerting. Someone had sent him an encrypted email from Plūcker's account. The code words authenticating the message being sent by the Irishman all seemed to be there. It was the way the message read that was different — word use, the way things were written, and the unnerving point of the need to meet in an alternate location, all seemed altered from what they normally got from the burly man in Bogota. Regardless, the message alluded to a serious security alert that required the Israeli's presence immediately.

It didn't take Dayan long, after he arrived in the Colombian city, to see the problem. The Ronin Club was nothing but ashes — burnt wood and rubble. The account from a local businessman running a nearby delicatessen explained that the club's proprietor had supposedly been murdered by some unsavory customers. Adding that news to the emergency communique, the Israeli assumed it probably had something to do with the Iranians. If so, that meant the Iranians were quickly figuring out who they were up against.

The mysterious communique now raised questions. It had been sent after the Irishman's death, leading Dayan to wonder who had actually contacted him. And, were they to be trusted? The communique had stressed that normal channels had been compromised. That was obvious from the wreckage of the bar. The new meeting place was to be a small hotel on the north side of the city. Plūcker was dead and Dayan's instincts told him to walk away now and cut all contact. However, their logistics man and contact to the black market was gone at a time when they needed equipment desperately.

Along with Oskar Perez and two of the Colombian mercenaries they had brought along, the Israeli found himself navigating the narrow streets of the city as he headed toward the north side. His instincts howling at him — this was a very bad idea. Everyone else agreed. They all felt the need to verbalize their thoughts. They all knew Plūcker had been their pipeline for equipment. Contacting Cohen and apprising him of the situation only verified the fact that the Irishman was their only contact for acquiring the equipment. After that, the katsa was at a loss to offer any alternative for procuring the needed materials. Their only hope was to meet this mysterious contact and see if they had a remote chance of reestablishing their pipeline.

The hotel Grenada was hardly a palatial establishment. Nor was it a slum-like hole in the wall. It was a modest four-story structure surrounded by a labyrinth of small shops and eateries lined up along the winding roadways. It was easy for the veteran soldiers to realize that whoever chose this location had done so with a strategic advantage in mind. Numerous roadways and a maze of businesses and backroads made for a complicated situation if someone were trying to follow or abduct anyone. A potential target had multiple ways to and from their residence and numerous places to escape to if they were being chased.

Pulling the car off to the side of the parking lot, the men exited the vehicle. One of the Colombians was left behind to watch the vehicle and for any suspicious activity. The rest of the group started toward the hotel. The doorman inside was a small, round man in his mid-fifties, sporting a pot belly, had a balding round head, and a lengthy handle-bar mustache. He had the appearance of a cartoon character.

His wife, who busied herself in the back room looked almost identical minus the baldness and the handlebar mustache.

"May I help you, Sẽnor?" The hotel manager with a big toothy grin asked pleasantly. Dayan and Perez stood back as the Colombian mercenary, Gabriel, took the lead and spoke to the man.

"Yes, can you call room 304 please?" The mercenary beamed a charming smile at the little man.

Obligingly, the manager picked up the phone on the counter and rang someone. Handing the phone to the mercenary, the manager went about his work, oblivious to the world.

Gabriel handed the phone to Dayan. After a few rings, he heard a woman's voice on the other end of the phone answer. "Hello?"

Dayan didn't recognize her voice, but the twinge of fear he heard in her voice led him to think they were not walking into a trap. "We're friends of Plūcker's, his friends from Buenos Aires."

That had been the code they had agreed with Plūcker to use early on when he discussed the operation. Figuring any reference to Uruguay might cause exposure, they settled on 'friends from Buenos Aires' when identifying the Israelis.

For what seemed like hours, there was silence. Then the woman spoke. "Meet me in fifteen minutes — room 207."

Dayan heard the phone click on the other end. Dropping the receiver back into its cradle, he nodded to his compatriots. The three men made for the stairwell. Ascending the gray, tiled steps one after another, the three men walked up the stairs keeping a few meters apart. If this was a trap, they would be spread out enough not to be taken out in one burst of gunfire or start tripping over each other trying to maneuver.

The hotel was quiet and built in such a way that one had a good view of the hallways and areas from the vantage point of the stairs. The establishment was not built to accommodate an ambush. Keeping their tactical distance, the three made their way to the second floor and started down the hall. Gabriel stayed at the entryway to provide security as Dayan and Perez proceeded further.

Reaching room 207, the two men stayed to the side of the doorway aligned with the neighboring room. Carefully extending his arm, Dayan lightly knocked on the door. A woman's voice answered, "Yes?"

"The friends from Buenos Aires," the Israeli replied.

Everything was silent as the woman hesitated. Then, the sound of locks was heard being undone, followed by the slight creak of the door as it slowly opened. Assuming whoever was on the other side was likely armed, both men stayed off to the side. When the door opened about half a foot, the woman became more visible. Dayan recognized the face of the Negress, Plūcker's barmaid, almost immediately.

The relaxed look on the woman's face told him she recognized the Israeli as well. "Come in, please," she whispered with some urgency. Dayan stepped forward, but not before he gave a nod to Perez directing him to wait outside. Inside, the room was plain — a bed with cheap brown covers and a few other pieces of furniture.

The curtains were drawn tightly. The only light came from a single lamp on a nightstand. Dayan took a position near the door and remained standing. The Negress moved towards a small chair near the bed.

"My name is Raizza," the Negress murmured.

"What happened?" Dayan asked.

Tightening her lips, Raizza raised her arms to rub her shoulders. "Some men I didn't recognize came. A few were Colombian sicarios — guns for hire. The rest of then looked like you, Middle-Easterner types. They stormed in through the back while Ian, I mean Plūcker, was being distracted out front. They tortured him."

"I'm sorry," Dayan replied sympathetically. "Did he say anything?"

Raizza shook her head. "I don't know. I was hiding in the office in the back. I could only hear his shouts and screams, but they killed him. I saw the body; he didn't die from the torture. So, he must have served his purpose."

"But you don't know that?" Dayan asked, tapping his fingers against the wall.

She shook her head.

"Why did you contact me?" The Israeli started to move closer to her. "Why not just disappear when you realized how dangerous this had gotten?"

Sighing, Raizza sought to find the words. "He, Ian, I mean Plūcker, was like a father to me. He took me in when I was living on the streets as a kid. He looked after me, gave me a job and a safe place to live. He never laid hand on me demanding *payment*. I know he was in a very dangerous business. But I can't walk away knowing these people killed him. I have to see this through. You're fighting the people who killed him. You're as close as I will ever get to see that he gets some kind of justice. So, for better or worse, you're all I have."

The Israeli shrugged his shoulders. "I'm afraid we won't be doing much right now. In the current circumstances, your boss's death has crippled our operation. Plūcker was running our logistics. Without him, we don't have any other avenue to obtain what we need to finish what we've started."

Turning away from the Israeli, she reached behind the nightstand. She produced a small knapsack and proceeded to lay it on the bed. Unzipping it, she pulled out a sleek black laptop. Handing it to the Israeli, she exhaled. "I know I am taking a big risk right now. I have no reason at all to trust you, but this laptop contains all of Ian's documents pertaining to your operation. You're no good to me if you can't be effective."

Dayan's eyes lit up. "You mean this laptop contains everything regarding our dealings for this mission!" the Israeli groaned. He thought about how easily the whole operation could have been destroyed.

"It was well hidden," Raizza replied. "They searched the building and his offices and found nothing. But before you go making judgments, understand this. He was arranging for you to be in a lot of different places. Often on extremely short notice. You think someone can manage all those black-market deals and arrange such secretive logistics off the top of their head?"

Dayan didn't respond. She continued, "Your entire operation is right here."

Taking the laptop, the Israeli shook his head. "Even with this information, I don't have the recognition with suppliers and the other people Plūcker worked with for all this.

"I do," Raizza replied stiffly. "I often was with him when he made these deals. I even acted on his behalf, when he was too busy to attend to the matter. I can work with those you still need. I just can't let this operation die. Otherwise, they win, and Ian died for nothing."

Dayan could see the sincere hurt in the woman's eyes. The only man in her life who had been decent to her was dead, and she was at a loss to do anything about it. More to the point, he didn't have any other options. He would have to trust Raizza to work with the suppliers doing what Plūcker would have done. "All right, what you're telling me is you can still obtain what we require?"

Raizza looked back at the Israeli. "Right now, I'm all you have. So, what's next?"

"Do you have a new base of operation?" Dayan asked.

"I'm working on it," she replied, taking back the laptop. "I've been more concerned with staying hidden for right now considering recent events."

"We need to establish a new base." Dayan rubbed his chin. "However, I also need to prepare for a major operation, and we need to discuss the details."

CHAPTER 44

The echoing sound of gunshots erupted. A crashing knock pounded outside the door.

"We just made contact!" Shouted Oskar Perez. "Gabriel's taking fire right now," Perez shouted over the thundering sound of what was becoming a hail of gunfire.

Reaching under his dark sports coat, the Israeli produced a small Bulgarian Makarov pistol. It was from the tiny arsenal Plūcker had helped acquire for Dayan and his team to use while they were operating in Colombia. Opening the door, the Israeli found Perez wedged up against the neighboring doorway kneeling in a defensive position.

Looking down at the far end of the hall, Dayan saw Gabriel, taking cover against the corner of the hallway. His weapon was out, and he was exchanging shots with someone firing back from the lower stairs. The continuous hail of return fire the Colombian was facing indicated several people were attacking.

"What do we do?" Perez asked nervously.

Turning to Raizza, Dayan asked, "Is there a fire escape at the other end?"

"Yes!" she shrieked.

Touching Perez on the shoulder, the Israeli ordered him to take the woman and withdraw to the fire escape. Raizza had barely finished stuffing the laptop into her knapsack before the mercenary grabbed her and headed down the hall.

Shouting at Gabriel to fall back, Dayan crouched in the doorway and raised his weapon preparing to give cover for his compatriot. After firing a few more shots, the Colombian called back, "Moving!"

"Move!" the Israeli replied, his weapon at the ready. Gabriel lowered his weapon, turned and darted down the hallway. He was careful to remain out of Dayan's line of sight as he raced down the corridor. The Colombian had just moved past Dayan when men came to the top of the stairwell and took positions at the corner of the hallway.

"How many are there?" Dayan asked keeping his attention focused on the force massing at the end of the hall.

"I counted maybe six," replied a winded Gabriel standing right behind him.

Lining up his sights, the Israeli prepared to fire. "We will leapfrog our way back toward the fire escape. Fire a burst and move. We won't have much time to change magazines, so maintain fire control. Two rounds preferably, three at the most."

"Got it!" the Colombian shouted — his adrenaline kicking in. "I have to say these boys didn't flinch, and they move quickly for cover. They know their business, whoever they are."

"I'm not interested in finding out," Dayan replied. Behind him, he heard the clicking of Gabriel's weapon, as he changed magazines. The final click followed by the sliding sound of a round being chambered told the Israeli his cohort was ready.

By now, the unidentified adversaries had tactically assembled along the corner of the hall next to the stairs. They had moved slowly into position, assuming correctly that their enemies awaited them down the hall. Gabriel had been accurate in his assessment. These men weren't amateurs. Their moves were tactically sound and demonstrated instincts that only came with years of hardened experience.

Firing off his initial two rounds in the direction of the assailants, Dayan could hear Gabriel dart off, taking cover in a doorway at the other end of the hall.

"Set!" he called back.

"Moving!" Dayan cried out.

"Move!" Gabriel shouted.

Lowering his weapon, Dayan turned and raced past the Colombian to the next doorway on his side. Behind him, he heard the shots of enemy fire and the louder shots of Gabriel's cover fire. Stopping at the doorway, the Israeli turned. Issuing the command that he was set and ready, the Colombian called out and started down the hall.

Aiming, Dayan ignored the growing barrage of fire, as he blasted three shots. He watched the end of the hall as the head of one of the assailants exploded with a cloud-like mist and another suddenly grabbed his stomach. Dayan continued to hold his position as he waited for the command from Gabriel. There was nothing. Turning his head slightly, the Israeli looked down to see the Colombian sprawled out on the floor. Blood streamed from various wounds across the back of his body forming deep red pools spreading onto the floor.

Now on his own, Dayan began moving backward firing a shot with every other step. His Makarov only held eight rounds, counting the additional one already in the chamber. Knowing this, he conserved his ammunition as he sought to slow down the approaching attackers. The hallway seemed endless as the Israeli continued backing up. Each time he stepped back, he hoped he would finally reach the damned fire escape. His attackers were doggedly catching up to him. They were proving to be hardened professionals using a similar cover by fire method of movement Dayan and Gabriel had attempted to employ. This allowed them to steadily gain ground, closing the distance.

Dayan was startled by the familiar voice of Oskar Perez. "I've got you!!" The ex-legionnaire came up beside the Israeli firing rapidly. Down to his last shot, Dayan quickly changed magazines. Jumping back into action, he relieved Perez who had burnt through his ammo. Dayan's fire was equally rapid but directed. Between him and Perez, they managed to slow the movement of the pursuing aggressors.

Together they fired rapidly at the pursuers, as they backed up. Raizza had the door open and was screaming for the two men to hurry up and follow her. The breeze coming in from the outside was a relief for the two men, who were desperate to end the deathmatch they were locked in. Slipping outside, they quickly made their escape down the concrete staircase. Dayan knew they had to move fast to avoid being caught by the overhead fire they would run into when the attackers got outside. Luckily, there was only one flight of steps.

They were almost to the ground floor when they were

met by another barrage of gunshots. However, the gunfire was not coming from above them. It was coming from the same level. Checking everywhere, they saw a team of four men approaching them from around the building. It was an easy guess they were a backup team to the first group. Like the first team, these attackers proved equally proficient as they took cover along the corner of the building and behind some parked cars.

Ducking behind the staircase, the trio were pinned down and cornered. Assessing his position, Dayan realized that while they were protected from this new ground team. They were completely exposed from above. Soon, their original aggressors would be upon them, and then they would be cut down.

Shots were still being fired, but they were no longer coming in their direction. Looking around, they saw the other Colombian mercenary, who had been left to guard the vehicle, slipping behind the ground team. He had already killed the two men hiding behind the building and was now directing his efforts against the two wedged behind the cars. Taking advantage of the moment, Dayan and Perez jumped to their feet and commenced shooting at the two aggressors from the other direction. Unable to hold against both sides, the gunmen slid out from their positions and took off running.

Dayan and the others raced across the parking lot toward their car. They ran past the Colombian who caught up with them. Gunfire crackled behind them. Bullets whistling through the air felt like they were only inches from their heads. The original pursuers were back and attacking them again.

Less than twenty feet from the car, Dayan urged

everyone to keep running. At the car, Dayan flew across the hood to get to the driver's seat. The doors were all unlocked. The Israeli looked over to see the attackers in close pursuit. He didn't need to order it; Perez and the Colombian were already returning fire as they reached the car. Raizza was sliding into the backseat on the driver's side.

Dayan's initial instincts were to join in the gunfight, but he knew his men were almost out of ammo, and they needed to escape. Fumbling for his keys, the Israeli found the one for the ignition. Jamming it in, he was half expecting to have engine trouble that always seemed to come in tense situations. He was relieved when the car roared to life immediately. By now, the other two men were sliding into their seats. Keeping the doors open, they continued to fire.

Dayan shifted the car into drive and held the gas pedal all the way to the floor. Suddenly, he felt covered all over in warm liquid. He didn't have time to study it as he squealed out of the parking lot onto the main street. He nearly crashed into a small white pickup driving by.

The passenger side doors were wide open as the car sailed down the road. Dayan's attention was now focused entirely on escape. It was his great fortune that the roads, at that moment, were empty with the exception of a few service trucks which the Israeli expertly weaved through.

"Oh shit!" a voice cried out. Immediately Dayan's attention was drawn back to the vehicle. The entire front cab was awash in blood and brain matter. Turning to the passenger side, he saw the blood-soaked corpse of the Colombian mercenary. He had taken a bullet right to the temple — most likely a hollow point. Now the merc's half-exploded face was oozing out the man's vital liquids across the front seat and leaving a trail along the road.

Realizing they couldn't go any further in this condition, Dayan pulled the car onto a small side road. Believing they had placed enough distance between them and their assailants, he intended to focus on the immediate problem. The neighborhood was a collection of small adobe houses clustered tightly together. Everything was quiet and, aside from some elderly people going about their business entirely oblivious to the world, the street was deserted.

Pulling into an enclosed parking shed, the three exited the car. Raizza was clearly shaken as she clung to her knapsack as if it were a lifeline. Perez and Dayan, however, accustomed to violence and death of this nature, maintained their composure.

They started walking down the old dirt road, their eyes scanning for trouble and another mode of transportation. They found an old farming truck parked along the road surrounded by thick bushes that masked it from any nearby houses. They decided it was their best shot for transportation. Within seconds, they had cracked the lock and slid inside. A little creative wiring and the truck started up immediately. Pulling onto the road, they slowly drove back to the main road.

Surriman judged the situation with a mixture of anger and vindication. He had been right in his prediction that the young Negress would make contact with these troublemakers. His men had followed the young lady to the remote hotel. When it became clear she had checked in, they set up an observation post inside the hotel. The elderly couple who ran the place thought nothing of the strangers coming into their establishment and hanging out reading newspapers in the lobby or dining in its tiny café. To the couple, they were no different than all the others who spent their time congregating in their hotel. As long as money was spent, all was well.

The observation team was comprised of a couple of former members of the Policía Nacional de Colombia or Colombian National Police intelligence operations unit. They had been hired to monitor the facility and watch for anyone who tried to contact the woman's room. When three men, who clearly looked and behaved like professional soldiers, called her room, they knew they had found their quarry.

The trap had worked, and Surriman was elated that he had another chance to engage this enemy. However, he had failed to capture or eliminate them. And worse, he had lost his only link to finding them. He fumed bitterly and was completely oblivious to the first several minutes of Keppa trying to tell him they needed to escape.

It was the high-pitched screams of the police sirens that snapped him out of his angry trance. Looking around, he became aware of the carnage left in the wake of the gun battle that had taken place. Waving his hand Surriman shouted out his commands for the men to move out. Hiding their weapons under their coats and in their innocent looking backpacks, the gunmen casually dispersed through preplanned escape routes.

"These were professionals, Keppa. I'm sure of it," Surriman's voice was low and intense. "We have to find them. They could seriously fuck up our operation."

"Nouri," Keppa replied nervously. "We lost five men in the fighting."

Surriman stopped cold in his tracks, and for a moment he

was frozen. Then he looked over at his compatriot. "This is war, my friend. We lose people; they lose people." Turning to give his friend a cold stare, Surriman's face was forceful. "This is not over."

Nervously, Keppa nodded.

CHAPTER 45

Oskar Straudner nearly salivated over the news about another violent confrontation between police and student protesters. It seemed that the police had lost all restraint when a lit bottle of a highly flammable liquid was hurdled from the protesting crowd. It landed on a phalanx of shielded police. Though protected with the thick padding of their riot gear, the sight of police officers being set ablaze had caused panic among the leadership. They responded by authorizing the use of tear gas and firing volleys of it into the crowds. The result had been chaos — thousands of students crammed into a tight space suddenly were trampling each other and charging the police line in a desperate attempt to escape.

Straudner could only offer his thanks to Ulbrict Laudman, who had arranged for a dangerous incendiary liquid to be thrown from an open window of the university's second floor. It had been timed to be thrown at the height of the turmoil when tension and nerves were at their pinnacle. The campus now had the appearance of a battlefield. Everything had been done to ensure a deepening rift and growing hatred between students and police. When the politician took control of the country, he wanted an angry and frustrated police force working for him. He would need good secret police and cops who were unconcerned about using violence and brutality to curb any future political adversaries.

Pouring himself a small glass of Scotch, the politician circled the sofa as he contemplated his next move. Earlier in the week, he had met with one of his conspirators from the army on his smaller yacht. Pressured to initiate the coup at once, Straudner had convinced the man that the powerful elite of the country, whose support was vital, was not yet ready to back an all-out takeover. It had, of course, been a lie. The elite was pressuring him for the coup.

It was the Iranian support he needed and was waiting for. In the next couple of weeks, members of the *support militia* would slowly infiltrate into the city and countryside. He didn't relish the idea of having gunmen not completely loyal to him walking about the country. But he didn't completely trust his enlisted conspirators either. In the end, having two powerful armed bodies, but with different masters, vying for the same goal gave him protection against any double-cross from either side.

In the meantime, Straudner's ex-Stasi operative had been successful filling in for the recently destroyed leftist insurgency. The riots had gained so much attention, no one noticed the virtual disappearance of the terror wave that had started it all. It also helped that an underground leftist newspaper had magically appeared and was quickly gaining a considerable following. The newspaper was reporting on all sorts of atrocities and violent acts being carried out by right-wing vigilantes or, possibly, the police. The fact that the paper had been indirectly set up by Straudner had been easily overlooked.

The stories were bogus, which meant little in the current fervor of political turmoil. People were reacting to stories that amounted to pure gossip. Still, they were readily believed and stoked the rage among the right elements of society. In time, the politician would emerge as the master of a country that would praise him for bringing order. He would have a security force to do his bidding and destroy his enemies. At the same time, he would secure and protect the lands and fortunes of the wealthy elite against the communist menace and enjoy their admiration. It was even possible he would be loved by those who would oppose him by being the leader who would restrain security men anxious to exert personal forms of retaliation for dead comrades and family members.

Leaning back on his sofa, Straudner lazily reached for his oak humidor. Producing a long Meduro wrapped Churchill Excalibur, he clipped the end, then moistened it with his tongue. He applied the blue flame from the lighter with sword-like precision as he rotated the cigar. The first puff permeated the air with a sweet aroma. Taking a sip from his glass, he felt the golden liquid flow down his throat with a strong burn. His only thoughts were that everything was now coming together perfectly. In a few days, the militia would start crossing the border, and the final work on the plan would be complete. Uruguay would soon see the era of Straudner and the dawn of a golden age.

Solomon Gold stayed in the shadows. His dark leather coat and wool beanie helped protect him from any onlookers. As he had done every third night, he watched the building across the way. It was always the same — the convoy of sleek, black Suburbans pulled up alongside the front of the building of Bolivar Investments & Acquisitions. The times varied, often by of several hours, but the routine never changed. The convoy would not set more than five minutes before the doors of the building opened, and Elloy Mendoza, the CEO of the company, walked out. He was always flanked by his indoor security detail — three athletic-looking men — and would quickly slide into the backseat of one of the waiting vehicles. Once everyone was inside, the cars would cut into whatever traffic was on the road and speed down the street.

The convoy moved in an unpredictable pattern by changing routes of travel and even destinations. The Cuban had two or three houses throughout the city from what Gold and his boys were able to find out by tapping into their connections among the Jewish community. The Cuban also belonged to a couple of elite clubs that allowed for overnight lodgings as well as the unpredictable desire Mendoza had to stay in some of the city's finer hotels.

Gold had a few of his friends troll around the different houses belonging to the Cuban pretending to look for yard work as instructed by the Israeli commando. The watch reported back that the armed security patrolled the property around the clock. The irritation of having to deal with all these complications was not lost on the young radical. All these measures had been put in place by Mendoza as a result of the botched attack by the Guardians of Israel.

It didn't matter though. He had made a horrible mistake, and people he cared about had suffered for it — he needed to make it right. If he wanted the commando's help, he needed to make sure, they didn't miss a second time. Gold kept his guys on a tight leash and threatened violent repercussions to any of his people who were discovered or who thought to take a chance on their own. His orders were final. We will wait for the professional help to arrive before taking any action. There would be no more amateur adventurism this time around.

When the convoy departed in the same swift fashion it always did, Gold waited until they had long since passed. Sure they were gone, he pulled the beanie tightly over his head and started across the street in the direction of Bolivar Investments & Acquisitions. The Israeli's had not been disingenuous in their promise to assist. They had maintained contact with the Guardians over the last few weeks. They had received the reports from the Jewish radicals through the agreed-upon weekly meetings in remote locations prearranged by use of disposable phones issued after each meeting then thrown away.

Once across the street, Gold continued walking nonchalantly past the building. He had been warned by the old katsa and Dayan to use the corner of his eye to observe. Gold practiced this technique for several days before he felt comfortable enough to attempt this evening's recce. There were no visible signs of any guards or any other notable security in the front. He had been reminded before not to look for the obvious. A person such as Mendoza would not use such an overt means of protection. In his mind, the young radical kept reiterating the words spoken by the two Israelis — think like a spy, think like a spy.

Walking up the street adjacent to the building, Gold reached a small alley that led to the back of the structure. Maintaining his calm, casual manner, he slipped into the alley and continued walking. The alley was poorly lit leaving most of the walkway enmeshed in dark shadows. He could see that the concrete flooring had been greatly neglected. Wild plants, growing up between the large cracks, were high and full enough to practically whip the young radical as he maneuvered between the buildings.

Reaching what Gold was sure was the back of Bolivar Investments & Acquisitions, he walked up to what he assumed was the back entrance. He fumbled with his shoelaces, pretending they were untied. He had practiced this routine several times and was hoping his actions didn't look too phony. He wanted to give the impression of being slightly exasperated. Leaning down completely enshrouded in the building's shadows, he pretended to tie his laces. He looked around with irritation as if he was lost. In reality, he glanced at the higher areas trying to catch any gleam that might indicate a camera lens.

Gold had nearly finished when he caught the slight flash of a tiny red light in the far, top corner of the building. Assuming it was the lighting for some sort of surveillance camera, Gold did his next exercise. Rising to his feet, he turned to face the building. Unbuttoning his jeans, he leaned over as if preparing to urinate. He had only just started when the door he was near flew open.

With his eyes accustomed to the darkness, the sudden flash of surging white light came as a blinding force. Gold nearly fell over; he was overwhelmed by the powerful light. Then a deep, growling voice caught his attention. "What the hell do you think you are doing out here?"

It took the radical a few moments to notice a silhouette in the door. In a few seconds, his eyes adjusted enough to make out a large man, dressed in a navy-blue suit.

"I…I got lost in the dark and had to take a piss," Gold replied, playing the role of a dumb college kid wondering about. "I figured nobody would see me if I shot a load back here, ya know."

"This is a respectable business neighborhood you're in," the large man snapped. "And you're just wondering about here at night?" The man sounded suspicious.

Dancing about, somewhat like a normal teenager trying to play it cool, Gold responded. "Hey man, I came from the coffee shop down the street. They have this poetry reading once a week. My girlfriend's into all that deep, sensitive emotional shit. So, I spent the last few hours listening to a bunch glorified whining crap and now all that damn coffee is taking its toll. Ya got what I'm saying?"

"Listen here you little punk," the man growled. "Go find a toilet somewhere like a civilized person."

From the sound of the man's voice, Gold concluded that he was buying the story. "Well, you mind if I use yours really quickly?" the radical pushed.

Gold's eyes had now adjusted. The man had also stepped a little closer to the stranger in the ally. The combination allowed the radical to catch a glimpse of a firearm tucked under the man's jacket. The man also appeared to be a very athletic specimen. It was easy to see that he was part of Mendoza's security apparatus.

"Get lost you little shit!" the guard commanded.

Raising his hands, as if surrendering, Gold began to back away. "Whatever. I don't want any trouble." With that, the radical slowly backed away.

When the door shut leaving him alone in the pitch dark ally, Gold turned and began fumbling his way back out the way he had come in. He was breathing hard with adrenaline curling through his body. He had been amazed that he had pulled off his deception.

CHAPTER 46

Ali Anwar al Qalmini contemplated as he sat at his desk. The information reported back to him by Major Akim had not been good. The major reported that Surriman's team had found the logistics source of their mysterious adversaries. Documents had been uncovered that proved they were on the right track. The hope was they had succeeded with this latest action in neutralizing them as a threat. It had been much needed good news.

The more recent reports, delivered by Surriman himself, described the latest gun battle. They had killed two of their enemies. Without time to examine the bodies at the scene, Surriman found some people with contacts at the city morgue. They confirmed two bodies: one found from the hotel and another from a car matching the one the enemy had escaped in. The car was parked a few miles away. Both bodies were Colombian mercenaries. The unidentified enemies were, therefore, still at large.

Qalmini was ready to accept this update assuming that the intelligence and logistics wings of their enemies had been wiped out. Surriman, however, reminded him that they could not be sure of that. The girl they had been watching had gotten away from them. She had been the Irish gun runner's assistant in all his business dealings. This meant she could still possibly aid them. As for intelligence, Mendoza's ill-advised purging had failed to kill the woman who headed the Guardian Angel outfit. She too was still at large. Whether she was still working in the service of these nameless enemies was not yet known.

What Surriman had managed to obtain from the Irishman were two names: Kafka Dayan and Micha Cohen. Both names, the Arab was sure were legitimate and Israeli. With little else to work with, Qalmini took a dangerous though necessary risk. Reaching out to the Iranian intelligence service, he inquired about these names. The response came with a litany of objections regarding this gross security breach. Still, the results were exactly as he feared.

Micha Cohen was a long-standing intelligence officer with the Israeli Institute for Intelligence and Special Operations — better known as the Mossad. What was known of him was a record that spanned the world including probable missions in South America. He was also suspected as the mastermind behind several assassinations carried out against the Hezbollah leadership.

The report on the second name elicited even greater concern from the Iranian.

Kafka Dayan had served nearly seven years in the Israeli Defense Force where he held the rank of Samal Rishon. He was a platoon level non-commissioned officer until he was discharged. His military service had been entirely with the dreaded Shayetet 13, Israeli's most elite naval commandos, a group with a savage and fearsome reputation. Shayetet 13 had a history of successfully executing some of the most daring and complex missions in the world.

Nothing was noted in the report regarding specific missions of Dayan's — suspected or known. Israel closely guarded the secrecy of their special military units. It didn't matter. Qalmini only had to think back through the last seven years of commando missions undertaken by the Israelis. He pondered recent encounters his own people had had with their shadowy enemy to analyze what capabilities he might be up against now.

Rubbing his hands, the Iranian recalled those events, calculating the dangers these Israelis represented to his operation. Already they had succeeded in creating enough trouble for the seasoned operative to break the secrecy and reach out to his formal intelligence sources. His man, Surriman, had pointed out their adversaries were now on their blind side — whereabouts unknown, and their next move unpredictable. On the other hand, their intelligence network had been eliminated and their logistics source most likely neutralized. And, since Israel had so far not taken action, he suspected this might be a rogue outfit and not a sanctioned government mission. The whole situation had Qalmini feeling like he was gambling. He didn't like carrying out a mission with such a threat looming, but the situation had developed too far to be stopped.

Since all the actions by the Israeli team had seemed to only affect Qalmini and his people, he decided not to apprise Mr. Straudner of the dilemma. From the documents and other information recovered at the Irishman's place, it was a reasonable deduction that they had not yet found out about him. Besides, nothing is more difficult or irritating than dealing with a nervous politician.

Even with all the months spent trekking across South America, Dayan was unable to get used to the humid jungle environment — the night air was thick and muggy. The Israeli was continually pulling clothes off. The incredibly humid atmosphere dampened his clothing causing it to stick to his body.

Oskar Perez and the other South American mercenaries moved about silently as they unpacked their gear and weapons. Everyone was now garbed in dark green camouflage military fatigues, matching floppy camo-hats, and tactical web-gear secured from a source Raizza had inside the Brazilian army.

Raizza had proven to be a true protégé of her late mentor. In a very short time, she had procured a few boxes of ParaFAL M964 A1 rifles. For a long time, they had been the standard issue weapon of Brazilian paratrooper units. Now they were being phased out for upgraded A2 models. This left several warehouses full of these weapons still in good condition, gathering dust, forgotten by lazy supply officials. To everyone's amazement, she even obtained three FN MAG M971 medium machine guns and a claymore mine.

The rifles were pulled from canvas bags and issued to each of the men. Many clearly showed wear from years of hard use. Despite this, Dayan and his men found them still in well-kept condition. Klaas Vanderhook began issuing magazines full of ammunition. The men loaded the magazines into their ammo pouches spread across their web gear. For good measure, they added a couple of clips on pouches that also fit their web belts, since no one knew what to expect this evening.

Based on the conversation Oskar Straudner had with the Iranian, the Israelis were able to figure out the general time the Iranian parties would start coming over the border. Alyssa Rios, as part of her deal, had continued monitoring the Iranian camp and area near the border. Her sources had reported a collection of small hauling trucks being gathered at a deserted farmhouse not far from the border. This matched the timeline overheard in a conversation with the Iranian. Then, a few days earlier, a group of men who looked to be Arab arrived at the farmhouse. Micha Cohen decided this had to be the moment. Dayan agreed with him.

As the mercenaries collected their equipment and checked their weapons, a young man garbed in the clothes of a local peasant waited off to the side. He said nothing. As he sat quietly watching these camouflaged figures preparing for war, he was rubbing the neck of a little Australian sheep-dog. He had met these hardened soldiers only a few hours before. Alyssa Rios, his employer, had instructed him to guide these men. The peasant was disguised as a goat herder. He moved between the woodlands that encompassed the largely uncontrolled borderlands between Uruguay and Brazil. He was vigilant in keeping watch on the activities of the suspicious Arabs.

Dayan approached the young man, who looked back at him with a distrusting frown. The Israeli understood the young man's concern. The peasant made his living operating in the shadows and working through highly secretive and protected networks of communication. Now, he was meeting a group of strange men, dressed in combat fatigues and arming themselves in the dead of night. It couldn't have been the most comfortable of circumstances.

"I appreciate what you're doing for us," Dayan said in a soft, apologetic manner.

"My boss told me to," the young man replied in a quiet tone. "I guess you should know. I'm a spy, not a soldier, and I really didn't want to do this." He stopped himself. "I just felt you should know where I stand."

The Israeli nodded. "I appreciate your help and realize the risk you are taking exposing yourself like this. I don't intend for you to fight, and I will let you go as soon as I don't need you anymore."

The peasant sighed as he looked around. "As I told my handler, I saw the Arabs at the farmhouse move out with all the trucks in a convoy to a road that runs along the border. They stopped at a point near a collection of goat trails coming from Brazil. In the last few weeks, I have seen men from that mining camp patrolling those trails. I am sure they intend to come through that way from the Brazilian side."

"Good," Dayan replied. "First, I need you to lead us to the trucks. Then I need you to lead us to the openings of these trails. As soon as I know all the avenues of approach, my men and I will take it from there."

Looking somewhat nervous, the peasant nodded. "I will stay as long as you need me."

"Hopefully, it won't be for too long," the Israeli responded, trying to add some degree of comfort.

By now, the mercenaries were dressed with full kits. They gathered around one of the two trucks that had carried them out here awaiting their briefing. Dayan, followed by the peasant, walked over to them.

The sun was setting. In another hour, it would be dusk. Dayan figured the Iranians would start moving their forces as soon as it got dark. Based on the reports delivered by the young peasant, it would take about four hours for them to wade through the trails and make it to the waiting vehicles.

With everyone gathered around, Dayan began his briefing. The truck convoy contained ten to twelve hauling trucks. He expected a force of no less than a hundred. His plan was to move quickly, neutralize the drivers, and render the trucks inoperable. Then, with the help of their young guide, they would move to the entry points they expected the Arabs to use and set up an ambush.

Everyone grimaced in near unison at the idea. They hadn't done any prior reconnaissance. They had only been introduced to their intelligence source this very evening. And, as a force of only ten, they were badly outnumbered against an armed force of a hundred guerrillas.

Acknowledging their concerns, Dayan pointed out that their advantage was surprise. The Arabs were not expecting an attack and would not be capable of reacting, because they were hemmed in by narrow goat trails. There would be timed explosions and laying down heavy firepower early in the fight. That would be enough to confuse the enemy and send them retreating. If not, the combination of downed trucks and whatever casualties they could inflict would at least severely slow the Iranian operation down.

CHAPTER 47

No one liked the idea.

As seasoned military professionals, they all agreed they were flying blind, counting on a lot of assumptions. Everyone wished they would have had more time in the field to do their evaluations and preparations. They emphatically expressed their irritation that they didn't have a larger force for this operation.

"I don't intend this to be a suicide mission," Dayan stated in the best commanding presence he could muster. "Give them hell early on. If they drive through and press a counter-attack, we withdraw immediately. We'll have done the best we could. And, I'll pay an additional eight grand US to everyone on top of what you're already being paid for the additional risk I'm asking you to take."

His answer satisfied his men enough to press on with the operation. Throwing off their field hats, the men quickly rolled black balaclavas over their faces. This was preferable to dealing with cumbersome camouflage face paint. The peasant couldn't help but notice they were all wearing soft sneakers as opposed to the more typical combat boots.

"Sneakers and bare feet enable us to move more silently in the bush," Dayan said, noticing the young man's baffling look.

The mercenaries set off after making one last check of their weapons. The peasant took a moment to request a chance to tie his dog up and relieve himself before they departed. The Israeli gave a nod of approval. Racing down a small slope, the peasant came to the tree line. Placing the dog on the ground, he pretended to undo his trousers.

"Are you all right," a soft feminine voice whispered nervously from inside the bushes.

"I'm fine, Eva," he quickly whispered back. "But I fear these men will not be able to stand against all these invaders tonight."

"What are you saying," Eva asked nervously.

"Take the dog," the peasant replied shooing the dog into the bushes. "I need you to go to the village and tell them what is happening. Tell them they need to come here fast."

"Me?" Eva yelped before stopping herself as she realized she was being too loud.

"You have seen what I have seen," the peasant replied in a desperate voice. "You know the paths those foreign men were using. The ones we showed the patron. You know the base area where I said they would have to come out. Go and warn him now. Eva. I'm counting on you."

Hearing the girl grab the little dog, the peasant started to back away.

"I won't let you down my brother," Eva replied.

He heard her carefully back into the bushes as he started up the hill. The mercenaries were completely occupied with their final preparations. The peasant assumed he and Eva were safe. He went to find the Israeli, who was making a few last-minute checks of men and equipment.

"Everything all right?" The peasant asked the foreigner.

Dayan was fumbling with a pair of night-vision goggles. "Well, they work, but I am afraid I am not familiar with them."

The peasant didn't reply. The Israeli turned to face him. "We step off in five minutes. We'll need your help in taking out the drivers. Are you going to be good with that?"

"I have to be," the peasant replied calmly. "I'll be the only visible one there. If they see me, my life will be in danger," Dayan nodded and returned to fixing his gear.

It was still a little light out when the team, led by the goat herder, stepped off. Having walked the land so many times at all times of day and night, the peasant was well versed in his direction. Not more than ten minutes later, he led the mercenaries to a small ridge and cluster of trees. Carefully, they crawled up to just below the ridge break and hunkered down in a prone position.

They saw the convoy just below them. It was parked along a wide dirt road. Producing an ACOG scoping mechanism, Dayan peered down at the convoy. The trucks were parked ten meters apart. Everything was set up for the vehicles to be immediately ready to move.

The drivers didn't appear to be professional soldiers. They were clustered loosely around the lead truck enjoying cigarettes and sharing light conversation. The Israeli scanned the vicinity carefully looking closely for the presence of a patrol that might be keeping an eye on the surrounding landscape and the vehicles. After a few minutes of observation, he determined there was no patrol. The drivers clearly were unconcerned with any possible threats.

Dayan observed the AK-74 rifles collected in a corner away from the road. The drivers may not have been professional soldiers, but they were cognizant enough to stay close to their weapons and keep them out of sight on the off chance of passersby. He concluded that these drivers were probably seasoned smugglers well connected to the black market. Dayan took that to mean that while they didn't look it, they were at least staying somewhat alert to any possible trouble. It would not be an easy task neutralizing them.

Sliding back down the hill, Dayan and the mercenaries looked at each other. He could tell from their expressions, they had reached the same conclusion he had regarding the situation below. Observing the area around him, Dayan noticed that the ridge ran along the hill parallel to the road. He decided the best plan was to send a team of his men down the road, staying along the ridgeline. Some distance down, they would to the road. By then it would be dark. Coming up behind the trucks, they could neutralize the drivers.

Figuring it would still be too risky unless the drivers were caught up with some kind of diversion, the Israeli decided they would need something to keep their quarry's attention. The peasant offered to go down there pretending to look for his goats. The drivers would not be threatened by some local peasant, especially since goat herders were very common. The drivers would be anxious to drive him off since their operation would begin soon and there was the chance the peasant might stumble upon their collection of guns.

With no other option available, Dayan agreed, and the plan was put into effect. Perez and Ripley took four other men and quietly began working their way along the ridge.

They were to wait ten minutes for the team to get into place and the sky to darken. The rest of the team looked on nervously. The peasant took several deep breaths as he tried to control his nerves. He felt a hand gently touch his shoulder. Looking back, he saw the Israeli looking at him. "You'll be fine," the foreigner said softly, trying once again to provide some comfort for the young man.

When ten minutes had elapsed, the peasant got up and started down the hill. He began calling out and ringing a bell he had in his hand. Arriving at the base of the hill, the young man could see, even in the growing darkness, the cluster of men beginning to come toward him.

"You have a problem?" One of the drivers asked as he confronted the peasant.

"Forgive, sir. I don't have my dog, and my goats ran off. I'm trying to find them," the young man said as he held onto his composure.

As predicted, the drivers gathered around him and were casually trying to edge him away from the trucks. They definitely were concerned that, if he got a closer look, he would notice their guns along the side of the truck. "We haven't seen any goats, and we've been here for a while now," the driver who acted as spokesman replied. He and the others continued to walk up to the young herder.

Pretending to look all about, as any nervous herder would do, the peasant noticed a collection of silhouettes approaching. He had only caught a glance as they stayed along the opposite side of the road and kept to the shadows of the trucks. Continuing to play dumb, he kept looking around as if not knowing what else to do. The drivers fidgeted, shifted, eager to get rid of the peasant. The silhouettes were now passing the second to the last truck.

The herder decided he had delayed long enough. "Well, forgive me for interrupting you. I will look for my goats back up on the hill." With that, he turned away from the group of drivers and began hurrying back toward the hill.

At that moment, the mercenaries, led by Perez and Ripley, emerged from the shadows of the trucks. The unsuspecting drivers barely had time to realize what was happening when they were met by several flashes of gunfire. Bullets tore into their bodies as the mercenaries fanned out in a tactical line. The drivers shouted in fear as it began to register they were under attack. Some froze and were cut down instantly. A few attempted to run but made it only a few feet before they were shot down.

Though it felt like hours, the whole business lasted less than a few minutes. Despite the extensive fusillade of gunfire, the noise was silenced by the use of suppressors, and the road was now littered with corpses of dead Arabs.

Ripley counted ten drivers down. By now, Dayan and the rest of the team were on their way down the hill to join Ripley and Perez. Along the way, they picked up the peasant, who was breathing hard and lying in a fetal position on the ground. He was shaking and completely shocked by the cold way the mercenaries removed the dead drivers and continued on as if nothing had happened.

With the bodies thrown to the side, the road was clear. The mercenaries set about slashing the truck tires until all were completely flat. Then, crossing the road, they fired their rifles into the vehicles' engine blocks — a little extra insurance for making the trucks inoperable.

With no time wasted, the mercenaries were now back on the road, ready for the next phase of the operation. The peasant didn't need to be told anything. He moved up front and waved them toward the tree line. A few meters past some thick bushes, the team found themselves standing in a sizable opening.

The peasant proceeded to take Dayan across the opening. The young man slowly walked the Israeli to a collection of small trails hidden within the shrubbery and trees. Only with his night vision optics, could Dayan pick out the trails. They were well hidden and wouldn't be noticed, even in the daytime, unless someone stumbled upon them.

CHAPTER 48

There were five trails in all. At a distance, they all broke off as if going in different directions. But those directions were all leading toward the border. Dayan noticed the trails all met at the base of the clearing. It was a fortunate discovery, and he immediately saw the tactical advantages the area offered. Overlooking the trails was a hill that was heavily covered in thick vegetation and overgrowth. Mounting a machine gun on top of the hill would give them control over all the trails.

Dayan thought it would be a narrow window, but if they could initiate an ambush at the base of the opening, they would be able to catch the Arabs off guard inflicting serious casualties before they had to retreat. After further study of the terrain, the Israeli realized it was the only option they had.

Dayan and the peasant were soon joined by Ripley, Vanderhook, and Perez. The Israeli wasted no time communicating the general outline of his plan. After looking over the ambush zone, the three commandos concurred with their leader's analysis.

Quickly, the mercenaries set about preparing the ambush. Perez placed their one claymore facing the head of the trails. He connected the wires before sending a man to run the line across the walking path. He set the wires a few inches off the ground to ensure they were nearly invisible. Any good shot of moonlight might expose them, but if the wires were too low, several feet might walk past before anyone tripped and set off the claymore.

At the same time, Vanderhook was busy taking his team up the hill. Looking through the bushes and trees, it took the Dutch mercenary several minutes before he found a position that didn't shroud them from their target objective. Once a location had been discovered, his team commenced digging in fighting positions and sighting in the machine gun.

Ripley had taken two other men up the trail to provide an observation post. Some three hundred meters up, he thought he would be able to see any sign of the enemy before they could hear the mercenary force working. They were setting up an ambush that might get initiated in hours, or it could just as easily be discovered by the enemy force arriving too early and ambushing the ambushers. In either case, the commando kept still, peering into the distance through his optics.

The mercenaries worked quickly. As hardened combat professionals, they knew all too well the dangers of not having a well-established setup. It was nearly thirty minutes later when the ambush was finally ready. It wasn't the ideal setup due to the absence of time and the generally poor digging conditions. Still, it was adequate for what they needed. They had built dirt mounds for cover and collected enough foliage to conceal their fighting positions. Dayan didn't want his team distracted or exposed when they weren't sure when the Arabs would arrive. In the dark, with an unsuspecting enemy, they would have the advantage.

With everything done as well as possible, the mercenaries got into their positions. A quick squawk on the hand radio by Dayan alerted Ripley the ambush was ready. Minutes later, the Welshman and his men came through the foliage. The Israeli led them past the claymore and directed them to the other side of the clearing where the rest of the team waited at the ready. With his services complete, the peasant was given permission to leave. The young man wasted no time and quickly vanished into the vegetation.

Everything was in place. Vanderhook and his men had the machine gun set up with fields of fire covering the trails. The rest of the force was prepared to lay down massive fire. All that was left to do was wait. Hunched down behind the hidden fighting position, Dayan looked across their attack field.

In his mind, he still pictured the narrow width of the trails leaving little room for the enemy to maneuver. Once the attack began, he calculated five minutes for them to get over the initial shock and figure out where the attack was coming from. It would take another two to five minutes to estimate the size of the enemy force against them and for someone in leadership to take charge and initiate a counter-attack. In all, he assumed it would be ten minutes before his team would have to fall back if the Arab force didn't fall back first.

An hour passed before a squawk came over the mercenaries' radios. It was Vanderhook, ever watchful, alerting everyone that he had sighted someone coming down the path. The mercenaries readied themselves. Moments later, sounds of shrubbery and branches being crushed were heard. The sound of many boots on the ground was more distinct. No one had to see to know that whoever was coming, there were a lot of them.

What unnerved Dayan, and most likely the other mercenaries as well, was the absence of any talking — the noise he had hoped to hear. Whoever was coming was maintaining good noise discipline — the sign of well trained and disciplined soldiers. It had been the Israeli's experience that a soldier that participated in unnecessary conversation or otherwise made noise in the field was unprofessional and poorly trained. Such noises were not heard this evening. While crunching of branches and shrubbery and the thumping of booted feet could not be helped in such places, needless conversation and clanging of unsecured equipment were properly addressed. Those noises were not heard from the group moving toward them. This revelation had Dayan believing this force was going to be both trained and professional.

With weapons ready, the mercenaries waited for the upcoming fight. Dayan peered around his fighting position to observe. Through his optics, he could already make out the silhouetted figures of men coming down the trails. Taking deep, slow breaths, he worked to control his heart rate and his nerves as the enemy neared.

No matter how many battles the commando had been in, his mind still raced with thoughts of all that could go wrong. Would someone fire early? Would the enemy see someone who is too exposed? His adrenaline pumped as he prepared for the inevitable action. It was only the deep breaths he took to fill his lungs and relax his nervous system that caused his hands to stop shaking with anticipation.

Figures were now emerging from the tree line. As

expected, they were beginning to collect in the clearing. Sliding behind his mound of dirt, the Israeli raised his hands to his ears and opened his mouth. The coming explosion would be loud. Covering his ears would only do so much; opening his mouth helped balance out the shock.

The ground shook with the thunderous explosion. It reverberated with equal force under the mercenaries' positions. Instantly, Dayan lowered his hands and grabbed his rifle. The machine guns roared into action from both the hill and the ambush position. Leaning around the mound, the Israeli saw, through his optics, silhouettes racing about chaotically. By now, the noise discipline was gone as shouts and screams echoed from temporarily traumatized Arabs. Between the gunfire and the collective yelling, it was hard for Dayan to make out what was actually being said. He fired, along with the rest of the team, at any movement in the general location of the trails. He emptied his first magazine within seconds. With limited visibility, even with his optics, he figured he should be hitting hostiles. Quickly changing out another magazine, he started firing again using more controlled shots, aiming where he could pinpoint the most shouting.

Atop the hill, Klaas Vanderhook directed his men as they fired on the men who were caught on the narrow goat trails. Looking through a pair of night optic binoculars, he watched as the Arabs began to figure out the direction of the attacking fire. They dove behind trees and wedged into nearby thickets. As expected, these guys were trained. They weren't going to retreat, they were going to fight. It wouldn't be long before they counter-attacked. His men aimed down the trails firing controlled bursts. Assuming the other two machine guns were covering the front of the enemy formation, Vanderhook had his men aim toward the rear to catch those still confused and lined up. He could see several figures fall and crumple to the ground. He also began to see some of them being collected. Someone below was now taking charge and starting to deploy forces to fight back.

Major Akim had only been confused for a short while. He was a long-time veteran of far too many horrific battles to be easily shaken. It didn't take the Iranian long to figure out where the attacks were coming from. It also didn't take him long to realize they were being ambushed by only a small group. And, since the initial blast of the claymore wasn't followed up with more explosives, such as mortars or grenades, he knew the ambushers were lightly armed.

Grabbing several men standing nearby, Akim pointed out the source of gunfire that revealed the enemy location. He ordered them to round the clearing from within the tree line and attack from the side. The men immediately took off. Then, pulling more men forward, the major intermingled them within the trees and berms and had them lay down a returning base of fire. The Iranian looked at the flashes of gunfire coming from the adjacent area, an elevated location, most likely a hill hidden in the thickets. It took only a short time for Akim to realize there was only one gun firing from the hill, and that the machine gun was concentrating its fire toward the far end of the trail. Grabbing up another group of nearby men, he pointed to the location atop the hill. Pointing out the direction of the machine gun fire, he dispatched them to move in the opposite direction. The men moved out weaving past the established firing line.

Rounds whistled closely past Dayan's head. Bullets crashed into the mound, throwing bits of dirt and rock into his face. The volume of returning gunfire was increasing — becoming heavier — as more men from the other side joined the resistance line. From the cries coming from his own side, Dayan realized he had already suffered casualties. By his calculations, his team had just a few more minutes before the Arabs either pushed across the clearing and forced the mercenaries out or flanked them from either side. That would finish it. The only question left in the Israeli's mind was how much longer they could continue inflicting casualties before they absolutely had to fall back and withdraw.

If they waited too long, they would eventually be surrounded and trapped. In the short time he had been in this gunfight, he had burned through two magazines and was nearing the end of his third. He could assume that the rest of his team had gone through as many. He had to make a decision; they would need enough ammunition to cover their escape.

CHAPTER 49

Even from where he stood, the peasant could hear the rattle of gunfire growing as the battle ensued. Waiting off the side of the road, he felt droplets of sweat running down his face. All he could think about was if Eva had made it — if the patron had gotten the message. The young man was no combat expert. He didn't need to be to understand that the mercenaries were fighting overwhelming odds. He had seen these foreigners slipping across the border with his own eyes and knew they were trained professionals. His concern was that soon he would see the road filled with these Arab invaders — then what?

Suddenly, he saw a set of headlights in the distance, — a vehicle was heading towards him. Behind it was another set of headlights, then another, and still more. Eva had done it! His baby sister had come through. The vehicles swiftly approached and within seconds the first set of headlights materialized into a farm truck.

Stepping onto the road, the peasant waved down the convoy. The lead truck slowed to a halt just inches from where he stood. The passenger door swung open and out jumped a short, petite girl of no more than fifteen. Throwing her arms around the young man, she grabbed him tightly in an embrace; the peasant enthusiastically reciprocated.

"Eva," he said, with a relieved sigh. "You made it, you're safe!" He rolled his fingers through her mane of curly black hair.

"I did as you asked," she replied excitedly. "I found the patron!"

The driver's door opened and out stepped a man that, even in the darkness, stood tall and lean. The man moved into the headlights revealing Diego Mancha, the patron. He cut the perfect figure of a South American aristocrat. His long, silver-colored hair came to his shoulders. His well-trimmed beard was a matching color, completing his authoritative presence.

"Patron," the peasant said, excitedly, "you got my message."

Mancha looked off into the darkness, as he listened to the gunfire crackling in the night. "Sounds like we've arrived in the nick of time," the aristocrat chuckled. "I appreciate your diligence."

Turning away, Mancha began signaling the other trucks that had lined up behind him. Several figures leaped from the back of the big hauling truck and assembled in front of the headlights. They were farmers, still garbed in their work clothes — coveralls, worn blue jeans, and sweat-stained shirts. Some even wore the stereotypical straw hats. They were quickly joined by more people from the other trucks. All were similarly dressed in the various forms of work clothes of those who earned their living working the land. From their dress and stance, they were clearly not soldiers.

The one thing they all had in common was the guns they now held in their hands.

Long accustomed to the culture of radicalism and totalitarianism that had dominated their country, these farmers were experienced in carrying weapons to protect their community. When the latest wave of radical violence swept their country, they assumed chaos would follow. Left-wing rebels or right-wing vigilantes would lash out with violent military reprisals. Determined not to be victims of either, the people in the nearby villages banded together and made deals with black market elements to obtain guns. They turned to those such as Patron Diego Mancha, a retired professional soldier, who had served many years in the Uruguayan army. He helped finance the purchase of equipment and inspected the weapons bought. He, along with several other former soldiers and policemen, set about training the local townsmen twice a week in basic tactics, marksmanship, and drills.

The young peasant Rios had employed to observe the Iranian camp feared mercenaries would not be sufficient to fend off the invaders. She took it upon herself to alert the townsmen to the army and their perceived intentions building over the border. Due to her warning, Mancha had been training the townspeople in preparation for this night.

Diego Mancha looked his ragged army over. "Everyone!" He opened in a smooth but powerful voice that immediately captured everyone's attention. "You can hear the gunfire in the distance." The Patron turned slightly in the direction of the battle. Turning back to the crowd he said, "Right now, the battle is being waged between the group Pietro is helping, against a much larger group of invaders trying to sneak into our country." The Patron paused to look at the people before him. Even in the darkness, he could read the looks on their faces. They were nervous but willing. "The police are in no position to stop them and neither is the army. That leaves us. If we don't stop them, it will be our lands and our homes they attack first. Are we ready?" Mancha's question was answered with a loud chorus of cheers.

Calling on men who had been soldiers, Mancha turned to Pietro. Pietro immediately started down the road to direct the ragged force toward where the battle was taking place. With Mancha in the lead, the rest of the group followed.

Klaas Vanderhook could already see the beginning stages of the battle turning. The Arabs had by now headed to the trees to take cover behind rock piles to begin returning fire. Initially, the fire was erratic, a sure sign that the Arabs were shooting blind. But now the shots were becoming more concentrated and accurate. Looking at his watch, he figured that in another two minutes, he would have his team fall back and break contact. Sweat poured from his head and soaked through his balaclava. Adrenaline was rushing through his system. He was feeling the exhilaration of the battle he was so addicted to.

One of his men, a Colombian, manning the ammo belt feeding the machine gun called out that the box was nearly empty. The barrel was turning red from the heat of so much hot lead blasting through it. The end was nearing.

Suddenly the air grew thick with a powerful pungent odor that instantly overpowered the mercenaries' senses, followed by a blinding flash and deafening explosion. Seeing nothing but darkness and hearing only echoes, Vanderhook was at a loss to understand what was happening. The only sense that had not betrayed him was his feeling of sharp objects cutting into his shoulder and lower body.

His hearing gradually returned to the sounds of gunfire; only much closer than it had been before. This time, it was not coming from below, but from above. The sound of men shouting in Arabic was coming from only a few feet away. The sound of his machine gun had stopped. He called out to his men but received no answer. Reaching out, he grabbed the gunner's torso. He only had to touch him to realize he was feeling a lifeless corpse. More bullets tore into the former Dutch marine, they cut into his arm and thigh. Finally, a sharp blow slammed into his head. He slumped over into the dirt — a lifeless corpse along with the bodies of his men.

Dayan had seen and heard the flash of the grenade as it exploded near Vanderhook's position. The machine gun suddenly stopping told the Israeli all he needed to know — the Dutch marine and his team were dead. It was now apparent the Arabs were moving quickly in a counter-attack. They were well led and seizing the initiative.

Time had run out. Turning to face his men, whose outlines he could only make out from the flashes of gunfire coming from their weapons, Dayan screamed his commands to fall back. He heard the order repeated by Ripley, then Perez. The men began to fall back from their positions.

Soon after they slid deeper into the tree line, they heard more gunfire. Looking through his optics, Dayan saw a skirmish line of shadowed figures approaching from their flank, maybe ten at the most. They spread out into a battle line intermingled with the trees. They stood far enough off to be largely out of the line of fire from their comrades.

Then, the Israeli felt a slight thump just a foot or so from his leg. Quickly understanding what the object was, Dayan rolled over behind a thick buildup of dirt and shut his eyes tightly. The blast was ear-shattering! Even with his eyes shut he could sense the instant flash of blinding white light. Opening his eyes, he was relieved to see that he still had his night vision, but his ears rang, and he could only hear echoes.

Wasting no time, the Israeli grabbed his weapon. Turning in the direction of the newly formed flank of attackers, he began opening fire. His shots were in the general direction, but he doubted he hit anyone. As his hearing began to return, he realized that the main body across the clearing had ceased firing. The flanking force of Arabs continued advancing. Like well-trained soldiers, the Arabs moved, covered by fire, with every other man moving a few feet forward while the ones behind laid down covering fire to keep the enemy heads down. The flankers continued this assault in a slow methodical leapfrog-like movement, making it nearly impossible for the mercenaries to lay down adequate return fire.

The enemy was closing. The mercenaries tried to fall back. Whatever damage they had inflicted would have to suffice. The flanking attackers were about to overrun them. Ripley and a couple of others had slipped next to Dayan attempting to lay counter-fire. The Israeli shouted the command to withdraw. His order resulted in a chaotic gathering of men fighting for their lives trying to escape. Their gunfire was erratic as each mercenary fired wildly in the general direction of their pursuers while trying to back their way out through the vegetation and uneven ground.

Major Akim could follow the retreating enemy's gunfire across the clearing. Noting the distance they were from his men attacking their flank, he radioed the flanking team to stand fast. They held their ground and continued firing. Directing his main force to the location of the ambushers, Akim ordered a full assault. In a swift, coordinated movement, his main body began to move from the trees.

"Maintain cover by fire, every other man!!" the Iranian shouted as his forces moved into the clearing. Every other man fired a few shots, lowered their weapons and moved forward, while the men on their sides provided cover fire. The bursts were quick — three to five shots at a time. It was effective at keeping the enemy disoriented.

Dayan and his team were now receiving fire from both sides. It was all they could do to fire blindly in both directions while attempting to work their way through the thickets behind them. Trying to balance while firing was nearly impossible. Somehow Dayan and his few remaining team members managed to find a soft spot in the vegetation. From there, he could see a long line of dark figures moving across the clearing. The silhouettes were illuminated by the hail of fire they delivered.

A hand reached across and grabbed the Israeli in a firm controlling grip. Turning around, he saw the outlined face of Darren Ripley. Even in the darkness, the Welshman's facial expression could be read well enough to see he was desperate.

"Come on!" Ripley shouted to his commander. "Everyone who's left has made it through. Follow me!" With that, the Welshman jumped into a line of bushes with Dayan following closely behind. Twigs and leaves smacked the faces of the men, grabbing at their clothes as they fought their way through. It was on Dayan's mind and the minds of his team that they would be out in the open trying to escape with the Arabs close behind.

A sudden stop by Ripley brought the Israeli up short. "Someone's coming," Ripley whispered. "They're approaching from the road."

With his rifle in the ready position, Dayan took the lead. Moving to where one of the Colombians had taken up point, the Israeli followed the man's gaze to a collection of people moving in their direction. They advanced in a haphazard tactical line formation, and a closer look revealed rifles in their hands.

Not sure what to make of the situation, Dayan and his men moved up, ready to engage. Were these more Arabs surrounding them? All sorts of possibilities raced through the minds of the mercenaries as they tried to develop a reaction. No matter, the sheer numbers indicated that whatever decision they took, death was inevitable.

"Don't shoot the Brazilian soldiers," a familiar voice shouted out, leading some of the incoming figures. "They are the friends I told you about. Is that you, Middle-Easterner?" the young peasant asked.

"Yes, it's us. The ones your boss told you to lead here?" Dayan clarified.

Darkened figures started to trot through the bushes toward the mercenaries. Dayan and his men were able to make out the image of the peasant who guided them. The young man was excited. "These are my friends. They are the local citizen's militia. I've told them about these invaders, and they've come to help."

At that point, a tall lean figure moved up to join the conversation. "Gentlemen," he opened in a quiet and polished tone. "It looks as though you need some help." The figure spoke with the voice of someone groomed in the world of elite society. Diego Mancha, looked beyond the mercenaries as he listened to the collection of approaching gunfire. Turning to some men following him, Mancha ordered them to get their troops online and prepare to move forward.

At once the men turned around and quickly moved back to their waiting group. Within minutes, they were dispersing from their tactical groups, moving into a single line facing the mercenaries. Another group moved off to the side forming another line along the far flank.

"I appreciate what I think you are doing for my country," Mancha said to the Middle-Easterner standing before him. "Now, I think it is time for my people to fight. It looks like you have seen enough action for one evening."

Dayan was unsure what to do. He looked at the young peasant who nodded approvingly. The sound of gunfire was getting closer with a few bullets striking nearby trees. With few men left and running low on ammunition, it was an easy decision for the Israeli. Waving his men on, Dayan nodded to the peasant and Mancha, pressing on to disappear into the night.

"Hold your fire!" Major Akim shouted as he looked around noticing that he had not seen any return fire in several minutes. "Hold your fire!!" he shouted again. Gradually, the shooting became less and less until it was dead quiet. Akim and his force moved through the clearing. Advancing to the tree line, they met up with the flanking force that had held back to avoid friendly fire.

Ordering his men to a line, the Iranian pressed his men forward. A few steps into the trees, the Arabs were climbing over the mounds of their attackers' fighting positions. Akim knew they were the bodies of their ambushers. He saw three corpses, from what he could tell from his findings and the comments of some of his men, there were other casualties.

Commanding his men not to waste time with the bodies, Akim reminded them there were still enemies in the vicinity. The Arabs pressed on, maintaining their combat line, continuing their sweep as they progressed back into the tree line.

Diego Mancha had the composure of a professional soldier. He had seen a great deal of combat in his years as an officer in the army. That experience taught him that patience and timing were often decisive factors. His hope was that his people would prove steady, given what little training they had received in comparison to who they were about to engage. His question would soon be answered.

It wasn't long before the sounds of twigs cracking and bushes rustling were heard nearby. It was easy to conclude that whoever they were up against, they were coming in force. Gripping his Steyr Aug rifle, an informal going away present at his retirement, Mancha prepared himself mentally. Despite his wanting to give the order, he waited. He needed to catch these invaders at their most vulnerable to ensure a quick victory. Otherwise, his people might not be able to win a prolonged fight against a more highly trained enemy. He knelt down in the bushes and prayed no one would get nervous and fire early — hoped they would trust his judgment.

Less than ten meters away from his position, Mancha watched as the bushes opened up revealing a collection of combatants in a rough-looking tactical line. The moment had come. "Fire!!" the Patron cried as he let loose with his rifle into the line of men before him. His firing was soon joined by the noisy reports of guns opening up in a chorus.

Major Akim was surprised by the sudden explosion of gunfire that lit the night before him. His mind raced, as he realized this was not the few irritants he had fought only moments ago. The line of pale white sparks lit a line that seemed to go on forever. Bullets buzzed around him and his troops like angry wasps from a broken hive. The sheer force overwhelmed him and his men, who were being cut down one after another. "Return fire!!" the Iranian commanded. His men attempted to oblige. For a moment, a line of equal brightness emerged from their other side. The whole battlefield lit up.

It was a brief but intense ten seconds of fighting before Akim realized his men were outmatched. The battle was lost when more hostile gunfire came from the flanks, spraying into the bushes at his men.

"Fall back! Fall back!" the Iranian screamed at the top of his lungs. He could hear his men withdrawing slowly back into the thickets, maintaining their alternating fire and fall back tactical retreat.

Diego Mancha noticed what was going on and at once ordered his forces to move forward pressing the retreating enemy. Not wavering in the slightest, the villagers rose to their feet and moved on their opponents in a clumsy leapfrog fire and maneuver advance of their own. They were determined, as their commander had warned, not to give their adversary a chance to regroup or take cover.

Approaching the clearing, Major Akim could find no means by which to mount a counter-attack. Even if he could, the enemy had proven to be too large and was aggressively pursuing. With no other choice, the Iranian reluctantly called for his men to continue to retreat. Fighting through the clearing to the bushes, the Arabs gradually broke off from the attack as they melted into the vegetation and began racing back along the trails from which they had come.

Akim was almost the last man, as he watched the gunfire of the new opponents moving from the trees into the clearing. A hardened soldier through and through, the Iranian was not going to be the first to run and leave his soldiers. Grabbing the side of his belt, he pulled a single pineapple grenade from it. It was maybe three pounds, but at that moment, it felt like a cinder block. Pulling the pin, Akim gripped the last safety tightly. He waited until he could see the attackers out in the clearing. He didn't have to wait long. Shadowy figures soon appeared and began walking tentatively out onto the open ground.

With all his strength, the Iranian lobbed the grenade. It flew a fair distance before exploding in midair, right in front of the pursuing line. The screams and shouts of a completely surprised foe told the seasoned combat veteran all he needed. Akim leaped to his feet and began running down the goat trail toward the border.

At the edge of the clearing, Mancha called his forces to a halt. He could see the bodies spread across the ground, and the lack of return fire told him that the enemy had seen enough.

CHAPTER 50

The explosion at the seaside resort district in Carrasco was not debilitating to the country's overall economy. But in one of the most exclusive neighborhoods in Montevideo, the attack was as earth-shattering as an earthquake to the many of the country's wealthiest citizens who lived there. No one had come forward to claim responsibility for the atrocity that took twenty-nine lives and caused dozens of severe injuries. Nevertheless, rumors planted on recently developed, unofficial blog sites intimated the attack was the result of a new wave of left-wing violence aimed at punishing the wealthy elites of the country.

For Oskar Straudner, the incident could not have been better timed. The bomb had been crammed into a school backpack and left close to a beach party of teenagers from private schools. He played his role of the concerned government official well. He listened sympathetically to the mob of angry parents demanding action. His reactions were those of a man appalled at the violence and sincerely concerned for his people and the welfare of his country.

His mind, however, was intoxicated with the excitement

and self-satisfaction of a man enjoying his genius — his ability to manipulate everything to forward his agenda.

As the collection of bankers, business moguls, and old money sat around the table pounding their fists, Straudner called for calm and diplomacy. This response only served to heighten their already enraged emotions. Their demands were simple. Straudner had a duty to save the country and that meant taking any drastic measures that would bring back order and safety. Many were decrying the impotence of the government's response. Others were offering to lend financial support for the creation of their own vigilante force or, better yet, support the one that had already started taking action — like the group that killed the former labor president. He tried to downplay all of these ideas, as he promoted himself as a humble peacekeeper.

He thought about how to applaud Ulbrict Laudman, who had planned the bombing. It had masterfully achieved its intended purpose, tipping many who had previously maintained a reserved attitude toward handling violence, to advocating that drastic action was essential. Straudner couldn't help but think that Laudman himself felt a feeling of redemption. A devoted communist, Laudman probably saw killing so many children of privilege as a heroic act. It had to be redeeming for the old German spy, capping everything else he had done thus far for his master.

In any case, the bombing, while a calamity for so many, had given Straudner the last brick he needed. Rising slowly from his seat, he looked at the heated faces around the room. The angry chorus subsided.

"Gentlemen and ladies." Adopting his practiced, presidential presence, he took control of the room. "I empathize with you all. As much as I have tried not to believe it, I must now reluctantly admit our country is in the grip of anarchy. I fear revolution is the very next step."

The faces in the room were a compilation of terror and anger. It was the exact combination the politician was looking for. "Whatever action that is taken must not be separate from our security forces. However, this menace is one that I feel our president is refusing to acknowledge.

"Perhaps, it is a nostalgic sympathy, as he, himself, has a similar past. I don't know." He paused to let the words sink in. "But I do know our country, like so many in South America, has a history. A history of embracing extreme leftist ideologies that only drag us into degradation. These extremist ideologies have always come in the form of violent armed insurrection. It is not just the violence that I feel may be looming, but the type of government that will inevitably follow if such violence is allowed to continue."

The room was quiet. Eyes sparkled, mesmerized. He had transformed himself into their de facto leader, his words absorbed like Holy Scripture.

Determining that he had done enough, the politician gave a nod and started out the door. Further words were not needed. Those at the table lived in the world of superior education and control of large businesses. They understood that nothing more need be said. The politician had told them enough; his actions said the rest.

Micha Cohen was neither jubilant nor disappointed. His mood was one of uncertainty. He and his men had succeeded in stopping the first wave of Arab militia from crossing into the country. They had destroyed the Arab transportation. It had been a good mission exceeding the expectations of both Israelis. However, they had lost most of their force in the process. Dayan estimated he had, at best, five men left. This calculation was predicated on the idea that those remaining still wished to remain in their employ — a question that had not yet been answered.

Cohen wanted to know who in the hell these mystery rescuers were who had miraculously appeared at the opportune moment. He wasn't complaining. Given his subordinate's report, they had been the reason the Arabs were completely driven off, and the rest of the mercenary team was able to escape. Their identity and the nature of their involvement still remained a mystery. All he could ascertain from Dayan's report was they had apparently been a group with mutual interests — and, obviously, mutual intelligence connections. This group had been apprised of the Arabs and were led to the scene of battle by the young peasant working in Ms. Rios' employ.

Then there was the question of Plūcker. His recent demise had been unfortunate. What was worse; he had been the logistics coordinator and recruiter for this whole operation. What did his death mean for them going forward? Dayan explained that Plūcker's assistant had stepped up to take over for her former boss. In passing, the commando had also mentioned that she had been the Irishman's barmaid for the most part. This did not sit well with the old man. He thought about their operation and how risky he felt the situation had become.

Cohen was beside himself as he tried to make sense of the whole thing. In all his reflections, he deduced nothing as he felt he was working with too much speculation and not enough hard facts. For a veteran intelligence officer, it was an appalling position to be in. The katsa wanted to investigate the matter further. The men were recuperating, and Dayan had no sooner delivered his report before he was off to meet with the Guardians of Israel.

Cohen, in Dayan's absence, had started working with the young radicals as they collected intelligence and maintained surveillance on the Cuban. He didn't want to involve these young hoodlums in any of this business. However, as Dayan had pointed out, they would not go away and would only be a threat to the mission if allowed to work on their own.

The other problem was the assassination itself. Cohen had realized the need to blind the Iranians by taking out their intelligence source. What concerned Dayan was while his mercenaries would have no trouble killing a bunch of armed men illegally crossing a border, they would not be open to the idea of a cold, calculated assassination. And, after the recent battle, they would not be fit to carry it out in any case. This left the radicals as a necessary force. Provided they could be controlled and listen to orders, they were really the only solution to finding the help needed to complete this operation.

The katsa didn't like the situation, but the idea of letting Mendoza continue to operate against them was even worse. Nursing a glass of iced tea, he sank slowly into a chair in what was serving as his office. He looked out at the skyline defining the mountains. He was playing a very dangerous game — but it wasn't his first. Like so many other situations the found himself in, it was the rush of the risk…why he livid.

Ali Anwar al Qalmini rubbed his forehead with his thumb and forefinger. The news from Major Akim was distressing. Their first wave of troops had been driven back by some unknown force. The major's report spoke of a professionally set ambush that took them by surprise. This led Qalmini to assume that it was those meddlesome Israelis. Most likely, it was this Kafka Dayan fellow who had directed it.

Then the major went on to explain in his debriefing about the sudden appearance of an unexplained army that joined the fight, overwhelmed them, and drove them back across the border. In his mind, Qalmini recognized this mystery army could not have been the Israelis alone. The Major sent a small reconnaissance team to investigate a few days later. He found out it was the peasants from the local communities that had armed themselves and formed their own self-defense force. Someone had alerted them about a body of armed men secretly moving across the border, and they reacted in a most unexpected way.

Sitting in his office, Qalmini was beside himself. He was pleased that his initial reservation about their politician, Oskar Straudner, betraying them had proven false. That meant the operation could still move forward. He was, however, dismayed over the unforeseen problem the local militiamen presented — it was a dangerous new complication.

"I had planned to have to deal with security forces, issues with destabilizing the government, the possibility of that creep Straudner fucking us over," he said half chuckling, as he looked at Surriman standing quietly in the corner. "But I could not have anticipated a bunch of farmers being such a pain in the ass in this plan." The Iranian lowered his head and began to breathe deeply.

"So, what's the next step?" Surriman asked, emerging from the corner of the office to approach the Iranian.

Raising his head, Qalmini looked over at the young Arab now standing directly in front of his desk. "The problem right now is that this fucking peasant militia is in our way. But..." the Iranian waved his finger. "We can deal with them in the future. Our vehicles are shot up, and even if our men had gotten across the border, our transportation plan is ruined. We need new vehicles right now! That is our priority."

"Well," Surriman spoke up. "Do we obtain more the same way we did last time?"

The Iranian nodded his head, "We have to."

CHAPTER 51

The street housing Bolivar Investments & Acquisitions was eerily deserted at 0400hrs. Dayan and Solomon Gold watched the building from across the street on the far side of the coffee shop. Standing in the shadows, the two looked as if they were having a smoke after a night out before going home and sleeping it off. They had drenched themselves with whiskey to add to the effect. Dressed in jeans, T-shirts, and wearing baseball caps, neither man looked at all out of place.

Gold leaned against the wall next to Dayan. They searched for irregularities that might give them an indication of a trap or change in pattern from what they had been able to track. After twenty minutes, Gold pulled a small disposable lighter from his coat pocket, ignited a small flame, and passed his hand over it signaling the rest of his group who were waiting several meters down the street.

"Well, are you ready?" Dayan asked casually.

Gold took a deep breath and nodded trying to play it cool. He had promised himself he would be a professional. Not only because he didn't want to embarrass himself in front of the veteran Special Forces soldier, but because he couldn't fail again. Too much was at stake.

"Are they ready?" the Israeli asked indicated the assembled team down the street.

Gold responded, "They know what's at stake."

With no more words, the two men meandered across the street. The cameras from the investment office would only show two drunkards on a binge. The road remained empty, no vehicles approached from either direction. The two men took their time. They had completed crossing the street when the rest of their team, a group of four young men, began to follow. Like the two ahead of them, the quartet moved as though they were friends enjoying the last vestiges of the night.

Gold led the way as he and Dayan pretended to stumble along. Having looked at the intelligence gained from Gold and his people, Dayan pretended to stumble along. Having looked at the intelligence gained from Gold and his people, Dayan developed a plan. For over a week, he and these men had rehearsed this operation. The radicals were highly impressed with the Israeli, who quickly caused them to realize they really were novices. Dayan was equally impressed by the sincerity and commitment the radicals displayed during training and learning how to collect intelligence. Both Gold and the men he chose readily absorbed all the training tips and advice Dayan and Cohen had offered. Now, they were performing with discipline and sticking to the plan as rehearsed.

Approaching the back-alley Gold had recced a few weeks earlier, he and Dayan pretended to joke with each other; Dayan could feel the growing tension in the young man. It had felt like hours, even though it was but a few minutes when they finally reached the back door Gold had previously tested. Knowing that a camera was observing them, the two went about as planned. Gold leaned up against the wall, while Dayan pretended to start urinating.

As expected, it was only seconds before the door flew open and a large man burst outside to confront them. "What the hell do you think you are doing?" he growled, walking over to confront the Israeli.

Dayan continued facing the wall, his hands held down by his crotch. Gold approached the man trying to intervene. "Hey man, my friend suddenly had to empty his tank, ya know."

The large man turned his attention to the younger man now standing close to him. As he was about to speak, Dayan pulled a small, double-bladed knife from under his belt. Turning slightly, he took a few steps toward the large man now completely occupied with the young radical. When he was within arms distance, in one move that only lasted a second, the commando grabbed the man's head with one hand, while driving the knife blade deep into his brain stem. The man died instantly and silently.

Gold, nearly petrified, stood as he watched the Israeli's cold precision. However, he quickly regained his composure and continued trying to explain himself to the now-deceased guard. As he did so, he slowly stumbled back until he had a clear view of the inside of the building.

At the same time, Dayan quietly lowered the body to the ground. He rose up looking at the radical who was now clumsily raising his hand to his chin and extending his index finger pointing half-heartedly to the left. Gold then lowered his hand to his chest in an equally clumsy way, whereupon he extended his index and middle fingers in a scratching motion. It was the code the two had worked out. Pointing to the left with his index finger told the group following them to go left upon entering the building. The two fingers across the chest meant there were two more guards.

As Dayan rose to an erect position, he carefully reached under his oversized leather jacket as if straightening out his belt. Lowering his hands to his sides, he held a small Beretta 32 caliber pistol with a silencer. Slowly, he brought the weapon up under his arms as he leaned down pretending to be hungover. Shuffling toward the door, he saw two suited figures standing several meters away talking to each other. Both were holding coffee cups, neither one was paying the slightest attention to the door or the man now stumbling through it. It was early in the morning, near the end of their shift. As Dayan had anticipated, the guards spent so many weeks on the job with no action, their attention was elsewhere.

It took a second for one of the guards to realize the man in the doorway was not his comrade. He waved wildly attempting to alert his partner who was walking over to escort the drunkard out. That guard was completely surprised when he took the 'drunk's' arm and found himself staring at a small pistol. Tucking the barrel of the weapon tightly under the guard's chin, the Israeli fired two shots in rapid succession. Both rounds exploded out the back of the guard's head painting the wall behind him with a large splatter of blood. The first guard watched his comrade fall not feeling the two rounds entering into his own skull.

The whole action seemed to be frozen in time but had actually only taken a few seconds. Gold was again taken aback by the cold precision of the Israeli, as he rapidly executed all three guards in what felt like the blink of an eye.

Turning back to Gold, Dayan saw that the young man was in a state of shock. It was clear he had never seen someone killed so cavalierly or efficiently.

"Call your friends," the Israeli said calmly. Despite having killed the first guard in front of the surveillance camera, no alarm had sounded. Dayan assumed they had just seen the totality of the building's security force.

His wits returning, Gold pulled his lighter from his pocket and proceeded as if lighting a cigarette. Moments later the other four men in the alley joined them. Dayan stood beside the building standing watch as the rest of the team moved inside.

The other four members came in carrying large knapsacks. They joined the Israeli now standing over the bodies of the two guards. They took up positions next to him while Gold dragged the body of the third guard farther into the building, shutting the door behind him. The other four team members were aghast as they took in all the blood and corpses. Dayan snapped his fingers loudly to get everyone's attention. "We don't have time for this!" he barked.

With everyone inside, the team moved to another door. They found themselves in a well-appointed hallway lined with expensive leather furniture and collectible works of art. Continuing down the seemingly endless hallway, they reached the main reception area of the building.

Lowering their shoulder bags, they each pulled out a compact Uru model, 9mm caliber, submachine gun. They were additional stock Raizza was able to acquire from a well-stocked inventory on a farm whose owner was a former army officer. That officer had taken part in Operation Condor back in the eighties. With no current fear of a communist revolution in sight, the old officer was quite willing to part with the weapons for a decent price.

Dayan was planning both the border and Mendoza operations. The weapons would be useful in one or both of the other raids. Hiding them in crates of machine parts, Raizza arranged to have them moved onto a cargo ship bound for a maintenance company Plūcker had occasionally worked with in Buenos Aires. On this occasion, the company owner received a large number of machine parts at a very favorable discount. In return, he asked no questions nor made any protests when unexplained figures showed up and snagged one of the crates conveniently left detached from the others.

The men placed their weapons on the floor before digging into their bags. For magazines and ammunition, Raizza had tried to meet her clients' wishes in procuring a sizable quantity of hollow point 9x19m Parabellum subsonic ammunition and suppressors, but not understanding the complexities involved with matching suppressors to weapons, she had gotten a smaller size of suppressor than what was required. Although disappointed, Dayan was pleased with hollow point ammo.

Gold sat at the security station around a large, polished, mahogany desk. Checking video feeds from all cameras, he concluded the building was unoccupied. The other four men finished loading magazines. They handed weapons to Gold and Dayan along with three additional magazines the two men quickly placed in their coat pockets. It was for that reason Dayan ordered all members of the assassination team to wear oversized jackets with large exterior pockets. That way they could better conceal weapons while moving around the streets and have space for additional ammunition.

The Israeli checked to ensure the back door had been shut. He tested it to guarantee it wouldn't jam at an inopportune moment. He had seen too many well-planned operations fall apart by missing a small detail. He was adamant that they had a good escape route established. Immediate exfiltration was a critical point. The prospect of a well-organized escape after completing a mission was vastly different than trying to escape under duress.

Meanwhile, two of the bodies were dragged down the hall and placed in sitting positions. Dayan's plans called for this to be the first thing Mendoza and his security detail would see. If it worked, it would give the assassination team an edge. It was also to their advantage that the front doors of the building were solid oak, limiting visibility into the hallway.

Due to the inexperience of his operatives in actual combat, the Israeli was taking no chances. From the intelligence acquired, the men surrounding the Cuban were all former members of the Argentinian security services. His team was a bunch of angry youth barely out of boyhood.

Gold and his team silently marveled at the Israeli commando who now led them. He was the type of fighter they imagined they wanted to be. He was experienced, methodical, and showed no hesitation when carrying out his mission. Solomon Gold had grown up aspiring to be this type of man. He, like the others, was determined to prove themselves this day.

That was the driving force that had pushed them to take the Israeli's training seriously and work to maintain their goal of professionalism. Gold had felt shame when he froze up watching the Israeli so easily kill the first guard. Even though he had quickly rebounded to fulfill his responsibility, the very idea that he had even for a second froze in the midst of battle was totally unacceptable. Looking at the faces of his compatriots, he realized they felt the same inadequacy when comparing themselves to this commando. From this point forward, he was determined to prove himself by being the ultimate professional carrying out a mission.

It had been an hour since they had entered the building when a small handheld radio on top of the security system cracked to life. "Base, base, do you read? Over," a gruff voice asked.

The young team paused in confusion. The Israeli raced to the radio and grabbed the mike. Thrusting it toward Gold, he growled, but in a whisper, "Answer them!"

Taking the radio, the radical steadied himself before pressing the talk button. "Yes, we read you."

The gruff voice responded, "We're coming in. We'll be at the building in less than five minutes. Is the perimeter clear? Do you see anyone suspicious in the vicinity?"

Gold momentarily hesitated looking to the Israeli for an answer. "Yes, yes, everything's fine." Looking at the monitor, he saw nothing that would be suspicious. "All looks good — there are only a few people on the streets and none look to be doing anything strange."

"Good," the gruff voice replied. "We're coming in."

The radio went dead. Dayan looked around the room. The faces of his team had turned pale. "Keep your cool guys. Remember, don't fire until you see Mendoza."

All heads nodded. Turning to Gold, the Israeli gave him a cold, serious look. "Is your girl in position?"

Gold looked down at the video screen showing the sidewalk in front of the building and the buildings directly across the street. Giving it a quick scan, he looked back up at the commando and gave a sharp nod. "She's up for this. We're all trusting her, and she'll come through."

Dayan pulled his cap down over his face until only the slits revealing his eyes were left. The rest of the team followed suit and pulled their balaclavas over their heads. Their moment had finally come.

It seemed like years. The excitement was building in the young radicals. Within minutes, the camera screen showed a convoy of four Suburbans coming down the street. A few seconds later, they were pulling up directly in front of Bolivar Investments & Acquisitions. Breathing among the young radicals was becoming quicker as the moment approached.

Gold and Dayan watched as the doors of the vehicles opened and several athletic looking, suited figures jumped out. The bodyguards formed a perimeter around the convoy. No weapons could be seen, leading Dayan to believe they were all carrying handguns with the sub-machine guns and shotguns still tucked in the vehicles. A few minutes later the back door to one of the Suburban's opened to reveal the short and distinguished frame of Elloy Mendoza. The Cuban slid from his seat onto the sidewalk. He was well dressed and carrying himself as the ever-important corporate executive.

With his attention focused solely on the building before him, he started to ascend the stairs. He was soon flanked by four of the detail leaving the rest to stand guard over the convoy. Dayan's information proved correct — the main force stayed until Mendoza was inside the building. Only then did the convoy leave. This meant they would probably have to deal with the larger force, once the convoy heard gunfire from inside.

Viewing the video screen, Gold watched with anticipation. The four suited guards placed themselves in a diamond formation surrounding their charge. Mendoza walked up the stairs at a leisurely pace. The arrogance of the Cuban and his dire need to maintain appearances seemed to cause consternation among the men trying to protect him.

Dayan held his weapon tight. As he shifted glances between the door and his team, he could see the sweat soaking through their balaclavas. "It's just another training exercise," he whispered to help calm their nerves. "You've shot these weapons several times and know they work. You've heard the sound of the guns firing and know what to expect." He couldn't tell by their masked faces if his words were having any effect.

Lined up opposite the security station where they had propped up the dead guards, Dayan had positioned the four men near the corner in a side lounge — they had shadows and furniture for cover. It wasn't much, but it would add to the response time of the bodyguards. Dayan hoped the several weeks of mundane routine had served to dull the guards' reactions.

Dayan's team had been arranged in rows of two, with the first two kneeling on the floor behind a velvet couch. The next two were a few feet further back behind some plants and tall lamps. They remained standing, ready to provide backup fire. Dayan and Gold remained at the monitor behind the desk watching their target nearing.

CHAPTER 52

Mendoza and his entourage were on the last few steps before gaining the hallway and reaching the door. Tucking the weapon tightly into his shoulder, Dayan couldn't help but feel the awkwardness of the solid wood shoulder stock of this old weapon. It wasn't the type of weapon he normally used. The wood stock was not alien to his experience, but his preference was for the newer rubber framed fiberglass systems he usually used. Still, he had managed to use the weapon successfully during practice.

The Cuban was now at the door. Gold alerted the team just seconds before the doorknob began turning. Dayan and Gold tried to hide by ducking behind the control system. It was too late to remind everyone not to fire until the target was inside the room. Both Dayan and Gold could only hope that no one fired early. The continued nervous breathing did not leave either man with much confidence.

The door opened slowly. Immediately, the first two of the entourage walked in. Not expecting anything inside, their attention was focused on making way for their employer. Mendoza followed directly behind them. It took the guard's seconds after they turned to notice the blood-stained corpses sitting on the chairs, and then the masked gunmen in the corners. By then it was too late.

The members of the team who had knelt down opened fire. Their weapons exploded in a barrage of gunfire as they sprayed the doorway with a hail of bullets. But, in their excitement, they failed to take aim. Their bullets whipped around wildly managing to hit everything except their quarry. The instincts and training of the bodyguards quickly kicked in as they dove to move their charge out of the line of fire and grab for their weapons.

Realizing the situation was about to turn into a gunfight, Dayan drew his weapon. Emerging from behind the security desk, he had a calmness that defied logic and deliberately took aim. His first two shots caught the first guard drawing his weapon. Two direct taps into the guard's chest and heart cavity caused him to drop the gun he was lifting from his holster. Dayan's next rounds caught the head of another guard coming through the doorway. It was lucky none of the guards appeared to be wearing body armor. Looking around, the commando realized that aside from the two kneeling down, no one else on the team was firing. "Shoot, God Dammit!" He shouted to the near-catatonic young men watching.

Lifting his weapon, Gold lined his sights to where Mendoza was curled up in a corner with one of his body-guards attempting to shield him. Belching off a few rounds, he watched the bullets tear into the torso and head of the bodyguard. The guard's body slid down on top of a frantic Mendoza, who was now trying to crawl toward the door.

Outside, sitting in a coffee shop at a small table, a young woman of no more than nineteen years of age sat watching the activity at Bolivar Investments & Acquisitions. A longtime friend, Reima Caulter had agreed to help with Gold's plan. Nervous watching the gun battle, she took a deep breath and pulled a small, disposable phone from under her coat. She had been instructed to wait until the shooting started. If the guards around the convoy moved toward the building once the battle commenced, she was to push send for a pre-dialed number.

A loud echoing explosion suddenly startled the guards. Dayan wasted no time. Ordering his team forward, the six men quickly charged for the door. By now Dayan's team had regained their faculties, and the Israeli's training began to settle them. Three of the men took to the doors where they found themselves staring down at a stunned group of suited figures lying prone on the stair steps. A giant black cloud permeated the atmosphere along with a powerful burning smell.

Directly across the street, an inferno was burning wildly over the remnants of a car. The car, which had been stolen a day earlier, was wired with several sticks of dynamite. It was driven to the location by the four men now with Dayan. At the same time, Reima made her way to the coffee shop to continue sketching while she waited.

The car exploded, rocking the entire neighborhood and creating massive destruction. Startled to near panic, the young girl edged her way out of the coffee shop and saw the destruction just up the road. Turning the other way, she started down the street, walking as fast as possible, trying not to look obvious.

Gold's team went to the door immediately. This time, they took careful aim and began firing down at the guards below. Dayan grabbed Mendoza by the back of the neck as the Cuban attempted to slither away. The Israeli glanced at Gold, who had knelt down right next to him. The glance asked only one thing — who was to finish the job?

Gold looked down at the man who had commanded the brutal death of Myra, an innocent young girl. Even though his nerves were getting the better of him, he knew the deed had to be done by him. Forcing the Cuban onto his back with brute force, Dayan pressed against his neck and arm. Gold seized the other arm, pinning Mendoza down. Reaching for his knife Gold looked down at the squirming man now threatening greater reprisals if they killed him. Gold held the knife to the man's face. But suddenly he froze, unable to move any further.

Sensing the young man's problem and being pressed for time, the Israeli grabbed his own double-bladed knife. Gripping it tightly, he looked down at the Cuban until their eyes met. "I could kill you quickly and easily, but then you could have done the same for Myra."

The Cuban gave Dayan a puzzled look. Gold remained frozen. The Israeli raised his arm and in one fast, precise move he drove the knife directly into Mendoza's eye socket. Clear liquid burst from his eye and was followed by a rising sea of blood that poured from his head onto the floor. Gold fell back onto the floor aghast at what had just happened. The Israeli pulled the knife violently from the Cuban's socket. Mendoza screamed a curdling cry of immense pain as he proceeded to flop about on the floor like a fish out of water.

Gold tried to recover as he watched the violent display. Deciding Mendoza had paid enough given the time they had, the radical raised his sub-machine gun and fired. The

Cuban's head exploded in a volcanic eruption as blood and brain matters sprayed everywhere.

"Fall back!!" the Israeli shouted. "Fall Back!!"

Gradually everyone began picking up and moving down the hall toward the back door. Two of the young assassins shut the front door and slid the bodies of Mendoza and one of the guards up against it to provide a hasty blockade. Then everyone started out the back. On the way out, the Israeli quickly glanced at the monitors to see if anyone was coming up the back alley while the rest of the team gathered up their knapsacks. The alley was deserted. Flinging the door open, the radicals began slipping through the door in rapid succession. Dayan was the last one out. He pulled a stick of dynamite from his jacket pocket and lit it. It fizzled in his hand as the burn ate through the foot-long cord. Throwing it over to the security station, he raced down the hall. Sprinting the ten or so meters across the small back room, the Israeli practically dove out the door. Bursting through the fire escape door, he caught the tail end of his team.

The assassins were now running down the back alley, adrenaline rushing through their bodies. Seconds later, they heard another ear-shattering boom. It was the dynamite destroying any possible recording that the cameras may have caught of them. At the edge of the alley, Dayan stopped everyone and ordered them to stuff their weapons and additional magazines into their bags. After doing so, they raised their balaclavas and headed to the main road. Walking at a brisk pace, they made their way up two blocks. People who had heard the explosions began to accumulate in the streets. Confusion abounded and, in the distance, the police sirens and other emergency vehicles were becoming louder.

Finally, they saw a parked small, green van. Knocking on

the side door, it slid open revealing a tall, lanky figure with a crop of sandy blond hair that hung around his head like a bird's nest. The lanky figure said nothing. He just jumped into the driver's seat and started the engine. Dayan had insisted that the getaway driver not stay sitting in the driver's seat waiting. Hours of just sitting would eventually attract attention.

Piling into the vehicle, everyone scrunched up against the walls of the van. Gold was the last one in and slid the door closed. The van lurched forward and pulled out of the parking lot. Everyone sat in silence — it was a virtual mortuary. Once on the main road, the driver turned on the radio at Dayan's request, to help provide a semblance of normality.

It was less than two minutes before the team heard the familiar sounds of police sirens screaming past them on their way to the scene of the carnage and mayhem they had just created. Dayan caught Solomon Gold staring at him. The young man said nothing, he didn't have to. His facial expression said it all. He had been the one who wanted to inflict a painful death on the Cuban. He wanted to get the needed justice for Myra. But, at that moment, he was too scared to do so. The radical's look was one mixed with gratefulness for the Israeli doing what he couldn't and humiliation at the thought that when the time came, he couldn't avenge Myra.

CHAPTER 53

The Candelária Church of Rio De Janeiro is truly one of Brazil's great historical treasures. Outside, the castle is grayish-brown brick with white trim. Inside, it is a majestic, palatial creation of masterful design. Even for the Muslim, Ali Anwar al Qalmini, it was a breath-taking experience to walk among the long-standing monuments and feel the history.

However, tourism was not his purpose for today's engagement. Walking slowly to a polished, mahogany pew located in a deserted area of the sparsely populated holy site, the Iranian sat down. He leaned forward to give the impression of concentrating on his prayers. The men of his security detail fanned out in an arbitrary looking pattern encircling their charge but maintaining enough distance to not attract unwanted attention.

He waited patiently, admiring the stained glass windows of the cathedral's ceilings that allowed a heavenly light to brighten the otherwise gray gothic setting and the huge, lighted altar at the front of the building. The altar was the front piece to highlighting a large, emboldening picture of the Christian deity guarded by angelic lights. It wasn't long before a gorgeous woman walked past him making her way to the altar. He directed his eyes toward the ceiling to avoid staring at the golden-haired beauty, elegantly dressed in a white sports jacket, matching skirt, dark stockings, and black heels.

The Contessa Selena de Alvarez was as punctual as ever, even on short notice. To avoid any suspicious looks, the Contessa played the role of a good Catholic as she went before the altar and genuflected while making the sign of the cross. Turning, she made her way back up the aisle until she found a seat in the pew directly beside the Iranian. Illana Muricia followed the Contessa and took a seat directly in front of her employer.

In desperation, Qalmini had reached out to contact the Contessa. Their business had previously been conducted either in Paraguay or, more safely, in Argentina. The Iranian, however, feared the recent repercussions of Mendoza's assassination and the discovery of the Israeli terrorist compromised either location. The extent of the Israeli network was, as of yet, unknown, thus an uncompromised location was needed. Qalmini decided Rio De Janeiro would be far enough from previous meeting places to be a safe alternative. A veteran intelligence officer accustomed to secret meetings, Qalmini tended to disapprove of religious sites as spots for meetings. Though they may offer certain protections — such as a general location where all sorts of people could congregate and meet randomly, they also allowed spies and secret police to just as easily follow and observe unnoticed. Given the limited time and the idea that such a well-visited historical site would be discrete and provide security for their meeting, he decided it was an acceptable risk.

Qalmini came straight to the point. "Forgive the suddenness. I know this meeting was on extremely short notice."

"I also noticed that it is not being held in our usual meeting place in Buenos Aires," the Contessa replied, her eyes focused straight ahead.

"Recent developments have transpired that make Argentina untenable at this moment," the Iranian answered.

The Contessa sighed, "You mean the recent assassination of our Cuban friend?" she smiled. "I doubt he is the reason for your sudden message to meet you here."

Qalmini grimaced. "We have had a considerable setback. Our forces were stopped at the border by a group of saboteurs."

"So, you want me to find these saboteurs for you," the Contessa dipped her head slightly, "since your previous contact is no longer available?"

"We know who the saboteur is," the Iranian replied with bitterness. "They not only succeeded in obstructing our initial force set to go to the city, but these bastards destroyed the trucks we spent months procuring. Right now, we have no means of transportation once inside the country." Qalmini was careful not to mention Uruguay by name. "We need vehicles and fast."

The Contessa put her finger on her chin. "How fast?"

"Within the next week at the latest," Qalmini replied, trying to mask his desperation.

"It was a slow and methodical process under normal circumstances," the Contessa said, assessing the problem. "With all that is going on right now, sudden moves of this type will definitely attract a lot of attention."

The Iranian pursed his lips. "I'm aware of the risks and

difficulties involved. I'm willing to be quite liberal with expenses and fees to procure your services."

Bringing her hand to rest against her cheek, the Contessa considered the Iranian's proposal. Finally, she turned to face him. "It won't be easy, and I won't make any guarantees."

Qalmini nodded.

"If I'm entirely successful, my price will be a million in US currency. In addition to all incurred expenses."

"If not entirely successful?" The Iranian asked suspiciously.

"I'm a free market businesswoman," the Contessa smiled. "The million is contingent upon meeting all your needs. If I fall short, we will discuss, any discounts you'll be entitled to then."

The Iranian knew he was in a tight position with little room to negotiate. "Under the circumstances, it's fair. But please understand, time is of the essence." Sliding his hand toward the Contessa, he raised it to reveal a small disposable phone. "I don't want to waste time with the usual communication methods. This phone is from the location of interest. It has a pre-dialed number already in it. Call it, if you should have any problems, or when you have what I need."

With that, the Iranian slowly rose to his feet and walked to the other end of the pew. His security detail rose one or two at a time and casually followed their master out of the church.

Lowering her small white purse next to the phone, she slipped the small device into it. Then, with the Iranians gone, both she and Illana slipped out of their pews and started toward the large double doors at the front of the church.

"It just so happens I may have the means of obtaining

what we need very quickly," Illana whispered as she followed her employer.

"Good," the Contessa replied. "I'm interested in your ideas."

Oskar Straudner didn't have to guess who it was once he heard the reports from the police commander. A few nights before, an unidentified group of armed men attempted to sneak across the border. They were seemingly stopped by another equally anonymous group of armed locals who gathered quickly, confronted the first group in a remote location, and fought them off. What the police found were the bodies of what appeared to be individuals of Arab extraction. The police commander is working on the theory they were either terrorists or bandits from the lawless borderlands. Clearly, they were attempting to take advantage of the country's chaotic situation to loot the local communities.

The politician knew all too well who the unidentified invaders were. He fumed over the news. His Iranian allies had been stopped at the border by a few local peasants. It didn't speak very highly of the Iranian army that was supposed to help seize an entire country when they couldn't even defeat farmers with guns. What was more disconcerting was that the militia augmentation he was counting on to secure his position was not moving into place as planned.

Straudner thanked the commander for the informal briefing as he cordially ushered him out the door. Now, alone in his office, he began to pace nervously. What did all this mean? Was the operation now quashed? Was his Iranian support gone? Why had they not made contact to inform him of this setback? Disaster? What was he to make of this? Worse yet, if these additional forces weren't in the country after all that had been arranged, would he be on his own to carry out the takeover?

Nervously deliberating, the politician paced about his office trying to analyze the facts in an attempt to formulate his next move. Slowly and deliberately placing one foot in front of the other as he walked along the rich green carpet and blue Oriental rug, he found himself assessing the various contents of his office. The vase dating back to the Italian Renaissance, the polished oak table he used for meetings off to the side. It was as if his mind was determined to think of anything except the most urgent matter.

Finally, he concluded only one option remained. He needed to reach out for help to determine the disposition of the Iranians. It was not lost on the politician that even if he made contact, anything his Middle-Eastern backers explained would be, at best, dubious. What was important, at this point, was that they were still approachable. They had left a number, presumably to a burner phone, to be reached in Buenos Aires in case of an emergency. If he used the number and contact, he knew the operation was still a go. If the number was dead, it would tell him the Iranians had aborted the operation, and he was now on his own.

Knowing Ulbrict Laudman was still in Montevideo, Straudner reached for his phone and proceeded to call a number he had been given to an emergency disposable phone. The deep voice on the other end barely had a chance to answer 'hello' before the politician cut in. Straudner wasted no time with pleasantries before ordering the German to take the next flight to Buenos Aires. Laudman already had the number for the Iranian contact as well as the code words and phrases worked out to establish identity. It was understood early on that he was to be the politician's buffer.

The phone conversation lasted less than a minute with Laudman promising to be on a plane within the next hour. Alone in his office, Straudner took a seat, not at his desk, but the seat at the far end of his oak meeting table. Reaching for the large wooden humidor placed in the center of the table, he opened the lid and brought out a short tipped Meduro wrapped Robusto cigar. It was an Aging Room brand. Clipping the tip, he lit the end with the gold lighter he kept in the inside pocket of his jacket. The first exhale released a thick, fluffy cloud that danced innocently before rising in the atmosphere.

It was the cold, sour feeling of vulnerability. The politician was feeling very exposed. He wasn't sure what his next move should be. Nor was he exactly sure what he had to work with. It was a position he had spent his entire life trying to avoid. He had always been so careful, taking only risks that were perfectly calculated and necessary for his gain — either financially or politically. He always ensured he had something — a strategy, a proverbial back door to escape through, or some form of *insurance* to guarantee his protection. Not this time. This time he had gambled in a dangerous game of intrigue and treason — a game in which he had been assured of an ally with a great deal invested, an investment that ensured they would have a strong commitment to this endeavor. It was too late to go back now.

In his mind, he began to consider alternatives. Somewhere, lazily gazing at another bluish-grey cloud of smoke, he realized another option. If his Iranian backers withdrew, would his wealthy supporters among the country's now terrified elite fill the void? After all, many people already believed there was a vigilante force in existence engaged in combating the leftist terrorists. If Laudman could find mercenaries fast enough to build at least the image of a group, it would give the elite a cause to help finance. It would also serve to head off the security forces from any perceived power grab of their own.

Straudner ran several scenarios through his head. His conclusion was that none could even be initiated until he heard from the Iranians. Sitting back in the hardwood chair, he puffed quietly on his cigar, his next move was uncertain.

CHAPTER 54

Kafka Dayan's eyes darted from picture to picture. He stood before the assorted collection of surveillance photographs spread across a long folding table. They were all of Saratoga Manor — the location where Oskar Straudner would be meeting with the leaders of his conspiracy. Alyssa Rios had come through one last time before she and her assistant vanished completely. A professional, who was clearly no stranger to planning commando operations, she had managed to capture precise photos of every aspect of the surrounding grounds and every angle of the building itself. The Israeli marveled at the detail and could only wonder how she had managed to pull off this job.

In addition to the photographs, she had also provided a virtual treasure trove of supporting documents detailing the makeup and behaviors of the local populace. The report covered everything from police patrol schedules and habits to information on a pair of suspicious busybodies who kept watch over all abnormal elements in their neighborhood. Several sketches and official city maps depicting the greater neighborhood area and transit system had also been provided. There were biographies of the owner of the estate, Colonel Juan Rega and his family, as well as the tiny staff that maintained his premises.

"It all looks good," Darren Ripley commented as he viewed the photographs from the other side of the table. "From what I'm seeing, there is no security aside from the normal police patrols. Plus, we have quite a few exit and entry points leading to the target that we can exploit to our benefit."

"What we don't know," Dayan replied, picking up one of the photos, "is whether or not they'll have additional security on this particular night?"

"Even if they do, they'll have too much ground to cover," Oskar Perez spoke up as he walked up next to Dayan. "I mean, the neighboring estates seem to be equally unguarded. This gives us the opportunity to approach our targets from multiple directions."

"Possibly," the Israeli ruminated. "They don't have armed guards. But," he walked around the table to a small refrigerator to retrieve a can of beer, "they do have a homogenous and tight community. People who could decide to call the police. They could even call their neighbor directly to let him know he's got strange people running around outside his home. But that also means we aren't focused on armed security. We're mostly worried about neighbors whose actions could create unknown problems that could throw off our plans."

Since Plūcker's bar, the Ronin Club, was no longer habitable, Riazza had succeeded in finding an alternate location, a small warehouse on the Montevideo pier. The owner was willing to take cash and the simple explanation that some importers needed a temporary space to house merchandise they were bringing in from another country. The property owner found the answer sufficient after she handed him a considerable amount of cash he happily didn't have to report. Even if he was suspicious, the police were too busy with the rash of political unrest in the city to care about a petty smuggling operation.

Bursting into the room, Micha Cohen interrupted their planning. He had a grim look on his face. "Dayan!" the katsa snapped. "I need to speak with you privately."

With a disinterested shrug, the commando casually followed his commander out of earshot of the others. The calm subtlety of Dayan's demeanor only served to infuriate the already agitated Cohen. "I have just finished following the aftermath of your little excursion," were the first words out of the katsa's mouth. "The Argentinian press is exploding with stories about your mass assassination. They are referring to the horrid act of terror you unleashed!"

Dayan looked around the room. The rest of the team was busily going over the intelligence documents spread across the table. "Do they have any definite conclusions yet? Or is this all just a massive uproar?"

Cohen compressed his lips. "So far, they are just discussing your actions as an egregious act of terrorism, which is what they think it amounts to." The katsa shook his head with a look of real concern. "However, that's only what the official reports are saying. I haven't heard anything regarding what the police actually know. Since the loss of Rabbi Kovinski, I haven't any source that can get inside their security forces."

Dayan shook his head. "So, they could just as well speculate that this is the beginning of left-wing political violence now pouring over from neighboring Uruguay. Then again, they could be hot on the trail of our Jewish radical friends. We knew when we carried this out it was going to be loud, and it was going to get a lot of attention. The hope is that our young friends don't make any mistakes and expose themselves while the country is up in arms."

"Did you make sure to cover your tracks?" Cohen sighed showing signs of exhaustion.

"The weapons were carved up into pieces and scattered all over a scrapyard. The remaining ammunition is in the ocean, and the vehicles and clothing used in the attack were burned, then buried in a remote location," Dayan replied as he fired a questioning look at the katsa. "Whatever you may think, we did have missions like this back in the unit."

Slowly exhaling, the katsa nodded slightly. "I know," he looked up at the commando and met his eyes with a proud, fatherly look. "It is just that we are playing a dangerous game with a dangerous adversary at our heels. This attack brings a great deal of unwanted attention from all the wrong places."

"I agree," Dayan replied, his eyes revealing the soul of a man tired from all the action and intrigue. "But, Mendoza was the reason for that danger, and we had to eliminate him if we wanted to cripple our adversary's intelligence network. Otherwise, how long would it have been until they found us? Now, they either move blindly, or they approach Iran's formal intelligence network and risk alerting the western powers to their activities."

"It's doubtful they'll do that. It would mean exposing Iran's connection to this whole affair." Cohen folded his arms as he pondered the situation carefully. "The concern is those young hoodlums you used. They're not professionals. They haven't been trained for this and have no real experience in our world. I worry it will only be a matter of time before the police catch up with them — then we're exposed."

Sensing the conversation had hit its end, Dayan waved the katsa over to the planning table. "We're planning the assault on our good friend Straudner right now. We need to maintain our focus on that."

Walking back to the table, the two Israelis rejoined their team. Perez and Ripley were riveted on the documents before them. Dayan reached for a photograph of the front of the house. It showed a modest-looking two-story complex sitting comfortably in the middle of land surrounded by a manicured grass lawn dotted with oasis-like clusters of plants and trees.

The katsa rubbed his chin as he looked the photograph over. Dayan allowed his commander a few moments to study the document. When Cohen looked up, the commando spoke. "It has its benefits and weaknesses," he stated to the katsa, who obviously was still a novice at planning commando raids. "We are going over all the documents now. We're lucky. Our focus on this location is timing and surprise, not on defeating security. Our study indicates they will have limited security."

"But," Perez interjected, "we do have a couple of major obstacles: they have a community where everyone knows everyone, and we will be storming a location populated by police and military officers who may or may not be carrying weapons."

"If so, we have to presume they'll have experience using those weapons, and they won't hesitate," Dayan added.

"We also have to worry about the number of noncombatants," Ripley spoke up. "After all, we'll have family members who will be there. That presents a problem."

Dayan sighed, "We can't use explosives, that's for sure. Bad enough we'll probably not have much of a chance to hit these guys at a time when they're away from their families. Even if we just use guns, we risk hitting a lot of innocent victims."

Cohen scowled, "I certainly don't want a massacre." "We can't, however, let that deter us. Straudner and most of the conspirators have to die to ensure the Iranians have no one to use as an alternative."

"Whoa," Ripley interrupted as he waved his hands. "I understand knockin' off these conspirator types. They're soldiers, and they wear a uniform where killing and dying comes with the territory. I draw the fucking line at killing a bunch of innocent bystanders just because they're in the wrong place at the wrong time."

"I agree," Perez spoke up. "Your cause is not that vital to me to justify doing this and walk away. I'm not undertaking some killing field operation."

The faces of the mercenaries were grim. Cohen looked at Dayan as if seeking an answer that told him he was not wrong in his logic. He read the look in his commando's eyes that said he felt the same way as his men but he, like the katsa, understood the hard choices such operations sometimes demanded.

"If this were Northern Ireland, you'd understand Darren," Dayan said not taking his gaze from Cohen. "If this were a mission in North Africa, you'd have a different perspective, Oskar." The commando turned so he could face both mercenaries at once. "But, those were in wars where you were soldiers fighting for a country you served against an enemy you saw as a direct threat. It's easier to accept fighting such complicated battles under those circumstances.

You don't have those clear lines here. Even more, I feel now is the time to recognize a problem that we have yet to discuss. Fighting the Arabs, when they tried to cross the border was warfare. It was a bush war plain and simple. We didn't see the aftermath of fighting other soldiers in the middle of nowhere."

Dayan turned, once again, to the katsa, whose facial expression explained he knew where the commando was about to go with this discussion. "This will be an assassination. An assassination that even done cleanly with no innocent casualties will still result in the massive killing of several high-ranking military and police officials in addition to the killing of a civilian politician in a democratic society.

In the eyes of the world, no matter why this happened, this will be seen as an egregious act of terrorism. We can easily predict this action will gain serious world attention. Anyone involved will not just suffer the wrath of a global force like Iran, the world will see us as fanatics or gangsters." He looked around the room with a serious expression coldly displayed on his face. "We will not be walking away from this and simply be able to go back to our old lives."

"Are you saying you don't want us to be in on this?" Ripley asked.

Dayan sighed, "I'm saying, as this operation progressed, I resolved myself to the reality that this was going to end with me dead or as a hunted man with a very large target painted across my back and, eventually, I will die. I accepted this because I'm doing this for my country. I won't ask you to take such a risk when you don't have the same stake in this operation."

"You're gonna try and to do this all on your own?" Perez interjected — a puzzled look on his face.

"No," Dayan shrugged. "But, I also feel we need to get this issue resolved before we go any further. We've lost a lot of men so far, Vanderhook and the others. They died taking the risk expected of hired soldiers. Up until now, you've done only what a hired soldier would do — fight battles. When this war is over, you can go home or seek similar employment elsewhere. I accept the deaths of the others as a professional soldier in the world in which I live. If you continue from this point, it will not be something you can simply walk away from. I don't want to lie and tell you we have a plan for the aftermath."

Cohen stepped forward. "I agree. This is not going to simply be a normal act of soldiering. And, as my compatriot has pointed out, we have no real plan for what we'll do once we've carried out this operation. That said, I will authorize Dayan to pay any member who carries this out and survives a bonus of one million dollars in US currency in addition to the remainder of what's now owed you."

"I'll need time to think about this," Ripley said, as he leaned over the table glancing at the documents as if the answer to the decision he needed to make lay somewhere within the pages before him.

"Me to," replied Perez. "We also need to talk this over with the others and get their opinion."

The explosion was powerful. It was a loud, earth-shattering thunder that echoed for miles in all directions. It culminated in a large towering inferno that finally transformed into a giant, gray cloud of smoke and dirt that covered the vicinity like a thick blanket. In an instant, the Catedral Basílica de

San Juan Bautista — The Cathedral Basilica of Saint John the Baptist — went from a structure of majestic architecture that headquartered the Diocese of Salto to a smoking pile of rubble.

In the street, the destroyed church was now littered with the corpses and screaming casualties of those, who only moments before, had come to hear the new Archbishop of Salto make a press announcement denouncing the violence plaguing the country and asking for the government to show restraint in its handling of the matter. Instead, it had become the scene of a grisly massacre in the streets of Uruguay's second-largest city. A small truck bound for an open-pit mining site and packed with more than a ton of dynamite had been stolen.

The truck had been innocently parked against the gate of the church. To anyone paying attention, it was the type of truck used by the maintenance workers the church employed. No one thought anything about it sitting by the gate. The recent violence had been centered around the capital city clear on the other side of the country. For this reason, no one seriously considered any possibility of the violence from so far away affecting them.

There were no intelligence reports indicating their village was in any danger. Nor was any security seriously considered for an event hosted by the church. After the attack, this had all changed. The chaos that followed had been captured by hordes of news cameras and watched by the city's population on their televisions at home. At that moment, the largest city on the west side of the country, and the second-largest city nationally, was thrown into the violence they had previously only heard about.

Once again, the handy work of Oskar Straudner's agent

had proven effective. Ulbrict Laudman had reasoned that the west side of the country was still mentally disconnected from the violence. They had witnessed the chaos plaguing Montevideo through whatever media outlets they were paying attention to, but they had been only passingly exposed to any attacks in the countryside. This, Straudner felt, left an essential portion of the country in an ambiguous position. If they were not directly affected, they would be more ambivalent toward accepting a powerful military response, namely his planned coup. Another consideration was that security in Montevideo was becoming tighter. Any further attacks would prove too risky to undertake.

At the politician's behest, the old Stasi operative orchestrated the robbery of the dynamite with the help of contacts he had developed over the years. Finding out about the press announcement from the city's diocese, he figured it would be the perfect target. It would serve to create mass panic in the primary population center in Western Uruguay. It would, the politician calculated, further help by enraging the base of ardent Catholics throughout the country who would no doubt consider a violent act against the Papal church as unforgivable heresy.

They smuggled the explosives into the city. At an unused warehouse, they packed it all into the battered maintenance truck. Laudman opted for a timed detonator instead of a remote activation system that could be triggered with a cellular phone — with all the electronic devices that attendees would likely be using, rogue frequency waves might prematurely activate the bomb.

In the early morning, on the day of the press conference, one of Laudman's accomplices drove the vehicle up to the iron gates closest to the church. Leaving an assortment of weathered-looking tools in both the front seat and against the windows of the hatch, it would appear to any onlooker that the vehicle was owned by a laborer doing work for the church.

The detonator was set to go off shortly after noon when the conference was expected to start and have the highest number of people present. Straudner had demanded a high casualty rate for maximum effect. It was his plan that within a few days of the attack, his covert online underground news site for the revolutionaries would give credit to the left-wing radicals for the bombing. In the articles posted, the terrorists would state that they were taking the battle to the church, which they considered a protector of and conspirator with the corrupt regime.

It would be the perfect way to ensure the whole country would be paralyzed by both fear and desperate anger. The politician would exploit the situation to strengthen and energize his support for the upcoming takeover. He would now have the security forces, the backing of the wealthy elites and, soon thereafter, the profound backing of the Roman Catholic Church if all went well.

CHAPTER 55

Illana Muricia had no trouble convincing the old man, she knew only as Alonzo, that her need for ten used, but in good condition, hauling trucks were for a smuggling operation she was putting together. Alonzo was a longtime black-market operator. He had come in and out of her life over the years as a man her father worked with when he needed things to conduct his less than legal business endeavors. If something was required — vehicles, essential documents, or even facilitating introductions with other individuals who could assist in such dealings — Alonzo had always come through.

When the question of obtaining several short trucks came up, the young college graduate understood the problem immediately. With all the unrest, trying to buy numerous vehicles for hauling would create suspicion, especially without a compelling reason to justify the need. Nor would they have time to create the illusion of a business. The police might normally overlook something like this, but at a time when the police were incredibly distrustful, everything was subject to close scrutiny.

Alonzo knew the young lady from his years dealing with her father. He remembered her playing as a child while they conducted business. Later, as she matured, the play sessions stopped, and she accompanied her father as an assistant with full knowledge of their dealings. He didn't even think it strange that she was now conducting her own business with him. It was as if she had been groomed to do this her entire life.

Likewise, Muricia had grown up watching such deals and studying the men her father did business with. She wasn't naïve, she knew how easily betrayals occurred in the backrooms of such places. Alonzo wasn't a man she approached without careful thought. She knew his family was Armenian; that they had been driven out in the early 1990s during the war between Armenia and Muslim Azerbaijan.

A longtime black marketer and follower of the Armenian Orthodox Church, Alonzo and his family had seen the very ugly side of law enforcement, having been persecuted by the Soviet secret police — the KGB. He got his start in the criminal world smuggling weapons from South America to help his people in the conflict. Murcia's father had been instrumental in helping Alonzo. Alonzo proved himself to be smart, savvy, and highly unlikely to cooperate with any police. For these reasons, she chose to enlist his services for this particular task.

Sitting across from a weathered folding table in the backroom of a grungy auto mechanic shop, she nursed the coffee offered to her in a small ceramic cup. Alonzo, a thin, frail-looking man with salt and pepper hair and a thickly lined face, sat on the other side of the table looking over a collection of documents. Peering through his thick, bifocals, he reviewed the work very carefully. "This registration," he said in a heavily accented and gravelly voice, "will suffice for any policeman that might stop you. It will have all the necessary registration information and ownership under the name and company you requested."

"Thank you," Muricia replied quietly. She used few words — there was no reason for small talk.

"Your business is a small startup shipping company that deals in selling wool wholesale," he continued. "That will give you enough of an explanation for being out in farm country. It will also justify the reason for you carrying cargo. Wool has a powerful odor when taken from the farms directly. It should both mask the smells and effectively conceal what it is you are really transporting. Your trucks — I assume you have seen them. Do they meet your requirements?" She nodded in reply.

Muricia could only wonder how the ardent Armenian nationalist might respond if he knew the cargo she was smuggling were armed Muslim Arabs working for Iran. Then again, Iran did back Armenia over Azerbaijan in the post-Soviet hostilities. It wasn't a subject he wanted to know about, nor one she wanted to broach.

Handing over the documents along with a bag full of keys, the old man smiled through his thin lips. She returned his pleasantry with one of her own. "I always thought your father was a lucky man having you as a daughter," he said. The look in his eyes was one of a man enjoying the nostalgia. "Strangely, I find myself happier to see you here now conducting business, much like your father did, than if you had chosen a more traditional life. You were never meant to be a soldier's wife, having children and hosting parties. This is the world I always knew you were meant to have."

Muricia slowly rose to her feet. In her hand was a large purse. "My father always respected you, as do I." Reaching over the table, she lowered the bag before the elderly man. Taking it in his hands, he looked inside to see a large quantity of cash. "Your payment in full. You have delivered flawlessly." Her choice of a large woman's handbag was strategic. No one questioned a female carrying one, and men seldom paid attention to how often it changed hands. If she walked into a garage carrying one, it was because she, being a typical young lady, had several accessories she constantly needed. If she walked out without it, the obvious assumption would be she had forgotten it. Women were always leaving their purses somewhere.

The old man didn't bother to count the money. In one look he knew she had paid more than agreed upon. He smiled and nodded. "Welcome to the life you were always meant to have."

With nothing more needing to be said, Muricia collected the documents, turned and walked out leaving the old man watching after her.

The trucks were found in a lot a few streets over. Alonzo had several pickup places that separated his garage from his more illicit business. It worked for her because the group of Arab looking drivers might cause issues. Based on her specifications, the trucks were in good shape but had the look of vehicles that had seen much use over the years. Driving along the country roadways, these trucks would be less conspicuous.

Muricia walked down the line of trucks just as she had done before meeting the old man. This time, she matched the paperwork to each license plate as she walked past. She meticulously studied the keys as she matched the numbers on them to the license plates of the trucks. All had to be in order. There could be no mistakes, no hang-ups, or discrepancies. When she had verified all the paperwork and the trucks, she called the Contessa to inform her the mission was a go. She was told the new drivers had entered the country that morning.

The Contessa took the report from her young assistant with professional delight and contacted her client with the location. Afterword, she instructed Muricia to wait until the client's drivers arrived to ensure a smooth transition.

Muricia waited down the road across the street in the safety of a car she had obtained for this mission. She parked in an inconspicuous spot near the street concealed behind a large, steel dumpster and a collection of abandoned cars. The dumpster's shadow matched the olive-green color of the car providing fairly good concealment. To anyone surveilling the vicinity, she would not stand out. She was also careful to maintain a close distance to the driveway leading to a side road allowing for a speedy escape.

With no idea what to expect, Illana Muricia was taking no chances. If anything went wrong or looked suspicious, she didn't want to be near the trucks with no means of escape. The danger of what she was doing and who she was dealing with was not lost on her. It had been nearly six hours when she spotted a large, white van pulling in from the main street onto the side road. It idled slowly past the parking lot housing the trucks. The van continued the length of the lot then suddenly sped up to a normal speed and continued down the road.

Muricia watched this activity, but she didn't know quite what to make of it. The van could have been anybody: her contacts, someone lost, or possibly the very real danger of someone intending her harm. Deciding to stay in place, she leaned back in her seat and waited. A few minutes later the same van returned from the direction it had just left. Again, it slowed to an idle as it passed the lot. This time, the van made a sharp turn into the parking lot. Minutes later, two men exited the van moving carefully but with obvious uncertainty.

Muricia decided they must be the men she was to make contact with. Pulling her car onto the road, she drove adjacent to the lot. She stopped several feet from the two men. Keeping the engine running and her foot on the brake was her precaution for a fast getaway in the event of a problem.

The two men stood still as they studied the green car with the single occupant in it that had so mysteriously appeared and remained idling. Determining all was well, the two men approached. The first man displayed an innocent demeanor. The second man moved more cautiously. His hand was stuffed in his jacket — presumably gripping a gun in case of trouble. Muricia could understand their concern; she made similar arrangements of her own.

She watched as the first man approached her door, bending slightly to see her. His features were not of Spanish or mestizo ancestry, but more Middle-Eastern. The rough lines and contours of his face revealed a life spent in harsh living conditions. "Pantheon?" was all he said in a low, gruff voice.

It was the code word she had been given before she embarked on this operation. Nodding slightly, she replied, "Yojimbo." Her voice was cold and stern, in the tone of a person neither intimidated nor unprofessional. Mindful of the behavior of the second man, she slowly turned the wheel of her car in his direction. It was apparent he was only concerned about a gun being drawn. He stood in front of her car several feet away to enable a clear shot through her windshield. If he went for what she was sure was a gun, he was going to feel the hard steel of her car as she ran him down.

"You are the contact?" The first man asked, his voice still gruff.

Handing the packets of paper through the window, Muricia placed them in the first man's hands. "These are the documents you will need if the police or anyone else should stop you." The first man gathered the papers in his hands. She continued, "The packets are in the same order as the trucks in the lot. Start with the first truck on the left."

The first man stood up and looked at the trucks to get oriented. "Thank you," he replied coldly.

Muricia passed a bag out the window to him. "These are the keys. Each key is marked with the license plate number of the respective vehicle."

Taking the bag, the first man nodded. "Thank you. Do you have anything else for me?"

"No, do you have anything for me?"

The first man shook his head, turned and walked away. The second man held his ground until his compatriot was halfway across the road before he backed up and followed. Deciding her business was finished, Muricia drove away. Several blocks later, employing a series of evasive moves, she was comfortable that she had not been followed. Pulling out the phone she had been given, she called the Contessa. Her message was quick, "All has been accomplished."

Qalmini's mood was grim. He had just heard about the demise of Mendoza when Straudner's people contacted him. Straudner had heard about the incident at the border and was now demanding a meeting. The only good news he had received was that the Contessa had solved his transportation dilemma. He relaxed a little at the knowledge his people had taken control of the vehicles, they were on the road, and all was in order.

But the obvious problem still remained. The Israelis had succeeded in delaying the operation. Now, with the Cuban's assassination, his intelligence connection was gone. He was operating blind against the Israeli threat. His options were limited. The only recourse was to reach out to Iran's intelligence sources in the region. The risk, nonetheless, was all too apparent. If MOIS or Pasdaran intelligence organs became involved in this operation, it brought a severe risk of attracting the attention of western intelligence services. The American government would definitely move to neutralize it. Or, even more troubling, was the possibility of being exposed and embarrassing Iran internationally.

The Iranian deliberated over the situation. The Israelis were a threat, yet so far they had not succeeded in stopping the operation. Every derailment had been fixed, destroyed vehicles had been replaced, and Major Akim, in conducting a review of the engagement at the border, offered valuable recommendations for addressing future encounters with the local militia. In addition, the Israelis had suffered severe losses, and their supply and intelligence organs had been neutralized. It was conceivable, Qalmini thought, that they could still carry out the mission without the risk of involving Iranian intelligence.

Straudner was another matter. Predictably, the politician

had heard of the skirmish at the border. He had assumed, correctly, it was the first wave of the support force that had been hit. As it was a meeting requested as opposed to a demand to sever ties at once, Qalmini figured Straudner was still inclined to carry out the coup. The politician knew it was the local peasants who had somehow obstructed their force; he knew nothing about the Israeli menace. Keeping it that way seemed the most prudent way to handle the current situation.

However, the politician was neither a soldier nor an intelligence operative and was not one to understand the complexities of military operations. It would be necessary to provide assurance that the fiasco at the border was a setback that could and would be controlled in the future.

Qalmini sighed. He was in a dangerous game with too many assumptions and not enough certainty. As a soldier and an intelligence operative, one who had long lived in the shadows of the covert world, he was all too aware that gambling in battle was never a good practice — and he was gambling.

CHAPTER 56

The Saratoga Manor looked innocent. Surrounded by similar tasteful houses located among the vast expanses of manicured lawns and foliage, it hardly seemed suitable for nefarious dealings. Which was, most likely, why Oskar Straudner had chosen it for his final planning meeting. Dayan casually glanced at it through the window of the blue Datsun pickup as he drove by. It had been his third actual recce of the place. Each trip was in a different vehicle, and his personal appearance had been subtly altered each time. Between his review of the existing documents and his own personal intelligence collection from visiting the scene, he had learned several facts for this mission.

The police presence in the neighborhood was sparse. Many had been reallocated to the neighborhoods and colleges suffering riots and turmoil; however, the ones that remained were vigilant and professional. The Israeli got out of his car during his first recce and was casually walking down the street pretending to look for house numbers. It wasn't more than a few minutes before a police cruiser pulled up directly behind him. The cops had already exited the vehicle with the one on the passenger side taking a defensive position while the other came closer but maintaining a safe distance. They were not amateurs. They had responded so quickly it confirmed a note made in Rios' report — the neighbors in the area were mindful of strangers. With the recent violence, everyone from police to local residents was on edge waiting for the next attack.

To avoid any further run-ins with the police, Dayan stayed mobile by driving the area and exploring the various routes to get a firsthand feel for what was going on and identify potential problems that would have to be dealt with when trying to make a getaway. During his drives, he encountered road construction in two places that were extensive enough to negate the use of those routes during their escape. He also noted the general patrol pattern of the police, estimating the number of patrol cruisers, each staffed with two officers. Landscaping crews were the most frequent personnel present throughout the day but in unpredictable locations. Dayan thought the police might use the landscaping crews as cover throughout the day.

Dayan found at least three roads in remote locations that the police rarely patrolled. There was a collection of houses from the late eighteenth to the early twentieth century that currently housed members of the newer professional class: university academics, lawyers, tech company entrepreneurs, and the like. These professionals were less observant of their surroundings than the more developed estates of the older moneyed elites. They had not lived in their homes as long and did not have the closer connections apparent in other parts of the neighborhood. The Israeli believed it would be a good place to stage vehicles to aid in their escape.

After the mercenaries had been given time to consider

the future aspects of the operation, a few opted not to continue. Oskar Perez and two of the Colombians decided to take what was owed them and leave. This left Darren Ripley, who continued to have reservations, and two other Colombians. The team was stretched dangerously thin to carry out a mission that could easily become complicated.

There wasn't enough time to recruit more mercenaries. Even if they wanted to, with Plūcker gone, they had lost their means of vetting people. Since the mission was a high-level assassination, good professionals would likely have similar opinions to the ones that just quit. That left only one option — the young Argentinian radicals, the Guardians of Israel.

After the Mendoza killing, the police were looking for possible suspects. Unlike the movies, Gold and his accomplices were not told to lay low. Instead, they were told to keep to a normal routine and not arouse suspicion by suddenly disappearing or taking any action that would look suspicious. He had been hanging out and working on his usual routine as the Israeli katsa, Micha Cohen, had instructed. Buenos Aires had been heating up since the Mendoza killing that not only resulted in the death of a prominent business financier and a car bombing in the business district, it had also ended with the deaths of several active and former Argentinian police. The incident was being handled with intense personal interest.

When Gold was contacted by Dayan, he was surprised, nervous, and excited all at the same time. The Mendoza killing had been a sobering experience for the young man and his group. Yet, he experienced a certain adrenaline rush he had never felt before. He felt it during the gun battle at the building and, again when speaking to the Israeli and thinking about the possibility of repeating something like it.

Gold brought Yari Sholman and Ira Culper with him. They had been part of the Mendoza hit team. Gold had reached out to them at Dayan's behest. Besides Gold, Dayan had assessed Sholman and Culper as the most capable to help carry out the next mission. With the explanation that what they were being asked to do would guarantee they would never be able to go back to their old lives, he would have found few other volunteers.

Solomon Gold was breathing slowly, but deeply, as he looked out his window. The objective seemed ominous to him, like a fortress housing a crime lord or evil dictator. It was extremely intimidating thinking about where he was, and what he was there to do. He was still in shock from being contacted by the Israeli commando.

Sitting in a truck next to the man who had disposed of Elloy Mendoza, Gold was quietly breathing and rerunning the plan over and over in his head. The last few days had been spent going over the plan, and rehearsing the actions with a makeshift mockup of the location. It had all been very professional and serious.

The added bonus of working with Dayan's mercenaries — hardened professional soldiers with considerable experience — made the radicals feel like serious covert operators. It was the life Gold always wanted. The plan had been rehearsed and contingencies discussed over and over. It was now to the point where Gold felt it was the only thing in the world he knew. When Dayan finally explained to the radicals the reason for the attack — stopping Iran from orchestrating a coup — it was all the radicals needed to know.

Now, sitting in the passenger seat of the large hauling

truck, Gold once again looked out the window at the houses before him. It was strange, he thought, how he never envisioned doing something like what he was about to do in such a peaceful and serene place. Sitting next to him, Dayan stared intently out the front window as he drove. Neither man spoke during the entire drive. Looking out the back window, Gold saw his two friends and the Welshman, he knew as Darren Ripley. He guessed the three of them were feeling the same way.

Along the sides of the truck hung beaten metal signs with the words *Santo Brothers Yard Maintenance.* Finding out that yard and landscaping crews were a common sight in this elite part of town, Dayan planned for his team to fit right in as a yard crew. Raizza had managed to procure an old flatbed truck along with an assortment of used yard tools and equipment. It all helped to give the appearance of a small crew that had been in the business for quite some time. A small white Datsun with the same company information and logos painted on the sides was driven by the two remaining Colombian mercenaries.

Driving up the street, the mercenaries kept to a moderate pace to not attract attention. The neighborhood was quiet. There were only a few locals about, walking or tending to chores around their houses. The tension in the truck heightened as Saratoga Manor came into view. Despite numerous rehearsals and a live range firearm practice, the sight of the manor brought a sudden reality to the whole thing. For the radicals, it was the nerves they remembered when they carried out the Mendoza kill. For the mercenaries, it was the realization they were about to commit an act of terrorism. The idea that no one was going to simply walk away from this was sinking home to everyone.

Approaching the manor, Dayan saw the gathering of people, mostly women, congregating out front. He took particular notice of three suited figures standing together. He presumed, from their posture, they were security recruited for today's festivities. The fact that they were not making any attempt to blend in with the more casually dressed party guests, Dayan assumed they were off-duty policemen hired for the day, not professional bodyguards.

"All I see are women," Dayan said, turning to Gold. "That means the men are probably meeting somewhere inside."

Gold nodded nervously. He was about to yell back to the occupants in back, relaying what he was told. He was stopped by a sharp look from the Dayan. The truck pulled up to the curb far away from the collection of cars. They didn't want to be blocked by any late arrivals parking close to them. With all the polished, upscale vehicles on display, it was unlikely anyone would even consider parking next to a dingy yard crew truck.

The truck halted. Immediately, the three men in the back began unloading equipment. Dayan and Gold jumped out of the front, moving to assist. Dressed in stained, greasy jeans, T-shirts, and having neglected hygiene and a shave, the team looked every bit like a crew of yard workers.

As predicted, the men Dayan identified as security began moving toward them, their jackets remaining open. As they got closer, they shouted to the yard workers demanding to know what they were doing. They were met by the Colombian mercenaries who, by now, had exited their car and moved in between the two groups. As they approached the security men, they informed them they were scheduled to do a job at the manor today. Dayan could see the outline of guns

— they were submachine guns. He immediately recognized the HK SP5K models. They were the modern updates of the older MP5K models used so extensively by executive protection and counter-terrorist units throughout the world. Judging from the length of the magazines, it was easy to guess they were sporting fifteen round magazines, rather than the thirty. Clearly, the concern for discretion outweighed the more prudent decision to carry the maximum ammunition load.

Dayan and the others continued unloading equipment from the truck. The guards, by this time, were frustrated and confused. They didn't want to let these men start working during the party. However, it was evident by their hesitancy they hadn't been given any schedules or itinerary to verify the presence of the yard workers. To add to the frustration, Ripley set up the lawnmower and commenced mowing the lawn. This action furthered the uncertainty of the guards, who were now trying to control the situation. The yard workers continued. They completely ignored the guards, who were still being kept at bay by the aggressive Colombians who demanded that their people get to work.

As the lawn mower roared to life, Ripley began cutting the lawn. Dayan gave a quick nod to the Colombians, and he and the Jewish radicals grabbed up bundles wrapped in blankets and plastic covers and started for the back. Out of the corner of his eye, he watched the guards, expecting them to follow. Instead, they remained together dealing with the Colombians, who were still being belligerent. As he suspected, they were policeman sticking to their initial training and experience. They opted to remain together while dealing with a hostile situation.

Dayan and the radicals continued to walk to the manor

past the collection of guests who carried on as if the yard workers didn't exist. Rounding the corner, the four men found the back of the manor virtually deserted. The only people there were another suited guard and a couple of teenage girls sitting in chairs giggling with one another.

The four men were at the back of the house before the guard realized they were there. Quickly, he rushed over to stop the greasy-looking men. Dayan and the radicals carefully laid down their bundles as the guard approached. Dayan's eyes darted between the guard and the two young ladies.

Approaching them, the guard demanded to know why they were there. Gold began to tell them the same story that the Colombians were telling the guard's compatriots out front. Dayan walked alongside as Gold continued. When he got within arms distance, Dayan moved off to the side of the suited figure. Gold kept the man's attention on him, as Dayan slowly neared. The guard realized the Israeli was behind him when he tried to turn and was stopped by a hard, thrusting force of cold steel into the side of his neck. Dayan had used a long thin screwdriver to stab the guard in the soft tissue precisely where the neck and shoulder meet.

The guard's eyes widened in terror as he realized he was about to die. Almost instantly, blood sprayed from the wound — it was a gory version of a water fountain. The guard choked as he took his last breaths. He crumpled to the ground gasping, his heart pumping a few more times before finally running out of material to pump. Dayan was mindful of the two young ladies who had seen the incident.

He was not the only one who had been watching the girls. They no sooner leaped from their seats when Yari Sholman charged and pointed the Sig Sour 22 directly in their faces. His index finger pressed against his lips, as he held his gun close to the terrified young ladies. Both girls whimpered as they remained frozen with terror. Waving his gun as a command for them to rise, Sholman started walking backward keeping watch on the girls as he beckoned them to follow.

Slowly, the two young ladies did as directed. Dayan walked over to a door leading into a small storage room. While Gold and Culper busied themselves unwrapping the blankets and plastic sheets, they ordered the ladies inside. They quietly shut the door and leaned a chair under the knob to keep it secured.

Dayan and Sholman turned to see a pile of compacted AK-74 rifles laid before them along with several magazines of ammunition. The two radicals loaded the magazines into the rifles as they passed them and spare magazines to the two standing men. Because they anticipated being within close proximity to their targets, Dayan had Raizza obtain rifles in 5.45x39mm caliber, instead of the more common 7.62 caliber models. At closer ranges, the smaller rounds would have more impacting velocity and tumbling effect. The smaller rounds were more lethal in close quarter situations where they had no chance to confirm the kill.

With all four armed, they tied handkerchiefs around their faces and began to move around the manor.

With weapons held at the ready, the four men slid slowly along the manor wall keeping low to avoid being seen by anyone looking out the windows. It was the noise of men, several of them laughing that told Dayan he was near his target location. From a large, open window, the four men could hear men's voices. The conversation became more audible as they neared the next window.

CHAPTER 57

Oskar Straudner had seized the moment. The tray of whiskeys in the far corner of the office had been well attended to by the gathering of police and military officers. Their manner had eased upon hearing the politician deliver his plan to seize the country and give the security forces a free hand to crush the radical leftists. After the recent bombing in Salto, the patience of the officers had worn thin, and they demanded action. The bombing had resulted in the deaths of over twenty people including the Salto Diocese Archbishop, Juan Abdora.

Drawing on his Ashton cigar, Straudner viewed the faces of everyone collected around him. They looked like loyal supporters, a look he had come to recognize when working among the political sharks. At this point, he was sure of every man in the room.

"My friends," he said quietly, but in a commanding voice. "Today we begin the journey to bring stability to our homeland." He rose to his feet, a glass of gin raised high in his hand. "I want to make a toast to patriotism."

The men in the room rose, their glasses raised in a similar

fashion. "My friends," the politician began with a beaming grin spread across his face, "to Uruguay."

The men started to echo Straudner's words when many stopped. Their grins turned to looks of horror. "Assassin...," a man cried before the room exploded with broken glass and the deafening sound of gunfire.

Outside, Dayan and the radicals had lined up against the window panes facing the large meeting room. When they were all in position, the order was given. In one motion Dayan, Culper, and Gold rose to look through the windows. Yari Sholman kept watch. Seconds later the men sprayed the office with gunfire.

Bodies fell as 5.45x39mm bullets ripped into one screaming man after another. Men tried to escape but were cut down by Gold who kept his aim on the area near the door. Recognizing Straudner from his surveillance photos, Dayan sought the politician out among the crowd. He saw him, already wounded, crawling around on the floor. Taking aim, the Israeli fired a burst that landed directly into the back of the politician's head. Straudner dropped limply to the floor. With the bolt of the rifle locked back revealing an empty chamber, Dayan dropped his weapon to the ground and reached under his shirt. Producing a grenade, he pulled the pin, flipped out the spoon, and released the handle. Counting two seconds for the cook-off, he launched the explosive into the office. At that moment, Dayan and the radicals took off running. A second later, they felt the force and sound of the grenade as it exploded behind them.

Out front, the sound of bullets firing caught the attention of the security men. Even the loud sound of the lawnmower did not entirely conceal the noise being made out back. For the party attendees, they simply thought it was some practical joke or children's firecrackers. However, the officers, with years of experience in the police force, recognized the sound of gunfire. Turning abruptly, they listened in confusion to the deadly, appalling detonations. Clearly disordered by what they were hearing, it wasn't until the distinctive sound of an explosion echoing from the backyard caused them to move. Reaching into their jackets, the guards grabbed their weapons as they sprinted toward the sound.

With attention turned from them, the Colombians reached under their large shirts and grabbed the small caliber pistols tucked in their belts. Gripping the .22 caliber Sig Sauer pistols, they pursued the security men. The guards slowed, their instincts initially clouded by their need to react. The Colombians quickly closed the distance leveling the silenced weapons at their quarries' heads. The resultant sound was a whisper from the silencer and the subsonic ammunition. The scrape of metal on metal was a louder sound as the slides pushed back to re-cock and eject the casings.

Two of the three guards dropped to the ground instantly, as the small chunks of lead tore into their heads lodging in their brains. It took the third guard a moment to realize what had happened. He turned just in time to see the muzzle flash and the blast that tore into his eye socket.

Leaving the lawnmower running, Ripley raced to where the Colombians had just killed the three men. The party attendees were in a state of confusion following the blast. Unaccustomed to warfare, they were not sure what to make of the alien noise from the explosion. The crowd standing petrified gave Dayan and the radicals' time to gain ground and make it to the front of the manor. It wasn't until a woman, seeing the sprawled bodies of the three guards, screamed loudly directing everyone's attention to the sight. The chaos began with people running wildly in all directions attempting to flee.

The Israeli and the radicals met the rest of their team and ran to their vehicles. Seeing people desperately making for their cars, Dayan worried they'd soon clog the streets trying to escape. Grabbing the rifle off Sholman, he leaped onto the back of the truck and sprayed gunfire over the heads of the fleeing people. Fearing they were being shot at, those heading for their cars stopped immediately and took off running down the street in the opposite direction.

Emptying the rifle, Dayan dropped it to the ground as he dived into the back of the truck. Gold had already slipped into the driver's side pulling the gearshift into drive. They had left the engine running to facilitate their escape. Pounding on the cab, Dayan shouted they had everybody. The truck screeched as it pulled from the curb and rapidly accelerated down the road; the car carrying the Colombians and Ripley were close behind.

Gold pressed down on the horn with his free hand trying to clear the way through the people running in the middle of the road. He pressed his foot to the gas with every intention of running them down, if necessary. The horn blowing sufficed to get the stragglers to dive out of the way.

The truck sped along the road leaving Dayan and the other two radicals grabbing onto anything that kept them from sliding around. Behind them, the second car kept pace. The police were expected at any time. Given the light number of patrols in the area, they believed they would be dealing with single patrols. It was likely the patrols were just now receiving word of the attack and trying to figure out where and how to react.

After getting a considerable distance from the manor, Dayan banged on the back window of the cab, shouted for Gold to slow down. It was unlikely the police had enough information yet to know how to respond, but a lawn truck racing away from a terror attack would definitely be a tip-off. The radical slowed the vehicle to the legal speed. The car behind them followed suit.

It turned out to be a smart move. Seconds later a police cruiser, sirens screaming, flew right by on its way to the manor. As Dayan had predicted, it passed without the slightest interest in the yard crew cruising down the street.

Turning onto another street, Gold began driving toward the planned switch-off point. Ten minutes later the vehicles pulled onto a quiet side road, two lanes wide and deserted. They drove up in front of a house where they knew the owners would be away for the next few days. Exiting the vehicles, the team walked casually down the road in groups of two to avoid attention. Gold and the radicals wanted to burn the vehicles and destroy evidence. Dayan and the mercenaries cautioned against it, warning that setting a fire would take time and really attract attention. Instead, the mercenaries' grabbed bottles of chlorine from the back of the truck doused the insides of the truck and car.

One hundred meters down the road was a house with two cars parked along the street. With no fanfare, the team casually slipped into the cars as if visiting friends living in one of the houses close by. Dayan and the radicals slipped into one car, while Ripley and the Colombians took the other. Dayan and the radicals drove off first. The next car left a few minutes later. They would meet at a designated rendezvous point.

CHAPTER 58

The sleek bluish-gray yacht was waiting at the marina when Illana Muricia drove up. It was the first thing she recognized. She had taken a cab after dumping the car she used for the truck transaction. After she delivered the vehicles, she had taken a few days to tie up some loose ends before attending her next meeting with the Contessa. Notice for the meeting came with a disposable phone she had been given just before embarking on her latest task. That morning she received a call. The Contessa had told her the place, time, and name of the boat, *The Lady Queen.*

Painted proudly in gold lettering, the Lady Queen was glowingly displayed on the rear of the yacht. Armed only with a small, black knapsack, Illana slipped through the gated door attended by a large, dark-skinned man dressed in khaki trousers and matching buttoned shirt. He looked Illana up and down before opening the door and allowing her to enter.

The wooden boards of the dock appeared to be only a few days old. Muricia walked down a small stairway, then the length of the dock. There were few ships in the marina at this time. It was probably why her new employer had chosen it. The yacht was modest. It was seaworthy and definitely provided the comforts essential to one of the Contessa's status. But it was not nearly the extravagant floating mansion so common among the oligarch elites in South America. It had one main floor, consisting of a kitchen and living quarters below the steering room. It was small enough to be managed by a single person but could easily accommodate two.

The Contessa was waiting at the steering station when Illana approached. "Come aboard," she called as she descended the ladder to greet her. With a shrug, Illana entered the craft. She was met by a beaming Contessa who took her by the shoulders.

"Where is the menacing security detail from the house?" The college student asked looking around to see that the rest of the ship was devoid of any other humans.

"They fulfilled their duties for my time here," the Contessa replied. "I like to move without a large entourage. As we have previously discussed, I don't like to keep too many people too close to my operation."

"So, who all works for you?" Illana seemed unsure of the situation.

"I'm building," replied the Contessa. "You proved your abilities perfectly and will be my right hand. In time, we will solicit the use of people as needed to fulfill services to clients. I don't like having established organizations. I work with people as needed and dispatch them when not needed."

Illana cocked her eye slightly, "So, where does that leave me?"

The Contessa sighed. "I can't go it entirely alone. You

will help, so I am able to more easily handle complex situations. My need for you will be a constant so long as you are up for the task — like recently."

"I guess the question is, what now?" Illana asked looking around.

The Contessa smiled. "We leave. A coup is about to happen in this country. I will very soon become a liability to those who are the key to orchestrating it."

"We're leaving on a yacht?" the college student was slightly confused.

Nodding her head, the Contessa turned to take up the rope connecting the ship to the pier. "I find yachting our way to another country vastly more discrete than taking a private jet that is more easily monitored. It's also the reason why I don't have a crew and entourage. I like a low profile and not much tying me down should I have to move quickly. Right now, I can abandon this ship and disappear if the need should arise. If I only have you, then we can move more quickly than if I have a staff of people who could betray me or suddenly have to be accounted for in my plans." She started up the ladder well toward the steering room.

Illana nodded. For being so young, the Contessa clearly had an instinct for her chosen associate. As they had previously discussed, a lot could be learned while working for her. The engine came alive as the ship started out of the dock.

"Did you take care of your commitments?" the Contessa called down as she steered.

"I've got nothing here holding me if that's what you're asking?" Illana replied.

"Good," the Contessa shouted back, "because we're not

coming back here anytime soon. This boat ride is ending in Brazil."

Illana wasn't surprised. She suddenly realized her future from here on out was unpredictable. Stepping on the craft, she had made a decision. Her future was with this woman she hardly knew and a world that offered absolutely no certainty.

Qalmini was on the phone with Major Akim discussing plans for the next movement into Uruguay. It was a welcome bit of news to hear the major discussing the confirmation of the trucks. The major gave a coded but detailed report of the situation having compensated for the previous mistakes. Qalmini relaxed as the Major explained his preset reconnaissance security teams near the border to root out any ambushes or vigilante groups that might prove troublesome. It had worked. So far, every deterrent had been mitigated, and the operation was still functioning. The vigilantes would no longer be a threat, Straudner was continuing with the mission, and the Israelis had seemingly been neutralized as a serious threat.

The major was in the middle of his briefing when one of Qalmini's security detail charged into the office. Not wanting to cut off the Major during his brief, Qalmini violently waved his hand, beckoning his unruly subordinate to leave. The subordinate's face was grim, and his complexion pale as he nervously waved his hands; he was determined to obtain his master's attention. Exasperated, Qalmini pressed the palm of his hand over the speaking end of the phone and growled, "This better be damned important!! Because what I'm in the middle of sure is!"

Gulping nervously the subordinate pointed toward the computer atop the desk. "I think you need to see something, sir. It has to do with Uruguay and affects you."

Perplexed, Qalmini followed his subordinate's direction. He bent down to press in the security code for his laptop. Typing in Uruguay news, he observed the screen for only a few seconds before his jaw dropped, his face turned pale, and he sank into his seat. As he continued observing the screen, his eyes widened. The whole time, the phone remained wedged in his ear with Major Akim still talking away.

Pressing his hand firmly to his mouth, Qalmini clicked on a television news recording. A well-groomed young man was speaking into a camera. Standing outside an affluent-looking neighborhood, he spoke about the recent terror attack in the community. In it, several high-ranking officials of both police and military had been massacred along with the prominent politician and business mogul, Oskar Vlak Straudner. The reporter pointed out that no group had claimed responsibility, nor had the police any definite leads other than it appeared to have been a well-planned operation carried out by professionals.

Qalmini didn't have to speculate. He realized in an instant who it was. The Israelis had found his Uruguay proxy. His mind raced as he tried to think of a last-minute way to mitigate the disaster. In the end, his conclusions were all the same. He suddenly realized that Akim was still talking — delivering his plan for the evening's movement. Qalmini bit his lip as he fought hard not to say what he was about to. Finally, he cut his subordinate off. "Major," Qalmini said, the bitterness in his low sounding tone was all too apparent. "Cancel the movement."

"Cancel, Sir?" The reply from Akim was that of complete confusion.

Qalmini continued viewing his computer screen as if waiting for some miracle to occur — that Straudner would somehow emerge from the dead, or at least a report stating reports of his demise were premature. There was none. He spoke to the waiting and confused Major Akim. "Yes. Effective immediately, the entire operation has been canceled. Again, the entire operation is canceled. I'll give you further instructions later. As of now, initiate dismantling protocols and fall back to exfiltration plans."

"Exfiltration? Sir, we're pulling out altogether?" the major asked again, still in utter disbelief.

"Yes, that is the order." Qalmini felt the words leave his mouth as if he were eating dirt. "The operation is done. We're leaving, going home." With that, he hung up and raised his head from the computer to focus his gaze on the subordinate before him. "Call my security chief and begin exfiltration procedures immediately."

The subordinate nodded, his face still fixed with the same nervous look. He turned and started to walk out the door leaving his master alone to stare at the view outside the window and reflect.

CHAPTER 59

The Montevideo pier was bustling as workers strove to hurry and finish the last of their work. No one was paying attention to Dayan, Ripley, and the Jewish radicals strolling through the collection of cargo boxes and dock workers. The Colombians had made different arrangements with some of their old contacts from their paramilitary days. Once confirmation of their bonuses and the rest of their pay had come in, they went their separate way.

The assassination had taken place only a few short hours before. In that time, the team had dumped the cars, changed clothes to something more in common with merchant sailors and started on foot through the harbor. Cohen had contacted a sea captain sympathetic to their cause who offered passage out of the country. After a high profile killing, staying in the country for even a day would be too risky. The captain and his ship were scheduled for a port in Morocco. It was a place Dayan and the others felt was an appropriate distance to be for the time being.

At the north end of the harbor, on peer 34, they found *The Queen Beth* docked and being loaded with several large crates of cargo. The customs inspector was too focused on examining the crate manifests to give the slightest notice to the collection of men walking toward the vessel. Dayan and the men did not glance in the inspector's direction but kept a steady pace as they passed him.

At the gangplank, they were met by a pudgy man in his early sixties. "You must be Micha's friends," he said with a wide grin spread across a pleasant-looking red face. "I'm Charlie Murcher, captain of this rusty old tub." He leaned forward and extended a massive hand toward Dayan.

Dayan had been given the name Murcher as his contact on the docks. Taking the captain's hand in a tight grip, Dayan shook it firmly. "Thank you. It is nice to meet you, sir."

The captain chuckled. "I imagine it will be even nicer for you to be on board."

The relieved looks from the team said it all. They followed the captain up the gangplank. Halfway up, the captain turned to Dayan, who was right behind him. "Micha is waiting for you in the galley. He wants to see all of you right away."

"When do you cast off?" Dayan asked anxiously.

"We are loading the last of the cargo, and everything has been cleared. We will be shoving off within the next hour if all goes well." Captain Murcher reassured Dayan and his team, who were about to be the most wanted men in South America.

The men were led down the walkway and through a rusty steel door that led through a labyrinth of compact, darkened gangways, finally arriving at a door. With a powerful turn of a lever, the Captain opened the screeching steel barrier into a large, lighted room with a few long tables surrounded by chairs.

It was the ship's mess. Sitting at one of the long tables leaning against the bulkhead was Micha Cohen. He was talking to someone sitting across the table who Dayan had never seen before. Seeing the men enter, Cohen sprang to his feet and started over to them. It was strange to see the katsa dressed in jeans and a gray knit sweater, with a pair of rubber boots completing the strange attire. In his hand, he carried a brown leather briefcase.

"We will be leaving shortly," he said. "Captain Murcher is a longtime friend and ally whom I've worked with for many years. He is no stranger to our work, and he knows how to be discrete."

Dayan looked back to see the tired faces of his team. They were showing the effects of coming down from an adrenaline high. "Good, because I think my guys have gone as far as they can for now."

From the briefcase, Cohen produced a collection of papers. "These are the papers needed to prove you're merchant sailors. Please read them so you know who you're supposed to be and where you're supposed to be from."

Dayan took the papers from the katsa. Included were documents for himself and Ripley as well as the three radicals. Cohen had characteristically thorough in accounting for everyone. The katsa had held back giving the documents to the team for fear that if they were seized along the way, they wouldn't have anything implicating Captain Murcher.

Dayan passed the documents around and dispatched his team to go get food from the galley. The men didn't hesitate. They made for the food line and a moment later Dayan and Cohen were alone.

"I guess we're good until Morocco," the commando sighed, a bit defeated. "But are we on our own after that? What's next?"

The katsa bit his lip. "Well, that is what we need to talk about."

Micha Cohen led Dayan to a far table where a man sat dressed in clothing similar to Cohen's. Like Cohen, he also had neither the physical features nor the presence that suggested he belonged in them. His raven black hair was neatly cut to military standards. His face was cleanly shaved and his hands were washed. Despite his baggy clothes, Dayan could tell the man possessed an athletic frame on a body that regularly worked out. If the commando had to guess, the man was military, most likely an Air Force officer or a pilot.

"Thank you?" the commando replied, unsure of how to take the man's words.

"My name is Mosher Almog. I'm an aluf mishne or alam in the Israeli Defense Force," the man said pleasantly.

"Air Force, I'm guessing," Dayan said, still showing an attitude of uncertainty about the situation.

Almog gave Dayan an approving look. He was impressed by the commando's quick deduction. "Yes, I am in the Air Force. I flew combat jets for many years. I do work for military intelligence these days."

"Aman!" Dayan took a step back, tense.

"You seem concerned," Almog said.

"After what I've just done, I'm waiting for a .22 caliber Beretta to appear from under your coat, and a bullet to go through my head."

Almog chuckled. "I can understand your concern considering you just carried out a serious assassination that is definitely going to gain world attention in addition to the one you recently carried out in Buenos Aires. That one has also been heating up the South American news outlets."

The commando began to feel butterflies emerge in his stomach. He wasn't sure what to think. He sat quietly turning to Cohen to get some clarification. The katsa remained silent. Looking back to the Aman, Dayan waited for the inevitable bad news.

Sensing the commando was not going to speak, Almog continued, "Normally, what you have done would have been a gross embarrassment to our country. However, Cohen has been good enough to manage this operation very well keeping Israel entirely insulated from the damage while still keeping us abreast of everything of consequence. You and your team present us with a very unique opportunity we can't pass up."

Dayan remained silent. Almog looked at Cohen and then back to the commando. "You see, it is only a matter of time before you are discovered as being responsible for these attacks in Uruguay. Iran and Cuba will see to it that this happens. Yet, you were not acting in the capacity as an operative for Israel which shields us from any culpability. In the eyes of the world, you and your group were rogue terrorists acting entirely on your own and are wanted for the military officers you just massacred and the death of the Cuban intelligence officer, Elloy Mendoza, who the world believes was a respected businessman."

"Is this supposed to make me feel worse?" Dayan interjected. "I'm still waiting for the gun to be drawn."

Almog raised his hand as he waved his index finger. "No, it should make you feel better. You performed a great task in the service of Israel and her allies by staving off a serious power play by Iran. You have the ability to continue doing so for our country. We have many enemies, as you very well know. We have many who are insulated, and we cannot engage them directly as we would like to without serious repercussions.

"Since you are a rogue operative and a terrorist, you present us with an answer to those problems. I want to build a fictitious terror network around you and your team. A network the world will see as Jewish fundamentalists, Zionist radicals who are carrying out actions on their own. It will be supported by outside logistics systems and financial backers which would enable Israel to deny any connection to your activities, but you will be working quietly on orders from us. To the world, these missions will be terrorist attacks executed by a rogue former commando from our armed services. You will provide the leeway to execute needed military operations Israel otherwise would be unable to do."

Pressing his fist to his chin Dayan, again, looked back to Cohen. "What role would you play?"

Cohen had a ready answer. "I would be the go-between. My role in all of this was in the shadows. It is unlikely I will ever be seriously connected to any of what we just did. Still, as a retired, old burnt-out intelligence officer, I can still operate as the handler. I'll take my orders from Aman or, more precisely, the alam here, and pass them on to you."

"So, this means," Dayan pointed to Almog.

"That, as of now, I'm your new commander," Almog cut the commando off.

"I guess we don't have much of a choice," Dayan rubbed his hand against his forehead processing the ramifications of what he'd been told.

Cohen and Almog shot a glance at each other before

Almog looked back at Dayan. "No, you really don't. Once this ship lands in Morocco you're either working for us in this new capacity or, in a few months tops, you and your men will be dead or captured."

"I'll have to discuss this with my team," Dayan replied. "What about Darren Ripley? The others, Gold and his friends are Jewish and known Jewish radicals. They fit neatly into this narrative. Ripley is a Welsh mercenary. What about him?"

Almog cracked another smile. "He's in if he wants to be. He'll even enjoy being paid, as will you all. Just so he knows, like the rest of you, you're out there with a constant target on your backs."

Almog was right; there were no other options once the ship hit Morocco.

"I'm in," was all he said. From this point forward, he would no longer be a former naval commando of Israel's Flotilla 13. He would now be Kafka Dayan, the international terrorist.

EPILOGUE

Following the order from Qalmini, Major Akim called off the mission into Uruguay. With the help of Surriman, Keppa, and Avi, he directed the deactivation of the training camp and demobilization of the Arab militia.

Just as they had smuggled them in from Paraguay and Argentina, Keppa and Avi used the same mode of transportation to return the volunteers back to their places of origin. The weapons, being too risky to smuggle back over borders, were sold to some of the local criminal networks, along with any support and training equipment that could fetch a price. This money was allocated for any additional expenses returning the volunteers back to their homes.

Surriman, along with Keppa, and Avi, returned with the other Arabs to their villages deep in the mountains and jungles. Major Akim headed to Brasilia, Brazil's capital, where he made contact with the Iranian embassy and was quietly flown back to Tehran a few nights later.

Ali Anwar al Qalmini and his team destroyed all documents and data storage pertaining to the operation from the Argentinian headquarters. His company, Saleed United Real-estate and Acquisitions took measures to sell all properties in South America at virtually cutthroat prices to ensure quick sales. At that point, his government would be less concerned with profits than divesting themselves of any connection to the fiasco they were now in.

Both, he and his entourage left Argentina on the company's privately chartered plane. The flight to Iran was deadly silent as Qalmini contemplated his future.

Having lost his employer, Ulbrict Laudman decided his watch fixture shop was now his to enjoy, free of maniacal aristocrats. However, feeling a sense of remorse for the violence carried out on so many working people, he chose to atone with a personal act for his own conscience.

After the gruesome assassination of its president, the PIT-CNT labor coalition had fallen into the leadership of Felix Guzman Uraba, a move engineered by Oskar Straudner. Urbana had enjoyed his position leading the powerful labor force. With the death of his benefactor-blackmailer, he was now free to operate without any concern.

When Pietro Lazi and Manuell Cozmento, two high ranking deputies within the coalition, were mysteriously invited to a meeting at a small corner sidebar, they didn't know what to make of this mysterious old German who said little except, "You should know about your coalition president."

The German slipped a beaten, weathered file across the table to the two labor leaders, then stood up and left just as strangely as he had approached them. It was an old, secret police file, dated from the 1980s. The file contained the records of meetings between police and a secret informant, one Felix Guzman Uraba, who reported seditious behavior by labor figures at the time. Among the names mentioned as violent revolutionaries were Pablo Lazi and Edwardo Cozmento, the long since disappeared fathers of the two men now staring wide-eyed at the well-worn file.

For the violence in Uruguay, President Jose Mojica resisted the outcries and demands to take stronger police action against the radicalism. In time, with the bombings and terrorism suddenly coming to a complete halt, the momentum of the violence and protests gradually died down. Calm and normality returned to the country. With the central figure of any possible government seizure now dead, the idea of the coup simply fell apart and disintegrated.

As predicted, it wasn't long before the image of Kafka Dayan was sprayed across the world news as the terrorist responsible for the violent attack in Buenos Aires and the death of a prominent businessman and several policemen. The horrible massacre led to the deaths of an Uruguay politician and ten high ranking police and military officers.

Across news sites everywhere, reporters questioned what the emergence of this terrorist attack meant. Experts discussed the rise of a new Jewish terror movement and whether it was political or religious in nature.

All theories ended with the same message — a new terrorist had struck, and his name was Kafka Dayan.

SO, WHAT DID YOU THINK?

Thanks for reading! I hope you enjoyed the book.

If you have a minute, please take a moment to leave a review on Amazon.

Your honest review will help other readers make

informed decisions about which books might appeal to them. It will also help me to better understand my audience, what I'm doing right, and where I might improve the reader experience.

I greatly appreciate your feedback and your time.

—J.E. Higgins

CAST OF CHARACTERS

Major Rashid al'Akim — Iranian soldier from al' Quds unit working for Qalmini

Contessa Selena de Alvarez — Mysterious international broker of criminal services

Felix Augusto —Young professional killer; works for Zacha

Avi — Old friend of Nouri's; helping train Iranian recruits

Ramon Caldoza — Research staff ofr the Partido National in Chamber of Deputies

Manuel Culvera — Uruguay Minister of Interior

Kafka Dayan — Recruited by Micha Cohen to stop the Iranian coupe

Martin Derry — Irish mercenary hired by Contessa to train recruits & execute missions

Victorio Deigo — Owner of food van selling homemade meals

Major Semir Ali Essouri — Iranian soldier from al' Quds unit working for Qalmini

Solomon Cabriza Gold — Leader of Guardians of Israel; young group fighting for Israel

Ernesto Guevero — Commander in Uruguay army

Jewish financial reps — Plan presented to acquire funding for Israeli plan to stop Iranians.

Mr. Greentree
Mr. Cincade
Mr. Lupon
Mr. Comfort

Keppa — Old friend of Nouri's; helping train Iranian recruits

Rabbi Abraham Kovinski — Rabbi at Jewish Community Center

Ulbrict Laudman — Black ops coordinator for Straudner

Don Diego Francisco del' Meduriso, the Patron — The Contessa's contact for black market arms

Elloy Mendoza — CEO of Bolivar Investments & Acquisitions & Cuban Directorate Generale Intelligensia (DGI)

Jose Mojica — President of Uruguay

Illana Muricia — Recruited by the Contessa as personal assistant

Myra — Young teenager working at the Jewish Community Center

Professor Raphael Patrica — Recruits student revolutionaries for the Contessa

Oskar Perez — Mercenary working for Kafka

Ian Plūcker — Ferry Owner of the Ronin Establishment; mercenary broker

Ali Anwar al Qalmini — Leader of Iranian forces to destabilize Uruguay to overthrow its democratic government

Raizza the Negress — Waitress at the Ronin Establishment

Alyssa Rios — CEO of Guardian Angel Intelligence (GAI)

Darren Ripley — Mercenary working for Kafka

Oskar Vlak Straudner — Member of Partido Nacional or National Party in Uruguay. Recruited by Qalmini to be the next President of Uruguay

Nouri al'Marak Surriman — Recruited by Iranians to aid operations

Felix Guzman Uraba—Uruguay labor union leader

Klaas Vanderhook — Mercenary working for Kafka

Mr. Vargas — Strong arm operator working for Elloy Mendoza

Emil Zacha — Former operative for Argentina's Intelligence Secretariat (SI). Works for the Contessa

Venzuelo Zamora — Lead instructor/trainer for Contessa's student revolutionaries

ACKNOWLEDGMENTS

To Lewis R. Higgins, Gloria Higgins, Shannon Lasky, Bob Liepold for their time reading and editing, and to Shayne at Wicked Good Book Covers for the fantastic cover image, as well as all the many others who contributed to the making of this book, I would like to extend my sincere thanks.

ABOUT THE AUTHOR

J.E. Higgins is a former soldier who spent 12 years in the US military, first as infantryman in the Marine Corps and then in the military police with the Army. He holds a B.A. in Government and a Masters in Intelligence; intelligence operations.

You can reach J.E. Higgins at his website: www.thehigginsreport.com where he publishes monthly papers on international political trends.

Made in United States
Cleveland, OH
14 November 2024